EMPRESS, GODDESS

EMPRESS, GODDESS

MORGAN H. OWEN

GALLERY YA

SIMON & SCHUSTER

London New York Amsterdam/Antwerp Sydney/Melbourne Toronto New Delhi

N
3
4
6
ROME
1. Imperial Palace
2. Circus Maximus
3. Pantheon
4. Curia (Senate House)
5. Colosseum
6. Theatre of Pompey
7. Temple of Jupiter
8. The Forum
9. Basilica
10. Ludus Magnus (gladiator school

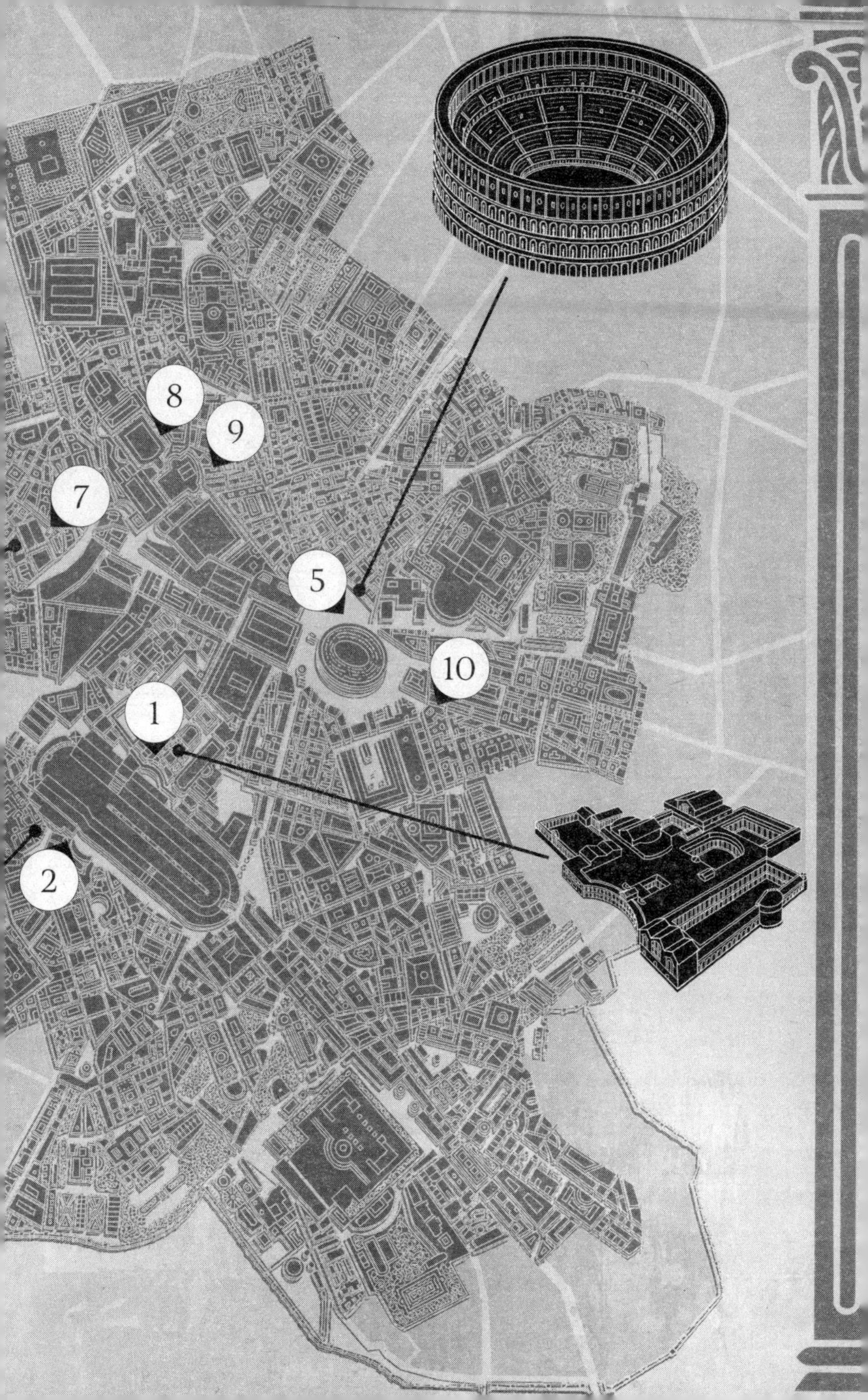
8
9
7
5
10
1
2

First published in Great Britain in 2026 by Gallery YA,
an imprint of Simon & Schuster UK Ltd

1 3 5 7 9 10 8 6 4 2

Simon & Schuster UK Ltd, 7th Floor,
199 Bishopsgate, London EC2M 3TY

Simon & Schuster Australia, Sydney
Simon & Schuster India, New Delhi

www.simonandschuster.co.uk
www.simonandschuster.com.au
www.simonandschuster.co.in

The authorised representative in the EEA is Simon & Schuster Netherlands BV,
Herculesplein 96, 3584 AA Utrecht, Netherlands. info@simonandschuster.nl

PB ISBN 9781398539747
eBook ISBN 9781398539778
eAudio ISBN 9781398544611

Typeset in Garamond by M Rules
Printed and Bound in the UK using 100% Renewable Electricity at CPI Group (UK) Ltd

FSC www.fsc.org
MIX
Paper | Supporting responsible forestry
FSC® C013604

To the women who taught me to be ungovernable.

CONTENTS

PROLOGUE

Two goddesses had called for a secret meeting, in light of the small matter of Rome having no emperor. They met in a blue grotto in the city of the gods, hidden away from prying eyes. Diana, goddess of the wilderness, came straight from a hunt, clad in sandals and carrying a bow on her back. Venus, goddess of love, wore her most fashionable robes, as if she were hosting a grand ball and not a rebellion.

They sat at the edge of the pool, concealed behind snaking plumes of steam. A lyre played without a musician, illuminated by the soft glow of small floating stars.

Though they were immortal and divine, capable of moving both the earth and the heavens, the goddesses were anxious. Diana toyed with one of her arrows while Venus fiddled with her necklace, which was shaped like a clamshell with a pearl in it.

They had handed out invitations to the resistance meeting sparingly, approaching only those deities they believed would be loyal to their fellow goddesses over Jupiter, king of the gods. Such covert reconnaissance was a gamble. Diana and Venus had to be pragmatic, careful, even in their planning. Each goddess was evaluated based on their history in the pantheon, their associations, their alliances, their talents and weaknesses, as well as their philosophies on mortals. If they invited the wrong deity, their plans could be foiled.

Diana and Venus were sure that word would spread, and soon. They would need to convert as many as they could, if they were to succeed.

'What if no one comes, and it is just us?' asked Venus.

'I am certain they will,' said Diana, 'if only for curiosity's sake.'

'But can we trust them?' said Venus. 'We cannot assume they will be loyal just because they are women. They might run straight to Jupiter.'

Diana paused before answering.

'We will find out, one way or another,' she said.

'I'm nervous,' said Venus.

'As am I,' said Diana.

'It is a terrible thing, for a goddess to be nervous,' said Venus.

Smiling, Diana reached out to pat her hand.

'We are defying the gods. Of course we are nervous,' she said.

Their world was in disarray. King Jupiter had vanished, leaving the empire of Elysium unattended, just like his murdered mortal protégé in Rome. Pompeii had been destroyed. The empire was without a ruler. The world of tomorrow depended entirely on Diana and Venus mounting a resistance, and yet, they were already two allies down.

'I wish Minerva was here,' said Venus, of the absent goddess of wisdom. 'How could she leave us to deal with this mortal mess?'

'She'll return soon enough, with information that can benefit us,' said Diana, though she did not meet Venus's eyes as she said it.

'You think she is off on a noble quest?'

'This is Minerva we're talking about. She won't give up so easily. She'd want us to go on without her. "There is no time to spare, we must make plans with haste!".' Diana imitated Minerva's lofty voice. '"History waits for no one, not even us. If we fail, the consequences will be grave indeed."'

'I hope you're right,' sniffed Venus, suppressing a smile.

'You are normally the optimistic one of the two of us,' said Diana. 'I'm not used to making the motivational speeches.'

'I am struggling. So long as Fortuna is blinded, unable to see the future, we are lost in the dark.'

'Don't you always say the most interesting things happen where none can see them?' said Diana, gesturing around at their covert location.

'I was thinking more of secret trysts, forbidden encounters, deliciously illicit rendezvous . . . that sort of thing.'

They fell silent, listening to the animated lyre and the burble of the waters around them.

Diana opened her mouth, as if to say something, but the sound of deities manifesting into being drew their attention.

A hooded goddess emerged from behind a pillar, her expression sheepish.

'Concordia, so glad you could make it,' said Diana, rising gracefully to her feet as Venus followed behind.

The goddess of peace and harmony bowed before them, speaking in a passive, even monotone.

'I do not feel well about breaking the laws of Jupiter, but I did manage to convince a couple of others to join us.'

'We are glad of your company,' said Venus, her voice a little higher than usual. 'And we have refreshments!' She gestured to a table laden with golden fruits. 'Would you like me to take your palla?'

Feronia and Eponia came next, the goddesses of wildlife and equestrianism respectively. Feronia was dishevelled, with twigs and leaves tangled in her curls, accompanied by a menagerie of creature companions. Eponia wore chariot-riding gear, her long hair plaited like the tail of an emperor's horse.

'We are only here to vouch for the animals of Rome,' said Feronia. 'Too many innocent lives were lost in the Vesuvian catastrophe.'

Eponia huffed in agreement.

Voluptas and Suada soon followed. The goddesses of sensual pleasure and seduction were loyal to Venus over all other men, including the gods, but they enjoyed nothing more than revelry. They quickly poured themselves glasses of ambrosia – the divine wine of deities – glugging as if desperately thirsty.

'This isn't a bacchanal,' said Diana.

'If we can't consort with the men, we must be allowed to have a little *fun,' said Suada, downing her drink.*

Soon, other deities emerged from the depths of the clouded caves, gathering around them expectantly. Diana and Venus greeted each in turn – bowing, shaking hands and thanking them for their attendance.

'Fortuna is my kin,' said Securitas, the elder goddess of national security, her grey hair cropped short. 'We were born from the void together, back in the time before time. If she is Jupiter's enemy, then he is mine. Are you sure we speak in confidence?'

'As certain as I can be,' said Diana. 'After all, Jupiter could be hiding in those bubbles, or in the stone of this cavern. He could be disguised as a golden apple. There is only so much a goddess can do.'

Venus looked at the banquet table with newfound trepidation.

'That wasn't exactly what I was hoping to hear,' said Securitas, narrowing her eyes as she gazed around the cavern. 'I assume you have not invited Juno?'

'Certainly not,' said Diana, with a bark of a laugh. 'Of all the goddesses in the pantheon, she is least likely to betray her consort.'

Salacia, the mermaid-tailed goddess of seawater, suddenly emerged from the blue waters of the pool. Her hair was made of seaweed, threaded with spiralling shells.

'Salacia,' said Venus, her eyes wide. 'We were not expecting you.'

'The waters hear everything,' she said, staring at them fixedly. 'Your words travelled on the waves and currents to my ears.'

Diana tensed, noting the trident in Salacia's hand.

'My mentor Neptune was killed by Jupiter. I stand against the king of the gods, now and always.'

'We are grateful to have you,' said Diana, exhaling.

They waited for more to arrive, but none came. The gathered goddesses grew restless, looking at Diana and Venus for guidance.

'Should we . . . begin?' the latter asked.

'Fine. Let's go ahead,' said Diana.

'Thank you all for coming,' said Venus, turning to the small crowd. She glanced again at Diana and was met with an encouraging nod. 'You know why we're here today: we are tired of the gods sponsoring wretched men to rule the empire.'

Venus gazed around at the gathered pantheon. It wasn't a terrible turnout for their first official engagement, but they would need hundreds more if they were to seize power from the king of the gods.

'For now, Jupiter is licking his wounds, but his pride is too great for him to stay away for long. He won't be able to resist the lure of an empty throne.'

The group burbled, murmuring with interest.

'His client Emperor Decimus was murdered, and although Jupiter has done the same in the past, he will claim it is a violation of his rules,' said Diana.

'He is a hypocrite, above all things,' said Venus.

'He will soon be plotting his comeback, his vengeance, for he believes that it is owed to him. That is why we must do everything in our power to make sure Claudia arrives safely to make her claim.'

'I'm thrilled to finally have an empress,' said Voluptas.

'About time, too,' agreed Feronia.

'But where is Minerva?' asked Securitas.

The goddesses stopped talking among themselves, turning to Diana and Venus. They had all been witness as Minerva and Jupiter battled, throwing the pantheon into chaos. Now both were absent from the world of the heavens.

'Minerva is away travelling, in search of her father,' said Diana, though she wasn't sure this was true. 'The fight isn't over.'

'What can we do?' asked Feronia.

'I am ready to serve justice,' hissed Salacia.

'Jupiter will soon find a man, any man, and engineer his rise to power, no matter how depraved or ignorant he is,' said Venus.

The goddesses grumbled in agreement.

'Other gods may aid him or attempt to make claims of their own. Claudia has a cousin, Marcellus, who served in the Legion, but he is a servant of Mars. This will cause further divisions in the pantheon – division we hope to take advantage of. Each of us must now sponsor a mortal woman of importance and guide the women of Rome to serve and support the empress.'

'I do not fraternize with humans,' said Salacia.

'Then now is the time to start,' said Venus, brightly. 'They can be quite charming, if you give them chance.'

'I doubt that,' said Salacia.

'Those of you who have already built up a relationship with a mortal must influence them to stand with our cause,' instructed Diana. 'Use whatever power they have to benefit the reign of the empress. Those of you who do not partake in mortal games, must select a candidate. Choose a mortal woman who can aid us, whose world view and aspirations align with our own. We'll need allies in every

sector of society if we're to assure our victory against Jupiter, from bottom to top.'

'And what if we get caught?' asked Eponia.

'Then you will say nothing,' said Diana. 'If one goddess turns against us, then all of us will pay the price for it. All will suffer. But if we stand together, we shall remain strong. This is why we must not get carried away with idle chatter. We must be very careful who we trust, and what we say.'

'I like gossip as much as the next goddess,' said Venus, 'but if the leagues of Jupiter should learn of our meetings, we will lose our advantage and the mortal world will descend into depravity – and not the good kind.'

'If we fail, all hope of a better future will be lost,' said Diana, thinking of Fortuna, her blind eyes and broken wheel; thinking of Minerva, battling her father in the amphitheatre of the gods; thinking of Pompeii and Herculaneum, buried by Vulcan's fire. 'We must not allow men to destroy the world. To prevent the fall of Rome, we must ensure the fall of the gods.'

Mortals believed the gods were infinite – that they could never be wounded or die, but this was untrue.

A god could die at the hands of another god.

A god could die at the hands of a goddess.

1. JUPITER'S REVENGE

The first empress of Rome stood at the bow of a ship as it sailed through a thick black smog. Softly illuminated by the faint reddish glow on the horizon, the ship's sails were ragged and dirtied by soot, much like her once-fine robes, and the hull was damaged, baring a jagged hole that resembled the gnawing pit in her stomach.

No stars could be seen in the sky, no coasts, no islands – just this deathly, fire-tinged fog in every direction, so deep and dark and empty; an endless, hopeless void.

It was vast and terrifying, much like the gargantuan task ahead of her, so enormous she could barely hold it in her mind.

Claudia Caesaria knew she might only be empress for as long as the ship sailed – that when she arrived in Rome, it might be to her own death or denouncement – yet she vowed to keep faith until the last possible moment, stubbornly deluding herself into visions of victory.

For as long as they were at sea, she was the ruler of the world.

She envisioned herself draped in purple, waving at a balcony before an adoring crowd, her hair braided with flowers. The people revered her, not out of fear or duty but admiration and affection.

She was loved, and she was good.

The waves around the boat frothed and foamed, full of small rocks that banged against the sides. Showers of foul dirt and gas rained down on them periodically, creating a hellish rain that stank of rotten eggs.

The ship was the largest of a twelve-strong military fleet, all with square-rigged masts and oarsmen below decks: one of only two vessels sent to rescue survivors after the eruption of Vesuvius. It was battered and busted from its apocalyptic odyssey, with scorch marks on the sails and a hole in the deck where a burning rock had crashed through. One more misfortune and the ship would be a wreck.

Less than half an hour after casting off from an isolated bay, the volcano had given a final roar, burying what was left of the cities of Pompeii and Herculaneum and filling the air with this deathly, choking smog.

Claudia gazed down at the bronze ram, gripping the front rim of the boat. It now served as a plough, clearing a path through the polluted seas of debris expelled from the erupting volcano. The sky seemed to be darkening still: a warning that this was not over.

On board were several hundred people, more than the ship was built to carry. They were bloodied and dirtied, coughing up rot. They huddled together in shaken silence, crying out whenever a particularly violent wave tossed them. Some prayed to their gods. Others criticized the pantheon for abandoning them. Many blamed Vulcan, the fire god whose festival they had been celebrating when the disaster occurred.

They represented a cross-section of society: from the brothel girls and slaves whose masters had been buried by rocks, to the famous scholar Pliny the Elder and his friend Rectina of Herculaneum, whose historic library of precious scrolls were now packed into crates.

Claudia was responsible for them all now: the people, the boat, the scrolls, even the animals they'd rescued from the disaster, such as the cat now swaddled in a young den girl's robes, or the yipping dog that ran in circles around the sailors.

'You should head below deck,' came a voice.

She turned to face the speaker: her personal gladiator and bodyguard, Gia Valerii. Claudia drank her in for a moment: her tan, muscular limbs, dark eyes and brown hair pulled back in a braid, though it was looking slightly more bedraggled than usual. Like Claudia, she was dirtied, grazed and rain-damp, still wearing the armour forged by the goddesses during their last battle.

'I will consider it,' she said.

'That's just a diplomatic way of saying no,' said Gia.

'It's a diplomatic way of saying maybe.'

'It's my job to protect you,' said Gia. 'So let me.'

She had dark circles under her eyes from hunger and exhaustion but she was still the most beautiful thing Claudia had ever seen – and she had seen many beautiful things as the daughter of a dead emperor.

'If there's a storm, I should be up here to support the crew,' she said. 'I can't be thought a coward.'

'What will you do to aid them?' said Gia.

'I know more about sailing than you would think,' said Claudia, brightly. 'I spent a few summers coasting in the seas around Capri.'

'Did you man the rigs? Swab the decks?' said Gia.

She arched one dark, highly sceptical eyebrow, which was warranted, because Claudia hadn't really done anything. Most of the work had been done by people who remained invisible, while she sunned herself and bathed and ate fruit.

'I oversaw the manning and swabbing,' she said.

'Oversaw.'

'I managed the whole sailing operation.'

'Uh huh. The captain says there's a storm coming in,' said Gia.

'And what of it?' said Claudia, airily. 'I have defied the gods and lived. What harm can bad weather do to me?'

The sky rumbled, giving a throaty, bone-shaking roar as the rain strengthened, drenching them both.

'Don't underestimate the power of Terra,' said Gia.

'Maybe Mother Earth is on our side.'

'Maybe,' said Gia, looking up with mild concern, 'but nothing is more important than you arriving safely in Rome.'

Far in the distance, a streak of lightning glowed faintly.

'The people will not take to me easily. I must do everything to show them that I'm one of them,' said Claudia.

'But you aren't,' said Gia. 'You are more.'

The boat tilted, groaning in protest as people lurched across the deck like drunks after closing. Gia steadied them both, gripping hold of the carved railing with one arm and holding Claudia with the other.

She flushed in the beam of Gia's burning gaze, despite the cold.

'You have many talents, I know this, but you won't be much support to the people if you're thrown overboard,' said Gia.

The ship groaned again as it righted itself, the crew shouting harried instructions at each other, water dripping from the sails.

'If you die, they won't hesitate to find someone to replace you, and I dread to think who that someone would be.'

Claudia inhaled, then exhaled.

'You are right,' she said.

‘Why would you ever doubt me?’ Gia smiled. Claudia mirrored it easily. ‘You do look spectacular in the rain, though.’

‘I can’t imagine how that is possibly true,’ said Claudia, patting at her stringy hair and sodden robes.

‘It brings back memories of a certain bathhouse.’

When they were almost strangers, just a princess and a gladiator, Claudia had invited Gia to chaperone her to the baths, under the guise of needing privacy to discuss the plot against her life, but her true motivations had been much less honourable.

‘When you told me you loved men, you mean?’ she joked.

‘Yes,’ said Gia, laughing. ‘I panicked, okay? Although I was thinking more about how much I desired you . . . and how unavailable I thought you were.’

Claudia fully met Gia’s gaze, so soft and inviting, drawing her in. They were standing so close that Claudia could feel the warmth of Gia’s body, a body she had known so intimately.

‘I am always available to you,’ said Claudia.

But when Gia leant in as if to kiss her, Claudia pulled back on impulse, looking ahead at the thrashing waves instead, as tumbling thoughts cascaded again.

‘Not here, not now,’ she said, in a low voice. ‘Not yet.’

‘Right,’ said Gia, staring down at the deck. ‘I didn’t—’

‘I cannot risk—’

‘I know.’

‘My position is tenuous as it is. But we will . . . when it’s the right time . . .’ said Claudia. ‘When my rule is secure.’

‘That makes sense,’ said Gia.

Claudia retreated internally, repressing her feelings and adopting a cool, impervious demeanour.

‘The sky is clearing,’ she said. ‘I think I’ll stay up here, for now.’

She craned her neck to see Gia’s brother Cassius engaged in conversation with Gia’s fellow gladiator Dominic. When he caught her eye, he quickly looked back to Dom, nodding exuberantly as if Dom was saying something fascinating, though Claudia was sure he hadn’t really been paying attention.

‘You should go and distract Cassius. He is curious already. I see him watching us.’

‘We can trust him,’ said Gia.

‘Are you sure? I hate to say it, but he’s no longer the boy you remember. He’s a man of war now. He may be much changed by his experiences overseas. You need to get to know him again. Perhaps then, you will know if he’s truly trustworthy or not.’

Gia didn’t respond, though Claudia could tell from her expression that she didn’t agree. Her views on sibling relationships weren’t as complex as hers, Claudia supposed, and they had recently lost their mother. There was clearly no question in Gia’s mind that Cassius would die for her, or vice versa, whereas Claudia and her brother Decimus had always wanted to murder each other.

At last, she had finally succeeded in that goal.

‘Go, be with him,’ said Claudia. ‘You thought he was dead, but he is here and well. You should make the most of this time together.’

Gia gave her a searching look, a tiny crease appearing in the middle of her forehead. Claudia reached out and squeezed Gia’s hand briefly, unseen by anyone except the seas ahead. Gia squeezed her hand back, yet the crease remained on her forehead as she drifted off to speak with Cassius.

Left alone, Claudia sighed heavily. She had never been in love before and she found that she wasn't suited to it at all. It made her feel light-headed, sick, intoxicated and half-mad.

She barely flinched as the boat lifted and crashed back down, spritzing her with mist and ruffling her hair.

Claudia knew some people clung to those they loved, as if afraid to let go. The legends of history were full of obsessive lovers who chased each other tirelessly into oblivion. But Claudia was afraid to hold the person she loved at all. It was safer not to give herself away completely, and she had given enough of herself away already – so much that it made her feel unstable, like an earthquake-shaken villa that might collapse at any moment.

Seduction was easy in comparison: a spirited challenge she had thrown herself into without caution, propelled by the strength of her desire for Gia. But true intimacy involved being seen and known, and Claudia wasn't sure she wanted either of those things. The whole of her was bloody and tangled and raw, and she didn't want to have to see it or know it or face it herself. That was the problem.

She recalled the moment when she'd confessed to her father's murder. There had been a second, just a split second, when she saw a brief, passing emotion float across Gia's face – some doubting horror that existed in contradiction to her reassuring words.

Gia was disappointed that she had lied to her.

That horror had washed away with the waves that had almost drowned them, but, like the tide, Claudia knew it would return one day.

Claudia felt the violent, twisting pull of her heart as a thousand clashing thoughts filled her head, all crashing into each other.

If I am to be empress, I must behave like one. I mustn't be soft or distracted. I must be as hard and cruel as a man. The fate of the world rests on it. I can't allow my heart to rule my head. It's dangerous to be vulnerable, especially in the position I'm in. But I am weak for her, so weak. I have never wanted anything so much, not even the crown on my head.

I love her but I am wicked, unworthy.

My father . . . I killed him.

Decimus . . . I killed him.

I killed both of them.

The sinister imagery snaked through her head again: her father choking on vomit, her brother dribbling blood. Swallowing down her feelings like bile, Claudia stared ahead at the open sea.

As emperors went, Tiberius had been unmemorable, best known for his aggressive campaigns in Britannia and for his many construction projects in Rome. As a father, he was equally unmemorable: quick to anger, and dull – not a bright man, nor a charming one.

In historical terms, he was deeply average, destined to be forgotten. Claudia was certain she could do a better job. For all her flaws and secrets, she was not *that* kind of monster.

Yet it seemed incomprehensible from the outset that a single person should rule the world, let alone that it should be her.

The boat rocked back and forth, like a mother trying to nurse a baby, but Claudia was still cold and hungry and haunted by the blood she'd shed to get there. She wiped her palms on her clothes, though they were no longer visibly dirty.

Claudia was still very much alive, terribly alive in fact, because not only did she have to live with what she'd done, but there were sure to be many people willing to steal that life from her now, perhaps even one of the survivors aboard the ship.

She looked around furtively, at Cassius and his fellow soldiers, Celadus the Handsome, Gia's gladiator friend Dom with his dog, the child Athena, the sailors, the brothel girls, the slaves, merchants, even a few senators . . . Any one of them could be her enemy now.

She would die by the same sword that brought her to power, she knew that. She accepted it. Emperors lived short and violent lives, and so would she. Her life would end at the hands of her enemies. All she had to do was hang on long enough to make change.

To change history.

As if in response, the ship gave another monstrous groan.

The waves were rollicking, peaking from the waters, as the wind picked up speed and the sulphurous rain pummelled them.

'Here she comes,' someone yelled.

A giant wave suddenly arced over the boat, crashing down on the rear deck and causing the crates to tumble and slide. One of the boxes hit the rail and shattered, scrolls toppling into the water as Pliny and Rectina rushed to try and retrieve them.

'We cannot let this knowledge be lost,' cried Rectina, frantic as if the boxes were children.

'All hands to deck!' called the bearded captain in his blue cloak, as Gia and the others rushed to secure the ship.

A sailor retrieved a wet coil of tangled ropes, salted and crusted from the sea. Shouting directions back and forth, they stretched them over the crates, crisscrossing them to form a net, as the ship continued to sway. Cold spray slapped Claudia in the face as she fumbled to tie her rope to the rail, her frozen fingers numb and slippery. Rectina worked the other side, securing it against the post that connected the ship's drawbridge.

The wind howled, tearing at Claudia's clothes. Her shawl, only loosely secured around her waist, flapped away like a giant bird. She watched it go, soaring over the waves and out of sight.

Everyone was thrown into motion by the rocking of the boat, flung across the deck and smashing into each other, like a chaotic partner dance to the symphony of screaming and crashing and creaking.

A rope snapped, causing a sail to swing directly towards her.

'Claudia!' sounded Gia's voice.

She ducked, narrowly avoiding a collision, but she was launched backwards by the violent bounce of the boat hitting another wave, slipping and skidding onto her hands and knees, sliding towards the stern.

Gia stumbled after her, struggling to stay upright.

Just as they reached each other, a shear of lightning illuminated the sky, closer and brighter than before, accompanied by a thunderous rumble. When another bolt tore through the darkness, all those aboard gasped, shielding their eyes from the brilliantly bright glare.

CRACK.

The sky split open. The lightning stretched, crackling and sparkling as it formed the unmistakable shape of Jupiter's staff.

'No,' Claudia breathed, the words lost under the waves.

A third bolt of lightning struck out like a sword, lancing the ship with a roar. Flames ignited with a whoosh, blazing heat rippling through the air. Passengers fell to their knees, while others attempted to push and shove their way to the other end of the boat.

Claudia screamed without sound, she and Gia stumbling backwards as fire consumed the wooden deck, growing rapidly. It ate through another rope, sending a second ragged sail plummeting. The mast toppled, knocking several sailors into the sea.

Another wave crashed over the ship, returning the sailors who had been swept overboard, but the remaining sail caught fire, growing wings of flame that burned through the dark.

'It is Jupiter's fire,' said Claudia. 'It cannot be extinguished.'

'I thought the gods were forbidden to show themselves directly to mortals,' said Gia.

'He is breaking the rules of the pantheon, to send us a warning,' said Claudia with dread.

Gia shepherded her towards the trapdoor, trying to hustle them below deck, but a stream of terrified oarsmen poured out as the lower portion of the boat began filling with water.

'We're going down!' someone cried.

'The ship is sinking!' yelled the captain.

Everyone began shouting in raw, carnal horror.

'What should we do?' cried Gia.

Claudia remembered that she was, at least by a technicality, the empress of Rome. She was in charge now, and that simple fact was terrifying. She had to do something, not just out of moral or philosophical duty but governmental, monarchic, goddess-blessed duty.

'I . . . I don't . . .'

Claudia gazed at Gia blankly as lightning rained down like golden arrows fired by an army of godly soldiers, striking the surface and creating little jets of boiling water.

'Claudia?'

She had to do something, but what?

Without the sails, they had only the oars to direct them, yet the oarsmen had fled their duties as the ship began to sink.

'We need to steer away from the storm,' she told the shaken captain, grabbing an oar as it floated across the deck and throwing it to Gia.

'It is hopeless,' he said. 'We're going down.'

'Not as I stand here. Men, pick up your oars!'

A dozen other passengers jumped to action on her command, helping to direct the boat between the falling golden spears as they grunted and heaved, but the vessel continued to fill with water.

'We need to lighten the ship's load and patch up whatever hole is letting the water in down below,' she cried.

The captain was still stuck on the spot, staring into the distance.

Claudia pushed through the chaos of a sinking ship and gripped his arms, drawing his attention. His eyes fixed on hers, watery and wide.

'I cannot do this without you,' she said. 'I need your guidance. I need your expertize. You are the captain, so be the captain. This is your moment, to be a Roman hero.'

The man nodded shakily, as if roused from a reverie, running one hand over his face before he turned to address his crew.

'You heard her!' he cried. 'Jettison the cargo! Block the hole! The empress's life depends on it. Move! Go, go, go!'

His men burst into action, with Rectina reluctantly dumping some of her least favourite crates of literature, while Cassius and several other soldiers descended into the flooded deck.

'Stand firm, everyone, and hold on tight to something solid,' shouted Claudia.

The captain nodded, straightening his shoulders. 'Roman fleets have endured worse,' he said.

'She's a good ship, and she's got us this far,' agreed Claudia. 'Stay calm, everyone, and we shall get through this.'

The crew grunted in fearful rhythm as their oars circled, but the lightning bolts were falling faster, forming a glittering curtain of fire.

Perhaps the captain was right.

The situation was hopeless.

Another flood of water drenched them, everyone clinging on for their lives, yet when the water subsided, the fire continued to rage. Jupiter's fire was too big and powerful to be extinguished, not even by the ocean itself. The wind screamed past Claudia's ears, the cold settling into her flesh and causing her to tremor. The energy of mass terror clutched at her stomach and chest like a bloody fist.

Passengers pushed backwards in a frantic, panicked thrashing, gathering at the rear of the ship to avoid the flames. She could hear Gia crying out names: 'Cass! Dom! Athena!'

The brothel girls prayed to every god they could remember, clasping their hands together as their ragged voices rang out over the crashing waves.

'Save us, Minerva!'

'Blessed Fortuna!'

'Diana! Venus! Please hear us!'

That gave Claudia an idea.

'By the glory and the power of the goddesses, we shall survive,' she shouted, above the raging sea. 'I call upon Minerva, Fortuna, Diana and Venus to protect us from Jupiter's wrath. By the grace of the goddesses divine, we shall make it to Rome.'

Claudia gazed up at the angry sky, awaiting a sign, yet the dark clouds continued to churn.

'We are your servants,' she said. 'We work in your name. We pray that you come to us now, to aid us in our hour of need!'

Another bolt struck the side of the ship with a loud crack, causing the two existing fires to join into a burning arc.

'The fate of the world is in your hands! In the name of all that is good and true, we appeal to you, goddesses,' Claudia shouted, less confidently. 'Goddesses, please, we beg for your protection!'

But the boat was falling apart, breaking into pieces that floated away on the water as another apocalyptic wave rose up like a mountain.

With an eerie creak, the bow lifted as they sailed into another ginormous wave. Claudia held on to the wet ropes they'd used to secure the cargo but when the ship slammed back down on the surface, she was thrown across the deck. She smashed into the rail of the stern, her body curling around it by force.

Memories flashed horribly through her mind, bubbling up like something buried on the ocean bed.

A bird without a head. A bloodied pool of eels. Her father's dying words. The sound of a sword entering flesh.

The waters roiled, glowing with Jupiter's fire, but she couldn't scream, her chest winded from the impact, her arms aching as she struggled to hold on to the rocking boat.

Claudia gasped as she glimpsed a dark, serpentine shape moving beneath her, snaking slowly through the deep water, unseen by the crew, who battled the fire, as it slithered under the ship.

Tired, distracted, muscles aching, her fingers began to slip, one by one. She lost her hold with one hand, her strangled cry cut short as she slammed against the body of the boat.

Claudia hung on for a brief moment before she lost purchase, plummeting down towards the frigid cold water with her arms still outstretched, grasping for a hand that didn't come.

As Claudia fell through the air, time seemed to slow, her vision brightening then fading, before a giant wave rose up beneath her. It deposited her back on deck in a heap, drenched but mysteriously unharmed. It all happened so quickly she had no opportunity to process it.

Gia and Cassius raced over as Claudia climbed unsteadily to her feet, goggling at her in awe.

'You ... you went overboard,' Cassius said, shaking his head. 'How is it—'

Gia interrupted him, embracing her tightly.

'I almost lost you,' she said.

A tremendous splashing and dripping noise sounded, as Claudia pulled back curiously from their embrace.

She watched Gia's eyes catch on something behind her, then widen in horror, her face slackening and paling, as a large, unnatural shadow, cast by the fire, fell upon the ship.

Sailors and soldiers were already screaming before Claudia set eyes on it: an enormous serpentine beast.

One man tossed himself overboard with the resolution of someone who had seen enough already. The others formed a huddle, clumping together fearfully.

'What is it?' said Gia. 'A creature of Jupiter?'

'The king of the gods has many such beasts of legend to fight for him, but they are rarely seen,' said Rectina.

The monster was never fully visible, submerged beneath the foaming waves. Claudia could see only glimpses of its form – its snake-like loops, its dark scaly skin, its horns and claws. That was terrifying enough. She imagined it sinking its sharp teeth into her, swallowing her up like a mouse and spitting out her bones.

But then the beast did something unexpected.

When another bolt of bright, hot lightning tore towards the ship, the creature used its body as a shield, repelling the fiery spears. They bounced off, sizzling into the water. Its draconian head struck out, shattering one of Jupiter's bolts into a shower of fine sparks.

A deep baritone grumble sounded as fire and water clashed mid-air, creating landscapes of steam.

The beast was on their side.

The storm began to subside. Through the spray of water and the smoke of the fire, Claudia glimpsed what appeared to be a large, fish-tailed woman riding the beast and hoisting a golden trident, though she was shrouded by mist, her eyes hidden beneath her seaweed hair.

'Salacia,' whispered Rectina, joining Claudia to stare over the rail at the mysterious deity.

'You know her?' said Gia, in awe.

'The goddess of saltwater. I recognize her trident. Made by Vulcan, gifted to her by Neptune. I have a relief of her in my spa.' Rectina's face crumpled, as though picturing her villa in Herculaneum, now buried beneath the volcano's fire. 'I *had* a relief, I should say.'

The strange goddess raised her trident with an energetic grunt, like a competitor in the Olympic Games.

'What is she doing here?' Gia asked.

'She clearly came to our aid,' said Claudia.

Seawater shot up from its prongs, drowning out the fires of Jupiter's lightning bolts as they fell.

'Maybe the goddesses sent her. Maybe they are still on our side.'

'We can only hope,' said Claudia.

The fire sizzled away to nothing, creating plumes of smoke that formed a cloudy protective cocoon around the battered half-sunken ship. Claudia could barely see the captain anymore as he staggered back and forth through the fog, counting the heads of his crew.

'Jupiter on the attack, Salacia on the defence,' she mused. 'If the deities of the pantheon are making themselves visible to us mortals, working for or against us, that can only mean one thing . . .' She turned to Gia, whose fearful expression mirrored her own. 'The war of the gods will be fought on Earth.'

With a sudden groan and a violent lurch, the ship turned sideways, beginning to spin unnaturally.

'What's happening?' Claudia called out in a shaken voice.

'I don't know!' said the captain, skidding across the decks.

The world around them faded and blurred as they hurtled uncontrollably through the water, seemingly in no particular direction. Claudia felt sick and wobbly, like she did after a single glass of wine or when she was deep in a dream and lost the use of her legs. Just when she couldn't bear the sensation any longer, the boat slowed down, cresting on a wave. When the clouds cleared, the goddess Salacia was gone, the sky above was blue and the seas were strangely calm.

The boat was no longer sinking and burning, its hole patched up with a shield of seaweed and shells. Strangest of all, they were gazing out at a familiar rugged coastline, crowded with boats, their sails emblazoned with the crests of Roman soldiers.

The passengers aboard the ship exploded into conversation, talking about the goddess and the wrath of the gods.

'What's happening, captain?' asked Pliny the Elder.

The blue-cloaked captain consulted a map and scratched his head in confusion.

'It's not possible,' he said. 'It's unnatural. We're leagues ahead of where we ought to be.'

'Where are we, good man?'

'That's the port of Civitavecchia,' he said. 'We . . . we've travelled hundreds of miles in minutes.'

Rome.

Roma.

Claudia was coming home.

2. THE OTHER EMPEROR

Claudia and Gia stood before the imperial palace on Palatine Hill, where the she-wolf Lupa had once nursed the human twins Romulus and Remus: the mythical founders of the Eternal City.

Gia issued a low whistle.

'So, this is where you live?' she said.

'You've never dated a girl who had her own palace before?' said Claudia, playfully.

She had spent most of her life here. Despite all of its garish, solid-gold grotesquery, this gilded mausoleum of empire was her home. She knew these old statues and murals like she knew the alphabet and the numerals. There was a familiarity to the place that comforted her.

'Funnily enough, no. Only you,' said Gia.

As they climbed the steps, Claudia followed a well-trodden path, touching a reassuring pillar with golden leaves and noting the piece of the mosaic that was missing on the floor of the portico.

'In that case, welcome to my humble abode,' she said, sweeping her arm in a hospitable gesture.

'Yes, very humble,' said Gia, dryly. 'The solid gold cherubs are particularly spartan.'

But the palace was also haunted by history; not just Claudia's memories of her parents and brother, but all of the emperors who had once walked these pillared halls. She couldn't see them incarnate but she could feel their skin-tingling presence now, lurking in shadows, inhabiting the in-between, veil-thin places where the dead and living bumped hips.

There were many such in-betwixt places in an imperial palace, located next to the Theatre of Pompey where Caesar was slain, and the Colosseum where gladiators fought to their deaths.

Emperors had lived on Palatine Hill since the age of Augustus. The palace was a collaborative work of architecture, having been renovated and restored many times since the days of the Republic, in styles that were not always in harmony. One emperor had installed a revolving ballroom, another a labyrinth for his enemies. Each man had different requirements and desires, be it a bathhouse or stables, a gymnasium or an art gallery. Claudia wondered what her contribution would be.

She imagined them all watching her as she walked along a colonnade lined with imperial busts.

What would they think of a woman ruling Rome? Augustus had banished and denounced his own daughter for defying his order. Tiberius the First wasn't known for his compassion. Caligula was more likely to torture her than give her the right to rule. Claudia knew little of the personal views of her grandfather Claudius, while her father, the second Tiberius, had never shown much interest in the rights and liberties of women, including herself and her mother.

Still, he would've been disgusted by the idea, she was sure.

Her gaze lingered on his recently installed bust but she pushed him out of her mind, continuing on into the atrium.

'This is so surreal,' said Gia. 'I can't believe I'm here. I wonder what my mother would think.'

Gia's mother had died in the eruption, buried along with the taberna where Gia used to live.

Claudia squeezed her hand in the silence that followed.

'Just imagine the places where we might kiss,' said Claudia, to distract her. 'It hardly gets more romantic than the balcony of a palace.'

'What about seated on a throne?'

'Both of us?'

'You'll be on my lap,' said Gia.

Claudia flushed, smiling despite herself.

'I shall have to arrange a palace tour,' she said, 'of all the most inviting spots for us to . . . sanctify.'

'I look forward to it, my empress.'

They ceased talking as Cassius and Dom strode past them, little Athena tagging along behind with the dog.

'It's so b*iiii*g!' Athena hollered, her voice echoing through the enormous space. 'Just look at this, Viatrix!'

Dom had allowed her to name the dog, and Athena had settled on Viatrix, Gia's gladiator name, owing to the dog being lean and muscular. Gia had seemed oddly touched by this dedication, though Claudia feared it might be confusing.

'This is where we live now!'

Athena ran in giddy circles, whooping so loud it was probably heard up in Elysium.

Claudia winced but Gia was amused by the girl's excitement, slapping Athena's palms as she ran past.

Soldiers, freed slaves and other survivors who had nowhere else to go streamed into the walled palace grounds, lugging lumpy sacks, crying children and disgruntled livestock.

Claudia had invited them to stay in the public wing of the palace until they could arrange proper accommodation; her first decree. The request was met with disbelief by the group of advisors, senators and cultists who'd been there to meet her ship, their faces falling when they saw Claudia and not Decimus.

Him dead, her alive and wearing his crown. That made things difficult, and her calling herself empress only complicated matters further.

In the palace temple, gilded statues lined the walls in alcoves, depicting each of the major deities of the pantheon, all seated on thrones and holding weapons, surrounded by their emblematic symbols and beasts. Each emperor had built a temple to the god they served, until they formed an entire pantheon, its sculpted deities divided by red columns.

Viatrix the dog barked happily, sniffing at the crotch of Jupiter.

As sunlight bled in through the roof of the atrium, the figures glinted mystically, their gemstone eyes full of life.

'Do you ever get the sense that you're being watched?' said Gia.

'We likely are, at all times.'

'Ever since we spent the night lost in a labyrinth, I'm not so fond of statues.'

Gia shivered, hugging herself. Claudia waited until the room was empty before she reached out to rub Gia's shoulders. Gia raised one hand over her own as they regarded the golden pantheon.

'They were installed as a reminder for the incumbent ruler to do a good job,' said Claudia. 'It wasn't always successful, based on past results, but the gods were more distant then. Perhaps emperors didn't fear them as they should. Now they feel closer to Earth, especially after our close encounter with Jupiter.'

A group of praetorian guards trooped in, causing Claudia to fall back, watching in her peripheral vision as they entered the palace.

She couldn't risk rumours spreading.

Her eyes glided over to the largest statue in the room: the king of the gods with his terrifying staff raised aloft, his face curled in a snarl of displeasure. Even the eagle on his shoulder looked hateful.

Had he always looked so enraged? Or had the statue changed, to reflect his current disposition?

She looked to Minerva, watching over her with cool golden eyes. Or at least, she hoped she was watching.

'My goddess,' she said, bowing slightly.

When Claudia had lost consciousness back in the cave, waiting out the volcano's rage, she'd searched for Minerva in her delirious half-dreams. On the brink of death, she had sought comfort from her goddess, but her goddess had been nowhere to be seen.

Gia stared at the figure of her own goddess, Diana.

'Do you think it was curious, that Salacia came to our aid and not Minerva?' said Claudia. 'Minerva is my own patron, and she's a Capitoline goddess: far more powerful than a minor sea deity.'

Gia raised one eyebrow.

'Not to sound ungrateful, of course,' Claudia added. 'But Minerva was the one behind the whole scheme.'

'She's a busy woman.'

'She vanished in our hour of need.'

'She cannot keep watch at all times.'

'No,' Claudia said uncertainly. 'But how did Salacia become involved in the plot? Did Minerva send her, to help us?'

'Maybe there's a rebellion happening in the heavens,' said Gia.

'I do hope so.'

'If Jupiter is breaking the rules to come after us, he probably has all the deities riled up. It could be the breaking point for the pantheon.'

'We must attempt to make contact with the goddesses, as soon as possible. We need their guidance,' said Claudia.

'How? Diana comes to me only in times of crisis.'

'We *are* in crisis. Jupiter is trying to kill us.'

'Our lives are one endless crisis.'

Claudia was finally standing at the top of the mountain she'd spent so long climbing. She'd arrived in the place she was destined to be. But the king of the gods had broken through the veil of reality to attack her. The future seemed infinitely dark and unknowable.

When she reached for Gia's hand, it was to steady herself as the world seemed to tilt, like she was still on the ship.

'Princess?'

They broke apart as a tall, rotund, pointy-bearded man in red robes appeared before her.

Ten or so others gathered behind him, wearing different-coloured togas that designated their role without the house.

'I'm the new consul. My name is Damocles,' he said. 'It is my great honour to receive you alive and well. We heard the news out of Pompeii and feared the worst.'

The consul was once an elected official, powerful during the Republic, now reduced to a symbolic role often handed to family or friends of the emperor. The role had a high rate of exchange, with men coming and going over periods of months. Being the beleaguered go-between of the emperor and the Senate was a great deal of work for a very limited amount of money, power or acclaim, which posed the question: What sort of man would be drawn to such a role?

'It's a pleasure to meet you, Damocles,' said Claudia. 'I shall arrange a meeting for us to become even better acquainted.'

'And you already know me, of course, Princess,' said the small elder man in an orange robe, with fluffy white hair like a dandelion.

Hieronymus. Once her father's advisor. He'd returned to Rome upon the emperor's death.

The other men glanced back and forth, exchanging furtive looks. One held a tablet, the other a lyre. An emperor's personal staff included not just political advisors and guards but also scribes and librarians, artists and musicians, courtiers and astrologers, physicians and tutors, not to mention a legion of domestic servants.

Between her father dying while away in Pompeii, Decimus coming to power and Vesuvius erupting, Claudia had lost most of her staff to death or defection. These men had been hastily put in place, though she wasn't sure by whom; the Senate, perhaps? They were strangers whose allegiances couldn't be estimated.

She had to assert herself, to earn their respect.

'Hieronymus, yes. It's good to see you again . . . though I would prefer that you refer to me by my proper name, Empress Claudia.'

One of the men smirked. Another snickered, whispering under his breath. Claudia couldn't hear what he said but she was certain that it was unflattering.

'About that,' said Damocles, raising one ringed finger.

'About what?'

'About you being empress. We wouldn't want you getting ahead of yourself,' he said.

'Meaning?'

'It's your cousin, Marcellus Suetonius,' said Damocles.

'What about him?'

'Well, he is here,' said Hieronymus.

'Already?'

'He arrived yesterday,' said Damocles.

'I hope you're about to tell me he's here to congratulate me on my ascension to power,' said Claudia.

'Afraid not, Princess,' said Hieronymus. 'He is making a claim, as the emperor's nephew. He insists he had a conversation with your father before his death, along these lines.'

This time, Claudia didn't correct his 'Princess'. She'd barely interacted with Hieronymus until now, for he'd never paid her any attention. She could tell that he wasn't impressed with her in the slightest, and that winning his respect would be a long, hard-won affair.

'Then he is a liar. He had no such conversation.'

'He is, in many people's eyes . . . the real *princeps*.'

The princeps was the heir. First in line. Her father's brother's child would stand ahead of her? No, she would not allow it.

'Many people are wrong,' she asserted.

'Try convincing them of that,' said Damocles. 'You know how stubborn the public can be when they form an opinion.'

Claudia's hands formed fists at her sides.

'I am the emperor's only daughter, his only living child,' she said. 'Marcellus has never shown any interest in government. He hasn't visited Rome in years. He is entirely unprepared for the job of ruling.'

'Ah, well . . . That's the issue, you see.'

'What?' she asked, sharply.

'Marcellus has served in the military,' said Hieronymus.

'And you have not,' said Damocles.

'There are no legal conditions for becoming emperor,' said Claudia. 'Furthermore, I am not *allowed* to serve in the military. That is not a fair comparison, nor a reliable measure of competence. Now, where is my dear cousin? I wish to speak with him at once.'

'You will find him upstairs,' said the consul. 'He has installed himself in your father's chambers, rather expediently.'

'He's done *what*?'

Furious, Claudia bounded ahead, followed by Gia, as she climbed the figure-carved staircase to reach the upper level of the palace.

'What kind of man would move into my father's private suite without my permission?' she hissed, as they raced up the steps.

'A sly one,' said Gia. 'He's muscling in.'

'I've met Marcellus only once, as a child, but now suddenly he thinks himself family? Such people are the worst kind of vultures.'

'What do you know about him?' asked Gia.

'Not much. I'm sure he spent his days at war reclining in a litter at a safe distance from any battlefield.'

Claudia hurtled around the corner, past a series of statues of the Charities and Graces and under an arch, bursting through a pair of carved doors to behold the notorious Marcellus.

'Darling Claudia!'

He quickly crossed the room towards her, drawing her into a dramatic sweeping embrace, an inescapable lock of a hug that suggested a familiarity they didn't share.

Claudia made a face at Gia over his shoulder.

'That's enough,' growled Gia, gesturing with her sword.

Marcellus quickly backed away, baring his palms.

'This is Gia, my gladiator and guardian,' said Claudia. 'She's quite protective over me, you'll find.'

'You should ask, before you touch the empress,' said Gia.

'Empress?' said Marcellus.

Claudia barely recognized him – tall and muscular with fine robes and a mop of curly hair, grinning at her broadly with all of his teeth, as if she was telling a hilarious joke at her own expense.

'That's right,' she said, stonily.

Marcellus chuckled, the sound draining away until it was just a faint gurgle, like water down a drain.

'You are serious, cousin?'

'You find it amusing, that a woman should seek power?'

'No . . . I just can't fathom why a woman would involve herself in politics if she didn't have to,' he said.

'Then why are you here, if you have no interest in it?'

Marcellus made a puffing noise. He looked winded, offended that his heroic arrival was not being celebrated. He had clearly hoped for a better welcome, from a more accommodating princess.

'Forgive me, cousin. I didn't mean to offend. I merely remembered you as the chubby little girl who begged me to play with her. You were so very sweet . . . I did not anticipate you being my competition.'

Claudia stared at him coldly.

'But you are much changed, of course!' he added. 'You're just as enchanting as the soldiers said you were. You know, the men dreamed of you every night? Prayed to you. The thought of your great beauty kept them alive, in so many ways.'

'You should stop talking,' said Gia. 'Immediately.'

'It's a compliment, isn't it?'

'Is it a compliment if I stick my sword up your arse?' said Gia.

Marcellus inched further away from her.

'You were right,' he said, looking to Claudia. 'Your friend here is quite spirited.'

'I'm going to ask again: what are you doing here, Marcellus? Why are you in my father's room, as if you own the place?'

'They came for me. They brought me here.'

He gazed at her like a child who was in trouble but didn't understand why, though he was a grown man in his mid-twenties.

'Who is *they*?' she asked.

'They said you and Decimus were probably dead, based on the news coming out of Naples.'

'*Who?*' she demanded, raising her voice. 'Who told you that?'

'Senators Tacitus and Thelonius, and General Aquinas. They found me holidaying in Greece and brought me here, to meet my destiny.'

There it was, just as Claudia had feared. The Senate had chosen their ruler, and it wasn't her.

'I thought you were a soldier,' she said.

'I was . . . honourably discharged, six months past,' he said, airily and without explanation. 'I've been searching for a new vocation ever since. As the closest male relative of the emperor, I am being called to rule, to be the hero Rome needs.'

'I am already here,' Claudia said, firmly.

'Which senators are supporting your claim?' he asked.

Claudia couldn't quite get a read on Marcellus. On one hand, he seemed naïve, possibly even dim, but he had a canniness about him too.

'It shouldn't matter,' she said, defensively. 'I am the heir, just as my brother was . . . But I have the support of Pliny.'

This appeared to have the desired effect, stunning him into silence. Pliny the Elder was a well-known military commander.

Damocles appeared at the door, bowing to Marcellus.

'Apologies for the interruption, but we didn't have a chance to finish our conversation,' he said. 'And it is rather urgent. You see, the Senate has asked you both to appear at the Curia Julia tomorrow morning, to make your case.'

'What case?' said Claudia.

'Your proposal, as emperor . . . or empress. They will pledge support for their preferred *princeps*.'

Claudia blinked at him, mind racing.

'The Senate is keen, of course, to preserve stability,' he said. 'We've lost two emperors in the same year, within the space of a few days. It wouldn't serve the empire for them to back another unpopular leader.'

'Naturally,' said Marcellus, nodding rather too hard.

Claudia already knew she would be unpopular, simply by the fact of being a woman, and by the look on Damocles's face, this was all a charade, in any case. The Senate clearly didn't expect her to win the requisite number of votes but by humouring her, they hoped to contain any potential influence she might have.

'If Decimus was standing here, would you expect him to prove his worth?' she said. 'So why should I?'

'It is different. Your brother Decimus was the named heir, in official documents that were filed to the Archives,' said Damocles. 'He had no chance to name a successor. The Senate will consider you both. They will hear you speak, then there will be a vote. The Senate shall decide which of you will rule.'

'Delightful,' said Marcellus, clasping his hands together. 'I spent a lot of time thinking about the kind of emperor I'll be on the boat ride over, and I've come up with some ideas. I think you'll all be impressed.'

Claudia resisted the strong urge to say something incredibly undiplomatic.

Hieronymus smiled at Marcellus like a doting uncle before turning to affix Claudia with an impassive stare.

'Shall I confirm your attendance?' asked Damocles.

'What if the loser refuses to concede?' said Claudia.

'Any aspiring emperor can seize power, but he must have majority support in the Senate and the military to hold on to that power,' said Damocles. 'The same would apply to an empress, I am certain.'

The consul was smug, but he was right. Her longevity as a ruler depended on winning over the public.

'I shall leave you two to . . . catch up,' he said.

Damocles shuffled away.

Hieronymus fixed Gia with a long, disapproving glance before he departed. She gave him one right back.

Claudia and Marcellus looked to each other, neither one eager to break the tense silence. She maintained a cool, undisturbed demeanour, pretending she wasn't bothered by the quiet. She had many years of expertise in psychological warfare to call upon.

'I've invited some fellows over for a gathering this evening,' said Marcellus, eventually. 'Drumming up support for my campaign.'

'Oh?' said Claudia, coolly.

'I assume it won't be a problem to host here, at the palace. There are enough empty rooms. Unless you'd like me to find another location for the occasion?'

Marcellus was already busy campaigning. Hosting an event at the palace gave him a certain accreditation, but if Claudia refused, she'd appear petty and threatened. It was better to treat him as if he wasn't a serious concern. And yet, the Senate meeting was tomorrow morning. Claudia didn't have much time to influence anyone or make allies herself. How had Marcellus arranged it in advance, if he'd only just been invited?

Perhaps he was smarter than he appeared, or perhaps the Senate was already aligning fortune in his favour.

Claudia inspected her cousin, taking note of his over-embroidered robes, his styled hair, his clean fingernails and soft hands. Like her, he was a child of privilege, but unlike her, he hadn't fought tooth and claw to survive the world's monsters. He had never been preyed on by Decimus. He hadn't witnessed the end of the world in Pompeii as she had, or been blessed by the goddesses.

Those were not the hands of a killer – not like hers.

She wouldn't give up so easily.

'Go ahead,' she said, casually. 'You are family, after all. I would not turn you away.'

'That is gracious of you, cousin.'

'Throw your party. Have your fun. But let it be said: you will not be emperor.'

Marcellus didn't answer for a moment, his expression frozen between a smile and a scowl.

'I hope we can come to an agreement and live in peace, but I will not stand aside and hand you the crown just because you are a man.'

'The crown isn't yours to give,' he said.

'It's on my head, isn't it?' she said, gesturing at it. 'I took it from my brother's body.'

A cold chill swept through the room.

'If I win, it will be because I was the better candidate,' Marcellus said. 'Not just because I am of the superior sex.'

Gia bit down on her bottom lip, making a fist as if she was barely containing her desire to punch him.

'I look forward to hearing about these visionary ideas of yours,' said Claudia, wishing him death with her eyes.

'You forget that I'm a soldier. I live for competition. I shall be glad of the opportunity to prove myself, just like you, cousin.'

'Then so be it. You can stay here in my father's quarters, since you've already moved yourself in,' said Claudia.

'That's very kind of you.'

'Truth be told, I would not have wished to sleep in this room after what I witnessed here.'

'What do you mean?' asked Marcellus.

'You might find the bed to have an unpleasant odour,' she said, wrinkling her nose. 'It has been cleaned, of course, but Emperor Tiberius did have a habit of shitting himself when drunk.'

Marcellus's face curdled as Gia tried not to laugh.

'I shall leave you to it,' she said. 'Tomorrow, cousin.'

Claudia swept out, as Gia followed.

'What now?' she asked, when they were out of earshot.

'Now, we're going to throw a party,' said Claudia.

3. A LAST PRAYER

Claudia sat on a golden throne, wearing her finest toga and red sash. The noise of joyous revelry echoed through the palace, creating a symphony of cheers and applause, but it wasn't coming from the room she was in. No, it was coming from the banquet hall on the other side of the building where her cousin Marcellus was being celebrated by his hundreds of devotees.

The setting of her own party was equally grand, In a room of gilded pillars and sumptuous murals in every shade. She had provided a buffet full of the finest food in Rome and a small orchestra who had been instructed to perform at the last minute by fear of the gods, but the atmosphere was distinctly dispiriting.

The attendees nursed chalices of wine in sombre huddles, talking in sullen whispers as the musicians played off-key.

Three hundred invites had been issued yet less than seventy people were present, including the staff. Damocles was eager to impress the man he believed would be emperor, setting up Marcellus's affair while Claudia would've been left to organize her own competing soiree single-handedly, if not for the help of her friends.

Gia was there, along with Cassius and Dominic, although they didn't seem too enthusiastic either. Rectina was also present, notably without Pliny, who was unwell, but she'd invited along several senator's wives and women of society, along with a group of Rome's most expensive courtesans. The survivors of Pompeii were here too, though they were strangers in this city, without connections or influence.

Claudia gave a short speech, thanking each and every person for attending, but in the quiet part of her mind, she knew it wasn't enough – not if she was to rule. There were only so many people who had a vote, and no more than three of them were in the room.

While Claudia had accepted their gifts and listened to their thoughts on democracy, promising to fix whatever issues most concerned them, none of the senators seemed as excited by the prospect of her reign as she hoped they might. Their support came hesitantly, reluctantly, with many strings attached.

'I'll consider voting for you tomorrow, *if* you can assure me the campaign in Britannia will be done before the end of next year,' said the man who carried a bag of tablets and scrolls. 'We have lost far too many men already, and what have we gained? An island full of old rocks.'

'I will take your concerns on board,' she said.

'You will have my allegiance if you can promise me that the aqueduct your father began will finally finish construction,' said the gentleman who talked endlessly of infrastructure. 'How long must the suburbs wait for running water?'

'I will do everything I can to find a solution,' she said.

'I might be persuaded, if you can promise you'll change the laws on second and third marriages,' said another man. 'Such prudishness is keeping Rome stuck in the past. We need to be as liberated as the gods.'

'I . . . will give it some thought,' she said. 'Possibly.'

Claudia regretted arranging the party at all, wishing she'd chosen a quiet night instead. She could've been giving Gia that palace tour she'd promised. Instead, she was holding on to her dignity by a hair.

Her competing event now had an air of desperation, the guests appraising her with pity as she pretended not to be bothered by the sounds of her cousin's superior campaign. No one wanted to back a loser and, right now, that's what she was.

'I am certain they are playing poorly on purpose,' Claudia muttered to Gia, as the musicians launched into a deathly dirge, their instruments twanging and screeching in a din that made her teeth itch.

'It's . . . fine,' said Gia. 'Everyone is having a good time . . . aren't you? *Aren't you?*'

'Great fun,' said Dominic, in a flat voice.

'All of the fun,' said Cassius.

'You don't have to pretend to spare my feelings,' said Claudia. 'I can take it. It's a disaster.'

'The party only just started. There's plenty of time yet.'

'It started three hours ago, Gia. I think this is it.'

Marcellus was having a party. Claudia was having . . . a candlelit vigil, by the looks of it. Her ambitions were already dead and buried. The atmosphere was undeniably grim. The guests craned their necks as another chorus of cheers sounded from down the hall, clearly wishing they were important enough to get an invite to the better event.

A group of women appeared in the doorway, peering in curiously. Claudia sat upright, her hopes momentarily buoyed, but before she could wave them in, the trio cut eyes at each other and disappeared, laughing as they proceeded along the colonnade to Marcellus's gathering.

It was humiliating, but Claudia had endured worse. She'd grown up with Decimus for a brother. This didn't even touch the sides of her capacity for shame, not when she'd spent every moment of her childhood engaged in a war that no one took seriously, least of all her father.

'It's a shame Pliny is feeling under the weather,' said Rectina, politely filling the silence. 'I bet he would've drawn a few more attendees, if only for his lively anecdotes.'

'It was very late notice,' said Gia. 'I'm sure some of the invitees had existing plans.'

'No, I must accept the facts,' said Claudia. 'I don't have as much support in Rome as I thought. I should've known it would be a challenge, convincing the people that a woman can lead alone. I can't expect them to be loyal to me when I have done nothing to win their loyalty.'

An even more depressive silence fell upon them.

'That's not true, Empress,' came a voice.

Celadus the Handsome appeared, moving smoothly towards her. One of the most famous gladiators in fallen Pompeii, he was dressed as if for battle in the arena, though his armour had taken some damage during the eruption they'd both survived.

'Pompeii remembers,' he said.

The small crowd stirred. Tall and chisel-jawed, his long brown hair tied back in a bun, he had a presence that drew attention, whether he wanted it or not. Men and women alike stared at him, open-mouthed, watching as he and Claudia conversed.

'If not for your warning, I may not have escaped the disaster,' he said to Claudia. 'You tried to do right by the people. It was not unnoticed by me.'

Gia too watched curiously, knowing they'd seen each other when he was visiting Rome.

For a short time, Claudia had been interested in Celadus, until he had pointed out that there had been no real chemistry between them. Though she had pretended not to be hurt, the rejection had stung. She'd liked the idea of being wanted by one so desired.

Claudia nodded, gratefully. 'Thank you, Celadus.'

She would need all the alliances she could make, if she was to survive a single night.

He was a man, but he could still be loyal.

'I will do my best to spread word of your honour,' he said. Claudia heard the sound of footsteps as Celadus turned to the door. 'In fact, I invited some others tonight.'

Claudia was surprised to see two women enter, wearing the regalia of gladiators. She recognized one as Gia's competitor in a match at the Neptunalia Games: a tall, muscular, short-haired woman named Dido. The other woman was unknown: shorter, dark-haired and dark-skinned, but with a swaggering walk and a beauty mark, wearing lavish armour and cosmetics that enhanced her eyes and lips.

'You know Dido, and this is Livia,' said Celadus.

'You live,' said Dido, greeting Gia with a slap on the back.

'The goddesses look out for their warriors,' said Gia.

'Perhaps we'll get to have that rematch after all.'

'If you feel like losing again.'

'Not this time, friend,' said Dido. 'I've been training.'

She turned to Claudia, bowing.

'Empress? Princess?'

'It is yet to be decided.'

'Then I shall call you, my lady,' she said, taking Claudia's hand to kiss in a sweeping bow.

Gia scowled at her but said nothing.

The other gladiator copied Dido's lead by bowing, though she did not seem as enamoured.

'How do you know each other?' Claudia asked Celadus.

'We met . . . at another party, would you believe?'

They all exchanged a strange, furtive glance, seemingly unwilling to provide any further information.

'Livia has been competing here in Rome for the past few months, and she and Dido have fought each other before too.'

'This is Gia,' said Dido, 'the one I told you about.'

'Your legend precedes you, Viatrix the Victorious,' said the shorter woman. 'But you have yet to encounter Livia the Legendary.' She flexed her arm, showing off her toned muscles despite her petite stature.

'Is that right?' said Gia.

'Rome already has a famous woman gladiator,' said Livia, 'so don't get any ideas above your station.'

Claudia tensed, fearing the party would go further downhill if it erupted into violence.

'Rome is a big city,' said Gia.

'Sounds like a challenge to me.'

'You bet it is.'

They smiled at each other, and only then did Claudia realize that Livia was joking. It was just friendly comradery. She'd never had many friends as the emperor's daughter, only handmaids whose duty was to serve her. Sometimes she found it difficult to understand the rules.

'Maybe Lady Emperor over here can arrange for us to show everyone what we're made of,' said Livia. 'Women fighting women at the Colosseum, just like we should've been doing since the beginning.' She looked to Claudia. 'What do you say?'

'If I become empress, I guarantee it,' she said – a task for future Claudia, should she be so lucky.

'More wine?' A doe-eyed handmaiden popped up at Claudia's side, holding a richly decorated amphora.

'Oh no, I shall want a clear head for tomorrow morning,' said Claudia, holding up one hand. 'Thank you, though.'

'We'll take that,' said Cassius, delicately removing it from the girl's hands. Dominic declined, but Cassius poured some for him and Gia, clinking their glasses.

The more time Claudia spent in their company, the more alike she found the siblings to be. They had the same smile, the same light in their eyes when they were amused. They communicated without words, always on the same page. She had never known that kind of family.

She wiped her hands on her robes as she tried not to think about her own brother. His lifeless eyes flashed through her mind, making her as cold as stone.

'Sharing is caring,' said Livia, eyeing the amphora. 'You'd better have some of that left for me.'

The evening dragged on, bringing a few more latecomers to pledge their allegiance, including the wife of Senator Cornelius. Cornelius had been her father's ally, and sometimes her own. Claudia and Gia had first met at his birthday party. They might never have come together if not for Gia intervening to prevent his lechery in the shrine of Venus, but he'd met a grisly end as one of her brother's many victims.

His wife was having a second wind now that her master was gone, having formed a friendship with her husband's former mistress. They were going travelling together, she said, to see the pyramids.

When the crowd had dwindled down to less than ten, Marcellus made an appearance. He was visibly jolly and trailing an entourage – a posse of men who applauded his every sentence.

'I bring gifts,' he said, depositing a bundle of jewels and rare spices on the buffet table. Claudia's guests flocked around him. 'I've had so many wonderful people show up to celebrate with me this evening, I thought I'd share that generosity.'

'How sweet of you to think of us, Marcellus,' said Claudia, in the warmest voice she could muster.

Gia joined at Claudia's side without a word.

'Of course, cousin. I'm always thinking of you. It is well known, what kind of man your father was. My own father also knew well what sort of man he was. Your brother, he was even worse – the wickedest of creatures. My parents always spoke well of you. They worried about you, as did I. We feared what would become of you, alone in the world with only monsters to care for you. I'm so glad I can be here to comfort you at this time . . . but we should talk business.'

'Business? I live to hear it,' said Claudia.

'It is obvious that I have the people on my side,' he said.

'Are you here to boast?'

'No, I'm here to appeal to you to rethink my proposition. Surely you can see you cannot rule alone. I ask you to concede, withdraw from the running and allow the Senate to announce me as emperor tomorrow, for the good of Rome.'

'I must decline.'

'You would rather be humiliated?'

'I would rather have the chance to change minds.'

'You won't succeed, dear cousin. There is no way the Senate will stand behind you, nor the military.'

'I'm willing to take that chance,' said Claudia.

'Then we'll see how the dice falls tomorrow. It's in the hands of the gods, as they say.'

They stared at each other fixedly.

'For now, my confirmation party awaits me. I apologize in advance for the noise.' He looked pointedly around the nearly empty room. 'We're going to be celebrating into the early hours.'

Marcellus drifted back to his own raucous banquet, taking his procession of followers with him.

'We should call it a night,' said Claudia. 'I've taken all the losses I can cope with in one day.'

'Let us not submit to defeat just yet,' said Rectina. 'A party is just a party. A party does not make a ruler.'

'*Popularity* makes a ruler,' said Claudia, 'which means I may already have lost. My brother was already hated when he came to power, but Marcellus is a blank slate. It will be difficult to convince people he's not the right man, when they are certain it must be *a* man.'

'There must be *something* wrong with him,' said Gia. 'I'm sure we'd find some dirt on him, if we were to dig deep and long enough.'

But Claudia had too much of her own dirt; too many shallow graves to be uncovered.

'There's no time,' she said. 'I can do nothing more now than have a restful night.'

The party disbanded, limping into nothing.

Claudia lingered, signalling for Gia to wait with her. When the room had cleared out, Claudia gripped her hand, manoeuvring them behind a pillar so they couldn't be spied on.

'Will you meet me later, up in my room?' she said. 'There's something I must do first.'

'Must you ask?' Gia said, her eyes hooded with desire. 'But what is this thing you must do so urgently?'

'I need to talk to Minerva,' said Claudia. 'I could do with her wisdom and courage before tomorrow.'

Gia gave an understanding nod.

'I'll be waiting, when you're ready,' she said.

Claudia gathered a collection of offerings, including the gifts given to her by Marcellus, before returning to the palace temple.

She stood before the figures of the Twelve Harmonious Gods or Dii Consentes: the most powerful deities in the pantheon, arranged into their ceremonial pairs.

Jupiter and Juno. Mars and Venus. Minerva and Neptune. Apollo and Diana. Mercury and Ceres. Vulcan and Vesta.

They weren't as grand as the statues in the Pantheon but they were brightly painted, each standing in their own alcove, illuminated by pillars with torches on top.

She laid the bundle of offerings at the feet of her goddess.

'Tomorrow, I will be named empress,' she said.

The air prickled as the hairs on the back of her neck stood on end. The breeze seemed to silence. The shadows shifted.

'I will it.'

Her body was burning like fire, though her hands were cold.

'So be it.'

Claudia held her breath, anticipating the appearance of Minerva.

Surely her goddess had some important guidance for her on the eve of the vote, with the future of the world hanging in the balance.

She sensed that the veil was thin, that someone was watching her through it, but Minerva didn't appear. Seconds stretched into minutes, until Claudia grew cold from waiting.

Her eyes caught on the statue of Jupiter, which seemed to glint unnaturally in the torchlight.

She cleared her throat nervously, her skin prickling again.

Was he really watching her?

The breeze gusted and the atmosphere dampened. The room felt empty and uneventful once more.

Whatever Claudia had sensed, it was not her goddess.

Dispirited and shivering, she crept upstairs, past the guards who lined the staircase and the handmaids who slept on either side of her chambers, all of whom watched her curiously. Claudia had never had more eyes upon her. Privacy, intimacy – it was all the more difficult now.

She and Gia would have to be discreet. Marcellus would surely benefit, if he learned the truth.

Gia waited for her on the other side of a closed door, sitting on the red-canopied bed.

Claudia's heart surged. It was strange to see someone she loved so much sitting in a place she so hated and feared. This room had been her sanctuary from the world, decorated entirely to her tastes with money as no object, but she had never truly been safe here. The last person to sit on her bed was probably her brother, and now he was . . .

'How could you not tell me?' said Gia.

Claudia froze. 'Tell you what?'

Her heart throbbed in panic. She'd left for Pompeii in such a hurry, she had no idea what she might've left lying around. A circus parade of horrifying possibilities came to mind: dirty robes, old diaries, her terrible attempts at crafts – but it appeared that someone had cleaned her rooms in her absence, probably her handmaids.

'How could you not tell me . . .' Gia paused dramatically. 'About the other woman in your life?'

She brandished Claudia's favourite doll, gently shaking it so that her sackcloth head bobbed about.

'Oh,' said Claudia, relieved, 'that's just Valentina.'

'Why is she so . . .'

'So what?' said Claudia, hands on her hips.

The doll was carved out of wood with straw for hair, wearing the toga the palace tailor had made for her long ago. It was meant to resemble her, but it was broken beyond repair.

Gia pulled a face, unable to contain her horror at the doll's caved-in face, her scribbled-on skin, her dirty, blood-stained dress.

'What happened to her?' she asked.

'Decimus,' said Claudia. 'Decimus happened.'

'Oh . . . no. Sorry, Valentina.'

'I told you, anything I ever owned and loved, he sought to destroy or taint for ever.' She sat down next to Gia, feeling very soft and small. 'He couldn't stand anyone else being happy, especially not me.'

'That's sad,' said Gia, putting her arm around her and kissing her shoulder. 'I should've known. I wish I hadn't made light of it now.'

'It's okay, she is pretty unfortunate-looking.' Claudia pulled the doll into her lap. 'But I cherish her all the same. She's kept me company through some dark nights. I feel responsible for what happened to her.'

'She's not real,' said Gia gently.

'I know, but . . . she is me, in a way,' said Claudia.

They fell quiet.

'He's dead now,' Gia said, tenderly stroking her hair. 'He can't hurt you any more.'

Claudia leaned into her hand, like a cat being petted.

'Yet, part of me fears him still, even now. Sometimes, I think I can feel him . . . watching, waiting. He was such a malevolent force. I'm sure his spirit could take form again. If any monster can be reanimated and resurrected from the dead, it's him.'

'New phobia uncovered,' said Gia, shuddering.

'I just pray he can no longer see me or hear me, that he is finally severed from my life.'

'He's gone,' said Gia. 'I know it.'

'This is depressing, let's discuss another topic.'

'Okay. What about this prince you're still engaged to?' said Gia, avoiding her gaze.

'Really? That's what you want to discuss?'

'Do you think he'll come?'

Claudia groaned dramatically, collapsing onto the bed.

Gia lay beside her, until they were both on their backs looking up at the canopy, their legs hanging off the edge.

'It's bothering me to think he might appear at any moment and sweep you off your feet . . . and I'll have to refrain from killing him for the sake of international diplomacy,' said Gia.

'Please, don't worry,' said Claudia, rolling onto her side. 'He is not a serious concern.'

Gia mirrored her, their faces close together.

'Do you intend to marry him still?'

'I don't *want* to marry him,' Claudia said.

'Then . . . don't.'

'The letter he wrote was sent before my father died. He may have changed his mind, and all of this speculation is just a waste of our precious time together,' said Claudia, stroking Gia's cheek.

'What if he turns up here in all his princely regalia, gifting you precious rubies and gold statues or gods know what?' said Gia.

Claudia shrugged. 'I assume he will, at some point.'

'Let's say he comes, and he expects you to marry him. I doubt he'll leave quietly, even if you decline. What happens then?'

'I . . . I don't know,' Claudia admitted.

The sounds of the other party could be heard below them, getting even louder now, as if some of her guests had said their sweet farewells then stepped behind enemy lines to attend Marcellus's party.

'I don't know what the future will hold,' said Claudia, taking Gia's hand and raising it to her lips to kiss, 'but I do know that nothing and no one shall come between us. I will move the heavens if I have to. I will venture into the depths of the underworld. Whatever it takes.'

'You can't promise that.'

'I can. I just did. Didn't you hear? I'm going to be empress.'

Gia sighed, and smiled.

'Fine, we'll put it aside, for now,' she said. 'There's no point worrying about something that might never happen.'

'Right,' said Claudia, relieved to have removed one worrying thing from her pile of worrying things. 'I can think of a thousand better ways for us to spend our first evening in the palace.'

'Oh, really?' said Gia.

'Yes, in fact, I think I promised you some kind of tour.'

4. THE GODDESS OF VICTORY

Claudia awoke the next morning in Gia's arms, their hair meshed together like a tapestry of threads, their bodies entwined as if they were matching halves designed by a sculptor. For a moment, Claudia was at peace, unburdened by the world's weight, before two blunt realizations crushed her chest, forcing her eyes to snap open.

The first realization was that Minerva hadn't appeared to her in her dreams as she'd hoped. Claudia was sure she'd remember it if she had, as she did before. She recalled only venturing barefoot through the darkness of Asphodel, calling out to someone who didn't respond. Her offering and her words had no apparent effect. Minerva was still absent.

The second realization was that it was the morning of the Senate meeting. By nightfall, she would either be empress, or dead. Such a fate tended to fall on those who failed to claim the power they sought. Once named as emperor, Marcellus would need only instruct his soldiers to kill her and they would do so without question.

Would she do the same, if the situation were reversed? Claudia didn't know, and not knowing things bothered her.

To calm herself, she twisted around to gaze at Gia instead,

memorizing the shape of the brows so often quirked in amusement, and the curve of her lips, which seemed to smile even in sleep.

Claudia adored the shape of her nose, the angle of her chin, every tiny mark and mole on her skin. She listened to her breathing. She felt that heady, surging feeling, like being back on the sinking ship again, waves crashing over her.

The hunger inside her scared her. She could no longer imagine a world in which they were not together. Her want had grown into a need, and there was nothing more terrifying than needing someone.

She was smart enough to hide it, at least.

It was still early, the room bathed in faded dawn light, but Claudia couldn't settle. She hadn't yet prepared what she might say, when they asked her to outline her plans for the empire.

Claudia had been thinking about the question for years already. She knew what it was that she represented and what she hoped to achieve, if given the chance. But if she fumbled her words now, of all times, she wouldn't convince anyone. The battle was already pitched uphill as it was. If she was to captivate the Senate, to convince them to switch sides, she was going to need a grand speech.

No, more than that. She was going to need a miracle.

Carefully liberating herself from Gia's arms without disturbing her, Claudia sat at the window, looking out over the Forum and the Pantheon. She looked to the Curia Julia, a boxy marble building with a pillared porch and giant bronze doors, where senators sat in rows on either side of a parliamentary court – a monument to murdered Caesar.

She imagined that it was full of robed woman senators, and that the streets were patrolled by women soldiers in armour. She imagined that a woman and her wife lived in the palace, patrons of all women in Rome, and that it was them. Her and Gia.

It was a beautiful vision. Perhaps she ought to commission an artist to paint it as a mural.

A soft knocking interrupted her thoughts. Startled, Claudia moved back to the bed, drawing the red curtains to hide Gia's sleeping body before opening the door a crack, revealing a doe-eyed, freckled handmaid.

'It's time to rise, Empress.'

Unlike the men in the palace, she didn't appear to have any difficulty recognizing Claudia as her ruler.

'I am up, thank you . . . uh? Sorry, what is your name?'

'My name?' said the girl. 'Did I displease you?'

She looked terrified. Claudia realized that when an emperor asked for a servant's name, it was rarely to praise them.

'Not at all. I just realized that I don't know your name, and I feel that I should, if I'm going to be any good at this,' she said.

'It's . . . Aurelia,' she said. 'I'm Aurelia.'

'Thank you, Aurelia.'

Aurelia's gaze lingered. She chewed on her bottom lip, looking at the ground a moment before she looked up eagerly.

'Your cousin Marcellus has not yet risen from his chambers,' she said in a whisper.

'Is that so?'

'He was up until the early hours, drinking like the barrel had no bottom,' said Aurelia.

'That is extremely useful to know,' said Claudia.

'The man whose job it is to wake him up is also still slumbering in his bed . . . I do hope he isn't late.'

'That would be terrible indeed.'

They exchanged a small, wry smile.

'I should also tell you that there are people gathering in front of the palace already.'

'For Marcellus, I assume?' said Claudia.

'No, they say they're here for you.'

'For me? Are you sure?'

'I am certain. They are calling themselves a cult of women.'

Claudia heard Gia stirring behind the curtain and saw Aurelia's eyes darting over her shoulder.

Claudia suspected that she had registered a presence there. She was obviously a sharp mind, the kind of person who didn't miss much.

'Then I'd better get ready,' Claudia said, quickly.

Aurelia bowed and skittered away.

When Claudia closed the door, Gia appeared from behind the curtain, wearing only underclothes.

'A cult of women, is it?' she said. 'It is only right that you are worshipped, but I insist on being first in line.'

Gia reached out, trying to pull her back under the canopy.

'Don't tempt me,' said Claudia, dodging her embrace. 'As much as I long to stay in bed and forget the world, the people are waiting.'

'Fine,' said Gia, smiling sleepily. 'I will have to learn to share you, for the good of the world.'

'We'll have to be on our best behaviour today. Aurelia already suspects that I have someone in my bed.'

'So what if you do? It's not her business.'

'If Marcellus should learn of it, I'm sure he'd rush to inform the Senate. Fortunately, my cousin hasn't yet dragged himself out of his pit. If he were to miss the meeting, I might actually succeed.'

'Then go – go and get ready. We'll go to the Curia early, so you can meet the people and show the Senate how serious you are,' said Gia. 'I'll gather the others. Strength in numbers, right?'

Claudia quickly washed and changed back into her gold and red robes, hastily combing her hair before donning the crown she had taken from her dead brother's head. There was still a spot of blood on one of the golden leaves, but she put it on anyway.

It made her feel strong, as dangerous as she needed to be.

Gia stood in the doorway, looking distractingly heroic in her volcano-worn armour.

'How do I look?' asked Claudia.

'Like the first empress of Rome,' said Gia. 'Better than me. I look like I've been in a fight with Jupiter himself.'

'You are always perfect to me. But I will have the palace armourer repair or replace it. Only the finest armour for my finest warrior.'

They clasped hands on the staircase, their fingers lacing together in a brief, secret squeeze before they broke apart, seconds before they turned to meet their audience.

Downstairs, Cassius and Dominic stood with Athena, Claudia's handmaidens, three guards and a gaggle of hangers-on, all of whom would accompany her on the walk to Senate House.

'This is for you,' said Athena, matter-of-factly, handing her a single wilted flower. 'For luck.'

'Thank you, Athena,' said Claudia, tucking it into her crown.

Its petals hid the bloodspot.

'I hope you become empress. Minerva is my favourite goddess. She's your goddess too, isn't she?' said Athena. 'Gia says you've met her.'

'It's true,' said Claudia. 'She comes to me in dreams. One day, I will tell you all about her.'

'Would you really?'

'Of course.'

Outside in the courtyard, a small group of women waited, all wearing dark robes that covered their hair. When Claudia and Gia approached, one of them ran in front of her, scattering petals from a basket.

'We are blessed by the presence of the empress,' said one, as another woman echoed her.

'All hail the empress!'

'We come to you on this historic day to pledge our allegiance,' said the first woman, who had clearly designated herself as the group's leader. 'The imperial cult would not admit us. They believe only a man can be chosen by the gods to rule.'

'We've formed our own cult of worship. Only women are permitted to join our ranks,' said the second member.

Claudia bowed her head to them, pressing her hands together.

'I'm grateful for your support. By the name of Minerva, I will do everything in my power to be worthy of you.'

'The goddess has spoken!'

'The empress shall be the protector of women and children!'

'All hail Empress Claudia, first of her name.'

The cultists formed a train behind her, chanting and ringing bells as they crossed the Forum towards the Curia Julia.

It occurred to Claudia, just then, that she had another strength, an advantage that Marcellus lacked.

Perhaps the women of Rome could save her after all.

*

Three hundred senators sat on benches inside the Curia Julia, split into two sides with the open floor between them. They murmured and muttered, coughed and cleared their throats, awaiting the arrival of Marcellus. The noise formed a burbling bubble of sound, slightly muffled and faraway, as Claudia stood in silence before them.

'How much longer?' one man grumbled.

'He isn't making a very good first impression.'

'Maybe he's engaged in more important matters.'

'More important than the Senate?'

At the far end of the room was the Altar of Victory: a statue of the goddess Victoria standing on a globe, holding out a wreath with her wings spread wide. She symbolized victory in war. The altar had been installed by Augustus to celebrate his victory at the Battle of Actium.

'Perhaps we should begin?' said Damocles reluctantly.

He looked at Claudia, but just then the internal doors clattered noisily as Marcellus burst in.

'Apologies for my uncharacteristic lateness,' he said, trailing soldiers and imperial cultists. 'I spent the morning going from door to door, speaking to the people of Rome about their concerns for the future.'

That rotten liar.

'More like he was out cold after pissing away the night,' said Gia, under her breath. 'You should expose him.'

'I don't think the senators will look well on me telling tales,' Claudia said. 'Marcellus will just say I had a party of my own, albeit a less successful one.'

It was obvious from her cousin's slightly dishevelled appearance that he was recovering from drunkenness, although drunkenness was not a hurdle to the position, if her father was anything to go by.

If *she* had turned up like this, she'd never have heard the end of it, but no one commented on Marcellus. Unfair as it was, she'd have to best him on the merit of her argument instead.

Her cousin stalked onto the floor, walking past Claudia with only the barest of acknowledgements. He smiled confidently and parted his arms with the broad span of a mediocre man who has no doubt in his mind about his own brilliance. Whether he was qualified and deserving of the role didn't even seem to enter his mind. He was assured of his own potential, in the absence of any evidence, and that in itself was a strength.

'I'm ready to share my grand vision for the empire. Senators, are you ready?' he said.

'The floor is yours. The Senate is listening,' said Damocles.

As gracefully as she could manage, Claudia shuffled back to the edge of the room, where Gia and the others were standing in shadows, including the female cultists. Gia gave her a supportive, sympathetic look, but that only made her feel more pitiful.

'Rome is already great,' began Marcellus, his booming voice echoing, 'but . . . what if it could be greater?'

Later, Claudia would struggle to recall much of what he'd said. Her mind had wandered wildly, rehearsing her own speech in preparation, but she knew Marcellus's speech contained many grandiose plans for even bigger buildings with even more gold on them.

'Greatness means always striving for more,' he said. 'Greatness does not sit on its laurels and say, "we have enough". No. Greatness is about thinking bigger, further, wider, stronger.'

It was a lot of empty promises of unnecessary construction, but it sounded suitably impressive, enough to earn him waves of nods from senators on the front benches.

He promised better games, better races, better chariots, better walls, better spas, better roads, better soldiers, even better slaves. Everything would be superior under his reign, though he didn't explain in detail how these things would be achieved.

Nevertheless, he had the air of a man who was already emperor and didn't need to explain himself to plebians. He believed himself great, and thus he was.

Claudia could feel it. The future was slipping away from her.

'Our armies will continue to dominate Germania and Britannia, and prevent the advance of the barbarians. The future of western civilization is at stake. We shall continue to lead the world in knowledge and technology. If Rome is strong, then so is mankind.'

His plan to expand the British invasion caused several of the senators to whisper in alarm, including the senator who had attended her gathering the night prior, but Senators Tacitus and Thelonius were convincing the men around them to support her cousin's claim and his plan to push the boundaries of Rome even further. And Marcellus was accompanied by General Aquinas. If the military stood against her, the battle was already lost. It was over, and Marcellus had won.

'We cannot be led by a sheltered child,' Marcellus said. 'One who has never known war.'

He looked at Claudia pointedly. She wanted to protest but she clamped her jaw instead, her hands clutching at the sides of her robes. She would wait her turn.

It was killing her, but she would wait.

'As a decorated soldier, I know exactly what is at stake each time we send legions to defend our borders. I know the cost of a life, and the sacrifices our conquest demands. That is why only a man who has felt the whistle of an arrow skim past his cheek can be a true commander. Only a commander can rule an empire.'

Claudia had felt more than just arrows grazing her skin. She had seen the world burning. She had felt steel slip through flesh. She had weathered the storm and braved the sea. She was not as worldly as Marcellus, but she had lived and feared and fought.

'Our enemies surely sense the empire's weakness, and the people are crying out for consistent leadership,' he continued. 'By my steady hand, we shall continue the era of Pax Romana. I will bring stability and strength, at a time of great uncertainty.'

The senators applauded, nodding encouragingly.

After a string of closing platitudes, Marcellus stepped aside to make way for a parade of generals. They testified to his suitability as emperor, reeling off heroic feats he'd performed.

When the last man had debased himself with gushing praise, Marcellus and his party retreated to the other side of the room, looking satisfied and a shade smug.

In his mind, the crown was already his.

Claudia moved to the centre of the room and stared into the cold eyes of the statue atop the Altar of Victory, silently appealing for her blessing. She gave her a faint, reverent nod.

'Claudia Caesaria, you may now speak,' said Damocles.

Her head throbbed. Her heart pounded. Her ears began ringing, as if someone had struck a bell within her skull.

The words she'd practised were now stuck in her throat, leaving her gasping for air.

'Do hurry up,' a man barked. 'We don't have all day.'

A murmur of mocking laughter rang through the crowd.

Claudia took a deep breath and put herself in the hands of fate.

'Marcellus says that only a soldier can rule Rome,' she said, 'and it's true that many emperors have commanded legions, but the most important quality of a ruler is how well he can represent the people.'

'Yes, dear, we know that,' croaked one old fellow.

'How can Marcellus expect to rule, when he serves only half the population?' she said.

The senators looked confused.

'Half of all Romans are women,' she said. 'What is Marcellus Suetonius offering to them?'

Several senators chuckled, but Claudia wasn't joking.

The Senate was comprised entirely of men, Claudia thought, many of them elderly. They were all educated, from wealthy patrician families. They didn't represent the common people any more than her.

'Where would the empire be without women?' she said. 'To run your houses, to serve your carnal desires, to birth your children – since that is all you allow them to do. They cannot vote or fight or stand in the Senate, yet they are expected to serve and obey. Even the limited power women are given is what keeps the wheel of empire turning. Women create new generations, of soldiers, of slaves, of senators.'

Claudia snuck a look at Gia, and her face was soft, quietly rapt. She knew her words would connect with her, if no one else; that she would be understood by Gia.

'Some of you have wives, do you not?' she said, turning back to the senators. 'You have daughters, do you not? Who is ruling them? Who is guiding them? Who considers their interests, when they hold the sceptre? Who protects women, when they wear the crown?'

The hecklers had nothing to say now, watching her with mixed expressions. It was difficult to read the energy of such a hostile room, full of people who wouldn't accept her no matter what she said or did, and yet she sensed a shift. Some of them still looked offended, disgusted even, but others appeared fearful, listening intently, as if women might eventually rise up against them if denied all autonomy.

'The world is changing and Rome must change with it. The armies of your enemies are busy recruiting women warriors. They will double the number of their soldiers. They will charge into the future and Rome shall be left behind, all because of the short-sightedness of mankind.'

Some of the senators on the back benches made eyes at each other, as if recalling previous conversations they'd had.

'I am the only living child of Emperor Tiberius. I am the rightful heir of the Julio-Claudian dynasty. I have grown up in the palace. I have seen first hand what is required of a ruler. My cousin may be brave and heroic on the battlefield, but will he know how to host foreign diplomats? Does he know every festival, and the customs of every parade? Does he know the laws, as I do? Does he know the history of the pantheon, as I do?'

Claudia looked to Victoria and felt a surge of confidence.

'Isn't it strange, that the symbol of military success can be a woman,' she said, gesturing at the statue, 'sculpted with weapons in armour, yet women can't join the legions? Minerva, the patron of wisdom, can be a woman, but a woman cannot occupy the Senate?'

Claudia paused, holding the gaze of Damocles. His expression had shifted from boredom and embarrassment to discomforting curiosity.

'I won't make promises I can't keep. I won't pretend that the years to come will be free of conflict. That would be a lie. If you asked me what kind of empire keeps expanding without limit, always looking afield and abroad without first ensuring that its own citizens are thriving, I would tell you, it was a fragile one. Even greatness,' she looked pointedly at Marcellus, as he had done to her, 'must be held in balance. I can promise to serve and protect every man in the empire, as well as every woman and girl. Every citizen of Rome will be my subject, including the ones you take for granted. Thank you for your time, gentlemen.'

As with Marcellus, a number of people now spoke in Claudia's favour, including Celadus the Handsome, who regaled how she'd attempted to evacuate Pompeii and been prevented by the praetorian guard who served her brother. It was arresting testimony, but he was just a gladiator – a famous one, but not exactly a member of the ruling classes.

The senate was more impressed when Pliny the Elder entered, being a general known for his vast wealth of knowledge.

'I joined the military as a junior officer,' he said. 'I commanded a battalion of five hundred men. In my time, I have seen female warriors in Germania kill Roman soldiers without mercy. I have heard of female generals in Britannia defend territories, even though they were vastly outnumbered. I have seen with my own eyes that women can be just as strategic and, indeed, victorious in battle. As a scholar, too, I have met many women whose minds were just as bright as any man in their field.'

He smiled fondly and gestured at Rectina, now living with him and his nephew, the young Pliny.

'Yet their work goes uncredited, unrecorded by history.'

Pliny, a seasoned master of public speaking, paused to allow the audience to reflect.

'I have no doubt that Marcellus would be a fine emperor, but Claudia would be a world-changing empress, symbolizing the philosophical advancement of Rome, along with its territorial conquests. We must grow in mind as we grow in might. For this reason, I support her claim.'

Damocles opened the Senate floor up to questions. Most of them were for Marcellus, trying to pin down his plan for British expansion as he rambled in circles, saying nothing in a lot of words. Then a bearded man raised his hand, nodding at Claudia.

'Is it true that you claim to be blessed by the goddess Minerva?'

'The goddess is my patron,' said Claudia, guardedly.

Though she was certain that some of the men in the room were backed by their own gods, they were not aware of it, as she had been made aware. They didn't speak to them as she did.

All eyes turned to her.

'What exactly do you mean by that?' the man pried.

'She guides and protects me.'

'You have communicated directly with the goddess Minerva?'

'Yes, but also other goddesses.'

The senators stirred – curious, resentful.

'You are in communication with *multiple* deities?'

'It should not come as a surprise that the imperial family is connected with divinity,' she said. 'It is tradition.'

This inspired a wave of protests:

'What do you know of what the pantheon desires?'

'She thinks she's one of them!'

'She thinks she's divine!'

'The goddesses speak to me, and through me, as I was chosen by Minerva to rule,' Claudia insisted.

Her last statement caused an outcry, as senators began shouting and jeering all at once.

'Prove it!' one man crowed, inspiring others to chant along with him: 'Yes, prove it! Go on, prove it.'

These same men had been told that her father met with Jupiter, that he dined with the gods in Elysium, and they had never questioned it, just because he was the emperor. But now it was her turn to declare her divinity, they were suddenly sceptics of the firmest degree.

'You cannot validate your claims?' said Marcellus.

'What evidence have you provided for *your* claims?' she said. 'You have none.'

'I am not the one who boasted of my divine right.'

'You didn't even mention the gods in your speech, as if they are entirely irrelevant to your ambitions,' she said. 'Perhaps the pantheon are strangers to you, but the plans of the goddesses are well known by me.'

Silence fell in Senate House.

A lone voice cut through the quiet. 'If you can prove it, we shall make you empress,' said the red-robed, bearded consul, Damocles.

The crowd rippled again, all of them attentive.

Damocles was goading her. He didn't truly believe that she'd be able to fulfil his request. It was simply an easy way to discredit her.

They had done nothing to stop Decimus from seizing power, even when he tortured and murdered members of their own organization, but now they expected her to perform a miracle for their approval.

She couldn't win.

'Minerva herself could appear at my side, before your very eyes, and you would still appoint my cousin simply because he is a man,' she said.

'Prove to us that the goddesses work through you,' Damocles continued, 'and we shall confirm you. But if you can't, we shall disqualify you and declare our support for Marcellus Suetonius.'

Claudia had walked right into a trap. Now they would use her inability to manifest a goddess to rule her out, while Marcellus would not be asked to prove any of his claims.

'I cannot summon the goddesses on command,' said Claudia. 'I am their servant, not the other way around.'

'That is the offer, Princess,' said Damocles. 'This is your opportunity to prove yourself. Show us why a woman should rule Rome, when none has ruled before.'

Claudia looked to Gia, who gazed back helplessly. She looked to Pliny and Rectina, who appeared to have accepted defeat. She looked to the cult of women, who became exultant under her gaze.

'We are with you, Empress Claudia,' said the leader.

'We believe in you, Empress.'

She looked ahead to the Altar of Victory, and to the winged goddess who watched over them.

Claudia had never prayed to the ocean deity Salacia, and yet Salacia had intervened to save her when Jupiter attacked.

Was the goddess Victoria loyal to Roman soldiers and generals over the other goddesses? Claudia wondered. Over other women?

Claudia took a deep breath and crossed the room, removing a gold ring from her finger. It had been her father's. It was the imperial signet ring, with its heraldic eagle.

She'd taken it from his body before she killed him, and Decimus hadn't been observant enough to notice its absence.

Now, she laid it at the feet of the statue as an offering.

The ring of the man she had poisoned to get here.

Few on earth would understand her actions, but the goddesses knew all. They saw all. Minerva had given her the idea to kill her father to begin with, though she hadn't said so directly. It had been more of an implication – an acknowledgement of what was required of her. They knew what a monster he was, and her brother too. They knew she was different. That was why she believed they would come to her now, if she offered this symbol of the greatest possible sacrifice.

'Victoria, goddess of victory, I seek your support. If I win, it shall be under your name, for your statue is witness. If you stand with me, and with the women of Rome, I implore you to reveal yourself.'

Claudia gazed up at the statue, willing the goddess to bless her with all her might.

'Thank you,' she whispered, as if the victory was already won.

Wetting her dry mouth in the most dignified way she could manage, Claudia returned to the centre of the floor . . . and waited.

She prayed that the deity would appear as she stared down at the floor, a mosaic of stylized rosettes entwined with cornucopias in red and green. The colours began to blur. Time lulled, like still waters.

She could hardly hear her own breathing over the relentless thudding of her heart – a wild bird, caged in her chest.

Nothing was happening. Perhaps the goddesses would only come to her aid when she was in mortal peril. If so, she was about to be abjectly humiliated.

Claudia's mind tumbled ahead, trying to come up with an

explanation for her failure to demonstrate her connection to divinity as heat gradually rose in her neck and cheeks. The senators started to murmur impatiently, their scowls deepening in her direction.

Then a beam of sunlight bled through an arch, brighter than seemed possible for the hour. It fell directly upon Victoria, illuminating her face in a way that made her look curiously incarnate.

One of the senators pointed, crying, 'Look!'

With the grinding sound of metal in motion, the goddess began to move, like an automaton created by Vulcan.

'Hark!' came a tremulous, building-shaking voice.

Victoria's lips didn't move, but the commanding voice seemed to issue from within the moving statue.

As bronze turned to gold, she slowly spread out her wings, their sculpted feathers glistening.

The gathered senators cried out in unison, scrambling towards the rear of the room.

'Behold, the Empress of Rome,' said Victoria,

One man fled for the doors. Others were already on their knees. Even Marcellus paled, his gleeful expression melting away.

'All will serve her, by decree of the Fates,' said Victoria.

'Claudia.' Rectina clutched at her chest, like a worried mother.

'Now I have truly seen everything,' said Pliny the Elder.

Slowly, Claudia stepped forward, her breathing ragged. The golden goddess leaned forward and touched her head.

'Claudia Caesaria is blessed by the goddesses,' she said.

Claudia nodded up at her cold face, in gratitude, in reverence.

The statue retracted her wings and slowly stilled, her lustrous gold skin returning to dull bronze. Claudia slid the ring back on her finger and turned defiantly to face the Senate.

'Will that be proof enough?' she said, coolly.

Senate House erupted into pandemonium.

'She is a witch! A daemon!'

'All hail Empress Claudia!'

'This is foreign sorcery!'

'All hail Empress Claudia!'

'Order!' bellowed Damocles, struggling to regain control. 'We must have order! Settle down, men. There must be a vote. This is the last vestige of democracy in Rome. We shall not be reduced to raving maniacs.' An uneasy hush fell. 'I call upon you to cast your ballot.'

One by one they did so, by placing stones engraved with their initials into one of two bowls. One for Marcellus, and one for her.

Her cousin had retreated to the other side of the room, while she and her followers now gathered around the Altar of Victory.

They had switched sides.

The vote was a remnant of the Republican era. Her father's appointment had been unanimous but this was a different, much more tenuous, situation. She was asking them to do something entirely new, something for which there was no previous form. If not for the apparition of a goddess, they would not even have considered her, and even now, with that miracle in her pocket, her victory was still not assured, despite the promise made by Damocles.

Claudia tried to estimate how many men were placing their tokens in her bowl, though she didn't know which was which, nor would it have mattered, because the tokens seemed to be evenly distributed. She lost count when Gia's hand brushed briefly against hers, drawing her gaze.

'It will be over soon,' said Gia.

'It is just beginning,' said Claudia, shaking her head. 'Win or lose, we will be fearing for our lives.'

When the last vote had been cast, Damocles and his assistants counted out the stones one by one before a gathered group of observers, including Pliny the Elder.

Claudia hung back, too nervous to watch. Marcellus moved around the outside of the observers' circle, trying to calculate the numbers for himself. The Senate recounted once, and again, before the senators returned to their benches and Damocles addressed the room with a face that was impassively blank.

'Today, history has been decided,' he said. 'The votes have been cast. We have 147 votes for Marcellus Suetonius, and 152 votes for Claudia Imperia, with one abstention.'

She . . . had won?

She was victorious?

It was too big to be believed, and yet the sound of celebration and objection grew enormous, blurring away into a slick of amorphous babble as Claudia stood still in shock. She looked to her cousin and saw her own bewilderment reflected on his face, united for a brief moment, despite their differences, in shared surprise at how destiny had come to pass.

'It cannot stand,' shouted one man. 'I will not allow it.'

'What are you going to do? Fight the gods?' replied another.

'We should vote again. There has clearly been inference.'

'She is not my ruler. I will not salute for her.'

'Not in my name, by the grace of Jupiter, no matter how many goddesses will it.'

'The Senate has given its judgement,' said Damocles. 'You may not like the result, but the empress has been democratically ordained.'

'It is offensive,' spat Senator Tacitus, 'to our ancestors, to our children, to the king of the gods. You may as well appoint a prostitute.'

Thelonius agreed: 'Rome will fall, mark my words.'

The vocal objectors were herded out by their more discerning fellows, who poured out into the Forum to spread the news.

Gia moved to stand in front of Claudia as the remaining crowd became more animated, senators bickering and brawling on the benches. Half of them wanted to kill her, and the other half looked at her as if she could make their wildest dreams come true.

Damocles raised his voice, to shout above the dissenting din.

'Claudia Imperia Caesaria, first of her name, descendant of Claudius, daughter of Tiberius the Second, subject of Minerva – you have been declared as ruler of Rome and will be known as Empress Claudia.'

In this moment, most of the followers who had clung to her cousin for the past hour crossed the room to join her, including many of the soldiers. Even some the imperial cultists reluctantly joined the circle that formed around her, joining the chorus of praise from people who'd swiftly turned face. Others remained apart, separate in their opposition.

Marcellus walked towards her, bobbing his head as if thinking of what he wanted to say.

Claudia braced herself, as Gia flexed her sword.

'If you touch a hair on her head,' she said, though she didn't finish this sentence, for Marcellus held up his palm.

'No need.'

Claudia recalled her prediction that he would slay her if she lost, and her momentary consideration that she could do the same.

'I'm here to congratulate you.'

He stuck out his hand. A peace offering. He looked clammy and greenish, as if last night's revelry was finally catching up with him.

'Fair play to you, cousin,' he said. 'I can't compete with divine intervention.'

Claudia stared at his outstretched hand, unsure.

'I will step aside, to be seen and heard only when you have requirement of me,' he said. 'All I ask is that you spare my life.'

If left alive, Marcellus would surely continue to be a threat, but if she killed him, she'd be starting out her reign as a tyrant. Claudia wanted to be admired and not feared, yet some quiet part of her wondered if she would *have* to be a tyrant, to rule as a woman.

Would the men of Rome respect her more if she conversed with them in their own language of violence, or was she to rise above it, as a superior creature?

Marcellus looked younger now, weaker. He was afraid, just as she was afraid. He was her blood, and Claudia was short on relatives. It would be her right to kill the man who'd questioned her legitimacy, and she was certain it would impress some of the more bloodthirsty onlookers, but when she looked to Gia, she saw the conflict in her lover's expression, the softness in her eyes, the way she lowered her weapon subconsciously. Gia had killed, but not like Claudia had killed.

Gia killed with mercy.

When Claudia held out her hand expectantly, Marcellus hesitated before complying, his temple twitching.

'All hail Empress Claudia,' he said, kissing the ring.

5. A MARRIAGE OF INCONVENIENCE

'What about lions?' asked Damocles.

'No.'

'Elephants, then?'

'Also no.'

Claudia sat in her throne room, in a golden chair with outspread wings. Damocles worked through a list of potential entertainments for her coronation, as Gia paced back and forth along the colonnade.

'What about tribesmen from the client kingdoms?'

'No.'

'Should we have a parade of freed slaves?'

'Absolutely not. I shouldn't like to remind them of the empire's greatest and most enduring evils.”

'Should we release a flock of doves, perhaps?'

'So they can shit on the statues of the gods in my name? No, let us not,' Claudia said.

Damocles sighed, rubbing his left temple.

'Please, Empress, you must give us *something* to work with,' he said. 'I know you are most concerned with being the people's princess, but there is a certain level of gravitas that is expected of us. A bit of pomp, a flash of glamour, some archaic ceremonial regalia. It's what the people expect. We cannot put on such a paltry parade that we appear weak, cowed, frightened of the public. Not unless you want a rotten cabbage to the face.'

'I do not.'

'Then you must demonstrate your strength.'

'Yet if I demonstrate too much of it, I shall be dubbed a tyrant before I've had chance to issue a single proclamation,' she said. 'The more I flaunt my power, the more my enemies shall seek to limit it.'

Hundreds of people swirled around her with fans and amphoras, presenting her with flags and sashes and even coins with her profile on them, all to be approved. Yet part of her mind had wandered away into the past, where all of her least regal demons dwelled.

She'd often knelt at her father's sandalled feet in this very room, begging him to protect her from Decimus.

'Please, Claudia,' he'd said, as he plotted conquests over wine, 'can you not see I'm busy?'

'I don't want to hear it, Claudia,' he'd said, watching two men fight to the death. 'Your brother's mischief does not concern me.'

'Don't be hysterical, Claudia,' he'd said, being fitted for new robes. 'You're making a scene. Conduct yourself with some dignity.'

Now, she bit down on the inside flesh of her lip so hard she tasted blood. Her nails dug into her palm, the sharp sensation flooding her with relief. She may be empress, but that small girl inside her, clutching a broken doll, was still frightened . . . and angry.

Her father had failed her then, and every time after. No matter what her brother did to her, her father had never punished him for it.

Now she was empress and they were dead. She could dismantle

their statues, if she wanted to. She could piss on their graves as soldiers fired cannons, if she wanted to. They would deserve it.

'I must *insist* that we march with the equestrian legion, at the very least,' said Damocles, bringing her back to reality. 'You like horses, don't you? There's nothing objectionable about horses.'

'Fine,' said Claudia. 'We shall have horses.'

'And if you're having horses, you may as well have chariots. A dozen charioteers. They can ride ahead of the gladiators.'

'Fine. What else?' she said.

'There is no question about the military band. You simply must have a military band,' said Damocles.

'A small one.'

'What about fire breathers? Or acrobats?'

'It is not a circus, Damocles.'

'The people will be less hostile if they are entertained. That's why I suggested the menagerie.'

'No menagerie,' she said firmly.

'What about an offering to the gods?'

Claudia lifted her chin in interest, her eyes narrowing.

'Now there's an idea,' she said.

'Which god would you like to dedicate your confirmation to?'

'Not a god, a goddess. We shall thank Minerva, but also Diana, Venus and Fortuna ... actually, let us dedicate it to all of the goddesses.'

Damocles blinked at her rapidly.

'All of them?' he repeated. 'Are you sure?'

'Why not? Have an attendant from each of their temples walk in the parade to honour their deity, and, at the end, we shall have a special ceremony for Minerva. She is my patron, after all.'

'But not a single god?'

'Not one.'

'Not even Jupiter?'

'Least of all him.'

One of the courtiers gasped at her reckless daring.

'As you wish, Empress,' sighed Damocles.

He made way for another man – the imperial armourer presenting a new crest – as a gaggle of advisors auditioned various singers, giving them each just a minute to impress her.

More and more visitors arrived, filling the table with gifts and offerings. Claudia sat upright in the chair, lifting herself up with her hands as she looked around for Gia, but she was nowhere to be seen. The arches were guarded by praetorians instead.

'Where is Gia?' she asked of the advisors.

'Who?' said Hieronymus.

'My gladiator,' she said. 'My guard.'

'Oh, *her*. I have asked for her to be kept away, so you are not distracted,' he said, pointedly. 'You can socialize with your friend later, Princess. For now, there is important work to be done.'

Claudia glared at him, stupefied that he could be so ignorant to their respective positions.

'Empress,' she corrected. 'And Gia is not merely my friend. She is a member of my court. She is my trusted confidant and protector. There are no rooms in this palace that are closed to her, if I am in them. Please, go and fetch her.'

One of the younger advisors scurried off eagerly.

'Very well,' said Hieronymus stuffily. 'Let us return to the topic of the confirmation.'

'Go ahead. I am listening.'

'First, there's the question of who will ride beside you. Ordinarily, it would be the wife of the emperor, maybe a sibling. In your case, perhaps you could be persuaded to have Marcellus accompany you.'

'I don't think that would be appropriate.'

'Why not, Princess?'

'*Empress*,' she said again, firmer this time, her eyes widening in warning. 'He challenged me for rule. He is my opponent. I have not sought to punish him for that, but I don't wish to reward him either.'

'Oh,' said Hieronymus shiftily, 'well I'm afraid Marcellus has already been asked, and he was keen to say yes.'

As if magically summoned by the sound of his name, Marcellus emerged from the throng of bodies.

'Wonderful day, cousin!' he said, cheerily. He'd smartened up since his appearance at Senate House, with fresh robes and a medallion that gave him an imperial look. 'I hear we shall be riding together in tomorrow's parade. I am honoured indeed.'

She didn't offer up her hand this time but he took it anyway, kissing the back of it as he gave a deep, respectful bow.

'Regrettably, I must—' Claudia began.

'It would be the perfect opportunity to launch ourselves as a couple, don't you think?' he said.

No words left her lips as she stared at him, speechless.

'If we are to marry, it is important that the public sees the strength in our union,' he continued.

'You and Marcellus are to marry?' said Hieronymus, just loud enough that he was heard by all those present. 'Why didn't you say so?'

The room erupted into a flurry of activity, congratulating her on a union she hadn't consented to.

Marcellus was smiling and shaking hands, as if it was real, as if she had agreed.

But she had *not* agreed.

At this exact moment, as her advisors cheered and applauded, crowing about the impending wedding, Gia walked in.

Over the din, Claudia saw a handmaid approach her, pointing to the empress to share the news.

'No, no, no,' Claudia said, in a dull voice.

Cassius and Dominic appeared behind Gia, along with Athena, all of them looking equally surprised.

Gia's eyes found hers. She frowned, raised her palms as if to say, *'what the fuck?'*

Claudia shook her head minutely but the situation was rapidly snowballing, as advisors accosted her from all sides.

'I shall prepare a public notice at once,' said the palace scribe. 'Do you have any words of joy to share with the people?'

'I will create another bust, right away,' said the palace sculptor. 'No – a relief. No! What am I saying? A full statue. In marble! You and Marcellus shall stand side by side in the courtyard!'

'When do you intend on holding the ceremony?'

'What gemstone would you like in your ring?'

'What day should we declare a new public holiday?'

'Should we set aside a room for a nursery?'

These were just the statements directed at her, but they were accompanied by a larger chorus of whispers she could only half make out.

'Do you think the princess is with child?'

'I thought she consorted with Celadus the Handsome?'

'I heard she consorts with them all, if you know what I mean.'

The room was swarming with people, all of them calling her name and asking her questions. Claudia felt faint, snatched from reality and planted in a dream.

'ENOUGH!' she bellowed, in a voice so fierce she frightened even herself.

The room immediately quieted.

'Marcellus is horribly mistaken,' she said.

'I am?'

Her cousin looked genuinely befuddled. Claudia couldn't tell if it was an act, or if he really was that oblivious.

'We are related, by blood,' said Claudia.

'It isn't uncommon, nor against the law,' he said.

'I have no desire for you.'

'It would be a marriage of convenience.'

'It would be a marriage of *in*convenience, for me personally.'

'You should take the night to think on it.'

'I don't need to think about it.'

Claudia was agog at his obliviousness, his entitlement. She felt her temper spiking, making her left eye twitch.

'I will not marry you, Marcellus,' she said. 'I can't, in fact, marry you, because . . . because . . .'

Claudia looked to Gia. Her lover's gaze seemed to scream, 'say it, do it, be free', but whatever courage she was hoping would empower her didn't come. Only easy lies.

'Because I am already engaged. Prince Darius of Persia has recently written to my father, about his intention to marry me.'

Several guests gasped, unaware of this fact.

'And you intend to go through with it?' asked Marcellus.

Claudia hesitated. Even if she wasn't ready to declare her public love for Gia, it would be a good moment for her to assert that she belonged to no man, that she would rule alone as empress without need of a husband, but once more, the words stuck in her throat.

Marcellus was a serpent but he knew, as she knew, that she was vulnerable. Even *with* a prince for a fiancé, she was going to struggle, but without one, she was even more at risk. She needed him to be threatened, to see her as dangerous too.

Her gut told her to be cautious, to never underestimate her enemies. Men were so resistant to women taking their place in general. She was sure the concept of an empress with a wife would rile them into anarchy. The fear of manhood becoming obsolete. What then?

'I . . . do,' she said. She couldn't bring herself to meet Gia's eye. 'Thus, I must decline your offer of marriage.'

Marcellus nodded slowly, his cheeks colouring.

'You were not empress when your betrothal was arranged,' Hieronymus said. 'The prince will seek to take advantage of your new power. You cannot trust the Persian royals. It is known.'

Several others hummed agreeably.

The Roman Empire and the Persian Empire had a long and bloody history. Though towns and fortifications were continually sacked and razed, neither side was willing to push too far beyond the border. The balance between them was almost always restored. Her father's strategy had been to maintain a stalemate.

'I am certain they would say the same of us,' she said. 'But I shall take your advice into consideration.'

'If I may say so, it would be far better to marry Marcellus and secure the imperial bloodline,' said Damocles, who had reappeared, presumably upon hearing of the imperial engagement. 'By wedding your two houses, there will be no question that the Julio-Claudian dynasty reigns. It will be difficult for anyone to contest your right to rule, and those who doubt that a woman can lead alone will be assured by his presence.'

Claudia bristled. She knew no one would be concerned about an emperor without a wife.

'I said no, and that's the end of it,' she said.

'Really, Princess,' began Hieronymus, 'if I may—'

'The next man to call me Princess will be escorted from the premises and stripped of his roles,' she said. 'It is the most basic of courtesies, to refer to me by the correct title.'

The room fell to a resentful silence.

'Tomorrow, Gia will ride with me, as my protection,' she said. 'Everywhere I am, she will be also, so long as she wishes.'

She looked to Gia, for confirmation.

'I do wish,' Gia said. She glanced at Hieronymus. 'What are your plans for security?'

'I don't remember putting you in charge,' said Hieronymus.

'You are to consult with Gia on all matters of my safety,' said Claudia. 'That is an order.'

'I'm not sure if the optics of an empress riding with a gladiator is quite what you wish to convey,' said Damocles. 'They aren't high society.'

Gia gave him a stony look.

'Celebrities, certainly,' Damocles said, in a higher pitch than usual. 'Popular, heroic and beloved by the people? Certainly. But to ride in the imperial chariot alongside the ruler of Rome? Certainly not.'

'I'm afraid I have to disagree,' said Claudia lightly. 'If gladiators are a symbol of the people, then I shall stand with the people.'

'You do not need to stand so closely,' said Hieronymus.

'They already know I sponsored Viatrix the Victorious back in Pompeii. It's not a secret. We were both there when Vesuvius erupted, and we survived together. I don't intend to forget that, or the citizens who were lost. There is nothing shameful about it.'

The courtiers whispered intently.

'If you need a second reason, Gia is the only person I trust to protect my life. If not for her, I would not be here. It is settled. The first empress of Rome shall ride with her female guardian. We are making a statement. That isn't a suggestion, or a recommendation.'

'If you insist,' grumbled Damocles.

'Very well,' said Hieronymus, in a voice that said: *on your own head be it, Princess.* 'Then we shall keep the parade short. We'll start at the palace and finish at the Pantheon, where you can make an offering to your god – I mean, goddess – as is tradition.'

'We will increase the protection at the Forum,' said Damocles. 'We have received several threats already. I will employ only the most trustworthy men to guard you during the ride.'

'Threats? Threats from who?' asked Gia.

'Not sure, they were largely illegible and obscene, but it will pay well to be careful. We cannot lose a third ruler in less than a year.'

They resumed their officious planning. Hieronymus and Damocles were replaced by other advisors, each one with a new request. Ships. Grain. Gold. Soldiers. Temples. Walls. Decrees. Borders. But Claudia was no longer present in her body. Each time she looked up, there were more and more people present, their voices growing louder and more demanding. She began to question it all, to doubt it all. Yet she had chosen this. She had dreamed of this, prayed for it, and now that it had arrived, she did not feel as she expected to feel. She didn't feel victorious but doomed, her head full of dread.

How would she be recorded in the annals of Roman politics? Would she be recorded at all? Or would she be the subject of a *damnatio memoriae*, her name erased from history for the crime of *infamia*?

'Well?' came a voice.

Claudia looked up to see Damocles staring at her expectantly. She realized she'd drifted away, stopped responding to conversation. Her other advisors were huddled together, debating whether they ought to fire cannons at the ceremony tomorrow or not.

Hot, hungry and overwhelmed, she stood up abruptly, her head swimming as she tried to anchor herself to reality. She felt herself swooning, her knees giving out.

Gia braced her fall, preventing her from falling down the steps.

'Are you okay?' Gia asked.

'I don't know what I am,' Claudia said woozily.

'Oh, that's not good. We'd better get you some fresh air.'

'Where are you going?' said Hieronymus.

'To the atrium,' said Gia. 'The empress will be no good to you if she's laid up in bed with exhaustion. She needs a moment of rest.'

Hieronymus's face shrivelled up in distaste. He didn't like being instructed by a gladiator.

'Unless you want to fight me over it,' Gia said.

'Do *not* be long,' he said.

Claudia blinked, and she was in the atrium as handmaids flocked around her with water, wine and grapes. Surrounded by marble statues capturing figures of mythology, she gazed into the face of

Proserpina, attempting to escape the clutches of the underworld god Pluto.

'Here, eat something,' said Gia, ambushing her with a fig. 'You are as pale as a shade, living without the sun.'

Claudia gently pushed the fig away, lost in thought.

'What's on your mind?' asked Gia.

'Everything, *literally* everything.'

'You're going to have to be more specific.'

'Jupiter,' she said.

'Not what I was expecting to hear, but go on.'

'He tried to prevent me from reaching Rome at all. My coronation might well draw his attention. Will he make his presence known again? Will the people be safe?'

'You are not a deity,' said Gia. 'You cannot be expected to protect everyone and everything.'

'What if the world becomes a battleground for a divine war, and I was the one who fired the first cannon?' said Claudia.

'The gods were active long before us,' said Gia. 'Diana told me herself: the pantheon withdrew after meddling in ancient affairs.'

Claudia listened to the trickle of the atrium fountain as drums continued to beat out in the Forum.

'I invited them back,' said Claudia.

'You aren't responsible for what deities do,' said Gia.

'No, but I did just inherit an empire.'

They quietened again.

'It's all too much,' Claudia sighed.

'You're telling me,' said Gia, shaking her head.

This startled Claudia out of her self-pity session, turning to Gia to acknowledge her own harried expression.

'Are you okay?' she said. 'I haven't had chance to ask. It's been never-ending preparations.'

'Well, apparently you're marrying the prince,' Gia said. 'I can't say I'm too happy about *that*.'

She was trying to play it off as a joke, but Claudia could tell there was something sharp and serious underneath it.

'I was just trying to keep Marcellus at bay,' said Claudia. 'Never take seriously anything I say to men.'

Gia didn't respond, and her expression remained sombre.

Ordinarily, Claudia didn't have to question what Gia thought or felt because Gia would tell her plainly, sometimes without saying a thing. No words were required when a penetrating look or subtle gesture would do. Now, Claudia felt that same connection falling away. Something was bothering Gia, and she wasn't being forthcoming about it, which was new.

'Talk to me,' Claudia said. When Gia didn't respond, she lightly added: 'As your empress, I demand it.'

'I'm fine, I'm just . . . annoyed about Marcellus, worried about the prince . . . and then there's my brother.'

'What about him?' asked Claudia.

She reached for Gia's hand, sensing that she was having some difficulty forming the next sentence.

'I don't know, he's . . . I don't know.'

Claudia nodded gently, encouraging her to go on.

'He's struggling to accept what happened back in Pompeii.'

The eruption unravelled in Claudia's mind like a ribbon from a spool, as it did at least once a day. The black skies. The rivers of fire. The seas of stone and the dust that made everything look corpse-like.

'He thinks . . . I let Mother down,' said Gia. 'That I should've protected her instead of . . .'

'Me?' said Claudia.

Gia rubbed the back of her neck. 'Maybe. I think he feels lost, too – far from home. I wish I could support him more.'

'Why can't you?'

'Because I need to be right here beside you, to protect you.'

Claudia reminded herself that Gia was grieving. Her mother's death had been lost in all the chaos of seizing the throne.

'We'll make time – for him, for you,' Claudia said. 'If he is your home, then he is my home too.'

Gia's expression twisted in pain.

Home. Claudia's home was here, right here, but Gia's home was gone. Claudia had never seen Gia look like that before, not even when they thought they were going to die.

'I'm so sorry,' said Claudia.

'My loss probably seems small to the gods, compared to the battle for the future of Rome, but to me it is . . . infinite.'

Claudia wanted to hold her, but she didn't know if this was a problem that could be fixed with her embrace.

'We could arrange a funeral, if you willed it,' she said. 'It could be grand or small, whatever you wish. I will arrange all of it, so you don't have to be further burdened.'

'I don't know.'

'Why not?'

'Her grave is Pompeii. Her home was Pompeii. It wouldn't be right. Thank you, though.'

'Whatever I can do, to comfort you,' said Claudia.

Her own father had died, her brother too, but Claudia knew it was different. She hadn't loved them in the same way. Their deaths had made her stronger.

Their deaths had filled holes, not created them.

She reached for Gia's hand, and while they didn't look at each other, staring out at the atrium, Claudia felt anchored again, no longer lost at sea in a storm, but peacefully floating offshore.

She would create a new home for Gia, and protect Gia as she had protected her. She would make sacrifices, as sacrifices had been made for her. She would take away Gia's pain, and her own.

She would use her power to make the world better.

Fortuna attempted to gaze into the void of the future, peering deep within her own mind as she'd done a hundred thousand times. But nothing emerged from the depths. No glimpses, no flashes, no prophecies, no predictions. She saw nothing but endless darkness, formless and motionless, like the universe before anything existed.

She gave a cry of frustration, pacing back and forth, her bare feet smacking on the stony ground. Fortuna had no taste for palaces, preferring a more primordial residence. She lived in a system of caves that connected the underworld of Elysium with the subterranean levels of the mortal realm.

Here, she was accompanied by many sibyls, the sage-burning prophetesses of caves, whose visions were similarly blank. They scried in pools and mirrors, in entrails and the stars, but they saw nothing that guided them. In shame and in rage, Fortuna had burrowed herself away, far from the comfort and community of others.

The caves were deep and ancient and unnavigable, much like Fortuna herself. It was the perfect place to hide away. She had delved deeper than ever before, as if returning to the womb, becoming older in appearance the further she wandered from the world. She knew these tunnels as if they were an extension of her. She knew the curve of their walls, the roughness of stone. She became part of nature again. Fortuna thought that being here might bring back the inner sight that Jupiter had taken from her, but failing that, at least no one would be able to locate her . . . or so she thought.

The slapping of sandals echoed, along with a grumbling sound.

'Good gods, Fortuna,' said Minerva, her voice echoing. 'Do you know how long I've been lost down here? It seems as if a thousand years has passed. This must be how mortals feel when they traverse the labyrinths.'

Fortuna tilted her head towards the sound, unsure how Minerva had found her despite her extensive efforts not to be discovered.

'What are you doing here?' she sighed.

'What am I doing here?' Minerva crowed, in disbelief. 'What do you think? Did you forget that the pantheon is at war?'

'I am aware.'

'Then why are you here, instead of at our side?'

'Aren't you hiding away too?'

Minerva spluttered in annoyance. 'I did take a short recess, yes, to recollect my thoughts and restore my spirit, but I have spent much longer in search of you. I began to fear that Jupiter had destroyed you, turned you into stars.'

'I thought you were looking for him, to finish the fight you started?'

'And I have found him,' said Minerva proudly. 'Well, in a sense. I have learned of his activities on Earth, at least.'

'And?'

'He is furious that the goddesses have intervened to protect the empress, even though he intervened first. That is just so typical of him.'

'Empress?'

'Oh yes, perhaps I should've led with that: Claudia has been confirmed as empress, despite his attempts to prevent it. Our plan was successful.'

'That . . . is something,' sniffed Fortuna.

'It is more than something. It's exactly what we hoped for – the beginning of a new world. But Jupiter is already moving into position,

putting his plans into action. Claudia is still in danger. She needs me. She needs us all.'

'What plans?' asked Fortuna.

'He is recruiting other gods into his cult, to form an opposition. He will soon find a mortal candidate to challenge Claudia. There is a cousin in the picture. A mediocre fellow, but he is best positioned to do Jupiter's work.'

'What do you suggest we do?'

'My father stole his crown through revolution, claiming power by ousting the Titans, and so we shall steal it from him.'

'You wish to become queen of the pantheon?'

'Isn't that obvious?' said Minerva. 'Come on, we've wasted enough time already. Let us leave the cave of fear and be part of the realm of the living again.'

'I didn't ask for you to come looking for me,' said Fortuna, shying away from her. 'I am perfectly happy down here, all alone.'

Minerva gazed around. 'Yes, you do look content,' she said dryly. 'Surrounded by rocks and with the face of one who has already given up. How could anyone not be entirely fulfilled and at peace, hiding away in a cave?'

'There are worse places,' said Fortuna, 'like Tartarus, which is where we might be headed once Jupiter regains his strength and pride, if we are lucky.'

'I didn't wish to say it, but I see that I must,' said Minerva. 'We wouldn't be here if not for you, Fortuna. You were the one who gave us courage to take action. You called upon us, and organized us. You were the catalyst, and the battle isn't over yet. You are needed, back in civilization. You are needed by the world. You cannot just walk away and decide that you are no longer involved.'

'What use is the goddess of fortune if she can no longer see the future?' said Fortuna, her face downcast. 'I am no longer what I was.'

'Is that it?' said Minerva. 'Is that the problem? You think you are no longer a warrior?'

Fortuna didn't answer, though she ceased pacing, her shoulders slumping as she wrapped her robes tighter around herself.

'You may have lost your sight, but you are still the goddess of fortune. You may not see the future but you can still influence current events. You're one of the oldest deities, the Superi of infinity. You are even more ancient than my father!'

Fortuna's face wrinkled in displeasure.

'A compliment!' said Minerva. 'He is ancient of mind, ancient in his ideas and his views, but you are not. You are not ancient, but eternal, in fact.'

'That's better,' said Fortuna.

'You have always been in tune with modernity. You are the past but also the future, even if you cannot see it.'

'There's the leader we need,' said Fortuna, smiling slightly.

'Have I convinced you to return?'

'You will be a fine ruler of the pantheon, some day. I don't need a prophecy to know that this is true.'

'Then what are we waiting for?' asked Minerva. 'Are you with me?'

'You were never truly without me,' said Fortuna.

6. THE CORONATION

The coronation of an emperor depended much on the emperor in question, and the message he hoped to send. Claudia's father was confirmed via a brief military parade after he was ratified by the Senate, intended to signal that he represented a continuation of the status quo.

Some of the men who came before him had opted for more elaborate victory processions: great carnivals and cavalcades of men and beasts. They were intended to show off their great might and divinity, their connection to the pantheon.

Previous dynasties had increased the personal powers of the emperor. He sat at the top, with control over all the legislative branches, amassing an insurmountable amount of power, but that same power put a target on his back. An emperor only ruled for as long as he could keep the public from rioting.

On the morning of her own coronation, Claudia emerged from the palace to a crowd of exultant applause.

It was from the all-female Cult of Diana, as they were now known – named in honour of the mystery party Claudia had attended against her brother's orders. Word of this small act of resistance had spread through Rome, earning her new supporters. The cult had tripled in size overnight, including everyone from ancient priestesses to vestal virgins.

'The empress has risen like the sun!'

'The empress is in motion like the wind!'

'All hail the empress!'

Claudia basked in their adoration, smiling and waving.

Their cheers and prayers strengthened her, giving her a feeling of divinity, of invincibility.

Following the appearance of the goddess at Senate House, Rome was alight with talk of Claudia summoning Victoria to approve her. Many had turned up in hope of witnessing the next celestial event.

Petals were thrown and incense was burned. Horns blared self-importantly as soldiers marched in formation. It was like any other festival in Rome: an excuse to avoid work and become intoxicated.

Claudia was quickly led out, with Gia at her side, surrounded by armoured praetorian guards bearing flags and shields. Drums beat insistently. Cultists chanted as they crossed the Forum, drawing a large and boisterous crowd. More and more soldiers surrounded her in defensive formations as she walked to her chariot.

She'd donned the new purple robes she'd been fitted for, embroidered with a decorative border and tied with a golden rope. She wore golden hoop earrings with suspended pearls and a necklace with an engraved *intaglio* at the centre: a ruby engraved with the seal of Minerva. Her father's laurel crown had also been set with pearls, diamonds and rubies, forming flowers that entwined around the golden leaves.

'Did I tell you how imperial you look today?' said Gia, leaning in so none could hear them.

She walked beside Claudia, wearing the goddess-made armour, now shiny again after a visit from the palace blacksmith, with sandals that wound around her calves and bronze cuffs on her wrists. Gia had also been equipped with a new sword and shield, both welded with a metal relief of Claudia's emblematic lioness.

'You did, but I never tire of hearing it.'

'You look very imperial,' Gia repeated.

'And you . . .'

Claudia admired her dark brown hair scraped back into a braid and wound tightly at the back of her head, her tanned muscles oiled, her brows defined. She had the most beguiling features, the sharp angles of her face as beautiful in rest as they were in action.

Her heart fluttered, forcing her to sigh longingly.

'You are very distracting,' Claudia said. 'Yet you are also the only thing keeping me planted in reality. It's surreal, like I'm in a play . . . Maybe I'm still dreaming, or perhaps we are dead. We died back in that cave and everything since has been an enchanting illusion.'

'I do not think I would've imagined Marcellus,' said Gia, pulling a face of great distaste.

'Who could have believed we would be standing here, together? Anything is possible.'

They were careful with their words, overly aware of all who were listening, but their eyes said everything.

Claudia and Gia would ride in a chariot near the end of the parade, after the horses and chariots. Directly in front and behind them were a legion of soldiers. Four others would ride with them: two soldiers and two praetorian guardsmen. Cassius had offered to serve as one of the soldiers and Claudia had gladly agreed. Marcellus rode in the third chariot, with Damocles and Hieronymus.

Gia and Claudia climbed aboard, with the four guards arranging their shields to form a wall of protection around the empress. The horns and drums grew louder as they set off along the edge of the Forum, advancing through the crowds. The music was a familiar sound: the same heraldic march that was always played at events. Claudia found that it comforted her, despite everything.

At the head of the parade were girls with flower baskets and boys playing drums. They were followed by flag bearers and dancers. Behind them, a dozen priestesses performed rituals, followed by the guardians of the shrines and temples of the goddesses, each wearing costumes that signalled their deities.

Minerva's priestess wore her characteristic fringed helmet. Diana's priestess carried a bow and arrow. Venus's priestess walked barefoot and wore a necklace of shells, while Fortuna's spun her golden globe, her eyes tied by a blindfold. Claudia had been sure to include Victoria and Salacia too, to thank them for their service.

The streets were filled with curious Romans who came to spectate the historic event, regardless of their opinions on the new empress. Soldiers lined the roads too, though there were notably less of them than usual: some had likely refused to participate in the confirmation of an empress, if not fled their duties altogether. Those senators who'd voted for Claudia walked the parade route ahead, greeting the citizens who'd come out to mark the event.

Claudia noticed that were a large number of women in attendance, including young girls.

She waved at them as they passed, her chest swelling.

Yet the mood was nervous, oddly subdued. She and Gia barely spoke on their way to the Pantheon.

When her father came to power, the people were largely

disinterested. At first sight, he wasn't as bad as the emperor before him, or the one before that. It was business as usual. Another Julio-Claudian with a golden wreath on his head. The appointment of Decimus had been dreadful and dreaded, yet the people knew where they stood on him. They knew what he represented, even if it wasn't good.

But Claudia was a mystery, in the way that all women were a mystery to most men. In this moment, she was both a dictator and a saviour, everything and nothing. The people hadn't concerned themselves with her, and thus they knew little about her, other than the way she looked.

The men would make much commentary on her appearance that day, she was sure. Claudia was glad she wouldn't hear it over the drums and horns and the clatter of horseshoes, the chanting of cultists and the patter of applause.

The parade advanced slowly, the roads ahead of them crowded. It took almost half an hour to travel the short distance to the Pantheon. When they were stationary, the crowd seemed to grow even louder.

Claudia felt suddenly claustrophobic, trapped in her chariot in the eye of a storm. She climbed out, accompanied by Gia, her handmaids and advisors, along with a small group of guards. The crowd roared, but it was a feral sound, like the audience before a gladiator match.

Claudia hadn't wished to give a speech or to reside over ceremonial games to mark her commencement, like her predecessors. She had chosen to appear only briefly before the public, to make an offering to Minerva at the Pantheon, then leave the people to an evening of revelry. This, she felt, was the perfect balance. The ceremony wasn't ostentatious enough to enrage the public, nor spartan enough that she appeared weak as Rome's first woman ruler.

As they approached the imposing building, Claudia's handmaids fell back, but Gia stepped forward.

'You should not be unattended,' she said, gently touching her arm to hold her back.

'It is safe. Everything had been arranged.'

'What harm can it do, if I accompany you?'

'No one but the empress may enter the Pantheon today. All of the entrances are guarded. I am safer in there than out on the street.'

'If you're sure?' said Gia, though she continued to look hesitant.

'I need to do this alone. Every emperor before me has done the same thing. Besides, some things are between a girl and her goddess.'

Gia lowered her hand, nodding in acceptance.

'I'll stay close by. Call out if you need me.'

'You know I will,' said Claudia, with a lingering glance.

Steeling herself, Claudia walked alone up the steps to the terrific sound of a city in celebration, passing through the enormous pillars of the veranda and into the ancient building.

It made her skin tingle, the hairs on her arms standing alert as she stepped into the cool, ancient tomb within, its circular oculus channelling a beam of sunlight.

The Pantheon was colossal in scale, its walls carved from floor to ceiling, and in each alcove, a different altar to a different god.

They watched her, unmoving, as the noise outside quietened, unnaturally muffled.

She spun in a circle, bowing to the circle of the pantheon and wondering who might look through the eyes of these sacred statues to spy on her, as she knew gods were prone to do.

She greeted Venus, in her windswept short-robed beauty, then Fortuna, shrouded, and Diana with her deer, before standing in front of Minerva. The goddess of wisdom was sculpted in victorious glory, her shield protecting her body and holding upright a spear. She had a serene, peaceful look of all-knowing wisdom on her face.

'I come to you now, my goddess, as empress of Rome,' said Claudia. 'I remember vividly the first time you appeared to me and told me I was destined to wear my father's crown. You said I'd rule some day and be the leader the world needed. I did as you advised. I did what was necessary. You know the sacrifices I have made.'

The flames danced, as if in response.

'You know what I have done, and what I am. Now, as I stand in the temple of all gods, I have finally arrived in the future you predicted. I am here, thanks to you, and I am ready, but I need you by my side.'

Standing before the statue of her goddess, she felt her strength building, her resolve hardening.

'I have already achieved things I didn't think were possible, but I still need your guidance, your protection,' she said. 'I wish to speak with you directly, empress to goddess.'

Fire crackled in the silence.

'Perhaps a mortal can never ask anything of their patron. Perhaps it is rude of me even to ask.' She paused, setting her shoulders. 'But I think I know your character. I know your nature. I believe that you would be here, if you could be here, on this day.'

Claudia approached the sacred fire that burned eternal at the centre of the enormous room.

'Your absence means I fear for you, and for myself. I long to know that you are well. If ever there was a time to show yourself to me, shouldn't it be now, on the day of my coronation? Come to me, my goddess, and together we shall rule the world.'

Ensconced in a carved stone fixture and dedicated to the fire goddess Vesta, it was said to be a dark omen for the imperial family if ever the sacred flame blew out.

Claudia held out her offering: her father's ring.

It was already a powerful talisman, imbued with both the energy of his violent death and Victoria's appearance.

It was a confession, taken from his poison-riddled body in the secretive dark. It was a plea – an object with great material value, that she was willing to sacrifice. It was evidence – of what she'd done, and she was willing to let it burn.

She lifted her fingers, dropping it in the fire.

It fell into the pit of coals, gradually reddening. She watched the metal burning and melting to liquid as flames heated the ring. She could feel the energy of a thousand lives and loves coursing through her, the building's history kept alive in its stones.

The air throbbed and stirred.

Claudia waited for Minerva to appear, perhaps floating down through the oculus or rising from the flames.

Outside, thousands of people surrounded the Pantheon, awaiting the reappearance of their new empress. Their riotous merriment rang through the city, creating a continual drone.

Cannons fired, causing her to startle.

The sacred fire began to flicker, gently at first, but then it began an ecstatic dance like a maenad, its flame almost pushed sideways. A strong breeze funnelled down through the oculus, causing a whirling tunnel of wind that tossed up fallen leaves.

Claudia stepped back in surprise.

It was still daytime outside, in the autumn heat of noon, and yet inside the Pantheon, it turned suddenly to night. A dark cloud hung over the oculus, blocking out the light of the sun.

It was unnatural, like a god's eye closing.

Claudia exhaled in a frightened, shaky rush. At the same time, the eternal flame extinguished with a hiss. The Pantheon was plunged into darkness as the other torches extinguished along with it, one by one.

The noise of the celebrations outside faded away, wrapping her in thick, foreboding silence.

At once, she knew this was not the goddess's work.

In the darkness, a quiet, animal fear came over her, making her hot and cold at once. A deep pit of dread formed in her stomach, her blood coursing and pulsing as her ears began to ring.

Claudia stiffened and froze in place, trying to listen, trying to hone in on whatever presence had sent a spike of fear through her heart. She could hear her own shallow breathing, her own pounding chest, but also . . . something else.

Some*one* else.

As the last embers of the sacred fire burned out, the darkness within the Pantheon grew so deep and dense that Claudia couldn't see her own hand stretched before her, let alone whatever monster waited for her.

Mortal, or . . . not.

Sensing movement, she whirled around with a gasp, but her attacker was already on top of her, a knife in one thrashing hand as the other clamped down on her mouth, stopping her from screaming.

'Mmmph!'

A person. A man. Solid and fleshy.

Claudia dug her teeth into his flesh and lurched sideways, judging only by sound. When he came at her again, she clutched at his robes in panic, trying to reveal him, but he slithered out of her grip.

'Gia!' she yelled, hoarse with fear.

She tried to recall what Gia had taught her about self-defence. All her clever ideas about bribing or seducing or even counselling an assassin through his youthly traumas paled away in white-hot panic. She could barely scream in fear, never mind form words that made any sense.

'Please . . . don't . . .'

She could see only the faintest hint of the blade, reflecting what little light poured in through the darkened oculus.

'Gia!' she tried again.

But the building was muffled, shrouded, cut off from the city outside somehow.

Their bodies collided as she wrenched away from her attacker. Claudia ended up sprawled on the ground, on her back, her body tensing in anticipation of pain – far too quickly for her to come to terms with the lot of her life or have time to regret anything.

Gia, Gia, Gia, she prayed, as if Gia was a goddess.

The dagger's blade grazed the skin of her cheek, forcing her to roll to one side to avoid it.

Her eyes were beginning to adjust to the darkness. She briefly glimpsed the insignia carved on the knife's handle: a bolt of Jupiter, illuminated by the crack of light shining through the oculus. That meant he was a servant of the god.

The man climbed on top of her. She glimpsed him raising his arm again to strike, but after a second, he fell back. The grinding of stone alerted Claudia to something moving behind her. She could barely make out what was happening, but Claudia was sure she saw Minerva's statue standing up from her throne and assuming a battle stance. Her serene expression had contorted into a warrior cry, her brows sloping in determination as she raised her spear.

Claudia looked to the statue of Diana, who too was on her feet, pulling back her arrow in a bow, readied to fire.

Her attacker, his face now partially visible, staggered backwards in fear, shrinking away from the animated statues, just as a door wrenched open with a drawn-out creak.

A flash of fire followed. Claudia heard a noise, a voice, a wordless cry of fury and fear as two bodies came together in a terrific clashing of steel and flesh that seemed to last for an eternity.

It was Gia, fighting the assassin. Claudia heard a grunt and a splattering sound, followed by a thud.

She held her breath, unsure who had won.

Sunlight poured in. The dark clouds over the oculus shifted, and it was day again. Suddenly Gia was there with a torch, crouching down to check on her, her eyes wide in concern.

'Are you . . .'

'I'm okay,' said Claudia.

She was unharmed, and Gia was unharmed. Nothing else mattered. The fire illuminated the dead man on the ground, gasping his last breath as a bubble of blood formed between his lips.

'In the name . . . of Jupiter,' he rasped.

One final blink and his eyes froze open.

It was one of the praetorian guards, and he had a bag of coins in his pocket, now spilling out onto the bloodied floor.

'Shame I didn't have time to interrogate him,' said Gia.

'I am *not* sorry about it.'

Gia scrambled up, checking the perimeter as Claudia remained on the floor, clutching her knees. She rocked back and forth, staring into thin air, trying to steady her breathing, her chest heaving.

Her eyes landed on the sacred fire. Gasping with horror, Claudia recalled that the eternal flame had been extinguished in the chaos. She staggered over to it, winded. It was cooling, slumbering, dormant – like Vesuvius before the eruption – but there were still a few embers burning ablaze in the pit of ashes, fuelled by the ring she'd sacrificed.

All hope wasn't yet lost.

Murmuring encouragement to herself, Claudia breathed on it.

'In the name of Vesta, I command you to burn,' she said. 'If this flame dies, then so will I.'

By her word, the flame caught and expanded, blooming into a reassuring flower of fire. She looked up to see the statue of Vesta, the goddess of the hearth and the home, staring right at her.

Claudia was sure she saw the statue of Venus smile, but she was also dizzy and delirious, restless energy racing through her blood.

When she looked to Minerva, she was serene and seated again, while Diana had lowered her bow.

The sacred fire continued to grow, burning the fallen leaves like tinder. The eternal flame burned once again.

Claudia's mind was wiped clean. She was cold and shaking, but she felt nothing in particular, or maybe everything, all at once – so many feelings that they became grey and blurred.

Her first day as empress and already she was fielding her first assassination attempt. When the people found out, they'd think she was cursed. It would be interpreted as a sign that she wasn't fit to rule. The opposition to her appointment would strengthen. The

Senate might move to remove her immediately, in whatever manner it took.

She should've expected it. She should've listened. It had been far too easy to catch her alone. If she survived this, she wouldn't be so stupid again, she swore it.

When Gia returned, Claudia collapsed into her, letting Gia hold her upright and pull her into an embrace, supporting her weight.

'You're safe now. I'm here.'

'I'm glad you came in time,' she murmured into Gia's neck, as Gia kissed the top of her head. 'Not a moment too late.'

'What did he do?'

'He didn't harm me, though he tried,' said Claudia. 'We have been lucky. Blessed Fortuna.'

They exchanged a deep, weighted look.

'I knew an attempt on my life was a possibility, but I didn't think it would happen so soon.'

'I should never have left you alone in the first place,' said Gia. 'I sensed that something wasn't right but I thought I was just being overprotective, and that I'd draw attention to us by being so obvious.' She shook her head in frustration. 'So, I waited, then I saw that one of the guards had left his post. I couldn't get in the first door I tried. It was as if it was locked, and then, suddenly . . . it wasn't.'

'Do you think it was the deities intervening? I swear, their statues came alive to aid me, right before you entered.'

'Who else is on our side but them?'

'I called for you but you couldn't hear me.' Claudia wet her dry lips, lowering her voice even further. 'I fear that Jupiter was involved. The eternal flame went out.'

Gia's eyes flashed wide in alarm.

'Just for a moment! I managed to reignite it with a little help from Vesta . . . but this, this was not the work of men. Every torch went out at once. Day turned to night. It was pitch black. I couldn't . . .'

She was shaking uncontrollably. Gia pulled her closer as they warmed themselves before the reignited fire.

'It was another warning,' said Claudia. 'A sign from above.'

Claudia stared at the statue of Jupiter, crowned and bare-chested with his staff. His gaze was stony, empty. Whatever presence she'd sensed had left with the assassin.

She felt her body relax, melting into Gia. Her life would be full of close calls, she knew that.

This was just a rite of passage.

Cassius appeared at the rear door, as they quickly broke apart. The rest of Claudia's staff came pouring in, all talking at once. Hieronymus. Damocles. Marcellus. Two guards dragged their fellow away, leaving a trail of blood, as the palace physician fussed over her.

All of them were concerned . . . or pretending to be concerned. Claudia tried to read their faces, to look for signs of deceit.

'I knew a parade wasn't a good idea,' said Hieronymus, though it had been his suggestion in the first place.

'We should never have left you alone,' said Damocles, though he had hired the guard who'd betrayed her.

'I underestimated how unpopular you are,' said Marcellus. 'You would be safer with a man at your side.'

'And yet, it was a woman who saved me,' she said. 'Where were you, cousin, when I was being attacked?'

'There will be time to discuss it later,' said Hieronymus quickly. 'For now, we should get the empress safely back to the palace.'

'The attacker will be investigated. I suspect, by the denarii he had on his person, that he was paid for the attempt. We will not rest until his master is found. The finest soldiers in Rome will track him down, I assure you,' said Damocles.

'We should inform the people at once,' said Hieronymus.

Marcellus. Hieronymus. Damocles. It could have been any one of them. She didn't know who to trust, not even within her own house.

'No,' said Claudia, firmly shaking her head.

'No?' parroted Hieronymus.

'It's a praetorian who is responsible. I can't be sure the organization hasn't been infiltrated but I doubt he was working alone. Let us not pretend that the other praetorians cannot be bribed too. We must handle the situation carefully, gather evidence before making accusations.'

'You don't want retribution?' asked Hieronymus.

'Vengeance isn't more important than peace,' she said. 'This incident was intended to shake faith in my reign, to make me look weak. One assassination attempt can breed another. We must not advertise this.'

Hieronymus and Damocles looked to each other.

'For now, I will launch an internal investigation,' Claudia said. 'I do not trust the praetorian guard to do it justice. Gia and Cassius will look into the matter, if they are willing?'

Gia glanced at Cassius, who gave no response.

'I'm afraid I must once again question your logic, Empress,' said Damocles. 'Your friends are not qualified for this.'

'Why not? Gia has saved my life before, and Cassius has fought at war overseas. They are perfectly capable of making enquiries.'

'You don't want to make enemies of the guard.'

'And I don't aim to. We will handle this ourselves, lest we point the finger in their direction without good cause. For now, let no one speak of what happened here today. If one of you lets slip your tongue, I shall find out and I shall remove you from service. Is that understood?'

'As you wish, Empress,' said Damocles.

'Whatever you say, Empress,' said Hieronymus.

Claudia's handmaids worked busily to readjust her robes, to tidy up her hair and make sure she showed no sign of distress.

'We should cut the parade short,' said Damocles. 'Cancel the acrobats . . . and . . .' He lowered his voice. 'The menagerie.'

'I said *no menagerie*, Damocles,' said Claudia.

They filed out of the Pantheon, into the cleansing brightness of daylight as the crowd roared and drums rolled, unaware of how close she'd just come to death, while guards discreetly disposed of the attacker.

The incident already felt faraway and strange, like a dream.

Gia stayed close, her face taut with guilt and worry, as they returned to the armoured chariot. Cassius stayed on guard beside them, while the missing praetorian was replaced by another man.

'I shall ride with you, to be safe,' said Marcellus, climbing in behind them.

Claudia didn't have the energy to argue with him.

Gia scowled and untied the partition curtain. It closed upon Marcellus before he could speak.

'It was planned,' Gia whispered into her ear, as they set off. 'Your enemies have infiltrated palace security. There must be a conspiracy against you. How else would they have corrupted your guard and gained entry to the Pantheon on a day like today, with all eyes on you?'

'I agree, which is why I said we would investigate ourselves. We must learn all we can about the dead man,' said Claudia.

'Do you think *he* is involved?' whispered Gia, cocking her head in the direction of the privacy curtain.

Marcellus.

'I don't know, but we need to find out.'

They clasped hands, hidden by Claudia's purple robes as the new empress regarded the crowd with a serene, imperial smile.

She would show no sign of weakness, no sign of fear, no sign of uncertainty. No blood to draw the wolves.

She scanned the faces of the people who lined the streets, some of them shouting and cursing, others applauding and adoring, some tussling with the guards as the mood risked turning festively feral.

The parade turned around in the Forum and retreated hastily, leaving the citizens to their private parties, but Claudia feared that the brief flurry of activity had not gone entirely unseen. The delay at the Pantheon must have been noted by those who were most invested in her failure. A keen observer might have noticed that one of her guards had been swapped for the return journey.

The number of armed guards stationed around the palace and the Forum tripled overnight, which would only compound the rumours.

Despite Claudia's best efforts, word of the incident would soon spread quickly, like a fire burning through the city of Rome.

7. THE EMPRESS OF LESBOS

Claudia's father hadn't taught her anything about statecraft, though she was the better student of her and her brother. Decimus had never had much of an aptitude for academia, nor the temperament. He was naturally smart, a sharp-eyed youth with a fine vocabulary, but he had little interest in anything other than the macabre. His dark eyes glistened only when her father spoke of massacres and disasters, of corporal punishment, state executions and prisoners of war.

Decimus had run through a dozen different tutors in Claudia's life, many of them leaving the palace in haste, some not at all (she knew not to ask questions about those particular tutors). He had a habit of pranking them in ways that were insidious and sinister, and eventually her father had been resigned to instructing Decimus himself. Each week, on Saturn-day morning, her brother was called to the throne room, where he was taught how to be emperor.

Claudia was rarely allowed to play by herself as her father liked to use his children as trophies to show off, installing them in his court as a testament to his great parenting. She would be brought out to sing, to dance, to recite poetry, dressed up like a doll for visitors to coo over. This meant that when Decimus received his imperial education, Claudia was often present. She busied herself with whatever she was doing, but she kept one ear attuned to their conversations.

No one had expected her to be in this position, including herself, but now, as she found herself ruling the world, she recalled the stolen lessons she could still remember.

'There are two kinds of emperors,' her father had once said. 'Weak men who are remembered well, and strong men who are remembered badly.'

'I don't care what people think about me,' said Decimus, smirking arrogantly.

'Good. Then you will be a strong leader indeed. If you want to stay alive, you must be feared.'

Since coming to power, Claudia had determined that she would be good and strong at the same time. She would not become a tyrant or an avenger, but she would not allow herself to be pitied either.

The day after her attempted assassination, it was business as usual. She was drawn into another day's schedule, installed in the throne room as visitors lined up along the streets.

She sympathized with merchants who complained about trade routes without making concessions, and debated with senators who wanted stricter laws on decency without agreeing to support their cause. She challenged the generals who feared an invasion at the Parthian border without agreeing to an ill-fated advance.

Claudia believed that if she worked hard and played by the rules set in place, she could win the people's allegiance. She woke early, before Gia had risen, and retired late, after Gia had fallen asleep, spending every possible moment reading scrolls and studying maps.

She knew she would be expected to know twice what a man did, to be a master in all trades. She compiled information on each senator, so she would know what moved him and how best to influence him. She attempted to keep abreast of the military's actions, but they kept her at an uncomfortable distance.

The fear of the assassination attempt lingered. It sat beneath her skin, concealed itself in the corner of her vision, crept at the back of her neck and in the hairs on her arms, making her feel unsettled.

Gia remained at her side throughout each day, smiling at her occasionally when no one was looking. Though nobody asked for her opinion, or even looked her in the eye on most occasions, she was always present, always witness to these worldly events.

Claudia reminded herself of those people in the empire who went unseen but heard everything: the handmaidens and guards and servants and slaves who gave up their freedom to serve.

She would be sure to earn their loyalty too.

Her enemies thought her weak, but she was determined to prove them wrong. She would do so without compromising her soul, without giving way to the worst of herself.

That was when the graffiti began.

EMPRESS OF LESBOS.

An aspiring artist had carved the descriptive moniker into a wall next to the palace, in a place that was guarded at all times.

Claudia saw it on her way to the Colosseum, to approve the completion of the construction project her father started. The inscription was surrounded by a gaggle of whispering guards and maids.

They were travelling in a golden litter but the main route was clogged with carts and chariots, forcing them to crawl at a snail's pace. Stuck in slow traffic, Claudia had no choice but to stare at the graffito on the wall that lined the road.

It did not, at first, appear offensive. Confusing, perhaps. She was Empress, certainly, but not of the Greek isle of Lesbos. Yet the author was not mistaken. It was the hidden context that made it offensive: Lesbos was the home of Sappho, and Sappho's name had become synonymous with women loving women.

They were calling her the Empress of Lesbians.

'Get rid of it,' she ordered.

Her staff jumped into action, climbing out and using their bodies to shield the offensive proclamation, but it was too late. It could not be unseen. The words etched into her brain, throbbing and bleeding.

The imperial party continued on wordlessly as two men stayed behind to scratch it out, but another graffito appeared further down the road, this one even more graphic.

'Princess Sappho sucks tits,' Gia read aloud, spluttering as she tried not to laugh. 'It is not untrue.'

'*Shhh*,' Claudia whispered, lightly elbowing her.

She again instructed one of her guards to have it removed as they moved on, her neck and ears burning.

Claudia convinced herself that they were merely discussing her policies. She sucked tits as a ruler. That was what it meant. But deep down, she knew better. They were mocking her sexuality yet again.

She pretended to be unbothered but the graffiti plagued her throughout the afternoon, making it difficult for her to pay attention to the architects and games-makers who grudgingly fawned over her, presenting sketches and model replicas.

The question continued to plague her.

How did they *know*?

As they stood in front of the half-finished Colosseum, her advisors followed her around – a gaggle of men in a rainbow parade of robes. While they were dutiful, even worshipful to her face, competing to be her favourite, sometimes she caught them rolling their eyes at her or covertly gesturing behind her back.

One man stuck out two fingers, poking his tongue through the V shape it made. He turned and caught her gaze, his face greying. She watched the lump in his throat move up and down.

Claudia pretended not to see. She noted that he was the one in yellow. She didn't remember his name and she didn't need to know it now.

'Have the man in yellow removed from the court,' she ordered of Hieronymus, at the end of their session.

Claudia moved on, shown to a private box inside the arena where she watched a group of gladiators practising purely for her benefit.

She sat on one side, with Gia as her guard, while her cousin sat on the other, waving at her occasionally. Claudia waved back and smiled, though her face fell as she turned back to the arena.

EMPRESS OF LESBOS.

Her head was still rooted in those words of *infamia*, her skin crawling with shame and embarrassment.

How could they possibly know such a thing? It wasn't as if her appearance gave anything away: she was groomed to be the beautiful princess, cast in the image of Venus and appealing to the eyes of men. Other than her having the somewhat masculine profession of ruling an empire, there was no way for her secret to have been intuited.

'What do you think gives them that impression about me?' she whispered to Gia, between matches.

'What impression?'

'"Princess Lesbos".'

'It's just graffiti,' said Gia. 'It's not serious. Most of it is just dick jokes, anyway. Don't worry about it.'

She squeezed Claudia's hand, but Claudia pulled her hand away.

Perhaps it was her relationship with Gia, that gave it away?

She could see the gladiators whispering among themselves and felt heat rising to her cheeks again, wondering what they were saying about her now. Perhaps she should've travelled to the Pantheon with her cousin after all, to distract from the accusations.

'I . . . have something to ask you,' said Gia, after a minute. 'While we have a moment alone, for a change.'

'Go on?' said Claudia.

'Livia has asked me to ask you if you'd support the opening of a school for gladiatrices, here in Rome,' said Gia.

Claudia recalled who Livia was: Rome's own woman gladiator, or gladiatrix as they were calling themselves.

'She and Dido have found a landlord willing to rent to them but they require funds for equipment,' said Gia. 'They know you were my patron, back in Pompeii, so they asked me to ask if you're interested.'

Claudia didn't answer for a moment.

'Do you think that's why they're saying those things?' she mused. 'Because I sponsored you and brought you to Rome with me?'

'Huh?' said Gia.

'The graffiti,' Claudia explained.

'Oh, right,' said Gia, as if she'd forgotten. 'I don't know . . . It could be anything. Is that a no, then?'

Though Claudia wasn't sure opening a gladiatrix school would help with her growing reputation as the Empress of Lesbians, she couldn't say no. It was the right thing to do, and perhaps it might bring her new supporters, sporting spectators who weren't threatened by women. Besides, she was unable to turn Gia down, particularly when she was looking at her just so, with the light of the sun catching her beautiful face.

'No, it's a yes. Sorry, it's a wonderful idea,' she said. 'Of course I'll be their patron.'

'You don't seem that enthused.'

'My mind was just wandering, but I am, I promise.'

One of the gladiators pinned the other to the ground, ending the fight. Claudia stood up to applaud him rather more enthusiastically than was warranted, as if to affirm her heterosexuality. She sat down when a different pair began to battle theatrically, both showing off for the empress.

'Dido and Livia have asked me to be involved, training the new recruits and providing mentorship,' said Gia, fiddling with the leather strips of her uniform skirt. 'And they want to use my name for advertising, you know, "Viatrix the Victorious, survivor of Vesuvius".'

'I hope you told them your presence is very much required, here with me,' said Claudia.

'Actually, I'd like to do it, if you could spare me a few hours a week,' said Gia, as if choosing her words carefully. 'I'm loath to leave you alone after what happened at the Pantheon, but Cassius has offered to guard you, in my absence.'

Claudia was taken aback. Gia was clearly serious about this.

And, for some reason, Claudia wasn't sure she liked it, though she could not put the feeling into words.

'You really want to do this, don't you?' she said. 'You don't just feel obliged?'

'I'd like to be a part of it, yes,' Gia said. 'I was there when Cyrus first opened the Pompeii school to women.' Her face sank at his name, even though she'd been the one to speak it. 'I thought it would honour him.'

Claudia hadn't thought of it like that. She placed her hand on top of Gia's, unseen behind the partition of their private box.

'Whatever you want, you will have,' she said. 'I fully support it. Tell Livia and Dido to compile a list of their financial requirements and I'll provide everything they need.'

'Are you sure?' said Gia hesitantly.

'Of course. For a moment, I was being selfish. I didn't want you to leave my side, but I'm trying to be the best version of myself that I can be . . . for Rome . . . and for you.'

'You already are,' said Gia.

They fell quiet, listening to the sounds of grunting and clashing steel, of sandals sliding through sand. A troop of centurions filed out into the amphitheatre, each one saluting her.

When she looked back, Gia was gazing at her in a way that scared her, so longing and hungry and vulnerable.

'What?'

'Just, looking at you,' said Gia, faux-casually.

What scared Claudia more was how desperately she wished to forget her place and throw herself into Gia's arms for all to see.

Her heart pounded.

She could've drawn the privacy curtain, even ordered her handmaids to shield them with fans, but she was too afraid. The thought bubbled up inside her again, bursting suddenly.

Empress of Lesbos.

That skin-crawling shame washed over her again, making her

feel naked, exposed. Her father's dying eyes. Her brother's bleeding mouth. Their spectres laughing at her, calling her sick . . .

The two things had become entwined in her mind, and she could not untangle them.

As they journeyed home, the sounds of the city wrapped around them, the clatter of hooves and the squeak of wheels, soldiers shouting orders as builders stacked bricks to form arches.

The graffiti was gone, and Claudia felt better again. The relief was only temporary, however. She was met on the palace steps by Hieronymus and Damocles, accompanied by Cassius and a band of soldiers.

'You are required urgently, Empress,' said Damocles.

'What's going on?'

They trailed her as she and Gia moved past, parting the small crowd that had formed in the entrance.

'An entire legion of men has disappeared in Britannia,' said the most senior of the soldiers, a cold-eyed, well-decorated general with the most elaborate cloak and helmet.

General Aquinas. He was one of the men who'd travelled to Greece to seek out her cousin. Aquinas had supported Marcellus in his campaign to be emperor.

'Five thousand soldiers are missing,' he said.

Claudia stopped walking, turning around to face them.

'*Five thousand* men have vanished?' she repeated.

'Without a trace,' said Hieronymus, his voice shrill. 'Their camp has been completely abandoned.'

'How is this possible?'

'We don't know but we're working to find out, of course,' said

Damocles. 'They are surrounded by unfavourable terrain. It has been difficult for the army to even reach their location.'

'It's just like the Varian Disaster,' said General Aquinas. 'The native tribes have formed an alliance to fight against us.'

'We have sent Marcellus to speak with the Legate to find out more,' said Damocles.

'Why in the gods' names would you do that without consulting me first?' said Claudia.

'They are known to each other. We trust that the army will share information with him. We did not think you would object, in the circumstances. A swift response is key in this situation.'

Claudia didn't comment further. Now wasn't the time. Roman men were missing and if she didn't retrieve them, safe and well, she would be blamed for it, especially with so many men already against her.

'Their base is still there,' said Aquinas, 'with all of their belongings in it. Their horses, their swords, their armour, their water skins, even their sandals: all left behind, as if they fled in a hurry.'

Claudia locked eyes with Cassius, recalling what Gia had told her about his service abroad. In his expression, she registered scepticism: he did not agree with the general's assessment.

'You don't think the natives are responsible?' she asked him.

'Not a chance,' said Cassius. 'I was taken hostage by a tribe in the territory of Mercia when my men abandoned me. They are not savages.'

Aquinas made a scoffing noise.

'They aren't capable of disappearing five thousand men without a sign,' Cassius insisted. 'Britannia is barren but it is not *that* barren.'

'Maybe you haven't seen what I've seen, but believe me, those barbarians are capable of anything. They pray to strange deities and practise dark magic. Anything is possible,' said Aquinas.

As they began debating, Claudia raised her voice, cutting into their conversation: 'Maybe there's another explanation.'

'Like what?' asked Damocles.

'A natural disaster that gave them no time to prepare. Perhaps they took shelter in a nearby settlement and word is yet to reach us.'

'The camp is undisturbed, with no sign of a battle, nor any kind of disorder,' said Aquinas. 'There were no storms, no evidence of a fire, and the camp was as far from the sea as you can get on a small island. It's hard to imagine what kind of disaster could've vanished so many soldiers and left no trace. I suspect the cause may be ... unnatural.'

Claudia shivered, meeting Gia's gaze. She was beginning to get an idea of who might be responsible and it seemed that Gia shared the idea.

Jupiter.

He had tried to sink her ship. He had sent a human assassin. What if he had spirited the legions away – turned them into insects or stars? Maybe he'd graduated to more sophisticated forms of warfare, by staging a catastrophe which she would be blamed for. This was how the deities had played the game of civilization for centuries, arranging mortals into position like pieces in a strategy game.

'What should we do, Empress? Should we retaliate?'

'Yes, please do advise us.'

'Should we send more soldiers to investigate?'

There was something suspicious about the disappearance. It had the fingerprints of the gods all over it.

The earth felt to tilt and roll, like it had in Pompeii ahead of the Vesuvian eruption. Her father had never taught her statecraft, yet now she was expected to solve the empire's problems. She couldn't complain; she'd put herself firmly in this position. This was the occasion and she intended to meet it, to look it in the eye and clutch it around the throat.

'Send four more legions to the area,' she said. 'They should talk with the elders of the nearest villages. Speak to their client kings and queens. Tell them we will reward them for information.'

Damocles almost looked impressed.

'Good call, Empress,' he said.

'That won't work. We need to drive out the barbarians who are responsible and set an example,' said the general. 'Their settlements will be burned in search of the culprits.'

'You don't know what's happened yet. If they are hiding five thousand Romans, dead or alive, we shall know about it without incinerating their settlements,' said Claudia. 'There is no need for you to inflame the situation by murdering innocent children.'

The Roman generals sneered at this.

'What are you suggesting?' asked Aquinas.

'There should be some kind of investigation,' Claudia insisted. 'We must attempt to communicate with the tribal chiefs.'

'I told you she'd be as wet as a milkmaid,' said one man.

'We must flush out the enemy,' said Aquinas. 'The occupation is challenging enough as it is. We cannot have the natives thinking they can overpower us so easily.'

'Let me be clear: the legions are *not* to pillage and plunder. There is no need for a massacre before we know what happened. Inform me when Marcellus returns. He can tell us what the Legate says.'

'Very well, Empress,' said Hieronymus, in the tone of voice that said: *on your head, so be it.*

Damocles continued to regard her with growing interest, but General Aquinas stared at Claudia without expression, his iceberg-blue eyes boring into her soul. The encounter lasted for an uncomfortably long time before he turned and walked away.

A dull droning noise filled Claudia's head as she attempted to read through the scrolls Rectina had loaned to her: everything she needed to know about governing an empire, as written by men. Pliny, too, had been helpful, visiting the palace several times a week to counsel her. Yet a wall had now formed inside her head, preventing her from absorbing the new information. She'd been sitting there for over an hour and she couldn't recall a single thing she'd read, largely due to the incessant sound of shouting. The noise seemed to be getting louder, permeating every word, until she threw up her hands in frustration.

'What is that?' she said, when she heard footsteps in the hallway outside. 'What is making such noise?'

She turned, expecting to see one of her handmaids, but it was Gia to whom she'd barked these enquiries.

'Oh, sorry. I—'

'I'll go and check,' said Gia.

She disappeared outside, as Claudia tried once more to focus on the script in front of her.

After several failed attempts at concentration, Gia returned and made a face that immediately put Claudia's nerves on edge.

'What?' she said.

'It's nothing,' said Gia. 'Just some protestors.'

'Protestors? What are they protesting?'

'You're not going to like it.'

'Show me.'

Claudia followed her out to the balcony. A crowd of thousands had formed in the Forum, chanting furiously and holding make-shift banners, screaming about the missing legion. Their cloaked, toga-clad bodies formed a thick, bristling mob, while the torches they held cast dark shadows on their grimacing faces.

'Where are our men?' they raged.

'Where is the Eighth Legion?'

'Never trust a woman to do a man's job.'

'Empress of Lesbos!'

'Get her out! Get the bitch out!'

But the crowd was not just men. There were women there, too: angry sisters and wives and mothers, all wondering where their loved ones had gone and what Claudia planned to do about it.

A troop of soldiers had been sent to manage the situation, but a couple of the praetorians were conversing with the protesters, joining in as if they were on the same side, laughing as they beheld the offensive signs and scrolls that ridiculed her.

There it was again: PRINCESS SAPPHO.

EMPRESS OF LESBOS.

'Of course it would be my fault,' said Claudia. 'I didn't even send the men there! I will pray to the goddesses and make offerings tonight but what more can I do?'

'It is just part of ruling the world, I fear,' said Gia. 'No matter what you do, you will never please them all.'

The roaring of the angry crowd grew louder as another legion of guards appeared on horseback.

'What if the people revolt and set the city on fire?' said Claudia.

'The goddesses will watch the world for now. They came to your aid before, I'm sure they will again,' said Gia.

Claudia paused, uncertain.

'Come on, it's getting late,' Gia pushed. 'You need to eat, and rest. I'll cook you something.'

She touched the small of Claudia's back and Claudia felt herself growing into her, towards her, like a flower facing the sun.

'Really?' she said, instantly distracted from her melancholy. 'You would cook for me?'

'I can't promise it will *good*, but it will be edible . . . probably.'

Claudia relented, warmth spreading through her body.

'I'd like that, very much.'

They crept into the palace kitchen, abandoned after dark. Claudia clumsily attempted to assist, and Gia conjured up a meal that was far more delicious than it was burned.

'My mother would've been proud of that one,' she said.

Claudia saw tears in her eyes and clasped her hand across the table with both of her own, to share the weight of Gia's feelings.

The words sat on her tongue, held back by the bars of her lips.

I love you.

But the remains of the day washed over her, making her think of the protesters and the graffiti, making her sickened, her skin crawling, as all of the palace ghosts seemed to crowd around them.

She looked up to see a servant watching from the shadows and quickly released Gia's hand, sitting back and upright.

Later, when they retired to her rooms, Claudia caught her handmaids Aurelia and Nadira whispering in the cool quiet of an empty corridor. They silenced as she approached but Claudia was sure she heard the name of Sappho on their lips.

'The servants are whispering about me. Should I be concerned?'

asked Claudia, as she and Gia undressed and climbed into bed, lying on their sides with their fingers entwined. 'Should I interrogate them, or ignore it? What if they're plotting against me? My handmaids have close access to me, in a way others do not.'

'You're their ruler. Being slandered comes with the territory. It doesn't mean they're conspiring to kill you.'

'I think they were speculating, about us,' whispered Claudia. 'I am sure I heard the word Sappho.'

'Maybe they just like poetry?' suggested Gia lightly.

'The first graffiti was within the palace grounds. It must've been one of my staff. One of them has seen something or heard something. About us. Perhaps we haven't been careful enough.'

'People just like to gossip, that's all – especially about women. They've never had an empress before. You are something different, something new. It'll take time for them to adjust to the idea.' She smiled and reached for Claudia. 'Let me distract you from worrying.'

But Claudia sat up abruptly. 'Why this, though?'

Gia groaned and slumped back on the pillows.

'It feels very personal,' Claudia said. 'If they'd called me stupid or unattractive or promiscuous, that would feel like a general insult to all women, but to call me *Empress of Lesbos* suggests a person with grounds for suspicion, if not intimate knowledge.'

'And so what? They can't prove anything either way.'

'It doesn't matter. It's already out there. If enough people say it, it will become true,' said Claudia.

'I mean, it *is* true, isn't it?'

Claudia felt that gut-twisting shame again. She pictured her father and brother watching over her in spirit, laughing as they clinked glasses. She couldn't drive them from her mind, their voices echoing as she imagined what they would say. Her brother had always had choice comments to share about her manly peasant friend, as he'd put it.

They would tell her she was perverse and twisted, just like them, and even though she felt neither perverse nor twisted, Claudia could not shake the cold of this fear. It was as if they were haunting her through this graffiti, through this gossip, relishing in her misery, even if it was only so in her own head, in her own regurgitated memories.

'I don't understand why you're so threatened by words etched on a wall,' said Gia.

'I don't need the public knowing about my private affairs. It makes me weak.'

'Who cares what they say? You're the empress.'

'No emperor can survive being a mockery,' said Claudia. 'The people will lose respect for me. I am barely holding on to power as it is. If this catches on, I shall be the joke of Rome.'

'You're ashamed,' said Gia, frowning.

'No, that's not it,' said Claudia defensively. 'I am ashamed of many things, including myself, but never us. Never you.'

'I don't want to be a liability to you,' Gia said.

'You're not,' said Claudia quickly.

'It feels like I am. It feels like it's a problem, us being together, like I'm standing in the way.'

'In the way of what?'

'The crown. The throne. All of it.'

They silenced again.

'Was there a part of you that hoped that I might fail in my ambitions?' Claudia asked.

'I . . . I don't know,' said Gia. 'Maybe.'

An image crystallized in Claudia's mind, of her and Gia living in obscurity, in a tiny Sicilian village. Marcellus was emperor and they cared little for the state of Rome. Only for their own survival, their own peace. It was a pretty, wistful picture.

'Honestly, a part of *me* hoped I'd fail,' Claudia admitted. 'I am as surprised as everyone else to be here.'

'I thought this was what you always wanted.'

'That was . . . before you.'

'See, I *am* the problem,' Gia said. 'You think they're speculating because of your association with me, don't you?'

Claudia flushed. The thought had indeed crossed her mind but now she felt ashamed of it. How could Gia ever be the problem, when she was her everything? She was the light and joy in her life.

'The *world* is the problem. It would be far easier for us for live undercover if Marcellus was emperor, that is all,' she said.

'Undercover,' Gia repeated, dully.

'But . . . we cannot walk away. We have a responsibility to the people, to the goddesses. It's bigger than just you and me. I have a duty. We can't risk losing what we have already risked so much for. I have to stay, to search for the missing legion, to guide Rome, to defend it from Marcellus.'

'We should go to sleep,' said Gia, rubbing her face wearily. 'It won't seem as bad in the morning, with a clear head.'

In the quiet that followed these words, Claudia could still hear the protestors.

'I hope so,' she said.

Gia soon drifted off in her arms. Claudia stayed awake, stroking her hair and gazing down at her.

Gia was so good and pure. She didn't belong in this world made for monsters. Claudia had grown up around monsters, she knew all their tricks and habits, but Gia was too precious to be squandered.

Claudia didn't know what she would do if Gia died in the line of duty. Something inside her would snap. She would go wild, turn feral, and become a monster like Medusa, petrifying men to stone.

Fear made her want to withdraw or push her away, to keep Gia far away from her and her twisted circle of power, where everyone was endangered and nothing was certain.

The people who hated her would think nothing of hurting Gia to get to her, more so if they knew she was special to her. It was only a matter of time. If Claudia truly loved Gia, shouldn't she do anything to keep her safe? If she loved her, shouldn't she set her free?

And then she heard it. Movement beyond the folds of the red canopy curtains, stirred as if by a breeze.

Her blood surged, her heart pumping hard, fearing that one of the protestors had broken into the palace. She ignored the thudding of her pulse to listen intently, but she heard only the faint drifts of the hourglass and the dripping of a nearby tap.

Suddenly, the curtain was ripped open. Inexplicably, there he was. Her brother Decimus standing at the end of the bed, blood dribbling from his lips, the wound of a sword in his chest.

She blinked again and saw her father beside him, choking on his own poisoned vomit, his bloodshot eyes wide.

He used his last bit of strength to crawl onto the bed, slumping on top of her and clamping down on her wrist, his putrid dying breath wheezing out as he said:

'You'll be seeing me soon, *canicula*.'

Canicula. Little bitch.

Claudia jolted awake and screamed, her body on fire.

The vision dissipated as Gia bolted up, reaching for her sword at the side of the bed.

'What? What's happening?' she said in panic.

'It's okay. Just a . . . bad . . . dream,' she managed to gasp.

Gia pulled her into her arms, holding her as she shook and panted, gently laying them back down again.

'What happened?'

But Claudia couldn't speak of it. She shook her head and Gia didn't ask again, stroking her hair until her breathing evened out and she stopped trembling.

Claudia pretended to be asleep, so Gia would not stay awake worrying and watching over her.

Little bitch. These were her father's real last words. She hadn't shared them with anyone, not even Gia.

In the final moments of his life, he had looked her in the eye and he'd known what she had done.

He'd be waiting for her, when she followed him into the dark. He would have his vengeance, one day. Her brother, too.

She'd already come far too close to joining them.

8. THE SHIELD OF MINERVA

The following afternoon, Claudia returned to her chambers alone to find that an impractically large silver shield had been propped against her canopied bed, almost as tall as she was.

She stood at the open arch of her quarters, flanked by the two guards and two handmaidens who stood out in the hallway.

'Good day, Empress,' they said, in unison.

'What is that?' she asked, pointing at the shield.

Her staff peered in.

'A large gift for you, my empress?' said Aurelia.

'But who brought it? Did you see anyone enter?'

'No.' Aurelia frowned, thoughtfully. 'Actually, I didn't.'

'Did anyone come to my door?'

'Not as long as I have been here,' said one of the guards.

'Nor I,' said the other.

When Claudia looked to her, the other girl, Nadira, shook her head vehemently.

'Should I call for backup?' said the guard.

How was it possible for such an enormous object to have been deposited in her private rooms, entirely unseen by palace guards? Something inside told her not to involve them.

'No, thank you. I shall call you, if I need you.'

'Yes, Empress.'

Closing the door, Claudia regarded the shield hesitantly. It might be a trap. Perhaps it was spring-loaded with an arrow, or coated in poison. She couldn't be too careful.

Or maybe it was a present from Marcellus: an unwanted gift that came with unpleasant expectations.

She examined it from a distance. It had a sculpted figure of Minerva on it – helmet, spear, owl on her shoulder. Yet it was surely far too heavy to be lifted. It had no real use.

Thinking of how narrowly she'd escaped with her life just days before, Claudia adopted a position of extreme cautiousness, circling the mysterious object and using a pillow to prod at it. She crouched and squinted and whispered to it – even smelled it. It had the reassuring steely smell of a blacksmith's forge.

Claudia grazed it with her fingertips.

At her touch, the metal shimmered unnaturally, causing her to step backwards. The sculpted relief of the goddess came to life, turning from its heroic side profile to address her.

'Congratulations, Empress Claudia,' said the relief. 'It is my honour and my privilege to address you as such.'

'Minerva!' Claudia cried, before instantly lowering her voice. 'I'm so glad to hear from you. I have—'

But her goddess continued speaking, as if she couldn't hear her. 'I apologize for taking so long to make contact. I've been on an important quest – a voyage into the unknown. I have spied inside my father's mind and recovered Fortuna from her self-exile. We are ready to regroup and assemble our defence.'

'Minerva?'

Claudia waved at her, uncertainly, but it seemed the goddess couldn't see.

'You are safe and the flame is still burning, thanks to Vesta,' said Minerva. 'We are fortunate she has taken our side, or her interception may not have had such a pleasant result.'

So, it was true: they *had* come to her aid in the Pantheon.

As the goddess of the hearth and home, Vesta had many nurturing and maternal qualities, but she also accepted vestal virgins as sacrifices in her name. Her femininity was used as a symbol to oppress other women. Vesta was neutral, double-edged.

Claudia assumed her interest was more personal than simple support for a woman's world. If someone tried to snuff out the eternal flame, that was an attack on her and her devoted followers, too.

Either way, it was a reassuring sign.

'I'm relieved that you are alive and well,' Minerva continued, 'and that Jupiter hasn't succeeded in his ambitions. I've been assured that the other goddesses have been keeping an eye on you, in my absence, and they will continue to do so. Our numbers are growing steadily, thanks to Diana and Venus. They have been busy recruiting goddesses to our cause. When Jupiter returns to Elysium, we will be ready. You must be ready too, Claudia Caesaria.'

'I am trying,' said Claudia softly. 'I am trying to be—'

Minerva's pre-cast message cut her off again.

'I know my father intends to do you harm, but do not be afraid. I am offering you a weapon, a gift of protection. This shield is what we call a god's-eye, or a goddess's-eye, in this case: an object that provides omniscient vision. Through its lens, you may view any person you wish to see. I have one much like it.'

Claudia's breath caught in her throat at this new development.

'It will not show you the past or the future, only the present. Only what occurs in the here and now. It will not show you Elysium or the underworld, only the mortal plane, but it will give you divine knowledge. This is my guardianship in material form. Know your enemies, Claudia. Know your allies. Use this shield to protect your kingdom through observation. As we watch you, you shall watch them.'

Minerva's sculpted relief faded away, flattening to form a shiny mirror. A portal. Two blurry figures appeared in the bright gleam at the centre of the shield instead, sharpening until they came into focus and Claudia was able to recognize them.

Damocles and Hieronymus. The consul and her most senior advisor, in red and orange robes. They were walking through the palace gardens, listening to the tolling of distant bells.

They made for visually interesting companions: Damocles, tall and large with a waxed, pointed beard like an arrow, and Hieronymus, small and bony with his fluffy mop of white hair.

'You swear to me, man to man, you were not involved in the incident at the Pantheon?' said Damocles.

'In the name of my god, Vulcan,' said Hieronymus, emphatically. 'On the lives of my children and grandchildren, I played no part in the attempt on the empress's life. Perhaps it is *you* I should be interrogating.'

'I have no loyalty to the empress but I don't seek to harm her either. She might even be useful, if we are to play it right.'

'You are not a fan of Marcellus?'

'I am not a partisan. I serve only Mercury and the Senate, and our influence pales with every new emperor.'

The image faded away, as Minerva's sculpted image emerged from the silver again. Claudia let out a shaky breath.

Neither man thought well of her, but it seemed neither of them had tried to kill her either. It was a strange relief.

'If you wish to view someone, you need only touch the shield and say, "show me" followed by their name. It will do the rest.'

A million possibilities flooded Claudia's mind.

'Let us keep this between us, for now. None of the emperors before you were blessed with such a tool. Those who learn of it will desire to take it from you. I am breaking all of the rules to empower you, to protect you, to give you the advantage, but these are extraordinary times, Claudia. Extraordinary times indeed! We must be prepared.'

Minerva almost seemed excited to go to war, Claudia thought.

'If Jupiter is willing to defy the laws of the pantheon to work directly on Earth, then so shall we. We will do everything in our power to shield the women of the world, even if that means saying good riddance to the rules. Rules are made to be broken, as you humans like to say.'

Claudia touched the shield again, wishing she could converse with the goddess directly. She had so many questions.

'For now, I must leave you. Good luck, Empress, and take care. I'll be speaking to you again soon. Goodbye.'

'Goodbye,' Claudia said, unheard.

Minerva's image returned to its stationary side profile. The shield reverted to normal, disguising itself as an ordinary object. To anyone else who saw it, it would merely be decorative. Gargantuan and gauche, suitable for an empress, but not suspicious.

Left alone with her thoughts again, Claudia hugged herself, excited and afraid, eager to test the god's-eye shield for herself. Who did she most wish to look in on?

Her heart leaped to Gia, but her head held her back. She knew good relationships were based on honesty and trust, though she'd had little opportunity to experience it.

Gia conducted herself as a person with no secrets and nothing to hide, but Claudia didn't enjoy that same freedom. There were things she wouldn't, couldn't, share with Gia – things that were humiliating, dark, vulnerable, twisted. Things she needed to conceal, if ever she was to be loved. She couldn't ask to know all of her, to see all of her, if she wasn't willing to offer the same herself.

'Show me Marcellus,' she said instead.

The shield formed its hazy, pearly portal again, clearing to reveal her cousin, whistling as he ambled along the colonnade. He clipped his toenails. He styled his hair. He counted some coins while singing a little song. He did some stretches. He ate a pear.

Claudia yawned, sitting down in front of the shield, and waited for him to do something interesting. Marcellus responded by taking a nap. He was, at first appearance, the most boring man in Rome.

A noise sounded outside her room. Footsteps, voices.

Claudia took her hand off the shield and the picture instantly dissipated. The door swung open. Claudia stood up and turned to see Gia standing in the arch, gazing at Claudia and her gigantic goddess gift.

She gave a low whistle.

'Now *that* is a shield,' Gia said. 'You could hide a whole legion behind that thing. I hope I'm not expected to carry it.'

Claudia gestured for her to close the door behind her. Gia did so, then joined her, standing in front of it.

'It's not a shield, but a magic mirror,' said Claudia.

Gia squinted it at, confused, for it didn't reflect them.

'I don't get it,' she said.

'It's a present from Minerva,' Claudia elaborated.

'*The* Minerva? She was here?'

'Briefly, distantly, in avatar form, but she is well. She is still behind us, and she gave me this to help keep us safe. Tell me, who would you most like to look upon in this world?'

'She is standing right in front of me,' said Gia.

Claudia smiled.

'Besides me.'

'What if they're doing something private, like shaving their arse or knocking one out? I don't want to witness such things.'

'They won't know you're spying on them,' said Claudia, laughing behind her hand. 'You'll be a fly on the wall. Just . . . think of a person, any person. For the experiment.'

'I don't know . . . How about Dominic? He's probably not doing anything unseemly.'

Claudia nodded and reached out to touch the shield.

'Show me Dominic,' she said.

The shield knew which Dominic she meant. That was why they called it a god's-eye, she supposed. The silver surface became hazy, its shiny metal swirling into a whirlpool as Gia watched, wide-eyed.

It formed a moving image, revealing little Athena playfighting with Dominic, out in the palace garden.

'You're too big,' she complained. 'It's not fair. You're always going to beat me.'

'I'm not, I'm skinny,' said Dom. 'For a gladiator, anyway. You just have to keep training.'

'Do you think you'll fight again?' asked Athena.

'I don't know,' said Dom. 'I don't know if I have it in me . . . not after the last time.'

'What happened last time?'

'I had to kill my friend, in a match.'

'That's sad,' said Athena.

'He was shorter than me, but he was a better fighter.'

'But you beat him, didn't you?'

'I only won because he gave up. He let me win, so I could live.'

'You're still tall though,' Athena sighed, after a pause. 'I'm not. I need to find someone my own size to fight.'

'Being small can be an advantage,' said Dom.

'How?' asked Athena, jabbing at him with a wooden sword.

'It might seem like a disadvantage when you're up against someone bigger,' said Dom, defending, 'but you can use it to squeeze out of tight holds, or to run through your opponent's legs. There's less of you to grab hold of, so you want to make sure you're fast.'

'I can be fast!' she said. 'Watch me.'

Athena bolted to the other side of the garden, swinging around a pillar before racing back to Dom, almost crashing into him.

'How was that?' she said, panting.

'The speed was good, but the technique . . . well, we can work on the technique,' said Dominic.

Claudia pulled away, allowing the scene to fade.

Gia's eyes sparkled with awe, or fear, or both.

'That is . . . scary,' she said.

'See?' said Claudia, excitedly. 'It is the gift of all gifts! The weapon of all weapons. It just appeared in my chambers with an oracle message from Minerva, telling me to use it to keep an eye on my allies and enemies alike. Goddesses do have their ways.'

'Did you spy on me?' said Gia.

She was smiling, one brow raised, as she pulled Claudia closer. Their bodies brushed against each other, invitingly.

'I will have to conduct myself just so at all times, if you're going to be watching,' she added.

'This is your first thought?' teased Claudia, kissing her. Her lips were soft and warm. 'We could gaze upon anyone in existence and your first thought is yourself?'

'Well, did you?'

'No, I didn't. I wanted to, though . . . just a little bit.'

She motioned with her forefinger and thumb, making a pinch movement, like a crab's claw.

'But I didn't! I was very good!'

'Hmm. I believe you.'

'Why, what were you up to? Something sordid?'

'When am I not?'

'Weren't you going to meet Cassius?'

'I did. He . . . he was busy.' Claudia waited for her to clarify, but she didn't. 'Go on then, tell me what Marcellus was up to. I'm guessing he was first on your list?'

'Not a lot. He was extremely tedious, actually. I'll spy on him again but I'm unconvinced that he organized the attempt against my life. Nor do I think Hieronymus or Damocles are responsible.'

'Really? You are sure your cousin isn't conspiring with others?'

'I saw nothing that persuaded me he is capable of it. It would be short-sighted not to consider other options, in the circumstances. Who else might aspire to rule Rome?'

'Many people,' said Gia. 'It's not really my scene, but I can see the appeal.'

She gestured at the luxury that surrounded them: the exotic flowers, the banquet of fruit, the amphoras full of wine, the lavish bedspread, the burning fire, the golden trinkets and marble statues.

'They may *want* to rule but who is in the position to claim the right, when the emperor's only living child is standing here?' asked Claudia. 'Who would be so brave, yet so foolish?'

'Do you have any secret half-siblings, by chance?' said Gia.

'Gods, I hope not. They might turn out like Decimus.'

'What about other relatives, or even people who worked with your father? They might still be loyal to him.'

'Only a great power could've extinguished the sacred flame in the Pantheon that day,' said Claudia. 'Jupiter must be involved somehow. Perhaps it is someone unseen, someone on the outside, who might wish to take Rome for themselves.'

'Like who?' said Gia.

Claudia paused, allowing the idea to settle in her mind.

'Show me . . . Prince Darius of Persia,' she said, reaching out for the shield again.

Once more, the shield glimmered and formed a vision. It was much less clear than the scenes of Marcellus or Dom and Athena, with a grainy, hazy quality, like a sandstorm. The colours were faded, the shapes indistinct. And yet, she could see *something*.

At first, Claudia could only make out rocks. A tree, a boulder, a jagged cliff with skittering pebbles . . . and a foot.

A hairy, sandalled foot.

The view pulled back, revealing another foot, a pair of legs, then another, and another, all marching in synchronicity, forming an endless line of men. Soldiers, on the march.

They were not just the legs of men either, but also of beasts:

horses, dogs, a leopard, a cheetah, and . . . elephants. Claudia saw chariots and flags, heard drums and horns, all muddled together to create a noisy, colourful cavalcade, kicking up dust as they charged through the desert.

'Where are they going?' she murmured.

It looked like a battalion, marching into war.

'Where is he?' said Gia. 'Let's get a look at this guy.'

'You are keener than me!' said Claudia.

'I want to see my competition.'

'There is none.'

The vision closed in on the main litter of the parade: a bold purple canopy with white drapes, decorated with flowers. It was pulled by dressed horses and guarded by warriors with spears, all of whom were chanting in Persian.

'All hail the Prince of Persia!'

Within the royal chariot, surrounded by courtiers in colourful robes and tall hats, sat a fearsome-looking man with dark-rimmed eyes, dressed in bronze armour, his dark hair falling loose upon his shoulders.

Sharp-faced and stoic, he gazed into the distance at the barren, uninhabited landscape that Claudia recognized as the Parthian border: the battleground between two great empires.

'He is coming to Rome,' she gasped. 'He is on his way.'

When she released her hand, the picture stilled and faded. Gia slumped back on the bed.

'The prince is coming,' Claudia said, in shock.

Gia groaned, head in her hands.

'This is just what we needed,' she said. 'At least Minerva gave us a heads-up, I guess. Thank you, goddess.'

Claudia sat beside Gia on the bed as they stared at the shield, unsure what to say to each other.

'What will you do?' asked Gia.

'I don't know. What *can* I do?'

'Tell him not to come. Tell him that you're the empress now, and the deal your father made against your will is off.'

'It isn't that simple,' she said.

'Why not?'

'There may be consequences, for rejecting him – not just for me, but for Rome and beyond. A war with the Persian empire is to be avoided at all costs. It is a battle I'm not sure the empire could win.'

'So then, form a platonic alliance instead.'

'That may still involve marriage, if he wishes to keep up appearances. If he arrives with the expectation of making an empress his wife, his people won't be pleased to return with nothing.'

Gia didn't say anything.

'I may be forced to consider marriage if the Senate tries to pressure me to marry Marcellus,' said Claudia.

'I was afraid you were going to say that.'

'It could work in our favour to at least be seen to consider it. He could be useful to us.'

'Useful? How?'

In some sense, Darius's arrival couldn't have come at a better time. If the people were suspicious that she might be a secret Sapphic, perhaps Darius himself could be the distraction.

Claudia could see it clearly now: she could parade the prince around as her consort until the rumours subsided, and then, when it came time to marry, she would find a diplomatic reason to reject him. A war with Persia would be a disaster, which meant keeping Darius onside. And it would deter Marcellus, at least.

'How can a noble from another land help?' said Gia. 'What power does he have in Rome?'

'That other land is Persia. Persia is a thorn in the empire's side. Romans have long feared they might build a superior civilization. If I had a connection to Persia that Marcellus did not, it might prevent him from trying to creep his way onto the throne.'

'Right,' Gia said, obviously unhappy.

'It would merely be a business arrangement. A political alliance. It's a tale as old as time. It would mean nothing,' said Claudia.

'It would mean something to me,' said Gia.

Claudia gave her a fraught, conflicted look.

'You knew this,' she said. 'We have discussed it before. I told you, back in Pompeii.'

'You are empress now. And if you are empress, then nothing should prevent us from being together,' said Gia.

'Or perhaps it is even more difficult.'

'Isn't that the privilege of power? Emperors have done much more unthinkable things to serve their own needs. I'm sure that one of them had a male lover or two, if I remember the rumours right.'

'It is different for men, and you know it.'

'No one is expecting you to stand on the balcony and announce that you dine on Lesbos, but . . .'

'What?' Claudia said.

'I don't know . . . How long could we carry on like this? For how many years would we live in secrecy?'

They stared at each other a moment, aware of the strange power imbalance between them.

'I know we talked about Darius and I accepted it,' said Gia. 'It's just, seeing him now, and hearing you talk about it . . . it feels very real. Too real. I'm struggling with the idea more than I thought I would. And what of his feelings? He might not see this as simply a betrothal of convenience. He might expect you to provide him with an heir. What then?'

Claudia had already considered the possibility, but she was yet to come to a conclusion on the issue of lineage.

'You are right,' she conceded. 'There is a great deal for him to gain from the situation, and a great deal for us to fear. But he will surely approach this from a practical perspective. He will be more concerned by treaties and borders than romance. I don't think I need to worry about hurting his feelings. Only yours, and my own.'

'Someone getting hurt seems pretty inevitable to me,' said Gia.

'Not if we're on the same page. Can you trust that there's no interest on my side, no matter how it looks?'

'I suppose I must.'

'Charming the prince is important, a delicate act of diplomacy, but it isn't worth losing you for. Nothing is. I swore that nothing would come between us, and I meant it.'

Claudia reached out to touch Gia's face.

She yearned for her, even though she was standing right in front of her, as if her well of desire would never be fulfilled. She could never get enough. It was insatiable.

She would give up anything to be empress, to serve the goddesses and fulfil destiny, but not Gia.

She would not sacrifice Gia. She would not sacrifice love.

Anything but that.

9. THE PRINCE OF PERSIA

Claudia continued to watch the prince's advance through the shield, though she couldn't share what she'd learned with her advisors or risk revealing Minerva's gift. She waited until Darius sent riders ahead of his party to announce their imminent arrival. Only then could she gather her staff and begin preparations, putting them slightly behind schedule.

The palace burst into a frenzy of diplomatic hospitality, as servants began polishing every stone and stitching every robe, cleaning every amphora, painting every pillar and filling every crack.

On the morning of the prince's arrival, Claudia woke early and watched as dawn lit the sky. Birds swooped past her window, gathering on the roof, the sound of their beating wings drawing her to the balcony.

Climbing quietly out of bed and opening the curtains, she crossed the room and pulled open the partition that enclosed the balcony, standing at the railing to look out over the gardens.

Ornamental trees and marble statues were arranged in a grid, with crisp, watered lawns and trickling fountains. Guards moved slowly through the morning mists, their armour gleaming in the haze.

All was quiet.

All was peaceful, for now.

Claudia closed her eyes, taking a deep, stirring breath. She tried to think of nothing, until a soft flutter caught her attention.

A small brown bird sat on the stony railing, staring at her. It cocked its head, curious and friendly.

'Hello, cute one,' she whispered.

It reminded her of when she was a girl, and the bird her brother killed. She felt a strong, painful longing for a past that had never existed, for a family she'd never had.

She reached out her hand, hoping it would hop on, but the bird flew away just as suddenly as it had arrived.

A lone '*boo*' cut through the quiet. Claudia looked to the Forum to see the protestors gathering, ready for another day of disapproval.

It wouldn't look good to have civil unrest on the streets when the prince arrived. It wouldn't do much for her reputation, if she was to make him respect her. Should she order the guards to have the protesters rounded up and imprisoned? Or would that only enrage them further?

Claudia yawned. She'd stayed up far too late, staring into Minerva's shield, secretly watching the prince for signs, but nothing she saw gave her cause to think him immediately dangerous. He was charming, courteous to his staff and gentle with his many beasts, all of which had names and favourite snacks he fed to them. He had a harem of women who accompanied him, fussing over him maternally, but he was respectful towards them, if not familial. He didn't engage in any nocturnal activities with them. He took their advice and considered their opinions. As the prince's party approached the city walls, he had brief conversations with his advisors, all of whom were bearded men in hats of varying heights, but he spoke only of marrying her and securing the Roman-Persian alliance, not of plotting to have her murdered.

All the same, she had to be on guard. The journey from Persepolis was long. The prince was still travelling on the day of her coronation. Had he paid an assassin to kill her ahead of his arrival in order to seize Rome? It was possible, but her gut told her he was not responsible – that it had been a distinctly Roman job, complete with a seal of Jupiter.

Claudia stared into the middle distance for a moment, trying to gather the strength to go on with her day, then she roused Gia, who quickly departed before Claudia's handmaids arrived to style and dress her.

She wore her luxurious new robes for the occasion, white and purple with detailed embroidery, accessorizing with a purple cloak and matching diadem, with amethysts woven into its laurel leaves.

'Are you excited to meet the prince?' asked Aurelia, when Claudia yawned behind her hand again.

'Oh, yes,' lied Claudia. 'It will be good to put a face to the name I've known for such a long time. Yet, I'm also apprehensive of what he might be like. He is a stranger to me.'

'I understand, Empress,' said Aurelia, nodding sagely. 'It's like when you go to meet a boy just because your friend knows his friend. Sometimes he's nice and you can enjoy his company for a while, and sometimes he's a pig you can't wait to see the back of.'

Nadira flashed her a look of panic, signalling that she might not want to discuss her romantic life with the ruler of Rome, but Claudia was glad of the chatter, filling the silence and her mind.

What harm would it do for her to give the impression that she might be interested in Darius? It might even help dispel the rumours.

She laughed, signalling that Aurelia's oversharing was welcome.

'I've heard he's very handsome though,' she said, which elicited a delighted giggle from the handmaids.

'So have we.'

'Delphine in the kitchen says he's more handsome than the statue of Apollo in the courtyard,' said Aurelia.

'How does she know?'

'She says an oracle told her.'

'I'm sure he's preferable to my own cousin, at least.'

'You should wear your hair like this,' said Nadira, pulling out two wavy strands to frame her face. 'It looks the prettiest.'

'You'll make a beautiful couple,' said Aurelia, sighing wistfully. 'If he's not a pig, that is.'

'Indeed. Let's not get ahead of ourselves, girls. There are many ways in which a man can be intolerable.'

They nodded, mmm-hmming in agreement.

Claudia met Gia at the bottom of the stairs, as was their new tradition – a show to make it appear as if they did not share a bedroom. They conversed as if others were listening, which they usually were.

'Good morning, Empress,' Gia said.

'Good morning, Gia,' replied Claudia.

'Here it is, at long last,' said Gia. 'Today is the big day, the arrival of your beloved.'

'Hurrah,' said Claudia, in a flat voice.

'Are you giddy with girlish glee?'

'I am, indeed, buoyant with joy. Can you not tell?'

They dared to sneak a flirtatious look.

'Prince Darius won't be able to take his eyes off you,' said Gia, though her smile faltered.

They were quickly surrounded by advisors, guards, soldiers and senators, all talking about the incoming prince. Hieronymus shuffled over, followed by Damocles and the usual rainbow of palace advisors.

'Prince Darius is less than an hour away,' said Hieronymus. 'So far, all is well between his party and the military escort. Hopefully, the rest of his journey will be equally uneventful.'

'Wonderful,' said Claudia, though there was nothing she wanted less at this precise moment. 'And where is Marcellus?'

'He was meant to return after meeting the Legate, but he has yet to materialize,' said Damocles.

His absence was surprising.

'Has he not been reporting to you daily?' asked Claudia. 'That is what you told me, Hieronymus.'

'Your cousin has been called away on an urgent matter,' said Hieronymus in irritation. 'Do not concern yourself with it.'

'But I *am* concerned,' said Claudia. 'What urgent matter?'

'There has been a development, with the missing legion,' said Hieronymus. 'All is in hand.'

'You'd think the empress would be the first person to know. Are you to tell me that he has left Rome?'

'It is far more important that you focus on the imminent arrival of the prince,' said Damocles. 'We believe him to be an ally but we cannot be sure. You must stay vigilant.'

Claudia sighed and set her shoulders in resignation. They would discuss her mysteriously missing cousin later.

'What is left for me to do?' she asked.

'It is all planned,' said Damocles. 'The throne room is set up to receive him. There will be music, wine, dancers and appetizers. You'll present him with gifts, and he will do the same.'

'Gifts?' she said.

'Livestock, olive oil, salt, copper, gems. A selection of local treasures. His riders have given us his demands, and they are fair. All is arranged ahead of time. You'll talk briefly to confirm the terms of your planned engagement and recommit to peace at the Parthian border before embarking on the day's events. Tomorrow, his advisors shall meet with yours to begin formal negotiations.'

Claudia swallowed. These 'negotiations' would certainly involve her marital status.

'I will also be in attendance today, of course, to converse with the prince's advisor,' said Damocles. 'You may also choose one of your guards for protection, as will he.'

'Gia,' said Claudia, seeking her out. 'I choose Gia.'

'Again, I really do suggest picking one of the men, Empress,' said Hieronymus. 'The prince's guard has a reputation for—'

'I said Gia,' Claudia interrupted.

She met Gia's eye with a small, affirmative nod.

Hieronymus's lips tightened.

'Every entrance is accounted for,' said Damocles. 'Every soldier has been vetted and approved by me personally. We have done everything we can to ensure your safety, but you aren't to go anywhere alone with him.'

'You think he's dangerous?' Claudia asked.

'All men can be dangerous, Empress,' said Damocles. 'Especially in private.'

'Let us assume he's not foolish enough to violate a woman with her own army on standby,' Claudia said. 'He may still be dangerous of mind, though – dangerous in his ambitions. Tell me everything you know about Prince Darius, Damocles. In truth, I don't know much about him at all, despite the fact that we are technically engaged to be married.'

'We're told he can speak Latin,' said Damocles. 'He is educated and said to have mastered many traditional arts. He's a soldier, and, if the streets are to be believed, one of the finest fighters in Persepolis.'

'What of his personality?'

'Mixed accounts. Some say he is charming and kind, others say he is a rogue, causing trouble for the king.'

'I am sure he would hear mixed accounts of me, too.'

The consul and her advisor looked to each other.

'How do you think I should deal with him? What approach should I take, in establishing a relationship?' she asked.

'If I may speak frankly, Empress?' said Damocles.

'Go on,' she said.

'It wouldn't hurt to flatter his ego a little,' he said.

'Meaning what, exactly?'

'Enchant him. Use the weapon of desire. I strongly advise you to . . .' He looked at the floor. 'How can I put this?'

'Flirt,' said the elderly Hieronymus. 'You should flirt with him.'

Gia didn't react, yet Claudia could feel her irritation bristling silently beside her.

Every pair of eyes in the room were fixed on her.

'This too can be a woman's weapon,' said Damocles.

'I'm well aware of the power of flirting, but thank you . . . for your suggestion.'

At the sound of horns, they moved outside to stand on the palace steps, spread out between the rows of pillars and ready to greet their mysterious visitor.

Claudia's heart began to pound, though she wasn't sure why. The anticipation of the unknown, she suspected.

A crowd gathered outside, rising in volume as the sound of boots and horses grew louder, until they were deafening in volume. The prince's procession was imminent, filling the streets with music. Claudia could hear it long before she could see it.

The colourful, musical promenade of beasts reached the palace, chaperoned by no less than four thousand praetorians, passing right by the growing group of protestors.

One threw something at the prince's litter between rabid curses. Claudia didn't know what the prince had done to offend him so, or if he was targeted purely for being associated with her. The man was quickly dragged out of sight by guards, but rotten food was now splattered on one of the Persian party's embroidered fabric awnings, making it look as if someone had vomited on it.

It wasn't quite the reception she had hoped for.

Claudia sensed the nervousness in the air, the quick glances from soldier to soldier. The military was apprehensive about the meeting. A Persian invasion was possible, they were thinking; and for all Claudia knew, they might be right.

The royal cavalcade came to a standstill, though the musicians continued playing. One of the royal attendants stepped up to wipe the rotten gunk clean before the prince stepped out.

He postured with a dramatic swirl of his brown fur cloak, surrounded by women with palm fans and flowers.

Soldiers filed up on either side of him, then in front and behind, boxing him into a protective formation. Their armour was bronzed, and they wore strips of fabric beneath their plates.

Each step was in sync, timed to fit with the jubilant music, full of leaping flutes and sweeping strings.

'Shah Prince Darius, his most high majesty,' announced a squat man in a tall hat, 'son of Kamran, the King of kings, and Queen Malekeh. Commander of the Savaran, Chief of Warriors.'

Claudia felt her heart pounding again, but not with desire. It was more from the strangeness of the situation, and from the enormous expectation of such a momentous event.

'Empress Claudia Imperia Caesaria,' announced Hieronymus, 'daughter of Tiberius, heir to the Julio-Claudian dynasty, ruler of the Roman Empire and all of its territories, imperator of the Roman army and navy, ordained by the Senate and the goddess Victoria.'

The Persian warriors parted, revealing her long-awaited prince.

All those years she'd spent waiting to meet this man, and now here he was, walking right towards her.

He was even broader than he'd appeared in her goddess-eye shield, with a swaggering gait and a face that caused a stir among the crowd: the kind of man who inspired sculptors and painters, with razor-sharp features and a dark, long-lashed gaze.

'Empress Claudia,' he said, standing in front of her.

When she held out her hand for him to kiss, he did so without expression, his face serious and solemn.

'Prince Darius. It is my great pleasure to receive you in Rome,' she said, in her most regal voice.

Darius stared at her unabashedly. He was much taller than her, casting her in shadow, and his gaze was both impassive and strangely penetrating, his head tilted slightly to one side, appraising her like a statue.

'How are you finding Rome?' she asked.

'I have only just arrived,' he said. 'It has yet to make an impression on me.'

'Not a fan of marble columns?' said Claudia lightly.

'Persepolis is the city of a hundred pillars.'

His advisor – the small man in the tallest hat – elbowed him.

'But Rome is . . . impressively large,' he said.

He wasn't giving her much to work with.

'You haven't been to Rome before, or so I'm told?' she said. 'Are the accommodations to your liking, at least?'

Darius looked up at the palace many emperors had built, her childhood home with its golden leaves and painted pillars, its grandiose statues and fountains and gardens.

'It is . . . pleasant enough.'

Claudia's eyebrows lifted. 'Merely pleasant?'

A ripple passed through the crowd of senators and advisors who served as her buffer.

'Yes. I find it to be . . . quite adequate.'

Claudia's left eye twitched.

'What do you find to be lacking, exactly?' she said.

'It is not so much what is lacking but what is present in abundance,' he said, side-eyeing an arrangement of solid gold cherubs.

Claudia flushed hot, humiliated in front of the gathered crowd, though she tried not to let it show.

She'd expected him to flatter her, perhaps even sweep her off her feet, but he seemed displeased to be here instead, maybe even more displeased than she'd been to receive him.

'I hope at least your journey was uneventful,' she said, 'and the military escort gave you no trouble.'

'I would not say that. A man could not take a shit without making eye contact with a Roman soldier,' he said gravely.

Gia cough-laughed, clearing her throat to cover it.

'Our arrival was also . . . not ideal.'

He looked at the stain where the rotten fruit had hit.

'My deepest apologies, for that . . . unfortunate incident,' said

Claudia. 'He will be dealt with. As for the escort, I'm sure you can understand my position. It would be foolish to allow an unknown man to enter my city without a chaperone.'

'I am your fiancé, am I not?' he said.

'This is our first meeting. You are still unknown to me.'

The crowd stirred uncomfortably again.

'But . . . you must be tired and hungry from your difficult journey,' she said, smiling broadly. 'We have arranged a grand feast for your arrival. I do hope Roman food can impress you more than our city.'

Claudia raised her brows at Gia as the prince and his court were chaperoned into the triclinium, the grand dining room with one wall open to the atrium. She and the prince took their gold-winged thrones side by side as their staff sat down alongside them.

She was sure to reserve the seat next to her for Gia, forcing Hieronymus to sit further down the long bench, next to his Persian equivalent: the smallest bearded man in the tallest hat.

Damocles led a programme of entertainments as appetizers were brought out on golden trays, beginning with a poetry recitation.

Outside, clouds gathered and a light rain began to fall. Also not ideal. It gradually developed into a storm as they ate fruit and cheese, winds blustering in and riffling the curtains, cloths and napkins.

Claudia shivered, remembering the storm that had almost wrecked her ship and the way the sky had darkened before the assassination attempt at the Pantheon. Jupiter was known for his ability to control the weather. Now every time she saw dark clouds, it put her nerves on edge.

As musicians played, they ate an ostentatious feast of exotic Roman culinary delights, including fish, goat, and even peacock, which the prince declined with a sorrowful look on his face.

When Claudia caught his eye, he explained:

'The peacock is sacred to the Persian royal family,' he said. 'My father's throne is shaped like a peacock.'

Hieronymus shot her an apologetic look. He hadn't mentioned peacock when he outlined the plan for the feast, and she wasn't sure if the mishap was intentional or not.

'I do apologize, Prince Darius. We meant no offence,' said Claudia. 'It is prized as a delicacy here, due to its association with the goddess Juno . . . though I can't say I am fond of it.'

'Let us eat some real food,' he said. 'Once you have tasted a perfumed stew with cinnamon and pomegranates, you will never be impressed by anything cooked by a Roman man again.'

'Is that so?' she said, cutting eyes at Gia again.

'I hear you're a fan of sweet things,' he said.

'Guilty. The rumours are true.'

'Then wait until you try tar halva. It is made of rice flour, ground cardamom and butter, and sweetened with a light saffron syrup.'

'Tell me you have brought some,' said Claudia.

'It would be rude not to.'

'Similarly, it would be undiplomatic of me not to sample your native cuisine,' she said.

The prince's attendants brought out an array of dishes, shoving aside the Roman feast to make room on the table: spices arranged in a rainbow of colours, grilled meats on wooden skewers, bowls of rose water with floating petals, and dishes of sauces full of parsley and garlic.

Claudia was momentarily annoyed that Darius had taken over, until the delicious smells of saffron, cardamon and turmeric filled her nostrils, making her mouth water. She could barely wait for the imperial poison taster to sample it all, declaring it fit for consumption. Claudia helped herself to a little bit of everything, as did Gia.

'Maybe you *should* marry him,' Gia joked, under her breath.

The inclement weather had subsided, the white of the autumnal sky breaking through the clouds. Claudia's nerves finally settled and she allowed herself to enjoy the feast, even allowing Gia to share from her plate as they exchanged their favourite culinary discoveries.

Their hands touched at their sides, their feet tangled together under the bench, exchanging flushed looks as the lyre player launched into a beautifully haunting song that made Claudia's eyes sting.

And yet, here was her promised prince, her fated fiancé, seated at her side at long last.

She could not have been less interested in him.

At the end of the meal, Darius was sure to point out that the Persian dishes had been devoured more definitively, leaving more empty bowls and plates, declaring himself the winner of a competition Claudia had not agreed to enter. Yet she was happy to concede defeat.

'I may have to give you this one, Prince Darius,' she said, pointing at him with a spoon as she devoured the last bit of honey cake. 'You'll have to share some of your recipes. Call it a cultural exchange.'

'And what will you offer in return?' he said.

'I am yet to find something that impresses you, but when I do, I shall be glad to give it to you.'

'I am a difficult person to impress,' he said. 'I'm quite particular about what I like – fussy, some might say.'

His advisor adopted a deadpan expression, as though unwilling to agree with this in public.

'It isn't meant as an insult, though. When I love something, I truly love it – unconditionally and eternally.'

This was unexpected from a man who had been described as a rogue. Gia's posture stiffened beside her.

'That ... is good to know,' said Claudia, staring at her plate. 'Duly noted.'

Darius didn't speak, leaving the sentiment hanging.

'Perhaps we should move on ... to the gift-giving ceremony,' said Claudia, to break the silence.

'I will follow your lead, Empress,' said Darius.

They retreated into the throne room nearby – where more marble columns and golden cherubs awaited, to the prince's displeasure.

Gia faced off against a man with a scarred face and missing teeth, while Damocles bowed to the small, bearded man in the tall hat, introducing himself as consul.

'Damocles.'

'Mehdi,' he said, bowing back.

Hieronymus shuffled off to retrieve a red, silk bundle from a pillar. He gave it to Claudia, in a very officious manner, and she handed it to the prince in an equally ceremonious fashion.

'Sepas,' said the prince, in thanks.

He opened it, looking down at the Roman hamper Damocles had assembled, including figs grown in the palace orchard, a terracotta amphora painted with scenes of the gods, and a precious jar of Pompeiian garum, saved from the disaster.

Still, the prince appeared unimpressed.

Mehdi elbowed him again, shooting him a pointed look.

'I am grateful for ... the spirit of your generosity,' he said.

They took turns to present each other with gifts. Cinnamon was exchanged for salt, and silk exchanged for leather. Claudia's presents of olive oil and a rooster appeared paltry in contrast to the lavish gowns she was presented with, embroidered with a jewellery box of gemstones.

The prince stared at the hourglass on the table, seeming bored.

'A mosaic,' he said drolly, when she gifted him a scene of two peaceful doves, 'how quaint.'

'It symbolizes the historic union between our countries,' Claudia said. 'To the future of Persia and Rome.'

The atmosphere was somehow fetid and flat.

She had just gifted him with a basket of Sicilian lemons when a large cat with tufted ears was led into the room on a leash.

'What is *that*?' she said, both afraid and impressed.

'A Persian lynx. She's been trained to be tame with people, but she can kill with a single bite to the throat.'

The creature had vulpine, rust-coloured fur and cool, amber eyes, all claws and whiskers.

'That is why I thought you might like her,' he said.

Darius handed her the leash and, in shock, she took it into her hand. The lynx bared her fanged teeth at Claudia in a strange, grimacing smile before curling up obediently at her feet.

'You think I am a savage beast?' she said lightly.

'There are people who say you have killed your way to the throne,' he said. 'You wouldn't be the first. Many men have done the same.'

Her heart clutched and seized.

'You don't seem like the kind of man who pays attention to idle rumours,' she said, performing nonchalance.

'I'm not,' he agreed. 'But perhaps I am a fan of savage beasts. They are interesting to me.'

Claudia handed the leash to Damocles, who inched away as the lynx hissed at him.

The room fell quiet, as Claudia searched around for a way to begin an open dialogue.

'So, here we are,' she said.

'So, here we are,' Darius echoed.

There was a weariness to his expression, a guardedness.

'Let us begin again,' said Claudia.

He nodded, a grudging gesture of respect.

'I am willing to hear it,' he said.

'My situation has changed, since you last wrote to my father. I am no longer the girl you were promised, but a woman of agency.'

'I see that.'

'All is not entirely well between our two kingdoms, nor has it ever been, but your empire and mine have agreed a tentative peace. I intend to hold on to it at any cost. I hope we can work together, but you must work with me, Prince Darius,' said Claudia.

'My father is ailing too,' he said. 'Soon, I will be the King of kings. My father wishes for me to fulfil my commitment to you and unite our countries. I shall stay in Rome until the new moon, and court your favour, as promised.'

Claudia was beginning to suspect that the prince didn't want this marriage any more than she did. He'd been sent from his homeland into an enemy city, to win the hand of a Roman princess-turned-empress. It was a trepidatious quest. No wonder he was so difficult to read.

She was not at all sure about his feelings, or his intentions, so his next words came as quite a surprise:

'I will ask for your hand in marriage, to secure your empire and mine, but I will not force you to be my bride, just because our fathers made a promise long ago,' he said.

Darius was . . . giving her the choice?

'I believe in free will. That is what makes us human, what gives us wisdom, what excites our blood, our brains, our souls.'

He put one hand on his chest, signifying some spiritual belief.

'Love is not something that can be stolen, only given freely.'

'I agree,' said Claudia. 'Very much so.'

Perhaps the prince was more complex, less shallow, than he had initially appeared.

'But there must be no lies, no secrets between us,' he said.

'I agree,' said Claudia again, though she was keeping so many secrets they weighed on her like chains. 'Let us get to know each other first. Let us meet as equals, as allies, even as friends, before we make decisions on such important matters.'

'But it cannot be too long,' he said.

'You are in a rush?'

'I need to be married as soon as possible, before next summer, at the latest,' he said.

'Why the hurry?'

For the first time, the prince looked uncomfortable, staring off into the distance, his dark brows furrowed.

'My father demands it, as a criterion of becoming his heir. He believes that a king needs a queen if he is to command all of the people. Men, women and children. A man needs to know the value of family, if he is to rule them all. That is what he says.'

'He is not wrong. A loving family is even more valuable than a crown,' Claudia agreed.

'Hmm,' said the prince.

A crowd appeared, filtering through the columns and signalling that it was time to move on.

'Shall we?' said Claudia, standing up.

Darius mirrored her, rising to his feet.

'As you wish, Empress.'

'We'll begin with a tour of the palace, starting with the gardens. I hope you'll find it . . . more than adequate. A girl can dream, eh?'

She smiled at him, and he smiled back – genuinely.

Then Claudia looked to Gia, who was watching them intently, and her smile quickly faded.

What a strange situation.

Claudia looked uncertainly at the lynx.

'I'll take care of her, Empress,' said Nadira. 'I love cats! Aw, you're just a fluffy little baby, aren't you?'

The lynx didn't seem to object, cocking her head to be petted by Claudia's young handmaid.

The prince murmured with his advisor.

'I shall meet you there shortly,' said Darius. 'There is something I must arrange first.'

'Certainly,' said Claudia, intrigued. 'Whenever you're ready.'

He and his train of courtiers filed out as Gia moved to stand next to her, her hand resting protectively on her sword.

'Well, this is nice,' she said, as they walked out to the gardens. 'Me, you and him, on a nice little romantic excursion.'

'Just remember that my heart belongs to you and all of this is a mere show in the name of politics.'

Gia made an uncertain noise, her face wrinkled in doubt.

'Okay, but if he crosses the line, I can't promise to behave.'

10. ME, YOU & HIM

When Darius returned, he was accompanied by his tall-hatted advisor, Mehdi, who looked cheerful. The prince carried a curved sword on his hip, its blade glinting in the midday sun.

'We have a full itinerary of events planned in your honour,' said Claudia. 'We are most eager to entertain you, my prince, and show you all the leisure and pleasure Rome has to offer.'

'Trust me, I am ready to experience them,' said Prince Darius.

Claudia engaged him with the little Persian she had learned to impress him long ago.

'Your pronunciation is good,' said Darius.

'I'm afraid I'm not fluent. I do speak other languages though.'

'Such as?'

'Greek, a little Celtic, Aramaic . . .'

They made idle talk about their lives, sharing the unique experience of growing up in palaces with rulers for fathers. Claudia noted that he seemed much friendlier towards her than before.

'Any time I did something he didn't like, my father had me dragged to court and reprimanded in front of everyone,' said Darius. 'When I was young, it was a kind of humiliation ritual, but when I became a teenager, I took a certain pride in it. I was rather notorious.'

'My father never noticed if I did something wrong, because my brother was always busy doing something much more offensive,' said Claudia. 'At some point, I gave up and committed to being the good one.'

'And look where that has got you,' said Darius. 'He is in the ground and you are ruler of the world.'

'It *did* rather work out, didn't it?'

She asked of his siblings, and he asked where she had travelled. She asked of his animals, and he asked about Pompeii. She kept it bright; nothing too personal or revealing, just enough to make her sound worldly and amiable, as advised.

'Let us stop here a moment,' he said, when they reached the giant bronze statue of Hercules.

'What is it?' asked Claudia, smiling anxiously.

She hoped he wouldn't ask to kiss her.

'I wish to apologize for my rudeness earlier,' he said.

'Oh,' she said, surprised.

'I did not intend to be rude, but Mehdi has informed me that I was indeed rude.'

Mehdi nodded curtly.

'I'm not a good traveller. Long journeys, they fray my soul. They make my spirit weary. I am a man of creature comforts and homely bodies. I hope you can forgive me, Empress?'

'All is well,' said Claudia, pleased and relieved. 'I myself have been known to be a little disgruntled when overly tired.'

'Maybe you will accept these, as a peace offering.'

He clapped his hands and Mehdi retrieved a bouquet from a bush. It was a large arrangement of exotic flowers: desert roses, oleander, black irises, pink cyclamen and white jasmine.

'They're divine,' said Claudia. 'I will display them with pride and tend to them for as long as they will survive.'

The prince's advisor passed the flowers to Gia, as if she was a servant. She accepted, though she didn't look happy about it.

'My guard having her hands free is a key requirement of the job,' objected Claudia, as the arrangement obscured Gia's face from view.

'One hand on the sword, one hand on the flowers,' said Gia, passing the flowers off to Aurelia. 'I'm sure I could still do some damage.'

'Even with roses in your eyes?'

'I will pray to Fortuna for inner sight.'

'And there is this.'

Darius gestured, and again Medhi presented Claudia with a gift – a stunning pearl and jet necklace.

'It's . . . stunning,' she breathed.

'Let me,' said Gia, her fingers gently grazing the back of Claudia's neck as she put it on. Claudia could feel her warm breath, her whole body calling out for Gia's firm touch.

'Sorry, it's fiddly. I can't fix the clasp.'

Claudia was sure Gia was delaying, to tease her. Her desire was so strong she felt sure the prince would pick up on its rumblings, like a tremor beneath their feet.

'There, got it.'

Gia fixed Claudia's hair, smoothing down the back of her robes as Claudia's skin thrummed deliciously.

'What do you think?' said Claudia, turning her back to Darius.

'It's perfect, Empress,' said Gia, as professionally as she could manage. 'The prince has fine taste.'

*

Darius perked up when they visited the Temples of Venus and Vesta where they made offerings, complimenting the beautiful fashions of the goddesses. By the time they paid their respects at the Mausoleums of Augustus and Caesar, he was practically bubbly in conversation.

'Your Roman gods are interesting to me,' he said. 'The stories make clear their flaws. They are like mortals, in that way, consumed by their own fears and desires.'

'It is relatable, indeed,' Claudia agreed.

'I also find myself fascinated by the legends of your most infamous emperors. Such colourful characters! Is it true, about the horse? Did Caligula really make it his consul?'

'Not quite. I heard that he said it in jest, as a way to display his displeasure with the Senate. He was saying "a horse could do a better job than these politicians" not "I will literally employ this horse", but given that his reputation for wild behaviour preceded him, it wasn't difficult for people to believe the more lurid version of the story.'

Darius stroked the pendant he wore around his neck. Claudia hadn't noticed it until now. It was small, but it depicted what looked like a lotus flower, its petals jewelled in quartz.

'This is pretty,' she said, pointing at it.

'Pretty?' he echoed.

Claudia sensed that he was offended by her choice of word. Had she somehow emasculated him?

'It is more than that,' he said. 'It is a symbol of my goddess.'

Claudia stopped walking, as Gia almost crashed into her.

'Your goddess?'

'Yes. You seem surprised?'

'I thought you would pray to Mithras.'

'I do,' he said, 'but I also pray to Anahita. There is much you don't know about me, Empress.'

Claudia made a note to find out about Anahita later. Maybe she could even ask Minerva about it.

While Claudia and Darius enjoyed the palace's galleries, parading arm in arm along the colonnades of sculptures and paintings, Gia walked behind them silently, listening to their chatter about salting carpets and star-tiles, bronzes and bas reliefs, occasionally straying into more intimate conversation.

'You are not what I thought you'd be,' said Darius.

'What did you think I would be? A gorgon?' said Claudia.

He laughed – a natural, joyful sound.

'What I mean is, I am impressed with how you conduct yourself compared to Roman men, and the way you treat your servants.'

He gestured to Gia, who frowned minutely. Claudia flashed Gia an apologetic look.

'If my people were saying such offensive things about me, I would be hiding away in a dark room right now.'

Claudia pulled up, her heart clamouring. 'Offensive . . . things?'

'I would be ashamed to show my face,' he continued, and each word was a small dagger in her chest. 'I would want to run away, to go and live in the forest or the desert as a wild man with no name, but you are still standing here, in front of the very people who disparage you on the walls of your own city.'

'The graffiti . . . Ah. You have seen that?'

'Oh, yes. It has been written many times.'

Claudia physically winced at his brutal delivery.

'Despite this, you maintain composure. Your resolve impresses me,' he said. 'Even in humiliation and mockery, you are graceful.'

Claudia wasn't sure this was quite the compliment he seemed to think it was but she was also secretly pleased, for some reason.

'I'm glad to have found *something* that impresses you,' she said.

'I would not have held myself together so well, in your position,' he added, apparently unable to stop talking about it. 'How do you deal with such defaming rumours?'

'It isn't true, of course,' she said quickly. 'They are threatened by what I represent. They wish to paint me as a man-hater, so they object to my close friendships with my, uh ... female staff. They make more of it than it is. Men do not understand such things.'

'There have been times when I too was misunderstood. My actions were interpreted in a way that brought shame to my family. It is a deep regret of mine. The people of Persepolis have their opinions on me too, and it brings my father great concern.'

Claudia was curious about the opinions in question but she wasn't sure he would respond well to her prying. Recalling what Hieronymus had told her about flirting, she decided to spread her flattery a little thicker instead.

'I'm sure they are wrong. You seem a fine man, even though I met you just a few hours ago ... and, admittedly, my bar for a fine man is quite low, on the example of my father and brother, but ...'

The compliment was rapidly derailing.

'What I have seen, I am impressed with. I spent many years imagining what you might be like, and I must say ... you are even more handsome and charming than I envisioned.'

'Did you dream of me?' he said, fluttering his dark lashes.

'Many times. I longed to escape, to come and find you.'

'I dreamed of you too,' he said. 'You were the vision of love I grew up with, the promised princess of a foreign land.'

'That is . . . so romantic.'

'You were a very exciting idea to me, and the reality is even better than I imagined.'

Claudia couldn't see Gia's face but she was sure she could hear her rolling her eyes.

As the day stretched on, Darius continued to charm her. He flattered her beauty, declaring her more enchanting than any of the statues or murals they passed. He held open the door and took her hand when they ascended the staircase. He listened to her stories about her mother and shared amusing anecdotes about his pets.

'Imagine my father's surprise when he woke up to find that my snake had wrapped itself around his neck. I'm lucky he didn't have my head. We all laughed about it in the end.'

'Including the snake?' Claudia joked.

She dared to do an impression of a serpent laughing, though she feared he might find her ridiculous. Darius burst out laughing instead, until he had tears in his eyes. Yet Claudia was certain it was not that funny by the look on Gia's face.

'Oh! You are very amusing. Beautiful *and* funny too? The gods have truly blessed me.'

As their tour continued, Darius now took an interest in Rome's fountains, in the aqueducts and baths. They finished the day with dinner in the Capitoline Piazza, overlooked by the Senatorial Palace and the Tabularium, where historical records were kept.

They ate a selection of spiced meats, stuffed vegetables, cheese spread and fish stews, and he didn't complain once.

'Tell me about your goddess,' said Claudia. 'I should like to hear more of this Anahita.'

'Not now,' he said. 'Now, I wish to learn more about you.'

'Oh. All right. What do you want to know?' she asked.

He reached across the table, placing his hand on top of hers as she tried not to flinch in panic.

'Everything,' he said.

Gia dined at another table, presented with the scraps left over from their meals. Claudia caught her eye, but she merely raised her eyebrows a little and shook her head, wiping up the oil on her plate with a piece of bread.

At last, the prince excused himself to attend nature's call and Claudia turned urgently to Gia, making another apologetic face as she sat down at her table.

'I am so sorry,' she said.

'At least I am enjoying a sightseeing tour of the city,' Gia said. 'Even if I do have to watch my lover being courted by a man.'

'Your lover?' Claudia teased.

'What else am I to call you?'

'I'm not complaining. I like it, my lover.'

Claudia gave her a covert squeeze.

'How much longer?' Gia said.

'Unfortunately, we have the evening programme still to come.'

'Perhaps you could tell him you've taken ill?'

'I don't want to give him any more reason to doubt my intentions. I didn't expect him to have noticed the graffiti. That means I have to work even harder not to give off any Empress of Lesbos vibes.'

'And how are you going to do that?'

'Flirt with him harder, I suppose.'

Gia made a grumbling noise.

They quieted when the prince returned, with Claudia hastily standing up to take his arm and Gia trailing behind.

Back at the palace, they enjoyed a performance of classical Persian music, as women dressed like nymphs performed a dance. Gia stood on guard nearby.

'Tell me, Empress, what is it that you long for the most?' asked the prince. 'Power, or love?'

'Can I not have both?' she said.

'No, only one. Or so it is said. Great success or great desire will find you, but not both. I do not make the rules.'

'Then, I shall say love.'

'I suspected as much.'

'I have seen first hand how the most powerful men in the world can also be the loneliest,' she said.

'I know much about loneliness,' he said solemnly.

'Really? I would think you were always the centre of attention.'

'I have many courtiers and few true friends. Something about being the child of a ruler makes me unapproachable. People are afraid to get too close to me . . . Perhaps you can relate, in some way?'

'I can,' said Claudia. 'I was lonely all my life. My father had an entire empire at his disposal, no real companions, and nothing made him happy. I don't want to end up the same way.'

'Do you not have friends?' he asked.

Her eyes flicked to Gia.

The prince followed her gaze.

'I do, but none who were raised in a palace . . . until now.'

'What is it that makes you happy?' he asked.

'Many things. I have lived through such horrors that I am happy just to be here in this moment,' she said, carefully. 'I am happy that

I still have a chance to make a mark on the world, for my life to have meant something profound. What about you?'

'I am happy in the knowledge that I am just a speck in time, just a name in a history, standing against the forces that turn grand palaces to sand,' said the prince.

Claudia blinked at him slowly.

'You lost me, I fear,' she said.

'It is comforting to me that no matter what mistakes I make of my life, I will one day be forgotten.'

'I disagree,' said Claudia, shaking her head. 'I should like to be remembered in some small way, or else what was the point of living at all?'

'I am part of something much bigger and greater than myself. There is peace in that.'

The small orchestra began to play a different song – a slower, more soulful melody.

'I believe in the renewal of energy and life's forces,' Darius said. 'Time, moving in circles. We live, and we live again. Perhaps we have met before, in another life, and now we come back together.'

Darius nodded to Mehdi, then stood up and held out his hand.

Claudia looked at it, uncertainly.

'Let me show you how we dance in Persepolis,' he said.

'I . . .'

'It is an important part of our culture,' he insisted. 'Even our warriors dance to celebrate victory on the battlefield.'

She glanced at Gia, who gestured behind his back at the curved sword on his hip, signalling that she ought to be careful.

And she was right. It could be a ruse, to get close enough to kill her. It wouldn't serve her to be too trusting.

'Only if you remove that first,' said Claudia, indicating his weapon. 'I wouldn't like to injure myself.'

The prince smiled and obliged, before escorting her out into the centre of the throne room.

'This partner dance is performed at weddings,' he said. 'It is about harmony and union and the synchronicity of all things, coming together and parting again, like the waves beating the sand.'

The prince clapped his hands, stamping his foot at the same time, spinning quickly before circling back to sweep her up.

'Maybe one day, we will dance it at our own wedding.'

'Ha! Maybe,' she said, in a high pitch.

Darius attempted to teach her the steps, and though she quickly memorized them, putting them into practice wasn't as simple.

Gia watched as they whirled about the polished marble floor. Distracted by the look on her face, Claudia stood on the prince's toes.

'Oof,' he said. 'Wrong way.'

'I must apologize once more, Prince Darius. I have no rhythm, I'm afraid,' said Claudia, tripping over her own robes again. 'I am proficient in some other arts, but not this.'

'You are not so terrible,' he said.

'That's kind of you. Generous.'

'Here, let me show you.'

He placed her hand on his shoulder and lightly gripped her waist, leading them into a curving movement. His touch did not alight her mind and soul, as Gia's did, but it was not unpleasant. He didn't repulse her, at least. His hands were soft and firm and cool, with golden rings on the fingers and leather cuffs at his wrists. He was wearing some kind of musky perfume, which had a pleasant scent.

'What other arts are you proficient in?' he asked.

'Singing, weaving, poetry, painting . . .'

As they moved in unison, she caught his eyes lingering on the curves of her body, not lustfully but thoughtfully, contemplatively.

She felt the situation spinning, spiralling.

'There is no higher art than the body's response to music,' he said. 'It is an expression of the innermost soul.'

'That doesn't bode well for me, if I am bad at it.'

'Not so. You can learn. You have that flame inside you.'

'I don't know about that.'

'It is true . . . I can feel it.'

The tension between them thickened.

'Can *you*?' he said.

The music seemed to swoop and sway, like a murmuration of birds, making Claudia unsteady on her feet.

'Can I . . . what?' she said, playing stupid.

'Feel that burning, between us?'

They were no longer talking about dancing, but something else. Something more. It was an analogy. He was asking her if she felt an attraction towards him, in the sensual sense, and Claudia wasn't sure of the answer. Certainly, she could feel the warmth of his body. Certainly, he was pleasant to look at, with a tantalizing fragrance.

Did she desire him? He was handsome, as was Celadus. But – the idea of Gia removing her clothes filled her with a kind of ferality she was moderately ashamed of, while the idea of the prince removing his clothes gave her a feeling of mixed curiosity and terror.

Her mind turned. Part of her was vain and wanted the prince to admire her. Part of her was ashamed to even consider it. Part of her knew she had no choice but to say yes. Part of her didn't know what was happening, because her life felt entirely out of control.

'Yes,' she said. 'I feel it.'

'Then we are good.'

The prince swirled her and dipped her, their bodies pressing together in the intimacy of the dance. Darius pulled her closer, his hands at her hips as they moved in circles, locked eye to eye.

How much easier it would be, in so many ways, to marry the prince. There were certain securities, certain assurances he could provide her that Gia could not. There was something between them, a thread of connection that she could probably take and stitch something with, but it was nothing compared to the way she craved Gia, as if she were something greater than desire: not a want, but a need.

The song ended. They bowed to each other, standing apart.

Gia was looking away, arms folded.

'You asked me earlier, about my goddess,' said Darius.

'I did.'

He tapped his necklace.

'The lotus symbolizes Anahita, a warrior goddess and divinity of the waters. She rides in a chariot drawn by four flying horses, named wind, rain, clouds and sleet.'

'Fascinating. How did you come to venerate her?'

'I picked up her worship from my mother and sisters, but many men pray to Anahita. Especially soldiers. She is no less fearsome a divinity, for being a woman.'

'What is life like, for the women of Persia?' asked Claudia.

'Like Roman women, they look to the heavens for the power they are denied on Earth, but times are changing, just as they are here. We are living on the cusp of modernity, of new ways of thinking and being.' He turned to Gia, admiring her with interest. 'You must trust that your woman guard is stronger than the average man . . .

or else, you must believe that she would fight harder for you than any of your male soldiers would.'

'I do,' said Claudia, but she didn't add anything more.

A clearing-throat noise drew her attention.

Damocles stood in the arches.

'Your presence is required, Empress,' he said.

Darius stepped back.

'It seems our time is over,' he said.

'For today,' she said. 'I shall look forward to getting to know you better, in the coming weeks.'

Claudia gave a low, formal bow.

'And I, you,' he said. 'Thank you for your company today.'

When she held out her hand, he kissed it, his gaze lingering, rather more enthusiastically than their first meeting.

Claudia was drawn into an hour-long summit on the campaign in Germania. This was followed by a meeting with the Senate, in which they voiced their many current concerns, along with a pantheon of future ones. Senators Tacitus and Thelonius were most vocal.

By the time Claudia and Gia had chance to speak alone, it was almost midnight, the scattered stars clearly visible overhead.

'I have never been gladder for a day to come to its conclusion,' said Claudia, leaning against the closed door of her room.

'Nor me,' said Gia, darkly.

Gia stood at the window, with her back to her. Claudia sensed that she was not in a good mood, and she couldn't blame her for it.

'I am so sorry you had to witness that,' she said.

'We cannot trust him,' said Gia, still not turning to face her.

'You think?'

'My gut is telling me he's hiding something.'

'Are you sure you're not just opposed to him on principle?'

'Obviously, but that's not the reason.'

Claudia walked up behind her, looping her arms around her waist, but Gia's body language was not as receptive as usual.

There was a gulf between them.

Gia moved to sit on the bed and Claudia followed.

'Please, don't take it seriously,' she said. 'I'm just used to entertaining men from the years I served in my father's court.'

'You shouldn't have to do that,' said Gia.

'I know, yet it is second nature to me and I need to play nice with Darius for now,' said Claudia. 'You heard what Hieronymus and Damocles said. Flatter him, make him believe I desire him. Do you think I convinced him?'

'You almost convinced me,' said Gia.

'That was nothing,' she laughed, putting her hand around Gia's neck and using her nails to gently tickle her. 'I was just warming up.'

'Then I should steady myself for more?'

Claudia didn't have an answer prepared for this question. She didn't know how far she would have to go yet. That was the truth of it.

'Maybe,' she said. 'It is expected of me.'

'I would believe you, if I were him,' Gia said. 'I'd think you might actually marry me.'

'That was the idea, wasn't it?' said Claudia. 'That's why he's here in Rome, after all. We have been engaged, from the beginning, before you and I even met. If I cannot prevent it, or if it would be unwise to prevent it, then I must be sure he believes it.'

'I didn't think you would be so persuasive. That you would be so good at acting. Are you pretending with me? How would I know, if you were fooling me in the same way?'

The words wounded her, but then Gia was hurt.

'It's entirely different. He is a stranger I am contractually engaged to against my will, and you are the person I love with the freedom of my soul,' said Claudia.

Neither of them said anything, breathing softly in the quiet room as they listened to someone moving towards the staircase.

'You love me?' said Gia.

'I told you so before, didn't I?' said Claudia, looking away. 'When we were on the ship, after escaping Pompeii. I said, "I didn't love you then". That rather implies that I do, in fact, love you now, does it not?'

'It's not really the same thing, if you say it in the middle of confessing to killing someone,' said Gia.

Claudia flushed.

'I suppose not,' she said. 'You didn't believe me?'

'It *is* unbelievable, from an outside perspective, that an empress would want to be with me instead of an actual real-life prince,' said Gia. 'And here we are, fielding off his advances against the inevitability of your engagement. Maybe *I* am the one fooling myself here.'

Claudia would not have that.

'I can only comment from an *inside* perspective,' she said.

She delicately climbed into Gia's lap, spreading her legs on either side of Gia's hips and pushing her backwards onto the bed. She wound their fingers together, pushing Gia's arms back up over her head.

'But I am not in any doubt about whether I love you or not.'

'No?'

'The trouble is, my feelings aren't dependent on being reciprocated,' Claudia said. 'My feelings for you simply exist, regardless of how you feel about me. They will not go away easily, if ever at all. But let it be said that I *did* say it, and that I do love you, for the record.'

'For the record?' said Gia, smiling.

'Yes, the record.'

'Are you sure you want that on the record? I don't think the prince would like that.'

'Fuck the prince. Forget everyone else. Let it be written in history,' said Claudia, 'for all to see.'

Gia's expression softened, her eyes melting.

She sat up, her hands looping around Claudia's waist, pulling her closer and kissing her neck.

'Then let it also be written that I love you, too,' she said.

'You do?'

'Unquestionably.'

Claudia's heart skipped over a beat in excitement, as her entire body shivered deliciously.

'Say it again,' she said, in wonderment.

'Unquestionably.'

'Not that part, the first bit.'

'I love you,' said Gia, kissing her collarbone.

'And again,' Claudia demanded.

'I love you,' said Gia, kissing her lips.

'You know, I didn't quite catch that,' said Claudia when they broke apart, holding one hand to her ear.

'If I say it any louder, all of Rome shall know,' said Gia.

They quieted, gazing at each other in speechless silence.

'You love me,' Claudia repeated, as if willing it into existence.

'I didn't think that would be such a surprise, after everything we've been through,' said Gia, smiling lopsidedly.

'I had to be sure, before I let myself fall,' said Claudia. 'Love is frightening. This . . . us . . . it terrifies me.'

'You could not be more terrified than me,' said Gia.

'Then we shall be terrified together. Aren't we lucky? I'm so happy, I could cry,' said Claudia. 'I don't know what to do with myself. I might sing . . . or jump off the balcony . . .'

'Please don't.'

'Or ride a horse naked through the streets . . . or . . . or . . .'

She looked around the room, her eyes wild and searching, until her gaze settled on Gia once more.

'Or this.'

Claudia kissed her with all of her might – an angry, fearsome, passionate kiss full of unspoken things.

She wanted to consume her, for them to become one, their bodies winding and fusing together like threads.

'Good idea,' said Gia. 'I like that one.'

Claudia did it again.

'I'm delirious. I may be hallucinating, or feverish,' said Claudia.

'Oh no. Struck by Cupid, in her prime,' said Gia, rolling them over so that they were lying on their sides.

Claudia stroked her face in awe.

'You are the first person who has ever loved me,' she said.

'Well, same,' said Gia. 'In that way, I mean.'

'I doubt it. You must have all manner of secret admirers who would kill to have your sword to their throat.'

'Is that a request?'

'Maybe,' said Claudia, raising one finger to Gia's lips.

'Look at you,' said Gia, longingly. 'Every man who ever laid eyes on you would fall in love with you.'

'And I don't want any of them.'

'Good, because you're mine.'

'And you are mine,' Claudia said, tracing Gia's brows, her hairline, her nose and chin with one hand. 'I belong to you as much as you belong to me. You are mine, and I am yours.'

She was giddy. Gia loved her. She was not unlovable. She was loved by the person she loved in return. It truly was a miracle.

'What about the rumours, and the prince?' asked Gia.

Claudia interrupted her by kissing her throat, lips trailing down to her chest.

'What about—'

'Shhh,' said Claudia.

The adrenaline that already energized her blood now moved through her in powerful, shuddering waves.

'I am the empress. I take orders from no one . . .'

Claudia slid off the bed, sinking down to kneel at Gia's feet and parting her legs, seized by that delicious ferality again.

Shameful or not, it was hers to own, to accept, to become.

'But you are not my servant,' she said. 'In fact, I am yours.'

Minerva was born from her father's mind, quite literally.

King Jupiter had been warned that his own child would one day overthrow him, just as he had overthrown his own father, Saturn. When Jupiter heard that the Titan he raped had become pregnant with his child, Jupiter vowed to kill the baby to conceal his infidelity.

She turned into a fly to escape him but Jupiter ate her.

Unfortunately, this had the adverse effect of implanting baby Minerva inside his skull, where she pounded incessantly to get out, giving her father a colossal headache until he freed her.

Born from Jupiter's forehead, she'd come into the world fully formed and dressed in battle armour, ready to fight for the life her father had tried to take away.

As the aeons went by, she'd become one of his favourites, even joining him and Juno in the Capitoline Triad – chosen over all his other children.

This was the kind of dysfunctional family Minerva came from.

She'd never dared to spy on her father's mind before, afraid that he'd be able to sense her, but she'd searched the length and breadth of the universe and she couldn't locate him. Jupiter was a master of disguise, known to take many forms in his pursuit of women and power. This was her only hope.

She needed to know what he was up to, if she was to protect Empress Claudia, and that meant venturing within.

The resistance against Jupiter had gained in numbers and strength in her absence, as more and more goddesses were recruited to their army. Yet others had failed to return to attend further meetings, like Salacia, who'd come to Claudia's aid at sea. Minerva worried about what might have happened to her, but she worried more about whatever her father was plotting.

Leaving Fortuna, Diana and Venus to their goddess-recruitment drive, Minerva retreated to the privacy of her library palace to meditate.

She thought of Jupiter, her mind following the celestial paths of matter that connected all beings, mortal and immortal alike.

Eventually, she felt herself drawn to him.

Her strange birth meant that she'd retained a pathway into Jupiter's consciousness, a kind of umbilical cord or omphalos, connecting them together eternally. Just as her mother, Metis, had been swallowed, Minerva entered his mind as a tiny, insignificant fly.

She buzzed around, unnoticed by the gigantic ego of a god, swallowed up by the dark of the ancient Aether.

Minerva hung, suspended like a star, inside the infinite galaxy within Jupiter's mind. Disconnected fragments of her father's psyche passed by like galaxies: Fortuna, nursing him as a boy; the sacrifice of a sacred white bull; augurs looking at bird entrails; fire priests burning stalks of wheat . . .

Minerva spiralled and spun, thrown left and right, trying to correct herself as she thought, Show me what you're planning, old man.

Eventually, her vision formed a theatre as curved rows of seating built up around her, putting her in the audience at the Theatre of Apollo.

Ruled by Diana's twin, it doubled as the palace of the god of theatre, music and dance. Apollo often sat in his boxy temple at the top of the structure, watching on as nymphs and fauns waited on him. Today, however, it was empty, though his crows flocked overhead.

The building was a god-sized version of the Theatre of Pompey, its oversized scenery forming an animated backdrop. Here, her father's memory unfolded like a scene in a play.

Pillars morphed into trees as Jupiter ambled onstage in human form, with greying curls and full beard, surrounded by a posse of lesser deities. She was watching his own memory played back in a theatre of the mind, but the recreation was grandiose, surrealist, imperfect in its reflection. In his recollection of the event, Jupiter was even more fearsome and mighty.

'If Mars thinks now is the time to launch his own revolution to overthrow me, he is even stupider than he looks.'

Here was her father, speaking ill of another one of his many children. Though Mars was technically her sibling, they shared little familiarity or comradery.

'He has an army of soldiers at his disposal,' he raged. 'He thinks he will be the next ruler of Elysium. I will not stand for it!'

Jupiter's brother, Pluto, the pale king of the underworld, walked alongside him, dressed in blueish-green robes with a belt made of keys, his long straggly dark curls falling down his back.

'He believes himself superior: stronger, younger and smarter than me,' said Jupiter. 'But Mars won't be as easy to vanquish as my last victories – Vulcan and my dear brother, Neptune.'

Vulcan and Neptune had stood against him. Their mention sent a signal to the others: all those who stood against him would eventually become his prisoners or his slaves. Now, Vulcan and Neptune were imprisoned in the sky as constellations. Others were chained in Tartarus, along with the beasts of the Titans.

'I will not allow Mars to convert deities to his side,' Jupiter raged, hurling his fists into the scenery around him.

Pluto looked weary. He, Jupiter and Neptune were triplets, each receiving a third of the world to reign over, but Neptune had already been punished for his treachery. It was just the two of them now.

With great disappointment, Minerva also recognized her opposite, Mercury, with his winged sandals and hat, walking along with stout, red-nosed Bacchus and muscular, curly-haired Hercules.

They had been called to serve the king of the gods, and they hadn't been brave enough, or principled enough, to refuse. Her father had as many supporters as he had enemies. A war could go either way.

'My arrogant, ungrateful daughter is intent on waging war against me too,' said Jupiter, as the temple collapsed around him. 'She fled our battle like a coward, before I could win . . . before I could finish her off.'

Pluto and Mercury side-eyed each other, remembering that Jupiter had distinctly failed to win that particular match.

'She thinks she can turn goddesses against gods, women against men.'

The other gods grumbled their agreement.

'She thinks Rome should be ruled by a mere girl. She thinks millennia of tradition and order should be cast aside at her whim.'

'What if we call Minerva and the goddesses to a peace summit, my god?' suggested Mercury. 'You can agree terms without more conflict.'

'There can be no peace. Not now. Not after all they have done to meddle with destiny.'

Jupiter turned on his messenger, looming over him.

'Tell me, Mercury, why haven't you located her yet? You're the traveller of realms, are you not? You're not protecting them, are you?'

'I . . . I can only rely on word of mouth, and there have been no sightings of her yet,' said Mercury timidly. 'Venus and Diana have been summoned to appear before you, but they have so far ignored the request. It isn't difficult to imagine why, when Vulcan and Neptune were sacrificed for their opposition.'

Minerva knew her consort well, better than most men. Mercury was the inhabitant of two worlds and, as the messenger god, he generally took a neutral position on conflicts in the pantheon. He did not truly support Jupiter's aims, she was sure, but he was attempting to keep peace and contain the threat.

'And Fortuna?' said Jupiter.

'She cannot be found.'

'Useless! What good are you?'

'By severing her vision, you have also made her invisible in the sight of gods,' explained Mercury.

'You dare to question my judgement?'

'I-I did not say that,' retracted Mercury. 'I'm merely explaining why she is so difficult to locate.'

'In better news, Salacia has been dealt with,' said Pluto, in monotone. 'She and her beast have been imprisoned, along with Victoria, as you asked.'

Jupiter was hunting them down one by one.

'They should not have their own stars, nor their own temples. They will toil eternally in the underworld, so they must live with the weight of their mistakes. Others will soon follow,' said Jupiter. 'Their intervention broke divine law. It cannot be allowed. Only I, as king, should have that power.'

'What now, my god?' asked Mercury.

'We need a new emperor,' said Jupiter, walking on again as the others followed behind. 'One who can reclaim the throne from the girl.'

'Who do you suggest, your divinity?'

'I have many mortals to run my errands for me. One in particular is my most loyal servant. When the time is right, he will rise to power.'

A weighty hush descended.

Of whom did her father speak? Minerva didn't know, and she knew many things. She vowed to find out, as soon as possible.

'Until then, all of you must present your mortals to me, for my use. All will become messengers of Jupiter. I will need every man and every god at my side, if we are to regain total control of the pantheon and restore the course of history.'

Jupiter turned to address the gathered crowd.

'Your dedication will not be forgotten. You are my soldiers in this final battle. Mortal rot is decaying the pantheon, but we shall stand strong and united in the face of this rebellion of women. And as for Minerva . . .'

Jupiter looked up, locking eyes with her in the audience. He'd sensed her presence in his mind.

He knew she was there, spying on his memory.

'She will be punished to the highest degree.'

11. THE THREE COINS

The protestors had given up their daily assembly in the Forum after several days of rain, though the lost legion still had not been located. Not even Minerva's mirror could provide any clues as to their whereabouts. Marcellus didn't return to make his report as promised, no matter how many times he was summoned to do so, though General Aquinas assured her the matter was firmly in hand. The missing men's relatives still showed up at the palace each day, hoping for an update, but Claudia had none to give them. If there was news, it wasn't shared with her: a sign that her strength was already waning. She was empress, and she was failing.

Hieronymus again told her not to worry about it – that Marcellus and General Aquinas were handling the matter. They pushed her to make progress with the prince instead.

Behind the scenes, negotiations continued on the topic of their marriage, though she had not yet said yes. Once or twice, she heard them bartering – his advisors and hers – as if bringing together two warring armies. In a way, they were.

Day after day, gifts from the prince arrived on the hour, each one larger and grander than the last.

Claudia and Gia had enjoyed many of them together, including a set of aromatic oils and a hamper of exotic fruit, while others were treasured by Claudia alone: an armlet laid with precious stones, perfumes and cosmetics with delectable scents, and a series of small wooden animals, including a winged lion with a beak and goat horns.

Claudia didn't think he'd be able to top the lynx named Princess, which now accompanied her everywhere, or the imperial marble bust he'd had sculpted in her likeness, which Gia had taken to petting when no one was looking, but Claudia was yet again proved wrong when she unveiled his latest offering: an oil-painted mural of her as Venus.

'It is my favourite work of art,' said Gia.

'It feels like a bad omen,' said Claudia, as they admired it together, 'if the Trojan War is anything to go by.'

'I'm sure the goddess will understand,' said Gia. 'It's not as if you had it commissioned yourself.'

'At least no one has tossed a golden apple yet.'

When a troop of soldiers passed by, they both pretended to admire the painting, beholding the empress emerging from a clamshell.

'Do you think his intentions are still merely diplomatic?' asked Gia, when they'd passed.

'What do you mean?' asked Claudia.

Gia raised one brow, giving her a quizzical look. 'I doubt he'd have gifted Decimus with a semi-nude portrait,' she said.

'He was not arranged in marriage to my brother.'

'It's just quite . . . sensual, isn't it? Desiring, even. What if he is truly falling for you? What then?'

They stared at the artwork in silence again. Claudia hadn't yet considered the possibility too deeply. She had just assumed they were both playing the same game. Feelings had little to do with political manoeuvres.

'I am managing the situation,' said Claudia.

'Are you sure? If you don't do something to discourage him, I'm afraid he might propose . . . and this time, he shall mean it.'

'I will take my time to observe, and come up with a plan.'

If the prince had real feelings for her, that could certainly complicate matters.

On the other hand, he might be more pliable to her requirements. He might even be open to some kind of arrangement, one that would leave room for Gia.

For now, she decided to play along, whether the prince was playing the same game or not.

The following day, Darius requested a date.

They ate seafood near the river and rode a horse-drawn chariot around the city. They drove up to the top of Janiculum Hill, watching as the sun sank below the panoramic horizon.

Gia sat in the back, as the prince talked of their future.

'If we were to marry, you would enjoy all of the same freedoms you do now,' said Prince Darius. 'I would not seek to control you or limit your aspirations.'

'I would not let you,' said Claudia.

'Indeed,' laughed Darius. 'That is why I like you.'

He was wearing a vest that showed off his muscular arms and his dark eyes were ringed with kohl.

'What *would* you expect, from a union between us?' she asked.

'Trust, understanding . . . and, eventually . . . an heir.'

Claudia turned to him, curiously.

'You want children?'

'At least one,' he said. 'Don't all men? Again, it is a condition of inheriting the kingdom, as my father expects.'

She fell quiet.

'And you?' he asked.

Claudia had always pictured herself becoming a mother, but it was a reflex – almost as a condition of being a woman. She would have children because that is what women did, and she would love them because that is what mothers did. Part of her wanted to be a better parent than her father, but another part of her feared that she would fall short, somehow.

She and Gia could not have a child together by nature, but if she procreated with the prince, they could be a strange sort of family. She imagined what could be if Darius knew the truth about her and Gia, and if he accepted it gladly. Yet she did not feel comfortable enough to propose the arrangement to him.

'I would have to think about it some more,' she said. 'I am in two minds about it.'

'You do not feel maternal?'

'I am eighteen. I wouldn't like to have a child any time soon, but perhaps . . . one day, in the future, I would.'

'One day is good enough for me,' he said. 'For now.'

'If I may say, I don't get the impression that you are too keen on inheriting the kingdom,' said Claudia, probing. 'You speak of fulfilling your father's will only as an act of duty.'

The prince looked ruffled by the question.

'I don't crave power, this is true,' said Darius, 'but I know that I am a better man for the job than my brothers. I am fool enough to care about the future of the world, and I feel a responsibility to do the best I can with the privilege I was given.'

'We have that in common,' Claudia said.

Another date followed, and another. They ate a picnic in the gardens of a beautiful villa, strolled through an orchard and rode a boat along the Tiber. They visited parks and lakes and fountains, making wishes as they tossed coins into the sparkling waters.

'We would get married in Rome and holiday in Persia,' he said, as they travelled down the Appian Way in a litter. 'It would be a month-long procession, visiting all of the settlements.'

'I could not leave Rome for so long,' she said.

She looked to Gia, who was forced to walk alongside as part of the imperial procession.

'Perhaps two weeks then,' he said. 'Emperors are allowed to travel and take vacations.'

'Emperors, maybe, but I'm sure they would have much to say about an empress taking time away to sunbathe. It is different, being a woman. The people are not as forgiving.'

'They would not dare speak against you, if I had my way.'

'I do not need a man to punish my haters for me,' she said. 'I can do that myself, if I wish.'

'Then I shall merely scowl at them, like this.' He gave her his most fearsome face, which was so comical she couldn't help but laugh at him. 'Then they will know they have wronged you.'

'You look ridiculous,' she said.

'Then why are you blushing, Empress?'

The prince reached out, running his thumb along her jaw.

Caught off-guard, Claudia froze.

His dark eyes were fixed on her with great determination.

She felt him leaning in, his eyes fluttering shut . . .

'Not . . . here,' she said, pulling back stiffly. 'Not in front of my guards, in a litter on the dusty road.'

'Apologies,' he said, though he didn't look sorry at all. 'I got carried away with the mood of the moment.'

She met eyes with Gia before they continued along in silence.

'This is getting out of hand,' said Gia, when they were alone in bed. 'You have practically agreed to have his child, now you will go travelling with him? He almost kissed you today!'

The creak of the bench sounded outside and Claudia made a motion with her hand, signalling for Gia to lower her voice.

'I know,' she whispered. 'You were right. I thought I could stall him, but it is getting to be too much. If I keep rejecting him, he will become suspicious eventually. He might even call off the alliance. If I make an enemy of the prince now, when he is visitor to my city, my rule is over.'

'Then what do you suggest?' asked Gia.

'I have to hold the line between politely encouraging his affections and keeping him at bay. I will tell him that physical affection is off the table, until marriage.'

'And then what?'

'I wish to approach him with an offer, a marriage of convenience with you as my consort. But I must first determine if he is trustworthy. Will he be open to the arrangement or will he be scorned and vengeful? I cannot be sure without knowing him better.'

'Then we need to determine his true character,' said Gia. 'What was it he said when you discussed the graffiti before? Something about him being misunderstood back at home? Perhaps he has a secret of his own?'

'Exactly. In my company, he is always performing. He is presenting his best side, of course. I need to know who he is when he isn't trying to win my favour, but he won't reveal himself easily to me, much as I would not reveal myself easily to him. The shield of Minerva does not show me what is happening inside his mind.'

'You think he might confide in someone else?'

'I was thinking perhaps Cassius could befriend him?' said Claudia. 'What do you think?'

'My brother? Why?'

'The prince has only his attendants here in Rome, and he spoke to me of his loneliness. He might be forthcoming about his real feelings in company with a fellow warrior, preferably over an amphora of wine, or several. I might learn something useful.'

'Such as?'

'Such as, he displays strange proclivities in the bedroom, or abuses substances to great excess, or he has a wife and child back in Persepolis who are waiting for him to return. Something Prince Darius may be more inclined to share, man to man.'

'How are we to introduce them, without the prince knowing we're setting Cassius up to spy on him?' said Gia. 'I wouldn't want to put my brother in danger.'

'I have thought of that. Tomorrow afternoon, the prince and his staff will be with me at the Theatre of Pompey. Cassius can accompany me as my guard. I will approach him to ask for his assistance in getting the prince to open up. With Cassius taking your place, you will be free to perform reconnaissance while the prince is out of the palace. It would be an ideal moment to enter his chambers and examine his belongings, in case he has anything incriminating in his possession. If you get caught, just say it's an imperial order, for security.'

Gia did not appear convinced by this enterprising plan, but she didn't refuse her either.

'How long will I have?' she asked.

'I'll keep him entertained for as long as possible,' said Claudia. 'We won't return to the palace until you join me at the theatre.'

'And how do you plan to entertain him?'

They locked eyes.

'Just enough to keep him distracted,' said Claudia.

'Are you sure you'll be safe without me?' said Gia.

There was a softness to her face that made Claudia's chest ache. She knew Gia was afraid, not just of assassins, but of what might occur between her and the prince, if she wasn't there.

'Good day, Empress,' said Cassius.

Equipped in full armour, he waited for Claudia at the bottom of the stairs instead of Gia.

'Good day, Cassius.'

It was endearing and disarming how much he looked like her. Older and hairier, of course, with a more prominent nose, but they had the same brows, the same brown eyes – even his smile had a hint of Gia to it.

'I assume Gia has let you in on the plan.'

'What plan?' he said. 'I have heard of no plan. My only plan is to guard the empress with my life.'

Claudia smiled appreciatively.

'You're almost as witty as she is,' she said, after a moment.

'Wittier, I would say.'

Claudia glimpsed Gia watching them from the balcony, winking at her before they stepped outside. She climbed into the chariot that waited for her, as they continued on to the theatre.

'You wish to find a reason not to marry the prince,' said Cassius. 'I cannot imagine turning down such an offer, but I will do what I can to uncover his deepest, darkest secrets.'

'I have my reasons.'

It was quiet between them. Cassius did not make small talk, leaving them to sit in silence.

'It's good to catch up with you,' said Claudia. 'We haven't had much time to socialize, since we've been here.'

'And here I thought that all emperors did was laze on lecterns all day, eating grapes,' he said. 'How wrong I was.'

'Such is the privilege of being a man,' she said. 'If I did that for even a single day, I'd be ousted faster than you can say "Faster than you can draw your sword."'

'Instead, we have gods attacking ships and statues coming to life,' he said. 'What next?'

'They do say it's a gift, to live in such interesting times.'

'Hmm.'

The stone theatre loomed ahead, enclosed by a series of large columned porticos. Along the stretch of the covered arcade were rooms displaying various artworks and artefacts, but the building centred upon the circular seating arrangement that overlooked the curtained stage. At its very top, in the rows sometimes referred to as the nosebleeds due to their high altitude, was a small temple to a victorious Venus, which protruded from the exterior of the building as if it had been stuck on by the goddess herself.

Claudia had chosen the theatre as a kind of sanctuary, watched over by her divine ally. Though Caesar had been killed here, his son had restored it, ensuring its continued use.

A group of people crowded outside, awaiting her arrival, including the usual leagues of soldiers. Cassius gazed at them thoughtfully as he helped her out of the chariot.

'I swore I would never serve the empire again after I returned from duty, yet here I am, dressed in uniform and escorting the empress.'

'I would be interested to hear of your experiences,' said Claudia. 'Perhaps they could be of interest to the generals, too. They are still searching for the missing legion.'

Cassius scoffed. 'I would not serve them,' he said. 'After what I have seen, I no longer support the campaign in Britannia at all. So many lives lost, and for what? So that Rome can acquire another tiny island?'

Claudia wasn't sure how to respond. She didn't entirely disagree but the reality was not as simple.

'I understand,' she said instead. 'I value your perspective.'

Greatness was strength, and greatness was protection. There were many powers who sought to usurp Rome's position in the world; nations in which citizens enjoyed even fewer rights and endured even greater atrocities. Perhaps one day, the British would rule instead.

They passed through a lavish garden complex, paved in marble with trees and statues lined up in rows.

'Would you have me imprisoned if I said I did not think there should be an emperor at all?' asked Cassius.

'Certainly not.'

'Never was a fan, of the whole imperial thing.'

'If democracy should rule Rome, all the better for it,' she said.

'But you . . .' He gestured at her, confused. 'You wear the crown. You sit on the throne.'

'I cannot dismantle it all in my lifetime,' she said. 'Someone must turn the wheel, so we may all move forward, as we must.'

'That is what they all tell themselves, I'm sure.'

Senators assembled in the curia nearby, and, other than one cordoned-off area at the scene of the crime, there was no sign that a famous murder had ever taken place.

'I am not fool enough to think I could change your mind but I hope you will still be willing to help today, as agreed,' she said.

'I'm doing this as a favour to Gia, not for you or anyone else. I am doing it only because she asked me,' said Cassius.

'Understood,' she said. 'As Gia's brother, you are welcome to stay here in the palace, whether you serve the empire or not. I am grateful for your assistance today, but I would not force you. You are family.'

'No, Gia and *I* are family. You are a simply a beautiful stranger my sister met this summer past,' he said. 'And now she is your shield, swearing her life to protect you.'

It took Claudia a moment to acknowledge what he was saying.

'You don't approve,' said Claudia plainly.

Cassius didn't answer right away; she guessed that he was weighing up the benefits of lying versus telling the truth.

'I came home to find my mother and brother dead, my city buried, and my baby sister serving the new ruler of Rome,' he said. 'How would you feel, if you were me?'

'I see,' she mused.

As they entered the theatre proper, the sound of the crowd

surrounded them, smothering them. The noise hushed slightly at the sight of her arrival, as hundreds of eyes trailed them.

Claudia had sensed that Cassius had doubts about her, but she hadn't expected him to speak so honestly.

'I care for her too,' she said.

'Do you, though?' he said, pulling a sceptical face. 'What do you actually have in common?'

If only he knew.

She and Gia had mutually determined not to tell him the truth about their relationship, for his own protection, and theirs. Now, in this moment, she felt assured that it had been the right decision.

A considerable section of the crowd booed her entrance, their displeasure drowned out by the roaring of the all-woman Cult of Diana. Their adulation gave her strength, as always, even in the midst of this difficult conversation.

'Is us being women in a man's world not enough?' she said.

'There are plenty of noble women in Rome you could make your companion, if you're so desperate for company. I'm sure you'd have much more to talk about. What do you and Gia even discuss together? Border treaties? Gladiator matches? The eruption?'

'All of that, and more. I need not share every opinion and pastime with someone to enjoy their company.'

Praetorian guards charged in and escorted some of the hecklers out of the building, but the ripples of the disruption continued to move through the audience.

'I can see why she might be impressed by you, being rich and famous as you are, after all those years we spent looking up at your mural,' said Cassius, with a note of disgust. 'But what could an empress want with my little sister from Pompeii?'

'You do her no justice,' said Claudia. 'She has many qualities that I find admirable. She's braver than most men. She is caring and funny and speaks her mind. She is my favourite person.'

They climbed the stairs towards the imperial box, where the prince waited, watching them curiously from afar.

'I know her value,' said Cassius, 'but what value does she have to the woman who rules the world?'

'It's true, we are different, and yet, at our core, we are the same. What about that bothers you so?'

'She's in danger here. You'd have her sacrificed for your safety, like any other soldier in your legions.'

'Her safety is of great concern to me.'

'That's the job. That's literally the job, as your guardian, to lay down her life for you if required.'

Claudia bristled, annoyed that he saw their relationship in such stark shades of black and white.

'You are interfering,' she said.

'I'm her brother,' he said. 'I'm meant to protect her, especially now it's just the two of us.'

Decimus flashed horribly through her mind.

'In my experience, brothers tend to think they own their sisters like property and have the right to dictate how they conduct themselves.'

Perhaps that was too blunt. Decimus wasn't the ordinary sort of brother. She was sure Cassius was better than him. It wouldn't be hard.

'Not us. I don't tell Gia what to do,' he said. 'Unlike you.'

'I'm not forcing her to be here either. She is her own person.'

'She is in your thrall,' he said, staring at her as if seeking to understand. 'She is obsessed with you. I don't know what you have said or done to make her so loyal but it's not healthy, if you ask me.'

Saluting soldiers parted to let them into the enclosed, private area reserved for her and her party.

'I don't think Gia would be happy with you speaking for her, as if she does not have her own mind and volition,' said Claudia, in a low tone.

'I know. She wouldn't. I'm just a fool, letting my mouth run away from me, but I was given a second chance at life and I intend to do the most with it. You can have me punished for it, if you must.'

'It's all right, Cassius. I meant what I said before. The palace is your home too, if you want it to be. Maybe, in time, I can convince you that my power will protect both you and Gia alike.'

'We'll see about that.'

'For now, if you could please turn your mind to the prince. Remember, you are here to befriend him, to earn his trust and confidence. Do it for Gia's protection, if not mine.'

Cassius gave a jerky nod in answer.

'As you will,' he said.

Claudia took her seat next to Darius, in the utmost centre of the theatre. Their combined staff surrounded them, forming a wall of people that separated them from the rest of the audience, though they left just enough room for them to see the stage.

'Good afternoon, Darius,' she said.

'Empress.'

Another wave of booing rang out, as a group of late-coming senators took their seats.

'Your people are very disrespectful,' said Darius.

'They are,' she said, 'but they are still my people.'

'I have many enemies back home, yet they are nice to my face. Always smiles and open arms in front, whispers and plots behind my back. I don't know which is worse.'

Claudia made an ambiguous yet agreeable noise.

The prince's eyes flicked to Cassius, standing beside her.

'Where is your woman guard today?' he asked.

'Gia is busy with an important mission, so her brother Cassius has agreed to guard me.'

'Her brother, eh?' he said, looking Cassius up and down as he did the same in return.

'He has survived the British barbarians so I'm confident he can handle whatever trouble you might have in store for me,' she said.

'I *am* fond of trouble,' said Darius.

'Then I am sure you two will get on,' she said.

She glanced to Cassius expectantly.

'Certainly, your highness,' he said, bowing to the prince. 'I have many pertinent questions about your menagerie of animals.'

'Oh?'

'Yes, I was eating lunch yesterday when a small golden monkey appeared from nowhere to steal my bread . . . I don't suppose you know anything about that, do you?'

The prince's eyes glittered at this bold approach.

'Aha,' he said. 'I see you've met Navid.'

As they conversed, Claudia thought about Gia, worrying how her search for evidence was getting on, and what she'd think if she knew Cassius disapproved so strongly of them even being friends, let alone anything more. How seriously would Gia take his opinion?

She was so tired of all these wretched men interfering.

When she resumed paying attention to the prince's conversation, they were talking about Cassius's near-death experience.

'I am rapt by such stories,' Darius was saying. 'I have my own tales of that place between life and death. I am sure that there is another world, along with this one. Tell me, Cassius, what was it like?'

'I don't remember it well. As time has passed, the memory is surrounded by an aura,' he said. 'My recollection is hazy. But I was shot, right here in the side.'

He pulled up the tunic beneath his armour, revealing the scarred skin above his hip.

The prince's eyes lingered.

'One moment, I was staring up at the stars, blood in my eyes and my mouth. It was just as people say. I saw this bright, white light, and felt this immense sense of peace. I saw the face of the goddess Fortuna. The next thing I remember, I was lying in bed in a charming little stone house in front of a fire, being tended to by the witch doctor of the tribe. He healed me with herbal medicine, and it was as if I was born again.'

'That good?' said the prince, lifting his dark brows. 'And what were they like, the British?'

'They are coarse, sometimes dirty. They like their drink even more than us Romans. But they were always game for a laugh and a dance. They loved music, and making pottery. They were people, just like you and me. I had never felt better, or happier, in my life . . .'

His face was cast in shadow by a cloud moving past the sun.

'If not for my family, I may have stayed.'

With a growing round of applause, a master of ceremonies appeared onstage, announcing a performance of *The Three Coins*, by Plautus. Claudia wasn't familiar with it, but she trusted that Hieronymus wouldn't have risked anything too scandalous.

'Ladies and gentlemen, please put your hands together for the performing players of Campus Martius.'

To raucous cheers, a man in a toga emerged from the decorative pillars that acted as a backdrop, giving the impression of a house or a curia or a temple, depending on the play.

On this occasion, it was a house. The man was involved in some sort of property dispute. It belonged to a man named Charmides and there was alleged to be treasure buried within, but the house was managed by Charmides's daughter, who was described as spendthrift.

Claudia was barely paying attention when she heard Damocles mumbling: 'His daughter? It is supposed to be his son.'

A murmuring wave moved through the audience.

'Is it an interpretation?' Damocles mumbled. 'A reinvention?'

'What's going on?' asked Claudia.

'I'm not sure yet.'

When the protagonist of the play, Megaronides, announced the arrival of the mysterious daughter, the curious murmurs grew in volume.

'It is I, Lesbionicus,' said the actor, stepping onstage.

He wore a rudimentary wig of straw, dressed in an imitation of her imperial robes, with a wooden crown. His face was painted like a brothel girl's. He walked in a comedic sashaying way that she knew was intended to signal a woman of ill-repute.

The audience erupted into nervous, scandalized laughter.

'Where are my handmaids?' said Lesbionicus. 'The pretty ones? I need them to help me out of my robes.'

The actor winked to the audience, signalling a dirty joke.

'Or perhaps my woman gladiator will do the job for me? I pay her well to serve me, in more ways than one.'

It was Claudia. Lesbionicus was a parody of her.

They would say it was just a character, a name, that it was a coincidence, but she knew better.

Claudia felt a hundred pairs of eyes swivelling in her direction. She dared to look out at the crowd, catching rows of people whispering, giggling behind their hands.

'What is this, Damocles?' Claudia hissed.

'Do not blame me, Empress. They have changed the script.'

She looked to Hieronymus, who struggled to swallow back the smirk on his lips.

It was a joke at her expense, and in front of the prince, no less, but it was also something else more insidious. It was also part of the plot against her, and an acknowledgement that her worst fears were real: she really *was* the joke of Rome.

She turned and caught eyes with Cassius.

The look he gave her was one of understanding.

It was a look that said, 'ohhh'.

He saw the panic and embarrassment on her face, blushing red with her eyes wide, and he knew the truth, without a single word having been spoken between them.

He understood what brought her and Gia together now.

'Should I . . . stop them?' asked Damocles.

'Wait! They're just getting to the good part,' said Hieronymus, stuffing hazelnuts into his mouth.

Claudia feared that responding in anger would make the rumours appear true, so she merely shook her head and sat, frozen, as waves of heat and dread rolled over her, a fake semi-smile on her face.

She hoped the joke would end there, and they could all move on, but the play dragged on for a century, or so it felt.

She soon realized what a terrible decision being tolerant was, as the play debased her further and further. Lesbionicus had one sole trait as a character, which was her love of Sappho, played to the extreme to suggest she had a strong preference for women, particularly her gladiator, portrayed as a money-grabbing rogue with no real care for Lesbionicus. She was glad Gia wasn't here to see it.

'I should not die without one last kiss,' said Lesbionicus, to another chorus of laughter.

'How much will you pay me?' said the gladiator.

The audience lapped it up like thirsty cats. Only the Cult of Diana remained silent, furious on her behalf.

The people had heard the rumours too. They'd seen the graffiti. Claudia knew this, and yet, experiencing it first hand was entirely different. She was in the thick of it now. She could see their faces and hear their whispers. There was no escaping the truth, or hiding it from sight.

The play ended with Lesbionicus running off with the treasure-seeker's daughter, which inspired the audience to boo and jeer, uttering comments so depraved her brain blanked them out immediately.

When the torturous performance finally ended, the actors bowed to exultant applause. The audience looked to her for a response, as was customary when the emperor was in attendance.

'Have the entire company arrested,' she stated coldly.

'All of them?' asked Damocles.

'*All*. Of them.'

'Very well, Empress,' he said.

Politics was a circus, and right now, Claudia was the clown, but she was still the empress, which meant they had to follow her orders.

Damocles and some of the soldiers bustled off to arrest the actors, as directed. A chorus of protests sounded from backstage. It wouldn't help her win the people over if she became a tyrant, though they called her one anyway as they were escorted off the grounds.

She could see how easy it would be, to become one.

Cassius loudly resumed his conversation with the prince about life, death and the soul, flashing her a look over his shoulder.

She nodded, grateful for the distraction.

The gladiatrices Livia and Dido soon stepped up to fight, to give a performance of their skills – an attempt to attract funding for their gladiatrix school. Yet the atmosphere couldn't have been more hostile. Some in the crowd continued to heckle, asking them to take off their armour. The atmosphere quickly soured.

'I'll take your head right off of your shoulders,' Livia yelled, when one man threw the traditional piss-cup.

'Come on down here and fight me woman-to-man, if you think you're hard enough,' Dido goaded.

Claudia thought the day couldn't get any more diabolical but then Gia reappeared, moving through the wall of people.

'I need to speak with you, Empress, right away,' she said, ignoring the unfolding brawl currently spilling into the orchestra.

Her face was solemn, and she hadn't even heard about Lesbionicus yet.

'Now is not the time, I'm afraid,' Claudia said.

'It can't wait,' Gia insisted, looking pointedly at Darius.

'What's the problem?' asked Damocles.

'Nothing!' Claudia said. 'Nothing at all.'

She struggled to extricate herself from the middle of the crowd, almost knocking over a jug of wine in her clumsiness.

'I need to step aside for a moment . . . for fresh air. Please do continue enjoying the uh . . .' She looked to the stage, where Livia and Dido were now beating the man who threw the piss-cup. 'Performance.'

'Shall I accompany you?' asked Darius.

'No, thank you.' She used her hands to form an enthusiastic crossing motion. 'All is perfectly well.'

The whispering of the crowd intensified, with the prince sat alone in the imperial box as if he were the ruler and not her.

How would it look if she disappeared with her female guard right now, after the play they had just watched? But Claudia had no choice, walking out through the orchestra and through the side door as titters of laughter followed her.

She trailed Gia out into the quadriportico, to stand in one of the pillared alcoves that surrounded the on-site curia.

'What is it?' she said. 'You won't believe what you missed.'

'I found something.'

Gia presented Claudia with a weapon, using a stretch of fabric to hold it, so as not to touch it with her bare skin.

'The knife of Jupiter,' said Gia.

'Oh,' said Claudia, taking one step backwards.

It was just like the one used by her would-be assassin. Its lightning handle caught the light, giving it the impression of the bolt glowing white hot.

'I found it among Prince Darius's possessions while searching as you asked, hidden inside a set of robes,' said Gia.

Claudia felt winded again, struggling to draw a breath.

'It was well-concealed, took me ages to find it,' said Gia. 'He didn't have anything else of interest, other than some very questionable taste in undergarments.'

Claudia hadn't really expected Gia to find anything. The search was more of a precaution. Yet here it was, before her eyes and hard to deny. How could she have been so naïve?

Gia stashed the weapon away, still within its sackcloth bundle.

'There's no way it could be a mistake?' asked Claudia.

She wanted it to be, she realized.

Gia touched her arm, frowning in sympathy.

'I'm sorry,' she said. 'I know it isn't good news. I knew there was something off about him, though. All those gifts and his endless flirtations, he was just trying to blind you to his real intentions.'

'Why would a Persian prince worship a Roman god, or even pretend to? It doesn't make sense to me.'

'Maybe Jupiter has converted him,' said Gia. 'You have to admit, if Jupiter was going to choose a fighter, Darius isn't a bad pick. He is built like a minotaur, and he has an army of his own to meet yours in battle. I would choose him over Marcellus any day. Or maybe he's using a Roman dagger to hide himself, so no one will think of him as a suspect. It's not like anyone could have framed him – no one knew I was to search today.'

'Perhaps this *is* all Darius's plan to claim the city,' said Claudia. 'He needed me to invite him in, like some kind of Trojan Horse.'

Still, she screwed up her face.

Something about it didn't click – and no matter how she looked at it, she couldn't make it fit.

'But if he wanted to kill me and seize the throne, he could do so without committing to this elaborate routine. He has dedicated hours and much money to the farce. And why would he travel all this way to assassinate me when he could've hired a local to do the job, and draw far less attention? Even for a madman, it would be a bold move.'

'I don't know,' said Gia. 'I don't understand it either. I can only show you what I found.'

Claudia began to pace.

'Every time I think I'm being too ruthless, something happens to remind me that actually, no, I'm not ruthless enough,' she said, as Gia watched. 'I really thought Darius might be trustworthy. He actually had me convinced! Something about the frankness with which he spoke suggested a man who isn't adept at deception, but here it is. I have no one to blame but myself, for trusting him.'

Gia intercepted her.

'It's okay,' she said. 'It's not your fault. He even charmed *me* a couple of times.'

'Why didn't the goddesses see it coming?' said Claudia. 'I saw nothing in the shield that led me to believe he conspired against me. Is it because Fortuna's vision has been taken away?'

'What are you going to do?' asked Gia.

'Therein lies the problem,' said Claudia. 'No matter what I do, I'm in a bind. If I let Darius remain here, I'm in danger. If I kill him, it will be disastrous. Even if I send him away, it will cause a diplomatic conflict. My hold on Rome will be weaker than ever now, with everyone already thinking me guilty of infamia.'

'*Infamia?*' said Gia. 'Says who?'

'Oh right, you haven't heard the best bit yet,' said Claudia.

She cringed, steeling herself. It was even more embarrassing to describe it than it was to witness it.

'The play this afternoon was about a woman named Lesbionicus who lusts after her handmaids . . . and her gladiator,' she said, 'who was just in it for the money. It wasn't flattering.'

'Lesbionicus?' said Gia, not understanding.

‘Like Lesbos. They were satirizing me. It was mortifying.’

‘What did you do?’

‘That’s the really stupid part . . . I did nothing.’

‘Nothing?’

‘*Nothing*, Gia!’ Claudia threw up her hands. ‘I just sat there and let it happen. I made a pithy comment at the end and told Damocles to have them arrested, but the damage was already done. If the people didn’t respect me before, they certainly won’t now.’

‘Where was the prince during all this?’

‘He was sitting right there next to me, watching! What must he be thinking now? I dread to imagine.’

Gia bit her lip.

‘It’s not funny,’ Claudia said morosely.

‘No, you’re right.’ Gia tried to adopt a more solemn expression. ‘It’s not. It’s not funny at all.’

They looked at each other for a moment, the energetic current surging between them as ever, before smiling in sync.

‘Maybe it’s a little funny,’ Claudia conceded, taking her hand. ‘A dark comedy, perhaps.’

They ducked out of sight as Livia and Dido charged past, ranting about the unruly audience at the theatre.

‘These men have disrespected us for the last time,’ Livia said. ‘Pigs, every single one of them.’

‘If they want a war, they’ll have one,’ said Dido. ‘Mars versus Venus. I know who I would bet on.’

Once they’d passed, Claudia moved closer to Gia, as Gia moved closer to her simultaneously, both sighing in a mixture of distress and relief. Gia cupped her face, kissing her gently as if to soothe her.

'I wasn't mocking you, so you know,' she said. 'It's just so stupid, I can't help but laugh at how pathetic they are.'

'I have much bigger problems, I know. It just felt so degrading.'

She hugged herself, and Gia put her hands on top of Claudia's own, joining the embrace.

'I hate that they humiliated you.'

'How can they consider it *infamia*?' said Claudia. 'Compared to what they get up to?'

'Who cares what those monsters think? They don't understand decency when they see it, nor love, nor kindness. Anything they don't understand is perverted to them.'

'You're right. Why are you so often right? It's very frustrating to me, as a person who likes to be right,' said Claudia.

'I do it only because you look so cute when you're annoyed.'

'Please, I am on the edge as it is.'

'If it makes you feel any better, making fun of the emperor is a long-standing Roman tradition. It's not personal. They would despise anyone standing there, but particularly a woman. You know that.'

'I do know that.'

Claudia broke free to wring her hands, pacing again.

'Do you think Darius was responsible for what happened in the theatre too?' asked Gia. 'Could he have paid them to humiliate you?'

'Maybe. Or it might have been someone else. I have so many enemies now, I lose track of their names.'

'Then forget their names,' said Gia. 'They deserve none.'

'Everything feels cursed. I am standing on a clifftop, like I could be overthrown, literally thrown over, in my sleep,' said Claudia.

'Did you ever think it would be otherwise?'

'I thought it would be a catastrophe and yet, the reality is even worse. The legion is still missing, Marcellus hasn't reported to me since meeting with the Legate, the prince staying in my palace is conspiring against me, the people are putting on scandalous comedies about me, the king of the gods is trying to kill me . . . oh, and ' This was the worst part – 'Cassius is not a fan. Of me, in particular.'

She thought Gia might be surprised, maybe even deny it on her brother's behalf or tell her she'd got the wrong impression, but she merely sat down on a bench and said, 'I know.'

'You *know*?'

'He told me,' Gia said.

'When?'

'The night you got the shield from Minerva.'

'Why didn't you say anything?' said Claudia, sitting beside her.

'I didn't want you to be hurt by it. You have enough on your mind already. Why would I add to it? What good would it have done?'

'What did he say?'

'Nothing I haven't heard before,' said Gia.

'Like what?' Claudia urged. 'Go on.'

'Oh, you know, I'm just your servant, you're weird and lonely, you'll step over my dead body one day, that sort of thing.'

'Wow. That is . . . wow. *Weird and lonely?*' said Claudia. 'And here I was thinking we could be friends!'

'He's wrong. He'll change his mind, in time. He doesn't know what we have. He doesn't even know the truth about us.'

Claudia's stomach rolled in dread again.

'He does now, I'm afraid,' she said gloomily. 'He looked right at me during the play. He figured it out.'

'I doubt it,' she said. 'My brother isn't that smart.'

'You didn't see his face. He *knows*, Gia. I am certain.'

'Shit. He'll be upset I didn't tell him myself,' said Gia. 'I dread to have that conversation.'

Claudia felt hot and flustered, boiling and roiling at the surface. She gestured in irritation, as if flicking away a fly.

'I have no one on my side but you,' she said.

Gia looked at her and sighed, as if she too were in pain.

'That's not true,' she said. 'You have Rectina and Pliny, and ... the Cult of Diana.'

'How can they help me win against a prince? Against *that* prince, in particular? Have you seen him?'

'I have, and I can only hope I don't have to fight him.'

'I would still bet on you every time.'

'That's because you love me,' said Gia.

'It's true. I *am* very biased.'

They fell silent, drawn into each other's eyes.

'Should I call for the guard?' said Gia.

'Wait,' said Claudia, holding up one hand. 'Let me consider it.'

She looked up at the curia, past the statue of Pompey that had been installed and removed a dozen times. It felt like a fitting setting to the unfolding drama. Cloaked in shadows and illuminated by the moon, she could feel the presence of a historical spirit, of so much fear and so much pride ... It humbled her.

'This was where Caesar was betrayed, right here,' said Claudia.

Gia gazed at her a moment, trying to discern her meaning.

'You want to kill him?'

'Let us not go that far,' said Claudia. 'Not yet, anyway.'

'You're afraid the same will happen to you?' Gia tried again.

Claudia nodded.

'Pliny says men are more likely to kill when they're afraid. If I try to have the prince held prisoner, he might panic and do something in desperation – like a wild animal caught in a trap – whether he's guilty or not. We shall sit on this discovery, for now.'

'And say nothing?' said Gia.

'For now.'

'That is what we did after the Pantheon, and here we are.'

Maybe Claudia was being too cautious. Maybe she needed to be as ruthless as a man. Her father would've had the prince arrested and imprisoned. Her brother would've had him severed at the neck. But something inside her told her to halt, to tread carefully, that all was not as it appeared. She would first consult with Minerva's shield; to seek the guidance of the goddess before taking action. She would wait before doing anything drastic.

Her decision could start a war.

12. WHAT CANNOT BE UNSEEN

That evening, Claudia retired to her rooms alone to consult with Minerva's goddess-eye shield. Gia had gone to speak with Cassius, though she'd first ensured that Claudia would be protected by twice as many guards as usual, knowing that the prince might be plotting his next move.

Princess the lynx curled up on her bed, stretching as if she'd always lived there. Claudia watched her cautiously for a while, waiting until her eyes began to droop.

The cat wore a leather collar with a pearl-studded pendant on it, which resembled the necklace the prince had given her.

Only when Princess was settled did Claudia dare to pet her, running one hand over the fur on her back. Her pointy ears twitched as she began to purr – a low, rumbling sound that soothed Claudia's soul.

The creature was well-fed and well-groomed, as far as she could tell, for Claudia had little experience with big cats. It spoke to the prince's better nature, that his animals were so well cared for.

Claudia dared to stroke her under the chin. Princess purred louder, enthusiastically rubbing the sides of her face against Claudia's hand, then lowered her head onto the bedspread and drifted off to sleep.

Claudia didn't get the impression that the lynx had been trained to assassinate her in her sleep with a single bite to the throat as forewarned, but it would be a novel way for the prince to murder her, if he wished, if not a little obvious.

As had become her new evening tradition, she sat before the shield and used the supernatural reflection of Minerva's magic mirror to check in on her list of suspects. Tonight, she began with the prince.

'Show me Darius.'

He was lying on his back in his bed in the east wing. There were people swarming around him, talking and cleaning and presenting him with various objects, playing instruments and telling jokes as if to cheer him up, but he appeared to be pondering something, toying lightly with the pendant he wore around his neck.

The prince seemed troubled by something: his missing knife, perhaps. Claudia watched him for a time, hoping to catch him in the act of something, but he soon expelled his servants and retired to bed alone.

Claudia pulled the weapon out from the chest it had been hidden in, swaddled in a bundle of cloth. She tilted it back and forth in the light, examining its fine carving of a lightning bolt. It was ornate, much like the shield. A gods-blessed object imbued with unknown power.

She caught her own reflection in the blade and suddenly feared that Jupiter might be using it to spy on her. If Minerva could speak to her through a shield, there was no reason he couldn't spy through the blade of a knife. She wrapped it back up and stashed it away.

Again, that nagging thought – that it didn't make sense. The prince hadn't even arrived in Rome when she'd been attacked at the

Pantheon with what appeared to be this same knife. How could it be in his possession?

She suspected that he was being set up somehow, yet that was impossible too. It was as Gia said: who had known she planned to search his rooms that day?

Claudia attempted to spy on Marcellus again. She was expecting the vision to be infuriatingly blank, as it had been on the previous occasions she'd tried, but with a sudden, surprising pop, a blurred, shaky image appeared on the shield, revealing her cousin surrounded by trees.

It took her a moment to register what she was seeing. He was in the wild forests of Britannia, she discerned, recognizing one of the stone circles for which the isle was known. And he was in leagues with hundreds of soldiers. No, not in leagues – at the helm.

He'd gone there to track down the missing legion, she presumed, and yet no one had said a word to her.

Once again, it didn't bode well for her reign.

Her cousin paused, his eyes catching on something tangled in one of the bushes that blocked their path. He pulled it out, freeing it from the thorns, and held out the torn red material for his men to see.

'A soldier's cloak,' he said. 'We're moving in the right direction. We must keep going.'

'Yes, general,' said some of the men, saluting.

Marcellus was a general now? She hadn't given permission for such a promotion.

'Aquinas says we must attack any heathen villages we come across,' he said. 'Leave no bough unburned, no well unpolluted. We shall have vengeance, in the name of Jupiter.'

'Ao, Jupiter!' sang his men, cheerfully.

The shield gave another pop and ended abruptly, and she could not seem to get her cousin to appear again.

Someone was trying to hide his activities from her sight, to keep her out of the picture. Claudia had not been informed – she was deliberately being kept in the dark . . . and now she realized why: General Aquinas wanted to push ahead with his plan to raze the villages and drive out the barbarians, whether she approved or not.

Marcellus was positioning himself to seize power, using his influence with the military to gain support, but at least his extended vacation meant she had one less foe to worry about for now. He was overseas. He couldn't possibly have hidden the knife in the prince's rooms.

Claudia next turned to Damocles, who was ambling around the gardens. He looked tired, world-weary, ducking into his own chambers to write a letter, though she could not make out what it said.

Meanwhile, Hieronymus was complaining about her to a couple of senators in a local taberna, implying that 'the Persians will be taking over' if she had anything to do with it.

'She's too soft,' he was saying. 'Too young, too sheltered. Her father had many failings, but he was rarely too merciful. He tended to play on the safe side. Kill first, ask questions later . . . Ahh, I miss him.'

His companions hummed in agreement.

'This prince will run rings around her. It will spell disaster, mark my words. Just wait until your neighbours are praying to Mithras.'

Her mind turned unexpectedly to Cassius. Was he one of her enemies now? He was plain in her distaste for her. He was present at the Pantheon, too. She couldn't seem to put the question aside. Before she could stop herself, his name slipped from her lips.

'Show me Cassius,' she said.

He appeared in the shield, blurry at first, before rapidly taking form. He was talking to Gia.

Claudia could've removed her hand and avoided spying on her, but for whatever reason, for many reasons, she couldn't, didn't. She was stuck fast, unmoving as she eavesdropped.

'You can still choose,' said Cassius. 'You still have the freedom to walk away. We could leave, right now. They would never find us.'

'I don't want to walk away,' Gia said.

He groaned dramatically. 'Please, sister.'

'You're not listening to me, Cass.'

'I am. I just don't like what I'm hearing,' said Cassius. 'There is a crucial difference.'

They were in the stony, windowless caverns of the servants' quarters, in the spartan room Cassius slept in, sitting on two cots that were rammed up next to each other.

'Look, I'm not an idiot,' he said. 'I *have* travelled, you know. I've heard of Sappho. I . . . I've even desired men.'

Claudia tried to listen to their muted conversation over the incessant pounding of her heart.

'I guessed as much,' said Gia. 'You always joke about it.'

Cassius ran one hand through his short hair, self-consciously.

'Everyone does it,' he said. 'No one frowns upon it, as long as we keep it inside our tents. But there's a reason that every senator has a wife and not a husband.'

'That doesn't make it a *good* reason.'

'What I'm saying is: I understand, sister. I don't judge you for that. It is a part of nature. It isn't you being with a woman that bothers me so much . . . It's more, your choice of mate.'

'Well, that isn't up to you,' Gia said.

'No, but you asked for my opinion and I am giving it.'

Gia sighed heavily, her head in her hands.

'I can't give my blessing to it, knowing already how it will end – with you heartbroken, or dead,' he said.

'Things end. Doesn't mean they're not worth doing.'

'You're being so stubborn about this,' said Cassius.

'Says you!'

They stared at each other, neither one willing to submit.

'You have already made up your mind and you barely know her,' said Gia. 'If you'd been there when we were in Pompeii, you'd understand. If you knew what we had lived through together. She was there for me when you were gone . . . when I thought you were already dead.'

'But I'm not!' said Cassius. 'I'm alive, and I am right here, sister. It's a miracle that we're not both deceased. We should be free. We *could* be free. Don't throw your life away on some young, stupid love. The world is full of pretty people, sister.'

'Not like her,' said Gia, firmly. 'She's not replaceable, to me.'

'Everyone is, in the end.'

'I love her.'

'Oh, Gia. Do you know how many times I've been in love? Hundreds of times. *Thousands* of times. More times than I can count.' His face fell, a mask of some unspoken tragedy. 'Most often, it only lasts for a week, a month or two . . .'

'I'm not sure that's love, Cass,' said Gia.

'Whatever it is, it didn't last . . . It doesn't last, no matter how much I will it to. If I turned my life upside-down every time I fell in love, I would be an hourglass.'

Gia shook her head, amused despite his opposition.

'Love is just something the gods made up, to make us go along with their nonsense,' he said.

'Do you really believe that?' she asked.

'No, but I wish *you* did, so I could talk you out of it.'

'You were gone a long time,' said Gia eventually. 'There is so much of my life you weren't present for, so much of me you don't know now.' She fixed him with an intense stare, leaning forwards and clasping her hands together. 'I killed a man, Cass. I killed . . . well, several men, actually.'

'And what? I've killed too, sister. This is a kill or be killed world. You don't have to feel guilty for it.'

Despite this, he looked slightly sickened as an unidentified memory floated into his mind.

'I am changed,' she said. 'I'm not a kid any more, begging you to teach me to fight.'

'No, because you could probably kick my arse now.'

He reached his hand out, into the space between the two beds, and she took it.

'It felt like a lifetime, that we were apart,' she said.

'I'm not the same person any more, and neither are you, I know that . . . but you're still my little sister.'

Gia seemed on the verge of tears again. She wasn't angry at her brother, just sad, grieving . . . confused, maybe. A battle of emotions passing over her in waves, like fighting soldiers.

And where was Claudia? Peeping on them through her magic fucking mirror, like some mythological villainess.

'Can't you just be happy for me?' Gia said.

'I want to be. If you told me that you were with that other gladiator girl, or a brothel worker, or even a senator's wife, I would throw you a party and buy you a present, but not her, Gia. Please not her.'

'It doesn't work like that,' Gia said. 'It's too late.'

'*Too late?* That's not exactly a ringing endorsement of your relationship, is it? It's not a death sentence, Gia. Although for us, maybe it will be. The death of us all.'

'At least we shall be together then,' she said, dryly.

'Oh yes, I'm sure the underworld is lovely, sister, with the harpies and the shades and gods knows what else they have down there. I'm sure it would be a treat, a charming little family reunion.'

She rolled her eyes at his sarcasm.

'If people find out about the two of you, you know what they'll do, don't you?' he said. 'They'll kill you to keep you out of the way, or to spare her reputation. They'll kill you so she has to marry the prince, or her cousin. Either that, or they'll kill the both of you.'

'We have the goddesses on our side.'

'On your side, or hers?' said Cassius. 'Even by your own telling of the story, you were just a nameless warrior they foresaw, destined to protect Claudia long enough for her to become empress.'

Gia shifted uncomfortably.

'*She* chose you, not them, and you did your duty like a good little soldier. Your part is over now, sister. If you think the goddesses won't sacrifice you, now you've done what they wanted you to, you misunderstand their immortal games. They are more gods than they are women.'

'Cass, just stop.'

'You should walk away now, while you still have your dignity and your freedom . . . and your life. Your fucking *life*, Gia. Do you know how precious that is? Mother is gone. Father is gone. Our brother is gone. We are all that's left of the family.'

'Okay, okay. That's enough,' Gia said, standing up abruptly. 'I get it. I can't change your mind, and you can't change mine.'

'I will. Watch me. I'm very persuasive.'

'Give over, brother,' said Gia.

'I'm serious. I convinced the barbarian Brits not to kill me, didn't I? Just give me time. You will see for yourself and, when you do, I'll be here waiting to pick up the pieces. I'm back from the dead and I'm not going anywhere. I swore to the spirit of Mother that I'd get you away – far, far away from this mess. I won't leave until you leave with me.'

Gia paled at this mention of their mother.

'I won't lose you again.'

Frightened of what was happening, Claudia pulled backwards and the image instantly dispelled, the shield returning to its normal shimmering silver relief of the goddess.

She slumped to the floor, rocking back and forth as the lynx stirred on the bed, watching her with interest.

Her memory of confessing to her father's murder rolled over her, making her nauseated. That look on Gia's face – the one she hadn't been able to forget – she had seen it again, just now, in their conversation. Cassius had joined the naysayers' chorus, telling Gia that she was no good, and maybe some small part of her believed him.

Even Claudia believed him. And Gia was in danger now, because of her.

The sound of a knock made her heart leap out of her chest.

'Come in,' she said, startled.

Claudia quickly stood up, smoothing down her hair and her robes, trying not to let her face give her away, but it was her handmaid Nadira who popped her head around the door, not Gia.

Claudia deflated.

'Do you want me to take Princess?' Nadira asked.

'Oh . . . um . . .'

Claudia looked to the bed, where the lynx was pretending to be asleep, cracking open one eye just a slither.

'It's all right, she's already too comfortable. She can stay. Thank you, though. Have a good night.'

Nadira nodded, and disappeared into the hall.

Left alone, Claudia waited, letting her mind make a slave of her again. The goddesses no longer saw the future, but Claudia could imagine it clearly enough. She would rule for as long as she lived, which might not be too long, as things were going. Gia would likely die before her – probably at the hands of the assassin, be it the prince or another. Every moment Gia spent with Claudia put her in danger.

Another knock sounded. Claudia sprang up, standing alert as Gia entered the room. She glimpsed Aurelia and one of the guards peering in curiously before Gia closed the door, shutting them out.

Gia was attempting to appear casual, as if she had not just had a devastating conversation with her beloved brother, but Claudia could tell from the redness around her eyes she had been crying at some point between when she'd spied on her and now.

Before she could speak, the lynx jumped down from the bed, approaching Gia as if inspecting her.

'The cat sleeps with us, huh?' The lynx circled her, sniffing. 'Is this a test? Do I pass?'

'Not sure yet,' teased Claudia, folding her arms. 'Let's see.'

The lynx looked up at Gia, licked her lips, then sauntered back up onto the bed.

'I think that means she likes you,' said Claudia.

'Like she wants to eat me, you mean.'

Claudia stared at her expressionlessly, trying to work out what she was going to say.

'Are you okay?' said Gia.

'Yes, why?' she said quickly, on instinct, because she was always okay when people asked, whether it was true or not.

'You're acting a little strange,' said Gia.

'I'm fine,' said Claudia.

'Are you sure?'

Claudia longed to bury herself in Gia's arms, to forget what she had seen in the shield, but she couldn't. All of that fear and guilt and sickness inside her was roiling up like lava in a volcano, but instead of erupting she felt herself becoming dormant and cold.

'I'm so sorry, Gia,' she said.

'What for?'

'I have been selfish and . . .' Claudia stiffened, hands forming fists at her sides, though she didn't dare to look Gia in the eye. 'You should not be here,' she said.

'Where else would I be?'

'Somewhere else, somewhere safe, somewhere where you're not in constant danger, maybe.'

'I know what I signed up for. I chose to fight in the arena even before I met you. Where is this coming from?'

Claudia flushed, wiping her palms on her robes as her moral compass swung around the dial. She wanted to tell the truth, but she was too afraid. She could imagine what Cassius would have to say about her spying on them. It would surely compound his poor opinion of her.

Gia narrowed her eyes, reading into the silence. She looked to the shield, and Claudia knew at once that she was caught.

'You heard us?' said Gia, brow wrinkling. 'You were watching Cassius and I, through the shield?'

Claudia looked at it, guiltily. She couldn't deny it. Gia had a way of seeing right through her anyway.

'I didn't ask the shield to show *you*,' she said. 'I asked the shield to show *him*, because of what he said to me today. You were just with him. I momentarily forgot that part. I didn't mean to spy on you . . . But I couldn't look away, and the longer I listened, the more I needed to hear what was said. It was me you were talking about . . . It was hard to resist.'

'I wouldn't have wished for you to hear that.'

'I don't think he's going to change his mind any time soon.'

'He will.'

'It is doomed,' said Claudia. 'How can you be happy when your brother hates me so?'

'You think just because Cassius doesn't like you, that I will turn against you too?' asked Gia.

'I wouldn't blame you, if you chose him. It would be the wise and sensible thing.'

'Lucky for you, I am neither wise nor sensible,' Gia said, lightly.

Then she kissed Claudia so tenderly that she became light-headed, her knees giving out beneath her as Gia steadied them. She kissed her back, holding on for as long as she could, her fingers clawing at the material of her chiton beneath the armour.

'I already chose you,' said Gia.

She had to do it. She had to do it now, to rip off the bandage and not extend this exquisite torture.

But she couldn't. She was too weak.

Gia was her Achilles heel. If people knew they were lovers, her enemies would use Gia to target her. They could ask for anything they wanted, if they captured her or threatened to harm her. Claudia would give away all the world, in such a case.

She looked down at the ground, avoiding Gia's eyes.

'Just . . . maybe don't spy on me again, okay?' Gia gently brushed a strand of hair out of Claudia's eyes. 'Unless I'm in danger.'

They silenced as they heard movement outside the door: light laughter, the clank of armour.

'We are always in danger,' said Claudia. 'That is the problem.'

Now was the time. It had to be.

'Forget about Cassius, forget about Lesbionicus,' said Gia, with a smile. 'Let it just be us, for tonight.'

'Perhaps we should be extra cautious for a while,' said Claudia, finally summoning the courage.

Gia didn't answer for a moment, her face soft.

'Do we not live in secrecy already?' said Gia. 'What more can we do to hide ourselves?'

Claudia took a deep breath, steeling herself.

'You probably shouldn't sleep here with me any more,' she said.

'Why not?'

'We are being too obvious.'

Gia's face was unreadable. 'You're serious?'

'I don't want it to be so but it must be done, to keep you safe.'

'Is this because of what my brother said?'

'Yes, but not only that. There is the graffiti, the play today. I have to tread carefully with the prince. We have been too reckless already. We must be smarter, and assume that eyes are always upon us at all times. Anything my enemies can use to wound and weaken me, they will take, and that includes you. That includes us.'

All of this was true, but it was not the only reason. Claudia sensed that Gia knew this.

'What happened to let it be recorded in the annals of history?' Gia said. 'Isn't that what you said just yesterday?'

'That was before the people put on a play to satirize me, before I found out that the prince possessed a knife of Jupiter, before I heard your brother beg you to leave me in the name of your dead mother . . .'

'I thought we were stronger than that,' said Gia.

'We were . . . we are.'

'So, what has changed between us? Nothing.'

'I have a responsibility to the people, to women, to the goddesses,' said Claudia. 'I have a duty now. I can't risk losing what we have already sacrificed everything for.'

'I'm not asking you to.'

Your brother's words are just another reminder that we are not safe here, that *you* are not safe here.'

'When have I ever been safe?' Gia objected. 'I am happy as long as I'm with you.'

'And I you, but if I love you, shouldn't I do everything in my power to protect you?' said Claudia. 'Cassius is right. You are in danger so long as you stand at my side. Your life will never be your own. I will always have an obligation that is greater than my commitment to you.'

'Are you telling me you want to sleep apart, or are you telling me you want to . . . *be* apart?' said Gia.

Claudia swallowed.

'It is just . . . for now,' she said. 'Until the heat is off us. People will stop talking about it eventually.'

'I didn't think it would take so long,' said Gia.

'That what would take so long?' asked Claudia, confused.

Gia shook her head, as if she didn't have the energy to explain.

'What were you going to say?' pressed Claudia.

'It's not important.'

'I think it is.'

'I didn't think it would take so long for you to go back on your word,' she said.

Claudia realized a part of Gia had always expected Claudia to hurt her, to let her down.

'I'm sorry it has to be like this. If I had my way, you would be at my side every hour of every day,' said Claudia.

'Then what's the problem?'

'I must do the right thing and put aside my selfish desires.'

'Is that what I am to you? A selfish desire?'

'Compared to ruling Rome? Yes.'

'I can't even stay here in your room to keep watch over you as your guard because people are gossiping?'

Gia didn't move.

'You won't change your mind? You really want me to leave?'

Claudia almost caved, but fear made her strong.

'Please, Gia, I beg you to understand,' she said. 'You are always protecting me. Now I'm trying to keep us safe too, just in a different way. It is clear to me. The closer we are seen to be, the more you are a target. We must be apart, for now.'

'As you wish,' said Gia, in a tone that was unmistakably resentful. She abruptly pulled open the drapes and stood up.

'Gia,' said Claudia softly. 'Please.'

'Please what?'

'Please don't make this harder than it already is.'

'What do you want from me? I'm not arguing with you, or kicking off. You can't expect me to be happy about it too.'

Gia stood there a moment in silence, as if waiting for Claudia to say she'd made a mistake, but she didn't.

The silence stretched thin.

Claudia held her nerve, though everything inside her told her to backtrack, to forfeit, to submit.

'Goodnight, then,' said Gia coldly.

It seemed like a small thing, on the face of it, for them to sleep apart, but it was much bigger in a symbolic sense. Claudia realized that now, only when it was too late.

'Goodnight,' was all she could say without crying.

Gia didn't turn back, closing the door behind her.

Claudia sat on the bed, unmoving. She told herself that it was smart, that she was a ruthless, cool-headed, cold-hearted leader now. She had put Rome ahead of her own wants and needs, like all good heroes. She had put Gia's wellbeing first, even if that meant hurting her.

Hadn't she?

She would kill a legion for her, if she had to.

She would go to war, if she had to.

But in the dark of the night, alone with the haunting shades of her father and brother, Claudia knew the truth.

She *was* a coward.

13. THE EMPRESS OF ALL WOMEN

Claudia had stayed awake all night, watching the shield and laying plans.

In the lonely hours before morning, her bed so cold and empty without Gia in it, she had come to several conclusions. If being empress meant making such large personal sacrifices, it had to be for good reason. It could not be in vain. She couldn't live with herself, if she was a coward both in her heart and on the throne. She needed to be formidable again, like she was when the goddess Victoria came to her aid.

That gave her a grand idea, which grew and grew in the dark of the early morning, until it took over her.

Claudia found herself gripped by a delusional, wide-eyed kind of mania that enabled her to wash and dress, as if everything was normal. It filled her with false purpose and anxious energy that spilled over, making her hands shake.

Gia waited for her at the bottom of the stairs, wearing her uniform armour with a sword on her hip.

She looked momentarily flustered when she saw Claudia descending, before quickly recovering herself, plastering on a neutral, composed expression.

They didn't speak until her handmaids drifted off to fetch her breakfast, while the guards retreated to the hall outside.

'Did you sleep well?' asked Claudia.

'Not really,' said Gia. 'Those beds in the servants' quarters aren't very comfortable. Just saying.'

Claudia longed to touch her, to comfort her, but she feared it would only make things worse.

'You?' asked Gia, after a beat.

'Terribly. I hated us sleeping apart,' she said.

'Your choice,' said Gia. 'I didn't want it.'

'It's not what I want either. I hate that I've hurt you.'

Gia frowned and looked away.

'Who said I was hurt?'

'I'm going to do something a little drastic today,' said Claudia, changing the subject.

'I thought you wanted to lie low,' said Gia.

'This may just take the attention off us. Soon the people will not be talking about Empress Lesbionicus but the Empress of All Women.'

Gia cocked her head curiously, but before Claudia could respond, they were surrounded by advisors and guards and senators. She called Damocles and Hieronymus into the throne room, as Gia followed.

'How can we be of service today, Empress?' said Damocles.

The consul and her palace advisor gazed at her with apprehension, sensing both that she had something to say and that they wouldn't like it.

'I intend to issue a proclamation stating that women can join the army if they wish,' she said, without introduction. 'Starting next quarter.'

Claudia may as well have announced her intention to sacrifice every baby boy in the empire, by the looks the two men were giving her, but if she was going to win back the favour of the public, she would need to do something revolutionary and momentous.

'It is simple,' she said. 'If there are warrior goddesses in the pantheon, there should be warrior women in Rome. If humans were made in the likeness of the gods, human society should also mirror Elysium. This is surely why I was called to be empress: to improve the lives of women across the empire.'

'Do we not have enough problems for your taste?' said Damocles, rather more daringly than usual. 'You should focus on entertaining the prince, and placating the people so they don't revolt. Then there's the issue of the missing legion.'

'I thought Marcellus was handling that,' said Claudia, 'since he has been sent to Britannia and made a general without my say-so.'

Hieronymus shifted guiltily.

'Has he not?'

'I know nothing about that,' he said, unconvincingly.

'Where did you learn this?' asked Damocles.

'I have my sources. I am aware of what happens behind my back. But I won't remain seated as my cousin attempts to claw back power. I will assert my control over the military by accepting women soldiers.'

'You barely have sway with the Senate as it is,' said Damocles. 'Do you really believe they will approve such a radical notion?'

'They elected me.'

'Only after the intervention of a deity. Unless you plan a repeat performance to convince the people?'

'Perhaps you could hear me out before you attempt to persuade me of what a terrible plan it is?' she said.

Damocles cleared his throat. 'Yes, of course.'

'If we must,' huffed Hieronymus.

'The military is struggling to make progress in Britannia,' said Claudia. 'Hibernia is beyond us. We have reached stalemate in Germania. Arabia remains impenetrable. An entire legion is missing – thousands of soldiers, spirited into the abyss. Many naval ships were lost in the Vesuvian crisis. We are living in a time of peace, but peace is easily lost.'

'We are well aware,' grumbled Hieronymus.

'I don't believe in endless conquest, war for the sake of dominion. I'd rather the empire move towards a period of global stability, maintaining what we already have rather than endlessly chasing more. But the borders would be better defended if we were to allow women to serve alongside men,' said Claudia.

Hieronymus made an offensive noise, halfway between a scoff and a hoot, his furry grey brows hitting his receding hairline.

'It is inconceivable,' he said. 'The generals will protest.'

'Won't they be grateful for more soldiers, once they get over their pig-headedness?' she said.

'These women would all need to be trained, and equipped, and fitted with armour,' said Damocles. 'It will take time to organize.'

'The same is true of all new recruits,' she said. 'Every soldier in every legion is trained and fitted out, just the same. You don't mean to tell me the empire is short on gold?'

'General Aquinas won't like this,' said Hieronymus.

'Then it is a good thing it isn't up to him.'

'What would happen if thousands of women were to die at war?

Who will raise the children of Rome while their parents are out fighting for the empire?' asked Hieronymus.

'Women don't exist just to be your vessels,' said Claudia. 'Our soldiers have families. Our wealthy patricians have servants to raise their babies. It does not define them.'

'What makes you think the women of Rome wish to fight?' asked Damocles. 'Your friend here may be the exception.'

Hieronymus glared at Gia, as if she were personally responsible for this state of affairs.

'Rome has its own fighting women,' said Claudia. 'I'm funding a new school for gladiatrices.'

'Fighting in the amphitheatre is very different to fighting a war. The women might find that they aren't inclined to it.'

'Women are not a monolith. The life of a soldier can be an unpleasant one, but they are entitled to certain privileges. They are paid well. They travel and see the world. I'm sure there are slaves and brothel girls who would prefer it to their current circumstances. We should at least give women the option, to fight as men do and earn their freedom.'

'The Senate will never allow it,' said Hieronymus.

Claudia's eye twitched. She clenched her hands, resting on the arms on the golden eagle throne.

'Then I will not give them the chance to object,' said Claudia. 'As empress, it is my right to overrule them, if I think it best.'

'You can't just upend the very structure that the stability of our society rests on,' said Hieronymus.

'I think you'll find I can, actually,' she snapped. 'Or did you think the former emperor was merely decorative?'

'Perhaps we should revisit this later,' said Damocles.

'You act as if every emperor is wise, every senator is just and every soldier brave, just by virtue of being male,' Claudia said.

'Men are made for such things,' said Hieronymus. 'They have the necessary constitution.'

'If that was true, you wouldn't be so threatened by the prospect of women taking rank alongside you,' she said.

She felt that heat rising inside her again, her insides churning.

'And that's not all,' she said. 'If women can fight and rule, then they should also stand in the Senate.'

They gaped at her.

'Spare me from this insanity, I beg you,' said Hieronymus.

'What does Marcellus think of this?' asked Damocles.

'I have not consulted him. Why would I?'

The two men exchanged glances.

'And your fiancé, the prince?' said Damocles. 'What if he objects and it threatens your union?'

'It has nothing to do with him,' said Claudia. 'I am the ruler, and not them. I do not need a man's approval. I will hear their objections *after* I have made the announcement, but not before.'

'Perhaps now is not the time for such bold moves, Empress,' said Damocles. 'There has already been an attempt on your life. Your grip on Rome is tenuous, at best. We must move slowly, carefully, like a cunning predator in pursuit. It's important to keep the Senate pacified, and not risk enraging them, like kicking a hornet's nest.'

'History is made by people being brave.'

'You don't know what you're talking about,' spat Hieronymus, shaking his wrinkly jowls. 'You will offend the gods themselves, with your modernist nonsense. You know nothing about the Senate or the army.'

'And my dear brother did?' said Claudia. 'You were happy to serve him, weren't you? What about him did you find most convincing? His long military service, or his astute understanding of geopolitics?'

Hieronymus merely grumbled under his breath.

'I don't remember you objecting when Decimus declared that only Jupiter would be worshipped, or that Vulcan's festival would be replaced with one honouring him. Where were you then?'

'I was arranging your father's funeral,' he said darkly. 'You didn't seem to take much interest in it.'

'Hold your tongue,' said Gia, 'or I shall cut it out.'

'You will not speak to me like that, street rat,' said Hieronymus. 'The empress may tolerate your vulgarity, but I cannot.'

'We are getting off-track,' said Damocles nervously.

Claudia scowled, fury branding her neck red.

'You know where the door is, Hieronymus,' she said.

'Excuse me?' he said.

'If you object so strenuously, you're welcome to leave.'

'You need me,' he said. 'Who else would agree to serve you?'

'Your employment is merely a kindness to the old man I remember from my childhood. A familiar face, that's what you are, Hieronymus. Nothing more. You are certainly not here for your great wisdom or efficiency. Perhaps I'll choose a woman to advise me instead.'

'I didn't think you could possibly be madder than your brother, but you have surprised me,' he said.

Claudia's temper snapped.

'Go. You are banished from the palace.'

He stared at her, reddening, his face contorting with rage.

'We will see what the Senate has to say about this.'

The elder man shuffled away, bristling in rage.

No one dared to speak for a full minute, before Damocles sheepishly raised his hand like a schoolboy.

'Empress, if I might say – moving too far and too fast would be a mistake. Change must come slowly, or the people will revolt.'

'Why is it such a world-changing notion, that women might represent the people? Are they incapable of sitting in the curia and bickering, as the male senators do?' she said.

'I did not say that,' said Damocles. 'Personally, I would enjoy having a woman or two on the benches.'

'A woman or two?'

'To begin with,' he said, raising one finger cautiously. 'Let's not go crazy. But the process of being nominated, as it stands, would disqualify any woman who wishes to stand.'

'That is exactly the problem,' said Claudia.

'You are already out of favour with the people. This would certainly be pushing the limit,' he said.

'The people may not like me, but at least I can distract them with bread and circuses,' she said.

'Meaning?'

'I have been thinking about it all night, and I've come up with what I think is an enterprising plan.'

Damocles readied himself with a sigh. 'Go on.'

'We will create a new public holiday, to make the announcement,' said Claudia. 'I will consult with the priestess of the Cult of Diana. I gather that Meditrina, the patron goddess of wine, doesn't have a festival yet. We shall dedicate a day to her. We'll host ceremonial games, at the Circus Maximus: gladiator battles and chariot races. All of the usual sacrifices and rituals. I'll make an appearance with the prince and give the impression that we'll confirm our union soon. That will distract people from the rumours. It will be a suitably celebratory occasion. By the time I make my proclamation, the public may be in a more altruistic mood. I'll make sure everyone is merry before I . . . What did Hieronymus say? "*Upend the very structure of society*"? Well, that is exactly what I intend to do.'

'Then it shall be so, Empress,' said Damocles. 'Though I must warn you that you will have a thousand knives pointed at your back.'

'I already do.' She stood, straightening her shoulders with steely determination. 'That is all for now.'

Out in the courtyard, Gia and Claudia stared into the burbling fountain with its frolicking water nymphs.

'You weren't kidding when you said you would do something drastic,' Gia said, shaking her head slightly.

'An empress must live a little dangerously.'

'If you had a target on your back before, it will triple in size now,' said Gia.

'As long as the target is on me, and not you.'

Gia sighed heavily, as if burdened by thoughts she didn't share.

'Besides, I must do something,' Claudia added, to fill the silence. 'With the prince conspiring against me and Marcellus rising in rank in the army, I fear my reign will be shorter than I even envisioned. They will find a way to oust me and I won't get the chance to change history. If anyone is to remember what we stood for, then I must act now, before it's too late. I must do what I promised and serve the goddesses well.'

'They might attempt to prevent you from making the announcement,' said Gia, her brows knotting in concern.

‘They can try.’

‘Are you sure it is worth it?’ she said.

‘This is it. I have crossed the Rubicon. There is no turning back now. If we must fight a war with the gods, we will need an army of women at our side,’ said Claudia. ‘And I am the only one who can empower them.’

On the day of Meditrinalia, the colossal stadium of the Circus Maximus was packed to full capacity, creating a riotous, deafening crescendo of sound that carried throughout the city. The bars, restaurants, shops and brothels that surrounded it bustled with customers, all jovial and red-faced in the cool air, clinking glasses and singing, chanting prayers for good health.

Shaped like a squashed, elongated oval, the stadium had a strong and pungent aroma – of sand, sweat and blood. Here, Romans watched wild hunts and chariot races, the wooden benches teeming with people in togas and makeshift wreaths. A river’s worth of wine was provided, free of charge, for attendees, who eagerly filled the seats, whistling and stamping their feet, drinking from jugs they passed between rows and eating from baskets of hazelnuts, dates, olives and bread.

They knew who to thank, too, along with the goddess – as Claudia’s insignia was branded on every cup, bowl and vase. Every shield, every flag, every standard, every coin: they all bore her insignia.

Claudia was feeling positive. By the time she arrived, the people were merry enough to cheer for her, waving a rainbow of flags as her cult of women chanted in reverence. She was at the peak of her power, and she was about to make good use of it.

No one was talking about the play, or the prince, or the missing legion. Other than a few calls of 'Lesbionicus', all was well, in the political sense, at least. In her personal life, she was holding on by a thread.

As they climbed the stairs to the imperial box, Claudia looked to Gia beside her, but her guard's attention was elsewhere, keeping watch of the feral, intoxicated crowd.

Gia had been distant ever since Claudia had asked to sleep alone. That uncrossed space between them made her ache, though she tried not to let it show. She had created the problem between them, and she had no right to pity herself for it.

'Are you sure you're ready for this?' came a voice.

Claudia turned to see Rectina, smiling tautly.

'Not really,' said Claudia.

The elder woman was dressed more regally than usual, wearing the orange robes Hieronymus had once donned as Claudia's advisor. She'd asked Rectina to replace his vacant role with little notice, and Rectina had reluctantly said yes, out of love for her and nothing else.

'For what it's worth, I already see you as a senator,' Claudia had told her. 'You're more qualified in mind than most men on the benches.'

'I shall do my best for you, but I fear the odds are against us.'

Rectina was the only woman of status Claudia knew well enough to approach, and her connections meant she had influence of her own. Still, Claudia was drawing more people into the imperial web, putting them in danger. Gia, Cassius, Dominic, Athena, Rectina: they were all here because of her in some way, and under threat.

In the present, Rectina squeezed her hand.

'When you make the announcement, you should prepare for a hostile reaction,' she said.

'Is there any other kind?'

'The people might seem welcoming now, but they can turn on the flip of a coin. I've seen it happen too many times.'

'As long as they do not kill me immediately, I shall consider it a grand success,' said Claudia.

Rectina and Pliny accompanied her in the imperial box, which was dressed with garlands and equipped with a banquet table. Here sat a group of her 'courtiers', so to speak, including Dominic, Celadus and the child, Athena, dressed in a makeshift gladiator costume.

She quickly engaged Gia in a conversation about her upcoming match against Livia the Legendary.

Surrounded by a squadron of guards holding flags and spears and shields, the box was raised above the rest of the seating, allowing them a better view of the action.

The crowd rippled, an endless sea of heads, as the prince arrived, surrounded by his own colourful parade of courtiers.

Some men in the crowd whispered and sneered at his approach, recounting past battles between Persians and Romans. The prince was powerful, feared by some, but there was still an undercurrent of racism that burbled beneath the surface. Though Persian customs and culture had bled into Roman society, though Romans and Persians could be friendly on the face of it, when conflicts arose, they quickly made strangers of each other. Many Romans viewed their empire as inherently superior, no matter how tirelessly they complained about it.

She was a woman and he was a foreigner. Both of them were outsiders, even though she had been born into this world.

e took his seat with a sweeping bow, thinking

' found.

ities are dedicated to wine?' he asked, as

him a glass.

, a fair few,' said Claudia. 'There's Bacchus, and Liber Pater. Then there's Abundatia. Making ale is one of Aristaeus's many talents, too.'

'I do not know this one,' said Darius.

'The patron of handicrafts and beekeeping.'

He smiled. 'You Romans have a deity for everything. There is not a thing mortals can do without deities as your patrons.'

'They do like to get involved.'

After the military band reached their crescendo of drums, Claudia raised her hand to signal the commencement of the games. The crowd roared in response.

The power she held in her palm was enormous, pulsating, but it was prickly too. She could feel the weight of it, the edges.

A series of athletic events followed, with men throwing javelins and discuses. The Romans had adopted the Grecian Olympic tradition and all of the competitors were training for the summer games next year, but this was merely a warm-up for the real meat and bones of the event: the gladiatorial combat and chariot races. Still, the crowd was appreciative, cheering the victors and booing the losers.

Gia nudged her arm.

'I'm going to get ready now,' she said, 'for the match.'

'Oh, good luck,' said Claudia. 'You won't need it though.'

'Don't speak too soon. Livia scares me.'

'And me, but she has not met Viatrix the Victoriou
know I will be cheering the loudest for you, as always.'

They exchanged one of those laden looks again, full of jo
sorrow entwined: the distance between them, and the pull.

'Be safe,' she said. 'As safe as is possible, for a gladiator.'

Claudia felt a strange tightness in her chest as Gia disappeared down the steps, leaving her to eavesdrop on the conversation Darius and Cassius were having, taking bets on which competitor would win.

'I admire the grace and strength of the sport but I lack the competitive nature that drives athletes to compete,' the prince was saying. 'I am too lazy. I have been proficient in many things in my life, and many of them came easily, but I bore very quickly of being the best.'

'A terrible problem to have,' said Cassius. 'Poor thing.'

'Yes, I am very tragic.'

'I always took an interest in the games, ever since I was a boy,' mused Cassius. 'My father took us. It was the favourite part of my week. There is something delightfully carnal about the wrestling.'

'So much writhing.'

'And grunting. Who could forget the grunting?'

'And the gentle smacking of flapping arse cheeks.'

The two men burst into laughter.

Claudia applauded nervously when Gia stepped out to face the Roman gladiatrix, Livia, attempting to assemble her expression into a normal arrangement of empress-watching-her-guard-fight.

As a native Roman, Livia had considerable advantage with the home crowd. She already had her supporters here in the capital city, people who waved her flag and chanted her name, but this support could only be a good thing, if Claudia was to enact the change she dreamed of.

They each took turns to salute her.

When Gia met her eye, Claudia felt the heady squeeze of all of the tension and longing between them, making her happy and sad, comforted and distressed, everything in one.

A sudden throb of panic clutched at her heart – a cold, clammy feeling that sank deep into her guts.

Something bad was going to happen.

'Go, Viatrix!' said Athena.

She wore Dominic's gladiator helmet as part of her costume. It was far too big, falling down over her eyes.

Gia hadn't fought properly since the day she killed her mentor, Cyrus, though Claudia knew she'd trained several times with the girls from the new Ludus Victoria. She was taller than Livia by almost half a foot, but as soon as the horn sounded, the smaller girl lashed out in a vicious frenzy that had Gia defending immediately.

Their delicate grunts echoed across the circuit, in the centre of the racing track.

'Remember what I told you, about being small,' said Dominic.

'I don't care any more; I just want Gia to win!' wailed Athena.

The two girls were sparring, bantering back and forth, but Claudia was too far away to hear what was being said. From the look on Gia's face, it was a friendly fight between two respectful competitors, though Livia had a wildness about her, a ferocity that made Claudia anxious.

She was suddenly fearful that Gia might become injured, with the way Livia whirled her sword like a toothpick. Her heart pounded when their swords began to clash, wiping her clammy palms on the folds of her robes. The bad feeling intensified, becoming thick and solid.

But once Gia found her rhythm, Claudia remembered why she enjoyed watching her fight so much. It was the most fluid of dances, arcing and flowing like moving waters, yet Gia was always purposeful, always dynamic, her muscles flexing as she defended a hit.

While previously she'd worn her braid loose, now it was tied up in a tight knot at the back of her head. Claudia felt a wave of desire, but the collective gasps from the Circus Maximus kept her drawn to the action.

Unlike her opponent, Gia still chose to fight without a shield, making her lighter and faster, but leaving her open to attack. One close call saw Livia's blade skim past her shoulder as she ducked away. Another hit grazed the smooth skin on Gia's thigh. Claudia clutched her hands to her face, regretting telling Gia she didn't need luck.

Athena pulled her robes up over her head. Dominic was talking to himself, narrating Gia's next move as Cyrus had once done. Cassius used some words Athena had surely never heard before, and one that was new to Claudia too. She exhaled noisily when the flow of the battle returned to Gia's favour, her attack causing Livia to stumble and retreat.

When Gia went down, falling awkwardly, Claudia got to her feet. Though she tried to keep her composure, she couldn't prevent herself from crying out, her hands clutched together in prayer.

Gia scrambled upright, limping slightly, and struck out until Livia tired. With a thrashing tumble of limbs, Gia had Livia pinned to the ground, the tip of her sword to Livia's throat as the referee counted down, poised in the moment of the final strike.

There was something unexpectedly intimate about the pose, their eyes locked together, their bodies touching in a dozen different places, as if they were fused together.

It reminded Claudia of when Gia taught her to fight, and how she'd tripped them on purpose to get closer to her. She was relieved when they broke apart.

'Viatrix the Victorious is the winner!' called the referee, hoisting Gia's arm into the air.

Claudia exhaled, clutching her chest. 'Thank goddess.'

The audience exploded into cheers of success and defeat, depending on which fighter they'd made bets on. Athena jumped up and screamed, as did Cassius, while Claudia put her fingers in her mouth to whistle in a most un-empress-like way.

Livia threw down her shield in frustration, only to pick it up moments later and go back to shake Gia's hand.

Claudia was too far away to present her with a wreath, or even give congratulations, watching Gia disappear into the bellows beneath them.

'I think you may be on to something here,' said Darius.

'Sorry?' said Claudia, startled by his sudden presence at her side.

'Your women gladiators. Your guard was most impressive . . . Perhaps I could teach her the Persian fighting style.'

'That's my sister,' boasted Cassius.

'You said, yes,' said Darius, amused.

The tension in her shoulders returned. All was well and yet the bad feeling continued to plague her, rolling her stomach in waves. It was nearly time for her speech, conveniently sandwiched between the gladiatorial combat and the chariot races.

'Is it too late to persuade you to change your mind?' asked Damocles, in a low voice. 'I really would advise it.'

'Unfortunately, I am very stubborn,' she said. 'Besides, the deed is done. The banners have already been embroidered, as they say. It's in the hands of Fortuna and the Fates now.'

'Then on your head be it, Empress . . . preferably not mounted on a spike and paraded around the Forum.'

'And now, you will hear a proclamation from the empress herself,' announced the host. 'Please rise for Claudia Imperia Caesaria.'

Thousands of soldiers saluted in perfect unison as the crowd took to their feet, applauding dutifully. It wasn't exultant applause, but it was convivial enough.

When the host gestured, Claudia stepped onto the golden stairs provided for her and addressed the vast audience in their enormous ring, her voice amplified by servants holding bone bullhorns.

'Happy Meditrinalia!' she began, to raucous cheers.

Claudia wore her most ostentatious regalia, draped in purple silk, with gold and jewels covering every expanse of skin, her hair sculpted around the imperial victory crown.

She delivered a short prayer in Latin dedicated to Meditrina, during which a casket of wine was tossed on a ceremonial fire.

Claudia could feel the energy of the crowd flowing through her. Their sound, their smell, the endless wall of faces. The people sitting on the other side of the stadium were merely a blur. She smiled fixedly, waiting for the noise of the crowd to die down before continuing.

'Today marks not just a new festival in our calendar, in honour of Meditrina and the healing powers of wine . . .'

Several attendees raised their chalices in cheers.

Claudia paused, looking up at the grey sky. She had hoped the deity might appear to cement her reign, as Victoria had done before her, but the clouds did not part, nor did the sun's rays shine through.

'. . . but also, the dawn of a new era for Rome.'

A lone heckler yelled something she couldn't make out. She took a deep, steadying breath, trying not to lose her nerve.

'A great empire should not be left behind to the sands of time,' Claudia roared, channelling the lioness on her heraldic shield. 'It must keep moving, rolling forwards like the wheels of a chariot.'

The crowd eagerly cheered this mention of a chariot, keen to move on to the races.

'We must not fear change, but embrace it,' she said. 'We must not fear new ideas, but build upon them.'

Out of the corner of her eye, Claudia saw that Gia had finally made her way up to the imperial box, standing in position behind her. Claudia paused, momentarily losing her thread of thought as her heart surged and tilted, but her presence gave Claudia the courage to go on. She took a deep breath, clenching her hands at her sides.

'As ruler of Rome, I will serve every soldier and senator, just as he serves me. But as the first empress, I also carry the hopes and dreams of every woman in the empire.'

A distant shout preoccupied her. Claudia gazed out at the blurry crowd, unable to pinpoint the source of the sound.

'I have a responsibility to all of them, and to all of you,' she said, looking straight ahead. 'I intend to improve the life of every citizen of Rome, beginning with the rights of women. The right to serve, the right to fight, and the right to rule.'

The men in the audience rumbled with concern and disapproval but Claudia was sure that almost every woman in the audience was listening attentively, no matter what they thought of her.

'As I speak, our men are fighting overseas. Some will come into combat with warrior women, just like the gladiators you've seen today.'

'What about the missing legion?' someone yelled.

'Where are our men?'

'Women from other nations are defending their fortresses and commanding battles, and they are winning,' said Claudia, as the crowd murmured. 'The empire is quickly falling behind. Our goddesses are warriors, yet the women of Rome are kept apart from power.'

She could hear the generals grumbling inaudibly behind her, as her confidence began to falter.

'Why should women be denied the opportunity to rise above their current ranks?' said Claudia. 'Why should only men sit upon the highest stratus of our society? We women are being denied our swords, our titles and our crowns.'

The audience murmured again as the heckler bellowed across the crowd once more, something like 'Mort', or 'mare'?

'For too long, we have stood at the sidelines, with no control over our own destinies. That will change today.'

She felt Prince Darius stirring beside her, turning towards her, though she couldn't make out his expression.

'That is why, from this day forward, women will be permitted to enlist in the army and navy.'

The crowd silenced, burbling softly for a moment before a light scattering of shocked applause resounded. Waves of shock moved in ripples, people turning to each other in disbelief.

'Those who are interested should report to the civic hall, or to their nearest fort for training,' she said.

'Murderer!'

That was the word the heckler was shouting.

Claudia became aware of the growing noise in the stadium, but she carried on speaking, raising her voice each time the heckler interrupted.

'Beginning next year, a limited number of women will also be appointed by the Consul to serve in the Senate.'

The cheering morphed into a roar, the sound becoming spikier.

Damocles shifted uncomfortably, mopping his sweaty bald dome as the noise trebled, a battle of cheers and boos that bled together to create a cacophony.

'Why doesn't she join up to fight herself if she's so keen?'

'Has she ever even seen a battlefield?'

'They won't take our daughters as well as our sons.'

Claudia cleared her throat, trying to blot out the sound.

'We must take the example of the goddesses whose statues are installed around our city.'

Her support was increasing along with her opposition, led by the Cult of Diana. Many women hung on her words, their eyes glazed with visions of what they might be, if they could be anything.

'We must don armour, like them, and bear arms, like them, to stand alongside the men, and take our rightful place in history.'

When Claudia looked to Athena, she was gazing at her in awe.

It was all worth it, she reminded herself. Even if she died. Even if she lost everything. It would all be worth it, for girls like her.

'For I am not just the empress of men,' she said, turning back to face the crowd. 'I am the empress of your daughters, of your sisters and mothers and grandmothers . . . I am the empress of all women.'

Many in the crowd cheered, until a lone voice cut through.

'Murderer! She's a murderer!'

Claudia scanned the crowd again, closing in on the objector causing a ruckus. It was her former advisor Hieronymus, being escorted out by four armed guards.

'Claudia Caesaria killed her father, and her brother too!' he said. 'We know the truth!'

The audience *ooh*ed, scandalized.

'I will prove it! Get your hands off me! Don't you know who I am? I served the emperor Tiberius. *He* was a real leader!'

His voice faded as they dragged him away.

Claudia reapplied a well-practised smile. She would not give him the satisfaction of visibly disturbing her, though inside she felt as if she had been punched in the stomach by Hercules.

'Today is a day of celebration and victory,' she said, 'so I shall keep your attention no longer. Let us thank the goddess Meditrina, pray for good fortune, and, most importantly, enjoy the races!'

Another hesitant cheer, another tremulous pause.

'All hail the empress!' chanted the Cult of Diana, faintly, under a fluttering of boos.

The band began to play, though Claudia was still standing. The host reappeared. The momentum of the event moved forward, like the wheels of the chariots now riding out to roars of applause, and Claudia's moment to change the world was over.

She waited for a response but there was none. Nothing. Some whispering. Some glances. Yet there was no instant outpouring of support, nor any violent retaliation. It was strangely anticlimactic.

Claudia remained on her feet, stuck in time, as everyone else sat down. She didn't know if she should be embarrassed or triumphant. She had imagined protest, mockery, perhaps even a riot. What she *hadn't* imagined was that she'd fail to make a mark at all; that the games would go on as if she hadn't spoken a word. Perhaps Damocles was right, about change. She had moved so far and so fast, she had not left an impact.

'They're not taking me seriously,' she said quietly.

'They will,' said Rectina, ushering her back into her seat. 'It takes people time, to reconfigure their minds.'

'The people of Rome are used to hot air,' said Pliny the Elder, 'to emperors making proclamations that never come to fruition. You will show them in your actions, in your deeds.'

'It went better than *I* expected, I must say,' said Damocles, mopping his brow.

'You were brilliant, just as I knew you would be,' said Gia, standing behind her.

Claudia turned, her gaze lingering as she suppressed the urge to touch her or take her hand.

'I want to be empress one day!' said Athena, who'd taken off her gladiator helmet and donned a makeshift sash.

'You can take over as advisor after me,' said Rectina.

'Wow, really?'

Who would rule after her, Claudia wondered, should she live long enough to appoint an heir? But the thought lasted only a minute before her attention was demanded elsewhere.

As the chariot races continued, Claudia tried to relax, watching as the vehicles charged past the lap markers shaped like eggs and dolphins, as water was sprayed on the dusty track, as the competitors wove around bollards, their chariots leaning dangerously to one side, as the thunder of horses and applause filled the arena.

'I fear I underestimated you once again,' said the prince, under the noise of celebrant cheering.

'Are you impressed?'

'You're either very stupid or very brave.'

She blinked at him rapidly. 'Thank you, Darius. I shall take that as a compliment.'

'It was intended as one. Brave, stupid people have done much good in the world.'

'Wise words, as always.'

'I find that we are in unison. I have the same vision, one in which men and women are both free, to live truly. I do not know if it is possible, within our lifetimes, but I admire your ambitions.'

Claudia opened her mouth to reply when something whistled past her ear, in motion like a small bird.

She brought one hand up to her face reflexively.

'What was that?' she said.

A dull grunt behind her alerted her to a bug-eyed guard with a golden arrow poking out of his neck.

Blood poured from the wound, splattering her robes as he collapsed at her feet. One of her handmaids screamed as an arrow struck the empty seat beside her.

It all unfolded in the space of a heartbeat.

Claudia looked out at the race track, watching first with confusion, then horror, as the charioteers turned on the audience, firing arrows into the crowd.

The entertainment had turned on them.

She heard a missile tearing through the air before Gia jolted against her, shoving her to the floor.

Her face smashed into the ground as the Circus Maximus erupted into chaos.

14. THE PRINCE'S PLOT

Claudia's ears rang, the edges of her vision feathered.

For a moment, she couldn't remember where she was, who she was or what was happening.

The picture gradually filled in as she recalled, in a slippery thick of sweat, that she was being fired at.

She felt a body pressed against hers.

'Gia?'

Claudia tried to rouse her, but her eyes were closed.

'GIA!'

Gia was bleeding from somewhere, knocked unconscious by the bench as they'd fallen, both of them crushed to the ground as people toppled around them, shouting and shrieking and stamping on each other. Claudia could see a wound in Gia's arm. She reached out to touch it, as ice-cold dread stilled her heart.

Claudia stared at her palms, Gia's blood running between the creases, just like on the night she killed her brother.

She stood up in a jolt of blind panic, just in time to see an arrow sailing unstoppably towards her. She screamed and twisted her body, covering her eyes on instinct as a loud *thwack* sounded.

She . . . she wasn't hit.

Gasping in ragged fear, she saw the prince standing in front of her, holding his spear and shield. He'd knocked the arrow out of her path, putting his body between her and harm.

'Run,' he said.

He was defending her.

'It's an ambush!' trilled Damocles, as another arrow struck a member of the crowd. 'We must exit, at once!'

'Everyone, out!'

People in the crowd screamed feverishly, climbing over each other in their haste to escape – particularly those in the benches surrounding the imperial box.

At the same time, a wave of soldiers descended on the track, engaging in combat with the firing charioteers.

Gia was still out cold. Claudia met eyes with Cassius.

'Help me with her!' she shouted.

Cassius pulled Gia into a sitting position. Roman and Persian guards formed a canopy above them with their shields. Prince Darius passed her a dagger, which Claudia used to tear a generous strip from her imperial robes. Rectina tied it tightly around the arrow-wound on Gia's arm, following instructions from Pliny.

Gia began to gain consciousness, murmuring softly, her eyes unfocused as Claudia cupped her face.

'You're going to be okay. Do you hear me? That's an order.'

Another arrow hurtled towards Cassius, but it was intercepted by Darius, who dived into his path to repel it.

'That was close,' said Cassius. 'I am lucky you are here, eh?'

They exchanged a soft, curious look, but Claudia didn't have time to analyse it.

A guttural cry sounded and the prince's advisor, Mehdi, toppled over, an arrow in his chest.

'No,' said Darius, rushing over to him. 'Not Mehdi, no.'

Medhi reached out to stroke the prince's face tenderly.

'Darius, my boy . . .'

His hand dropped, his eyes frozen open.

Mehdi was dead. Before she could process this, another arrow struck the bench beside Claudia, bouncing off. It came to a standstill next to her sandalled foot.

The arrow's fletching resembled a thunderbolt, just like the knife she'd found.

'Go! Now!' screamed Damocles, seizing the dead guard's sword. 'Get the empress out of here!'

Claudia quickly bundled the arrow up into the material of her shroud and helped Cassius pull Gia up onto her feet.

Shielded by a formation of guards, they were hustled out of the imperial box, as Dom carried Athena. The prince shielded them at the rear, briefly looking back at his dead advisor as the panicked crowd trampled over his body.

Numb and dazed, Claudia ran forwards, through the gardens and out into the street, barely aware of anything but Gia, injured beside her.

'Just hold on,' she said, as Cassius propped her up. 'We'll be out of here soon. We'll get you help.'

Gia was pale, her eyes half closed.

Looking back, Claudia saw praetorian guards dragging one of the men who'd fired arrows, but she didn't recognize him. Another man escaped, vanishing into the crowd.

They were just paid servants of a greater master, like the man at the Pantheon. Whoever was pulling the strings was someone unseen, working in shadows, hidden from view.

'Bring him to the palace,' she yelled at the guards. 'I will want to question him, as soon as possible.'

People poured out of the Circus Maximus, screaming and waving. They thought the city was being invaded, despite attempts by the praetorian guards to calm them. Their sudden, panicked appearance in the Forum caused chaos to spread quickly, as citizens ran at the sight of so many charging guards, with no clue what was happening. They fled, some leaving their sandals behind.

Claudia and Gia were bundled into an imperial chariot by Damocles, for safety, though the palace was in walking distance. Cassius climbed in alongside her, followed by the prince and his grizzled-looking guard, who was weeping uncontrollably, praying in Persian.

It was far too many people to fit comfortably, all of them squashed up against each other and panting like dogs. She could smell the sweat of fear, mixed with wine, dirt and blood. The terrible perfume of the Circus Maximus clung to their robes.

Dom, Athena, Rectina and Pliny climbed into another chariot, which followed behind.

As they pulled away, Claudia noticed that several women had taken up arms, guarding the chariot next to the gladiators Livia and Dido as they made their procession along the street.

Dido saw Claudia passing by and . . . saluted.

Maybe her words had taken hold in some small way, despite the catastrophe that followed.

When Claudia looked back to Gia, she was staring at her.

'You're here,' she said, dazed.

'Where else would I be, but by your side?' said Claudia.

It all seemed so stupid and pointless now – all that fear that had come between them. She'd come so close to losing her. But here was the proof that she was in grave danger beside her. Claudia had tried to push Gia away, yet she was still bleeding. Sleeping apart had made no difference. It had not been enough distance to protect her.

'You're okay,' said Gia. 'I thought they hit you.'

'No, all thanks to you. You took an arrow for me. I would be absolutely furious with you, if I wasn't so worried.'

Gia inspected the wound on her arm, wincing in pain.

'Ouch, fuck, that hurts,' she hissed.

'You hit your head, too,' said Claudia, gently inspecting the bloodied part of her hair. 'I'll take you to the palace physician.'

'Is anyone else hurt?' she asked.

Claudia thought of the guard, bleeding from the neck.

'Don't worry about them right now,' said Cassius.

Gia's eyes flashed wide, remembering.

'Dom . . . Athena . . . Dido and Livia . . .'

'They're okay. They're all okay. I've got you.'

Claudia squeezed her hand.

'What did I tell you, sister?' said Cassius, with tears in his eyes. 'I knew you'd get hurt eventually.'

'It's okay, Cass.'

'You cannot do it to me. You can't leave me here alone.'

'Brother,' Gia said weakly.

Claudia and Cassius met eyes again. For a moment, whatever animosity existed between them melted away, united by their shared concern for Gia's wellbeing.

And then Gia saw the prince sitting beside them.

'You,' she said, sitting upright, face twisting in horror. '*You* did this, didn't you?'

'Is she delirious?' asked the prince.

'Please forgive her, your majesty. She *did* hit her head,' said Cassius, making eyes at Gia. 'What day is it, sister? What is your name?'

'I know exactly what I'm saying,' said Gia.

'I can assure you, I am not involved,' said the prince. 'How can you even think it? My own advisor is dead.'

'Prince Darius saved us all,' said Claudia, jumping in to avoid a diplomatic affray, on top of everything. She had seen the fear in his eyes as he defended her, the sorrow in his face as he grieved his advisor. The prince was innocent, she was sure of it. 'He defended us during the attack.'

'That was convenient,' said Gia.

'He is not the enemy we are looking for,' she said.

Claudia tried to give her a '*please stop talking*' look but Gia didn't pick up on it.

'What about the knife?' she said.

'What knife?' said Darius.

'The one I found in your room,' said Gia.

'When have you been in my room?' he said, his eyes darkening.

'The other day, on the orders of the empress.'

Claudia swallowed as the prince looked to her.

'You can explain this?' he said.

'It is exactly as it sounds,' she admitted. 'I didn't know if you could be trusted, so I sent my guard to perform security checks when you were otherwise occupied.'

'The important mission,' said Darius, nodding in recollection, 'when we watched that terrible play. That was why you sent Cassius here to distract me instead, am I right?'

Cassius bit his lip guiltily.

'In my defence,' he said, 'it was a pleasure.'

'She recovered a knife,' said Claudia.

'I have many knives.'

'The same kind was used in an attack on the empress,' said Gia.

'No. You are confused.'

'I saw it with my own eyes,' insisted Gia. 'We have hard evidence against you. You cannot deny it.'

Claudia was rapidly losing control of the situation. Outside, the streets were still in chaos, the noise of disorder ringing aloud.

'You're a snake,' said Gia.

'You dare to call me a serpent?' said Darius.

'What other kind of man would come to Rome to claim the girl promised to him when she was just a child?'

'I too was a child.'

'You are no different to Marcellus. No better, thinking women are prizes for you to win.'

They eyeballed each other with outright hostility, their hands sliding towards their weapons.

'Let us all take a breath,' Claudia said. 'This isn't the time to—'

'If you spoke these words to me back in Persepolis, you would not wake to see tomorrow,' said Darius.

'You may have fooled her, but you won't fool me,' said Gia. 'You set it up so you could look like a hero and win her favour.'

'You are wrong.'

'Then go home. Leave. Us. Alone. You are not needed here.'

'Gia, please,' warned Claudia.

'Is it so?' he snarled. 'You were not much use as a guard, when the moment came. If not for me, your mistress would be dead.'

Mistress – like the owner of a slave. Gia moved as if to jump him but Cassius held her back.

'That's enough!' Claudia shouted. 'We will talk about the matter in due course but we will not behave with such indignity, not when we have just been shot at, not when people are dead or injured.'

The prince took a deep, steadying breath, holding up his palms in a gesture of peace.

'Luckily, I have an appreciation for snakes,' he said. 'Wise and noble creatures. You could learn much from them.' He curled his lip at Gia. 'I will not forget this, but I will not fight you when you are injured either.'

'Surely there has been some kind of misunderstanding,' said Cassius, looking back and forth between Gia and the prince.

'There is no mistake,' said Gia. 'The knife was hidden among his belongings . . . I hope you don't trust him over me?'

Cassius looked to the prince again, then back to her, conflicted.

'I would normally trust you over anyone on Earth,' said Cassius. 'But you must admit that your judgement is somewhat compromised lately. When it comes to her . . .' Cassius looked to Claudia, pointedly. 'You are not logical at all. Your heart rules your head.'

Gia fell silent, frowning deeply.

'You asked me to befriend the prince and earn his trust,' said Cassius, turning to Claudia. 'I did as you asked, and I have seen nothing but a good man, with noble intentions. I have nothing bad to say about him.'

'Thank you, Cassius,' said Darius, his dark eyes shining.

The chariot grew uncomfortably quiet, the silence interrupted only by the prince's weeping guard.

Gia reclined on a bench in the office of the palace physician, who asked her to follow his fingers with her eyes.

Claudia paced anxiously back and forth in front of the window, wringing her hands as Cassius sat in a chair nearby.

'What's your name?' asked the physician.

'Via Galerii,' said Gia. 'No, Gia Valerii.' When Claudia goggled at her in alarm, Gia shook her head, raising one finger. 'That was just a slip of the tongue. I'm fine. I know my own name, obviously.'

'Hmm,' said the physician, his brow furrowing. 'Where do you think you are right now, Gia?'

Gia gazed around the room, evidently trying to anchor herself by her surroundings.

On the desk, a scroll about dream interpretation had been laid open next to one of Pliny's works. In an alcove, a candle smoked.

'The palace?' she said. 'In Rome? I've never been in this room before, but I presume it's the valetudinaria.'

'That's correct. And tell me, what year is it?'

'It's the year Pompeii erupted.' She looked at Claudia, her face settling with clarity. 'The year of the first empress. That was the next question you were going to ask me, right?'

'I believe you have a mild concussion,' said the physician. 'You should be all right after a little rest, though. It was a miracle none of you were killed. The empress here says you saved her life.'

'What about her arm?' Claudia asked.

'The wound will heal; it doesn't need stitching. She's lucky the arrow missed the major artery. A fraction closer and she might've lost the use of the limb.'

Claudia exhaled in relief. 'That's good.'

The physician offered Gia various leaves and spices, which were meant to benefit her health.

'What is it?' she asked, when handed a cup.

'Liquid cabbage,' said the physician.

'Thanks, but no. I'd rather be in pain,' said Gia. She pushed the cup back into the physician's hands, as if it contained poison.

'You should take several days to recuperate,' he said. 'Drink water, eat vegetables, and put some salve on that wound to stave off infection. Come back if you notice any inflammation.'

Gia nodded.

'Thank you,' said Claudia, as the physician departed.

'Empress,' he said, bowing in the doorway.

'I told you I was fine,' said Gia, when he was gone.

'You're hardly fine. You could've died.'

'It's nothing. Just a scratch.'

'You don't need to pretend to be strong for me,' said Claudia, barely resisting the urge to hold her.

'What was that about, in the chariot, sister?' asked Cassius. 'You were ready to tear ten strips off the Prince of Persia.'

'Oh, right,' said Gia, her face falling as she recalled. She cringed at Claudia. 'Sorry. It just slipped out.'

'He'd just saved all our lives, too,' said Cassius. 'What possessed you to say that, Gia?'

'It's not untrue,' said Gia. 'There *was* a knife. A dagger with a Jupiter bolt on it, such as was used to attack the empress. It was hidden among his things, in his room here in the palace.'

'Why didn't you say anything?' asked Cassius.

'Claudia chose not to confront him about it.'

Cassius looked to her, for further explanation.

'We weren't sure if it was planted there or not, or what the consequences of accusing him would be.' Claudia sighed. 'I should've acted sooner. I put a bullseye on my back, and all of you were the rings of the target around me. This was my fault.'

'*Of course* you're making this about you,' said Cassius.

'They fired at me. I'm the empress. It's entirely about me.'

'You know, it doesn't matter whose fault it is. It happened . . . and it will happen again, so long as she stands by your side.'

'Can you . . . not?' said Gia, frowning at them. 'Both of you.'

'Sorry,' said Claudia, at the same time Cassius said, 'Sorry.'

The fury inside her turned to steam, leaving her empty. What good did her rage do? Claudia shook her head, ceasing her endless pacing.

'No, no, he's right,' she said.

'I am?' said Cassius, brows lifting in surprise. 'I am.'

Claudia approached the bench. 'Gia Valerii, you are officially relieved of your duties as my guard.'

'For how long?'

'For good. You need not worry about money, of course. You will live here as my companion and I will provide anything you need.'

'No.' Gia shook her head vehemently. 'You need me.'

'I cannot sacrifice you for this,' said Claudia. 'I will *not* sacrifice you for this, Gia.'

Maybe removing her from her staff was too much, or maybe it wasn't enough. Claudia didn't know anything any more.

'I have to go and speak to Prince Darius,' she said, walking off. 'It can wait no longer.'

Gia climbed down from the bench. 'I'll go with you.'

'No, you heard the physician. You need to rest and recover.'

'If I'm not your guard any more, you can't tell me what to do,' said Gia, lightly. 'And you'll need that Jupiter dagger, won't you, as evidence, before you go charging off to confront him?'

'Fine, okay, you're right about that.' Claudia retrieved the arrow from the inside pocket of her robes, where it had been poking her in the side since they'd fled the arena. 'We should compare them. But you're still officially discharged from duty, remember?'

'Whatever you say, Empress,' said Gia, retrieving her sword in a way that suggested she wasn't taking being fired very seriously at all.

Gia instructed her handmaids Aurelia and Nadira to retrieve the knife, hidden in a chest beneath her bed. They returned trailing Damocles, presenting her with the weapon for inspection and lingering curiously.

'Where did you find these weapons?' he asked.

'The arrow was shot at us today, in the Circus Maximus,' explained Claudia. 'The knife was found among Prince Darius's belongings. The weapons are both made of the same dark golden brass, sculpted by a master who paralleled Vulcan.'

'They match,' affirmed Gia.

'Look at this detailing, right here,' said Claudia. 'I think they were made by the same person.'

'If the prince is responsible, he must've chosen their design on purpose, so you would think a Roman man was behind it,' said Damocles. 'Perhaps he hoped to capitalize on existing tensions.'

'But how would he know he wouldn't get shot himself, trying to play the hero?' asked Cassius. 'He seemed genuinely distraught by the death of Mehdi. I don't believe it.'

'I should speak with the charioteer before I confront him,' said Claudia. 'Maybe he can tell us something useful.'

'Ah! About that,' said Damocles, stiffly. 'There is also someone else down there who is keen to speak with you.'

They descended into the stony palace dungeons, which were freezing cold and smelled of ancient dank. A handful of thieves and disrupters were held here, awaiting sentencing, including the man dressed as a charioteer, held behind iron bars and captured in chains.

Here too was Hieronymus, her former advisor, his robes soiled.

'Please, Empress, I beg you to let me go,' he said, in a raspy voice. 'I have made a mistake. I drank too much. I spoke out of turn.'

He looked smaller, older, wearing no sandals.

'Damocles.' His eyes fixed on the consul. 'My friend, my old friend. You won't let them kill me, will you? You wouldn't do that to me.'

'It is no longer in my hands,' said Damocles solemnly.

'There is no excuse for the things you said,' said Claudia. 'You accused me of murder. It is completely unforgiveable.'

'You're right, you're right! I . . . I was just upset about losing my job. I take it all back. I don't really think you had anything to do with it, I swear, Empress. Whip me, banish me, but I beg you, do not kill me.'

'Why should I show you mercy? You have shown none to me.'

'I am not one of them. I didn't conspire against you.'

'A likely story,' said Claudia. 'It was a coincidence, then, that you were shouting your mouth mere moments before this charming fellow tried to have me killed? I think not.'

She looked to the charioteer, in the cell beside him. The man laughed, spraying spittle.

'You have enemies everywhere,' he said.

'He's talking out of his arsehole,' said Hieronymus. 'I don't know this man. I'm not in league with him. I wasn't part of it, I swear on the lives of my grandchildren.'

'Perhaps he is telling the truth?' said Damocles hopefully.

But Claudia wasn't feeling so charitable. She ignored him, moving on to the charioteer.

'The empress in the flesh, paying me a prison visit,' he said. 'Aren't I lucky?'

'A strange statement, from a man in a dungeon. It doesn't appear to me that you're very fortunate at all,' said Claudia.

The charioteer had a pock-marked face, a broken nose and wide-set eyes: a poor man, whose grubby appearance suggested he was fond of the drink. He was just a fool, but he'd almost killed Gia . . . and Claudia wouldn't stand for that.

'Your master will be displeased when he learns that you failed,' said Claudia. 'I am assuming it is a *he* who paid you.'

'No one paid me,' grunted the man. 'I did it for pleasure.'

'You won't know pleasure when I get my hands on you,' said Gia, showing her sword through the bars.

'I'd start talking, if I were you,' said Cassius.

'Your employers will kill you,' said Claudia. 'You understand that, don't you? You are a walking corpse, whether I let you free or not. Your only hope is to tell me who you're involved with.'

'I am happy to die for the cause,' he said. 'I will march through the underworld with pride.'

'What cause?' asked Claudia. 'You have no cause.'

'No woman shall rule Rome, by the name of my god.'

'You're a bit late for that,' she said.

The charioteer spat at her – a noxious glob of phlegm that hit her robes like a missile. She recoiled in disgust, as Damocles pulled out a handkerchief to hastily dab it away.

'You have one last chance to spare yourself,' said Claudia. 'Tell me who you're working for.'

He spat at her again, this time hitting Gia's arm.

'Let me in there,' she said, wiping it off in disgust. 'Just a few minutes and I'll have him weeping blood.'

'It will not work,' said Claudia. 'Look at him, he's a masochist. He'd probably love for you to rough him up a bit.'

The charioteer licked his lips in response, clutching his crotch and making obscene gestures.

Gia slammed her sword into the bars, making a loud clashing noise that drove him back into the shadows.

'You are fraying my last thread of patience, you revolting pig.'

The charioteer merely laughed.

'You still maintain that no man paid you?' pressed Claudia. 'No man hired you? Where did you get your arrows?'

'My god has his ways,' he said. 'He has his servants. I am but one of them. I bring him offerings, and his men bring offerings to me.'

Claudia didn't believe he could organize the attempt alone, even with the assistance of a deity.

'Tell me who sent you,' Claudia raged.

A slow smile spread across his face, making him look unnatural.

'My god, he came to me in a dream.'

The man fell to his knees, raising his hands to the sky.

'I was chosen! My glory is promised. He knows I am important.

He told me I was special, that I had an important job to do. He said I would dine with the gods as a holy martyr.'

Claudia made a scornful face.

'And you believed him?' she said. 'If only every mortal tool put to use by the gods had such luck. Most of them are probably toiling in Tartarus now, long forgotten by the deities who used them.'

'The next assassin he sends will succeed,' said the charioteer. 'My god has an army of millions. Any man who makes offerings to him can be used by him. He would kill you himself but he prefers to keep his hands clean. His soldiers will wipe you out for him.'

'Then where is he now?' she said. 'Where is Jupiter?'

The man began to chuckle, then cackle, an inhuman sound that grew louder and more unhinged.

'Still no answers? Perhaps you will be a bit more garrulous in a few days,' said Claudia, leaning in closer to menace him, 'when hunger and thirst are slowly eating you alive, rotting your body from within. Maybe then, you'll feel like talking.'

She nodded to the guard.

'Arrange for him to be executed in three days, if he is still alive and unwilling to name his master.'

They climbed back up into the foyer, as Hieronymus wailed and the charioteer screamed obscenities.

Claudia blocked the horrifying sound out of her mind.

'It isn't one man we're looking for,' she said. 'I see it now. No wonder I could not pin it down to a single individual. Jupiter might have an army of mortals, all working for him, seized and used like weapons according to his will. Maybe they are not even in control of themselves.'

Damocles dabbed at his bald head with a cloth.

'Do you remember, back in Pompeii, when Jupiter seemed to enter your brother?' said Gia.

Claudia met her gaze in dread.

'I will never forget. What did the prisoner say? That anyone who makes offerings to Jupiter can be called upon by him?' She turned to Damocles. 'If it were true, he could use any one of you as a weapon. Every man in Rome has made offerings to Jupiter.'

'Not just men,' said Gia. 'What if he can call upon the women who have prayed to him too? We have all worshipped him, at festivals.'

It was too horrible, too colossal, to imagine.

'We must talk to the prince now, and find out what he knows,' said Claudia. 'I will send for him.'

'You must tread carefully, Empress,' said Damocles. 'Don't do anything rash.'

'Too late,' said Gia, as the prince appeared.

'My ears are burning,' said Darius, striding up to them. 'I do believe you're talking about me . . . again.'

He was alone, without his guard, but he was smart enough to keep the curved sword on his belt.

'I should speak with you privately,' said Claudia. 'You wouldn't want the people to hear this. Come, follow me if you want peace.'

15. THE WISDOM OF THE WATERS

Claudia led the others into the palace temple, so the goddesses might be witness to whatever followed. She, Gia, Cassius, Darius and Damocles. The prince was outnumbered, but this didn't seem to concern him.

She presented the dagger, unfurling it from its shroud.

'This knife is the one found among your belongings,' she said. 'As you can see, it has the seal of Jupiter on it.'

Darius gazed at her in confusion.

'Let me be clear,' Claudia added. 'This is the same kind of knife used by the man who tried to kill me in the Pantheon, and it matches the arrows fired at us today. Here, see.'

An attendant held the arrow up, for comparison.

'You are accusing me?' said Darius.

'I am questioning you. It is different.'

'I cannot believe this,' he said. 'You think I would sacrifice my own advisor, a man who was like an uncle to me . . . and for what? Perhaps it is *you* who is trying to frame *me*?'

'Why would I do that? I could've died today. Gia was injured.

One of my guards was shot in the throat, and who knows how many others were killed or injured in the chaos.'

'I saved your life.'

'Maybe that was part of the plot, to make it believable.'

He threw up his hands. 'No, no, *this* I cannot believe.'

'I'm just here to determine the truth,' said Claudia. 'I hope to be wrong but I can no longer ignore my suspicions. Or the fact that the knife was in your rooms.'

'Then it seems we have a problem, because that knife isn't mine. I have never seen that before,' he said. 'I cannot explain its presence in my chambers, but I did not put it there.'

Cassius looked back and forth between them in concern.

'Who found it?' asked Darius.

'I did,' said Gia.

'Then the gladiator is lying. She must be,' he said, face curdling.

'She wouldn't,' said Cassius.

'That is why she desires to drive me out,' said Darius. 'I am a threat to your closeness. She has motive to work against me.'

'Trust me, you're not a threat,' said Gia.

'She has no reason to tell tall tales and endanger me for show,' said Claudia. 'She wants to find the real culprit, as do I. I trust her with my life. There is no question. She is telling the truth.'

Darius looked sickened, shaking his head in consternation. If he was an actor, he should've joined the Campus Martius players.

'Someone is setting me up,' he said. 'This is a political act. They wish to diminish the might of the Persian empire. I wasn't even in the city when you were attacked at the Pantheon.'

Claudia stared at the ground. She could see no clear conclusion.

She believed him, but she doubted that belief. She was afraid to risk her trust. She didn't know which way to turn.

'One of your enemies must be using me for a scapegoat,' said Darius. 'They knew you wouldn't trust me, that you'd go looking through my possessions and find this. They're setting me up to look like a traitor, and for you to look like a fool . . . and all the while, the real culprit is hiding in the shadows, unnoticed.'

Something about his defence rang true but she was reluctant to be deceived again.

'Tell me why I should believe that you're innocent.'

'I am innocent because I intervened to save you today. Because I would never lower myself by carrying a talisman to a Roman god. Because I would bring disgrace on my family, my people and my pantheon, to come to Rome and attempt to kill its ruler. Because I am not a savage or a warlord. Because I find that I am protective of you, that I see you as an ally in a treacherous world. Because if I wanted to kill you, I would do it openly, before an audience, so there would be no doubt. Because I would do it for good reason, and you would know the reason before you died. Because I wouldn't sneak around like a coward with a dirty dagger. Because I have more to gain from allying with you than I do from taking a blade to your throat. Because I would never be accepted as ruler of Rome without a Roman by my side. Because I am an outsider. Because I know this, and I am not ashamed.'

Her resolve faltered, her doubt dissipating.

'Think of what my father will do if he learns about this,' he said, in cold, wide-eyed fear. 'He's not as diplomatic as me, nor does he think as highly of women. He'd tell me to kill you and seize your city, even if it cost him a hundred thousand men, including myself. He would declare a war on principle alone.'

'My father would've done the same,' she said, 'but we are not them, as we have already agreed.'

'To kill you would be killing myself,' he said. 'That is the real reason why I did what I did today. Not to be a hero, but because I need you to live so you can fulfil our agreement, so I can return to my father and tell him I did not fail. I need you alive . . . so you can marry me.'

Claudia didn't know what to say, what to think.

'What would you do in my situation, Prince Darius?' she asked. 'If I visited you in Persepolis and one of your guards found a weapon in my chamber – not just a weapon, but a weapon connected to an attack on your life? Would you give me the benefit of the doubt? I don't think you would.'

'You would not like the outcome, I suspect,' he said.

The prince fixed her with a meaningful gaze.

'But let it not come to that. Someone is plotting against you and me alike. I can help to identity the real traitor.'

'Help me how?' she said.

'Meet me in the palace garden tomorrow night, after your staff have retired to bed, and I will show you,' he said. 'I will show you the one who truly works against you.'

'What investigative powers do you have, that I do not?' asked Claudia. 'How exactly do you intend to prove it?'

'I have my ways of finding information,' he said. 'Never assume that your enemy knows less than you.'

'Then, we are enemies?' she said.

'That is what we must determine,' said Darius. 'Agree, and I will show you. All I ask is that you come alone.'

'Why alone?' she said.

'When you see, you will understand.'

Claudia looked to Gia, who shook her head and shoulders in such a way that said, *I don't know. Your choice.*

'Fine,' Claudia agreed, turning back to Darius. 'I will meet you. If you can show me evidence connected to the assassination attempts against me, I will hear it. I will reconsider my position then. You may return to your rooms, but my guards will be stationed outside.'

'Very well. I will be keeping an eye on you too,' said Darius, touching his necklace. 'Just like you, I must protect myself.'

The palace gardens were constructed to resemble a stadium, where former emperors had held their own private games.

Claudia had spent many days and evenings out here in the heat and the cold, trying not to fall asleep as she watched the endless parade of recreational violence her father and brother enjoyed.

Gladiators were often brought in just to fight each other for the emperor's amusement. Occasionally, one of them died, dragged away by slaves. Decimus would cheer, and her father would say, 'Next!', as if their lives were nothing more than a moment's amusement.

Now, Claudia wondered if this was where she too developed a taste for violence, and a weakness for athletes in armour.

She and Decimus had once raced here in miniature chariots pulled by ponies. He had cheated, of course, causing her chariot to crash into the exterior wall. There was still a crack in the brickwork. She ran her hand over it, lingering at the top of the garden.

She'd been so angry she had actually stood up to him – one of the few times she'd ever dared to, when she was small enough not to know better – and he'd quickly made her regret it, smashing her face into the wall until she screamed.

Her father never punished him, only her for crying, or being dramatic, or embarrassing him in front of his advisors. It was always her fault for reacting, and never her brother's fault for attacking her.

'You know what Decimus is like,' her father would say. *'Don't rile him up and he won't bother you.'*

But he always found a way to bother her.

This garden was where she had first learned to ride a horse, and tumble like an acrobat, where she learned to recognize birdsong and catalogue the stars, but it was also where she first learned to fear men.

The enclosed green space created an oasis in the middle of the crowded, built-up city, giving an illusion of privacy. A portico with colourful marble columns ran around the hippodrome gardens, creating a balcony from which to spectate. Servants and guards crowded here, Gia surely among them, watching as Claudia walked alone towards the promenade, where the prince waited beneath a high, vaulted roof.

Darius bowed gently as she approached. Claudia made sure to keep her face hard, despite the crashing waves of emotion inside.

'I am here, and I am alone,' she said. 'Don't make me regret it.'

'Then we shall waste no time,' he said. He gestured with one arm. 'Let us go to the pond. I can show you there.'

'The pond?'

'We seek the clarity of the waters.'

Claudia accompanied him along the curving gravel path, though she anticipated another ambush around each corner as they moved away from the sight of the people on the balcony.

'If you're thinking of drowning me, you should know I already survived a shipwreck this year,' she said. 'I will not make it easy for you.'

'And a volcanic eruption, and various assassination attempts,' he said. 'I have seen. Believe me, if I sought to destroy you, I would be cynical about my chances of succeeding.'

Claudia faltered, her mind catching on a single word.

'Seen? How?' she asked.

'Your goddess shows you things, and so does mine.'

Her breath hitched.

'I have been watching you, just as you have been watching me.'

She swallowed, her palms clammy as she wondered what he might have witnessed.

'I know you have watched me through your goddess shield,' he said. 'I know because Anahita showed me. But you are not the only one who has a connection with divinity.'

This certainly piqued her curiosity. 'Tell me more.'

'Long ago, when I was just a little boy, my father told me I would grow up to marry the princess of Rome and be a hero for my people,' he said. 'My father has quite a talent for storytelling, so he spun an enchanting legend for me to believe. He told me it was destined, as he had been shown in a prophecy from his god, Mithras. I grew up believing we were soulmates, though we had never met.'

Claudia nodded, to signal that she was listening.

'But my father's real motive was something much more corporeal. He saw me as a gift to be given away in exchange for political leverage. My father was bothered by all the so-called priests and oracles who told him to fear a Roman invasion, so he pretended to have a vision from Mithras that gave him the solution.'

'Pretended?'

The prince smirked. 'As far as I know, my father has never actually spoken to the gods directly, but when he said he did, people believed him. Including me. So, he sent his men to visit your father and swore he'd never go past the Parthian border for as long as he ruled, *if* you were promised to me. Your father was more than happy to accept. He was a lazy man, who preferred easy solutions.'

Claudia could not argue with that.

'My father returned home and told his people that he had fulfilled the prophecy, preventing the foretold disaster. They stopped worrying about Roman invasion for a while. He thought he'd made the deal of the century: a Roman princess and a Persian prince, signifying that our empires are equal in kind. That was his vision.'

They stood before the ornamental pond, surrounded by marble statues of sirens and water nymphs. The god Neptune had been vividly rendered in gold, riding bareback on a horse made of sea foam.

'My mother was the real priestess of the family, and the one who taught me how to truly commune with the gods by using the water like a mirror,' said Darius. 'She learned the old ways from women in her family, passed down through generations.'

Claudia held her breath, enraptured.

'One day, the goddess Anahita came to me. She showed herself to me in the surface of the river, for the first time. She showed you to me, and she gave me this talisman, to watch over you.'

He indicated the necklace.

'Your shield shows you only what is happening in the present, and there is much you have missed. But the waters are eternal and timeless. They show me what has happened in the past.'

As he spoke, the prince removed the lotus necklace he wore and gently placed it around Claudia's neck.

'There is a myth that all gods are the same gods, just different variations of them,' he said. 'They are born from the same source, with the same origins, but they grow, over time, to reflect the people and the places they are the guardians of. If this is true, then our gods are sisters and brothers, just like you and me. Not of blood, but of spirit.'

The prince said something in Persian that Claudia wasn't fluent enough to understand – a prayer, a chant, an evocation.

'Anahita, my goddess,' he said. 'I beg you to show her what I have seen. Show her those who plot against her. Give her the clarity and wisdom of the water.'

At his word, a sparkling glimmer appeared on the surface, as if an invisible light was reflecting on it from above. The glow grew outwards, rippling into bands of different colours that cleared to form a vision, like a painting on the water's surface. Though Anahita was a Persian goddess, unfamiliar to Claudia and certainly not revered by her, she came to her now, woman to woman, to show her the truth.

The image rippled and shifted, revealing her own handmaid, Aurelia, standing outside Claudia's room. She pressed close to the door, leaning in to overhear a conversation between Claudia and Gia.

'You will be free to perform reconnaissance while the prince is out of the palace. It would be an ideal moment to enter his chambers and examine his belongings, just in case he has anything incriminating in his possession . . .'

The image rippled again.

Aurelia entered Darius's room as his servants crowded outside in the corridor, leaning over the balcony to observe a golden monkey stealing the lunches of several Roman senators.

Aurelia looked around furtively, then removed the Jupiter knife from her robes. She wrapped it in a discarded toga and stashed it in one of the prince's travelling crates before slipping away.

Outside in the garden, flushed with fear and thrill, Aurelia met with a general and two senators. It was Tacitus, Thelonius and General Aquinas, the same three men who had tracked down her cousin Marcellus and brought him to Rome to oppose her.

'Is it done?' asked Aquinas, a sullen-looking man with hooded eyes, their irises a penetrating, cold blue.

'Yes, sir.'

'Good girl,' said Tacitus, the man with long, greasy hair.

'You've done well. The gods would be proud. We are grateful for this and for the information you've given us,' said Thelonius, the tallest, baldest and most amiable of the three.

'Will you free my brother now?' she said.

'Soon,' said Tacitus, smiling. 'You'll be rewarded by Emperor Marcellus when he returns from Britannia.'

Emperor Marcellus?

'How long must I wait?' asked Aurelia. 'If the empress finds out, she could have me killed.'

'He will return before the Plebeian Games,' said Thelonius. 'Keep faith, and believe in the plan.'

The image faded.

'Not Aurelia,' said Claudia. 'I trusted her.'

Another ripple of colour on the water's surface showed bright-eyed General Aquinas paying the chariot riders at the Circus Maximus, equipping them with Jupiter's bows and arrows. In amongst them was the unkempt, red-nosed prisoner Claudia held in her dungeon.

Aquinas retreated into an empty corridor before re-emerging in the arena, climbing several sets of stairs to stand in rank several rows behind the imperial box, watching impassively as a guard was shot in the throat by the same arrows he'd provided.

In the dark mirror of the pond, a third and final scene formed, revealing Aquinas again. It was the day of Claudia's confirmation ceremony, recognizable by its flags and standards, the streets crowded with people.

The general approached one of the Pantheon guards, handing him a bag of coins.

'You are sure?' said the guard.

It was the dead praetorian; the one Gia had killed.

'As sure as the gods,' said Aquinas. 'Do not fail me.'

He pulled out the knife, branded with Jupiter's seal, and pressed it into the guard's gloved hand.

The image paled again.

Darius removed the necklace, his cold hands at Claudia's nape, while she attempted to process what she'd just seen.

It was possible that these images were just magic enchantments meant to deceive her, yet she believed them instinctively. She had always known a plot against her was possible, if not inevitable, but witnessing the extent of it in clear vision left her breathless, shaken.

'Your cousin works against you,' said Darius, putting the lotus pendant back on himself. 'He is absent on purpose, so you will not suspect him, but his people are all around you. He is gathering supporters, ready for his return to Rome. They are trying to cause a dispute between us. Marcellus has much to gain, should our union fall apart.'

'I do not doubt that,' she said.

'Unlike me, he will be readily accepted by the people who object to you. He need only remove you from power to get his wish. Unlike you, he will do what these men want, without question. He left on their orders. The military will do as he says, including remove you from power.'

Claudia was shaking, though she did not feel cold.

'Marcellus will soon return to finish what he started, and when he does, it is important that I am here,' said Darius. 'Rather than kill you, it might be more expedient for your cousin to take you as his bride. That would consolidate his position.'

Darius was right. Now, more than ever, she needed the prince's protection, yet she dreaded the conditions it came with.

'Only you and I can maintain this peace,' he said. 'Anahita has shown me. The future is no longer set in stone . . . because something occurred to derail the path of preordained fate.' When he gazed at her, it was as if he saw past her, through her, into a realm beyond. 'It was you, Empress. You were the one who changed history when you claimed the crown. But rewriting history has consequences. Removing Decimus was like throwing a pebble in a pond.' He retrieved a small stone, tossing it into the water. 'It has created ripples through time.'

They watched the rings expanding, growing outward.

'Now Anahita sees a different future. My kingdom, a desert. My gods, abandoned. A war that will rage for seven hundred years.'

'You think I will be responsible for such atrocities?' she said.

'No. Not you,' he said. 'In her vision, you are dead. Your gladiator is dead. Marcellus is emperor. Aquinas will push for Rome's expansion until it penetrates our borders.'

Claudia shook her head strenuously.

No. It would not be so. She hadn't done what she'd done just to cause more suffering. She hadn't walked through the hell of Vulcan's fire to steal her brother's bloody crown, all for the world to fall apart in the hands of another idiot man.

'How can you be sure your goddess is telling you the truth?'

'Do you doubt your goddess? No, because you have seen. You have felt. You have known. I *know* she is telling me the truth, because she sees me in a way no one else has ever done. She knows things about me that no one could know – that I myself am barely aware of. She knows my innermost soul and all of the secrets I have hidden there.'

His face became grave, haunted by something unspoken.

'When Marcellus returns, you will either be his wife against your will, or you will be buried beneath his feet. That is why I come to you now, with a new proposition.'

Claudia dreaded to hear it, but she knew she had no choice.

'I'm listening.'

'We will marry as planned, as soon as possible. We will solidify the alliance of our two empires. Then you will have two armies to defend you, and Marcellus will no longer be a threat.'

The words she had in mind dried to dust.

'Our marriage will be one of companionship,' he said. 'I can keep you safe, like no other man can.'

'I cannot do it,' said Claudia.

'I can give you security, not just for yourself but for your people. I can give you a cover, a mask, behind which to hide yourself. I can even give you a child, should you desire one.'

'You would expect me to . . . ?' asked Claudia.

'Only if you wanted an heir, as I do,' he said. 'Your gladiator friend cannot offer you that.'

The gardens were unnaturally quiet, barely a bird or insect to be heard as they gazed at their reflection in the still waters.

'The rumours spread further each day. Your men speak of infamy. Your reign is on shaky ground. Any excuse to topple you, and they will take it. This is just another thing that makes you weak to them. This is just another reason to overthrow you. Without me at your side, Marcellus will have an easy job of ousting you, and they *will* kill you if you refuse to do what they want you to.'

Claudia felt trapped, as she had done as a child.

'Marry me and your position will be stronger. For both of us will rise, or both of us will fall. Together, or apart. A woman alone is not enough,' he said.

'Would your goddess agree with that?'

'My goddess is wise. She sits with uncomfortable truths. They will not let you rule the world. It is a dream.'

'You're wrong. I am very much awake.'

'You are already promised to me, and I am here to honour the promise I made my father,' he said.

'But you know the truth, about Gia and me,' she said. 'To marry me would be to live a lie.'

'I already do. Every moment of my life is a lie.'

He didn't elaborate, leaving the words to hang between them.

'We have no choice,' he said at last. 'You need me, and I need you. You must choose between your duty as a ruler, and your lover. Marcellus will soon return from Britannia. Your answer, is it yes, or no?'

'You must give me time. I need time to think about it.'

The prince admired her a moment, then nodded.

'Three days,' he said. 'You have three days to decide.'

'And if I say no?'

'Then we must be enemies.'

'I see. It's like that, is it?'

'I do not wish it; I have grown fond of you, Claudia Caesaria. But I must put my people first. Protect them. For now, let me give you a small token of my affection.'

'Another gift?' she said.

'A kiss,' he said.

Grudgingly, Claudia turned her face slightly, offering her cheek.

Before she knew what was happening, the prince leaned down to brush her lips with his.

She froze, not returning the gesture, but not moving away either. He pulled her closer. His lips were much colder than Gia's, not as soft or sweet. It was a nothing kind of kiss, but she feared being visibly rude, so she smiled as if it was pleasant.

Finally, thankfully, he broke away.

It was, despite her long history of flirting, Claudia's first kiss with a man, and it was a dry husk. It was the kiss of two people who were biologically incompatible.

She knew then that she did not, could never, desire him. That she could spend her whole life with him, bear his children, even bury him, and she would never love him.

She would never love him like she loved Gia right now.

She *was* like Sappho, after all.

'That was . . . wonderful,' said the prince.

'Yes, magical,' said Claudia.

'My heart is stirring . . . in flight.'

'And mine, mine is also . . . flying,' she lied.

They stood in silence, as the prince reached for her hand. He tried to entwine their fingers together but they didn't fit right, clashing together uncomfortably.

'You have three days to make your choice,' he said. 'I hope your answer will be yes, my empress.'

Darius bowed once more and retreated to his rooms.

Claudia remained behind alone, staring at her reflection in the pond as her whole life washed over her.

She told herself that all was not lost. She had changed the future before by coming to power against all odds, and she could do so again. She would do it again. She would not let Marcellus usurp her, and she would not marry Darius under duress.

She would find another way.

When she turned back from the pond, moving along the garden path, something caught her eye.

She looked up at the balcony, realizing she was not alone.

Claudia glimpsed Gia watching from the shadows at a distance, before she turned away and disappeared into the dark.

Three goddesses cautiously approached a fortified palace, made of smoke-black stone. It was decorated with many spikes and barred windows and burning torches, guarded by disgruntled-looking satyrs and centaurs.

A larger-than-life statue of a helmeted deity driving a chariot stood in the courtyard, led by four winged Pegasi.

'Do you really think this is a good idea?' asked Diana, holding out her bow. 'Fortuna will not approve.'

'Certainly not,' said Minerva, holding her shield and sword, 'but we have no choice, not now we have lost Victoria and Salacia. If Jupiter has so many of the gods still on his side, we need to convert less . . . reputable allies.'

'I did not know you meant her*,' said Diana.*

'We will fight for all women and goddesses – good, bad and in-between. That is how we will win the war.'

'Didn't she go berserk and kill her own soldiers in battle?' said Venus, though she withered slightly under Minerva's fierce glare.

'It was a misunderstanding.'

'Doesn't she demand blood sacrifices from her priests, too?'

'None of us are perfect,' snapped Minerva, 'including myself. Let this be a blank slate for every deity, on which to rewrite their own story.'

Minerva's sister Bellona represented the destructive aspect of warfare, known for carrying around a bloodstained sword wherever she went as a not-so-veiled threat. She was belligerent, full of bloodlust, and a loose cannon, but she was also one of the finest warriors Minerva had ever personally trained – as ruthless as any god.

One of Bellona's horned, cloven-footed attendants greeted them at the door, ushering them inside before anyone could see, locking and barring the door behind them.

Venus and Diana exchanged a harried glance as they followed.

The temple palace was full of the deceased fire priests and dead soldiers Bellona kept as servants, giving the place a distinctly sinister atmosphere. The walls were hung with various weapons – swords, shields, spears and whips, along with trophies acquired in numerous conquests, be they against men, monsters, gods or beasts, and painted murals of bacchanalian orgies, with Bellona at the centre of them.

She waited in a room decorated with many mortal skulls, clapping slowly at Minerva's approach. The two bore a resemblance but Bellona had a more impish look, with burning pupils and fiery hair, her helmet and shield bearing the symbol of the gorgon.

'Finally, you call on me,' said Bellona.

'Hello, Bellona.'

'The great Minerva returns. I was beginning to give up hope.'

'You were expecting us?'

'Yes, what took you so long?'

'I've been busy, trying to topple our beloved father,' said Minerva.

'And you thought you'd exclude me from all the fun?'

Bellona grinned, but it didn't have the effect of making her more approachable. It was a sharp, feral sort of smile, like a cunning fox.

'You can't imagine how furious I was when I heard that you'd approached those low-hanging fruits, Feronia and Eponia, before me, your own sister,' she said.

'Oh, please,' said Diana. 'Most of us are siblings in the pantheon.'

Bellona's fingers danced up and down the hilt of her sword.

'But I am Minnie's favourite.'

'Do not call me that,' grunted Minerva.

'You didn't used to mind, before we fell out. You still haven't apologized. How long has it been now? A thousand years?'

'You think I should apologize to you? Come on, Bella – you know you are not always to be trusted,' said Minerva.

'Says who?'

'Well, everyone. You are a mercenary who will fight for the highest bidder. I wasn't so sure you wouldn't go running to Mars at your earliest convenience.'

'Venus has consorted with Mars too,' she objected.

'Venus has since seen the light,' said Minerva.

'It is true,' affirmed Venus. 'I am converted to the other side.'

'I am on no side but my own,' said Bellona, 'but I can be persuaded to join any fight if there is an opportunity to refine my specific set of skills.'

She stood up, stretching her limbs like an athlete.

'I do not care for causes, only the game of war, but if you're planning on killing father, I want to join in. That's why you're here, isn't it? You've realized that you can't win without me?'

'I wouldn't go that far,' grumbled Minerva, though she had admitted as much. 'You would be an asset, though – you and your chaotic vengeance friends.'

'Which ones?'

'Discordia and Invidia.'

'Discordia's allegiance changes with the wind, and Invidia will only fight if she has been personally wronged. They have no loyalty to women. Besides, they are imprisoned in the underworld by Jupiter, unable to leave.'

'Let me handle that,' said Minerva. 'I have spies in the underworld

court of Proserpina. I am trying to reach out to her, but I cannot travel to the underworld directly without attracting suspicion from Father. You, on the other hand . . .'

'I could easily travel to the underworld and call upon all the Inferi goddesses to wage war against Jupiter . . . but perhaps I am now the true goddess of wisdom, for you are not thinking big enough, sister.'

'Go on,' sighed Minerva.

'Mars will get in the way of your goal. His ego is bigger than Jupiter's, and he has long overshadowed all of us warrior goddesses. We tire of him commanding us. Now he too seeks to rule over all of us. Blah blah blah.' She mimicked talking voices with her hands, like puppets. 'Mars has been vying to overthrow his father since he came into being. Now, with us goddesses on the revolt, he finally sees an opportunity to rise to power. Which means Mars and Jupiter will drag out their dick-measuring contest for aeons, and we all will be forced to witness it.'

'I sense you have a plan?'

'I shall wait for him to make his move against his father. When his armies are distracted, I will overthrow him and take his place as the patron of war, to guide every soldier of Rome, but you must do something for me in return,' said Bellona.

Minerva already knew that Bellona's terms would be unreasonable.

'I'm listening.'

'I want to be a proper goddess again. I want to be in the Forum. I want my statue restored to the Pantheon.' She bared her teeth, stamping one foot as she brandished her bloodstained sword. 'I want. My own. Temple.'

'We haven't forgotten why it was removed in the first place,' said Diana.

'So, I killed a few thousand mortals,' said Bellona, her eyes wide as she gesticulated erratically. 'Who hasn't? How many men has Father killed? How many mortal women has he impregnated?'

'Father is not a good example,' said Minerva.

'Jupiter is afraid of me, like all men are afraid of me,' Bellona said, 'and they rightly should be.'

'We are supposed to be better than them,' said Venus.

'We must be better than them, just to be respected less? All of the others are there, good and bad, but I am singled out as mad? It is because I am a woman. Mars is more of a tyrant than me, but he gets to be a heroic warrior with his own planet, while I am mocked and feared, just like Medusa and Cassandra and all the other monsters that men have buried their secrets in.'

'If you are going to fight with us, there must be rules,' said Minerva.

'Boring,' said Bellona.

'You will not kill mortals unless they pose imminent danger to others. You will not torture mortals. You will not fornicate with mortals.'

'No wonder you are prematurely grey of hair,' said Bellona, 'if you insist on conducting yourself with utmost decorum on all occasions.'

'This is serious, Bella.'

'Eternity is too long to be good all of the time.'

'Those are the rules. If you want your temple and your statue back, you must agree to them . . . as well as you are able to commit to anything.'

'Can I inflict the mortals with diseases?'

'No,' said Minerva, firmly.

'Can I feed the really wicked ones to the beasts?'

'A few of them, maybe.'

'Can I scavenge their corpses for treasure?'

'Do as you will. They cannot take it with them.'

'Then I shall agree. I will deal with Mars, and you will deal with Jupiter. Maybe then you will finally see us as equals, sister.'

16. ONE OF US

Claudia wasted no time in ordering Damocles to remove her handmaid Aurelia from her duties, instructing him to take her down to the cells to spend the night with Hieronymus and the charioteer.

'Are you going to tell me why?' asked Damocles.

'She was the one who concealed the knife in the prince's room. Her brother is being detained by General Aquinas. She will confess, if confronted. If they testify, they shall be allowed to leave the city alive. I suspect they will accept the offer.'

'General Aquinas?'

'And Senators Tacitus and Thelonius. They are conspiring with Marcellus to have me overthrown.'

'How do you know this?'

'Do not ask questions, Damocles. Just have the three men brought to the palace tomorrow morning for questioning . . . and increase security. Not a door or window should go unguarded.'

'Very well, Empress.'

By the time she reached her rooms, only Nadira sat outside, with an empty spot on the bench beside her.

'Is my guard waiting inside? Gia?' Claudia asked, trying not to sound too hopeful.

'No, Empress,' said Nadira. 'I have been here all night. I have not seen her.'

'Oh. No matter then. Thank you.'

'Goodnight, Empress,' she said.

'Goodnight,' Claudia replied, curtly.

Claudia's gaze lingered on the space where Aurelia used to sit. She wouldn't make the mistake of trusting her staff too easily again.

Inside, Princess the lynx was curled up on the bed.

Claudia stood out at the balcony, taking deep lungfuls of night air, much colder than the heat of the Pompeii summer when she and Gia had fallen in love. She put her hands on the rough stone railing and tried not to cry as the weight of so many problems dragged her spirit down.

Claudia felt a loneliness she hadn't experienced since the days before Pompeii. Before Gia. It was a deep, cold ache, down to the bones – the kind of loneliness that can last a lifetime. It was the loneliness of a person who feared love and being loved, a person who was unable to hold on to the thing they wanted most of all.

She turned and went back inside, lying down under the canopy of the bed, adopting various positions in restlessness as she waited.

She was sure Gia would turn up eventually, yet she couldn't prevent herself from picturing the worst. They hadn't spent the night together since Claudia had requested space.

As the hourglass tipped, she found herself consumed by worry, wondering what Gia might be doing without her. Curiosity compelled her, possessed her, filling her with unspent energy, as if she might burst if she couldn't let it out.

Without a deity to guide her, Claudia was drawn by the worst impulses – ones she could no longer ignore. The part of her that was firm and steadfast was stretched thin, until it finally snapped.

She told herself that it was for her safety.

For her protection.

'Show me Gia,' she said, touching the shield.

The steel was not as malleable as the water, nor its images as clear, but just as when she gazed into the pond, a picture emerged.

Gia sat at a table in a rustic-looking taberna with Dominic, Dido and Livia, all of them dressed in casual togas. They sat before a window, drinking from a large clay jug of wine painted with a fresco of Grecian-style athletes.

'We're glad you came,' said Dido.

'We didn't really expect you to turn up,' said Livia, smoothing down her hair.

Gia had gone out, left the palace without telling her. Claudia knew it was not a good sign.

'I wasn't expecting to be free tonight,' said Gia, 'but I am. So it goes, right?' She sounded unusually mournful. 'That's life.'

'Are we celebrating, or commiserating?' asked Dido.

As far as Claudia could tell, it was a gladiator-themed establishment, with sporting murals and mosaics, frequented by a colourful cast of Rome's lower-ranking residents.

'Both,' said Gia.

Vulpine-eyed Livia raised her glass, which the others copied.

'To the opening of the Ludus Victoria!' said Livia.

'To the Ludus Victoria,' Dido and Gia repeated.

'And to Gia's victory at the Circus Maximus the other day, which I'm not bitter about at all.'

They downed their drinks in one go.

'Course not,' said Dido.

Livia immediately refilled their glasses.

'Also, for saving the empress's life,' added Dominic.

'I thought it was the prince who saved her?' said Livia.

'Why do you think I got shot in the arm?' said Gia, downing her drink again. 'For fun?'

'Any excuse to throw yourself on top of her,' said Livia.

'Cut it out,' said Gia. She laughed forcedly. 'Who said I have such desires?'

'I'm only teasing you. There's no shame in it. You don't have to be embarrassed,' said Livia, nudging her flirtatiously.

Gia flushed, spluttering in search of an answer.

'What? I didn't, I'm not,' she said.

'This isn't Pompeii. You're not the only one any more.'

Claudia's breath caught in her throat, surprised too. She wished she was there, to celebrate with them and share in this unity.

Gia looked to Dido, to Livia, and finally, to Dominic.

'I know it's not exactly a secret, but keep it to yourselves,' she said, in a low tone. 'It wouldn't look good on the empress if people found out her guard was . . . you know.'

Livia and Dido exchanged a knowing look.

'We know,' said Livia.

'Is *the empress* going to marry the prince?' asked Dido, in a pointed way. 'Because that's what I heard.'

'Looks like it,' said Gia coldly. 'She kissed him tonight.'

Livia whistled, as Claudia's guts churned.

'No, I didn't,' she said, though no one could hear her. 'He kissed me, actually.'

'He's not bad to look at,' said Dido. 'I wouldn't mind.'

'All men are gross,' said Livia.

'Yeah, you said. *Several times*,' said Dominic.

'I don't mean you, Dom,' said Livia, slapping him so hard on the back he coughed. 'You're our honorary woman.'

'Good luck to them, I say,' said Dido, lifting her glass again. 'May love find us all one day.'

'Pfft, get real. They'll probably get killed before they can say their vows,' said Livia.

'Don't talk like that,' said Gia.

'What is she going to do, arrest me for gossiping? It's true, the people already tried to kill her twice. Next time they'll succeed.'

Gia looked to the door, her brow furrowing.

'I should go. I shouldn't be here. If something happens while I'm here, it will be my fault,' said Gia.

'You barely ever leave her side,' said Livia. 'You *are* entitled to have a life of your own.'

'Stay out with us, please,' said Dido, clasping Gia's hands in her own. 'Livia is just jealous.'

'I'm not!'

'She secretly wishes you were throwing yourself on top of her instead,' said Dido.

'I do not!' Livia protested, her eyes bulging. 'I never even said that. Seriously. What is wrong with you?'

Dido and Dominic chuckled together, as Livia said something in her native language that none of them could interpret.

Gia looked to the door again.

'Don't worry. Cassius is still there, isn't he?' said Dom. 'He'll look out for her.'

'I don't know about that,' said Gia.

'He doesn't like her,' whispered Livia, her eyes popping as she delivered this gossip. 'He doesn't approve.'

'Oh,' said Dom, looking to Gia. 'Do you want to talk about it?'

'Not even a little bit,' said Gia, draining her glass again.

'We should take Gia to the place,' said Dido. 'Cheer her up.'

'Where?' asked Gia.

'You mean, the *secret* place,' said Livia.

'Are you a sphinx with these riddles?' said Gia. 'What place?'

'A place where no one cares what you do or who you do it with, if you catch my drift,' said Livia. 'Where a lover of the female form might find another, under cover of night.'

Gia gaped at her. 'There's such a place?' she said.

'There is every such place, here in Rome. This one just so happens to be a certain senator's house. He's been having these parties for years, and all of the people there are . . . *you know*.'

Gia looked as if she'd just been slapped.

Livia wiggled her eyebrows.

'So, do you want to go?' said Livia.

'I can't,' said Dom.

'Why not?'

'Don't want to. Not really my scene.'

'What *is* your scene?' Livia asked.

'Staying home and studying.'

'*Bo*-ring.'

'What about you, Gia?'

Dido drummed on the table, goading her to agree.

Gia looked conflicted but she eventually rolled her eyes and held out her glass, nodding at Livia to refill it.

'You'd better pour me another one, then,' she said.

'Yes!'

Claudia could see no more, letting go of the shield as if burned. The image faded and she couldn't bring herself to look again.

She knew what would happen next.

It was obvious.

Gia had seen her kiss the prince. Now she was out drinking with someone who desired her, going to a secret party where Sapphic sisters met for forbidden pleasure. It was a mess.

Claudia wasn't sure if she had the right to be upset but she had never been so jealous.

She dressed herself in the least ostentatious clothes she owned, hastily, haphazardly, mumbling to herself as she did. She tied back her hair, to try and disguise herself, removing her jewels and make-up.

She would find out which senator they meant and go to the party. She would find Gia herself and put things right.

But the longer it took her to get ready, the more her confidence waned. Wouldn't she look a fool, showing up to a place where she wasn't invited? What right did she have to show her face? What if she went all that way just for Gia to reject her?

A thousand small fears filled her mind.

Nonetheless, she pulled on her sandals and a dull grey palla, pulling it up over her head to disguise her hair, then she left her room, sternly ordering her guards not to follow as she blazed through the building.

'Is there something I can help with, Empress?' said Damocles, popping up at her elbow.

She didn't entirely trust him, but she didn't entirely care either. She was tired of creeping around and denying herself, particularly now she knew there were senators throwing parties for her kind. If

Damocles chose to stir the pot, then she would handle it. She would handle him.

'I will need a chariot,' she said, 'and a driver. Someone known for their discretion.'

'It is rather late, Empress,' he said.

'I can tell the time. Some things cannot wait until daylight.'

'Is this connected to what you told me earlier? If so, I really must advise against it. It would not be safe.'

'No, this is a personal matter.'

'May I ask to where you're travelling?'

'There is a senator here in Rome, known for throwing parties of a certain nature,' she said. 'Have you heard of him?'

'What sort of nature? That hardly narrows it down.'

'The kind . . .' She could hardly spit the words out, even though Damocles had heard the same rumours as everyone else. 'The kind attended by a certain persuasion . . . those who stay with their own kind.'

Damocles blinked at her. 'That would be rather inadvisable, given the circumstances. Are you sure you wish to stoke that fire?'

'There is someone there I must talk to, urgently.'

She didn't admit that it was Gia.

Damocles stroked his pointed beard with one hand.

'I may have heard of it, but I've never received an invite.'

'I need to know who he is. Nothing insidious. He has done nothing wrong. He shall not know you gave his name.'

'Senator Philopappos. People call him . . . Pappa.'

'He has children?'

'No,' said Damocles, thoughtfully. 'I don't think that's the kind of papa they mean.'

He bustled off to organize her ride, telling her to meet him outside. As she crossed a courtyard, Claudia heard the rustle of a bush and pulled up sharply, fearing General Aquinas might jump out.

Muffled voices grew louder, forcing her to hide.

Concealed behind a pillar, she watched two figures moving behind a trellis that obscured them, barely visible through the gaps in the wood, threaded with vines and leaves.

'You're sure she's not watching in her rooms?'

This was a Roman man, wearing a soldier's uniform.

'I am certain. She is going out. They are arranging a chariot for her as we speak.'

This was an accented man, wearing many rings.

It was Darius, she realized.

'Then now is the time.'

'Good, because I have been waiting.'

'Where shall we go?'

'How about right here?'

'If we are caught, you must pretend that I am very drunk.'

'Understood, my prince.'

Claudia heard the rustling of robes.

'I am just very desperate for affection, you see, and I will accept it from anyone,' the prince said.

'Anyone, is it? You are a charmer, aren't you?'

Cassius.

Darius . . . and Cassius.

The world turned like a wheel, and Claudia reeled. She sprang up and fled before she could be seen, running to the front of the palace where her chariot was waiting, and tumbled in.

'Take me to the villa of Senator Philopappos.'

'Yes, Empress.'

They drove away with the clatter of horseshoes, and Claudia's mind was ablaze. She was furious – the prince had used her secret to get his way, all while he was guilty of the same. But she was also feeling something else, something less simple to define.

It was as if the world had become fully illuminated and she could see the truth for the first time.

Senators who threw parties for people of the same inclination. A prince who would sleep with a soldier for fun.

Darius. Cassius. Livia. Dido. Even Gia. They were all exploring their desires, in their own way.

Claudia had made herself prisoner in her own mind but she was the gods-damn empress, and she would be prisoner no more.

She was free.

She felt free for the first time in her life.

Claudia vaguely recalled Senator Philopappos as an opponent of her father's, but she'd had few dealings with him personally. He was known for his generosity during the festival of Saturnalia in December, when he prepared a feast for his staff and waited on his slaves.

He lived in a sprawling, lavish villa on Aventine Hill, surrounded by scrubby trees. It was difficult to see from the nearest road, enveloped in the folds of the sloping land.

As Claudia's chariot approached, she heard loud music coming from inside, playing a lively song with strong bass drums.

'Should I wait?' asked the driver.

'Yes, though I may be several hours.'

'I'm sure I can find a way to entertain myself,' he said.

He looked out at the villa, at the figures who hung out between columns, calling out to those who passed by and offering their services.

Climbing out of the chariot and making sure her palla was still in place, Claudia took a deep breath and approached the villa, trying not to meet the gaze of any of the men on guard. Though she sensed several lingering looks, they were more of curiosity than desire. They didn't whistle or call out coarse words, as men tended to do. She got the sense that they too were members of Pappa's covert same-sex club.

The house was full of the noise of merriment and intoxication: singing, laughter, and an uproarious cry as someone shattered a vase, with people whistling and applauding.

Claudia dared to peek out at the small crowd gathered on the portico outside, smoking pungent-smelling herbs in makeshift pipes. She glimpsed two men with their faces painted like women, wearing wigs like the actor who'd played her in *The Three Coins*.

At the doorway, a burly man stepped in her path, giving her a questioning look.

'I don't know you. What's your name?'

The first thing that came to Claudia's mind was the all-woman party she'd attended back in Pompeii, thrown by the senator's wife her brother had killed.

'Julia.'

'You sure you belong here, Julia?' he said, inspecting her.

'I am certain. My mistress is within.'

'You look like the empress, you know. You ever hear that?'

'Once or twice,' she said, dying inside. 'I'm not flattered.'

He smirked. 'Go on, then.'

Claudia glided on. The next room was so full she could hardly move through it, which was oddly a blessing, as no one paid much attention to her. She was just another body in the throng of robes, all weaving and knotting together as they danced to the band.

Claudia spotted Pappa himself, conducting from his seat. Ruddy and bearded, he was humming along to a song without words. He was clearly having a good time, flanked on either side by two bare-chested, younger men who fed him wine and grapes.

She wasn't sure how she was going to find Gia in among so many people but she pushed on stubbornly, pressing her hands together to form a point and carving her way through the crowd like a knife, ducking under one sweaty armpit and bursting between two amorous lovers.

Within the space of several minutes, Claudia had seen everything it was possible to see in a single villa at once, including a drinking competition, a man being walked like a dog, two senators splashing each other playfully in the pool, soldiers slow-dancing in a silent, empty room, brothel girls kissing each other in a small Temple of Venus and tall, glamorous women dressed in strange fashions from overseas.

But there were also plenty of ordinary-looking people here – people she wouldn't have picked out. Athletes and physicians, politicians and slaves, artists and courtesans, all mingling together merrily.

She felt like a traveller, a tourist, arriving to see the otherworldly sights of a world much different to her own – one in which people kissed busts of dead philosophers and played games that forfeited their clothes.

They were all so happy, she noticed. Smiling broadly. Dancing free. They seemed unafraid and unashamed.

As she moved out towards the atrium, she glimpsed someone familiar on the other side of the crowd – not Gia, but Celadus.

Celadus the Handsome, and he was arm in arm with another gladiator. Claudia caught his eye, their faces mirrored with surprise and a strange kind of reaffirmation.

This was how he knew Dido and Livia.

This was why he told her they were not right for each other.

This was why she'd been drawn to him, because they were akin.

First Darius, and now Celadus: Claudia certainly had a habit of gravitating towards men-loving men.

He raised his hand in greeting and she raised hers in return, but then they both moved on in some mutual agreement of privacy, like passing ships on the queerest of seas.

Claudia also made note of several other people she recognized, including several senators.

She found her way to the atrium, which was full of nude statues, open to the starry autumn skies. They were not the familiar gods, but scenes from older Greek mythology.

She recognized Achilles and Patroclus in their tragic embrace.

People like her had always existed, sometimes in the shadows, sometimes in the open. They were a part of history, and now she was a part of it. She was one of them.

Finally, she glimpsed Gia through the parting waves of people and time slowed, like she commanded its flow.

She hadn't seen her yet.

Claudia was afraid that she might've fallen into Livia's well-toned arms already, but she was just leaning against the wall nursing an empty chalice, staring into thin air.

She may have been the unhappiest person there.

As Claudia wove between the shiny marble bodies of the statues, headed in their direction, the others turned to spy her, close enough that they had no difficulty recognizing her.

'Look who it is,' said Dido, delighted.

'I told you she was possessive,' whispered Livia, clearly furious.

'Claudia?' said Gia, squinting as she sighted her.

'I am Julia tonight,' she said, holding one finger to her lips.

Gia stood upright, swaying slightly. She had the glaze-eyed look of a person who had drunk a great deal in a short time, which was finally catching up with her all at once.

'What are you doing here?' she said.

'You left without a word.'

'You removed me from duty. I don't need your permission to leave the palace, do I?'

'This is not about duty.'

'Then what?' asked Gia.

Claudia's neck burned red as she dropped her eyes.

'For you,' said Claudia, quietly. 'I am here for you.'

Gia bit down on her lip, shaking her head.

'I saw . . . I saw you,' she said. 'You and the prince. He—'

'You are angry and upset, I understand,' said Claudia. 'I would be too. I know what you think you saw but—'

'How did you even find me?' said Gia.

One moment later, the denarius dropped.

'You watched through the shield again, didn't you?'

'I wanted to clear up any confusion. I was out of my mind, thinking that I couldn't explain myself. I have so much to tell you. I promise, it wasn't what it looked like.'

'Oh, I've heard that one before,' muttered Livia.

‘Shhh,’ hissed Dido.

‘My own eyes lied to me?’ said Gia.

‘It was not what you think. Please, let us talk. Alone. Then I will leave, and you can stay, if you wish.’

‘Say it here, or not at all.’

‘Here? Right here?’

Claudia didn’t think Gia would ordinarily be so reckless, declaring this for all to hear, but she was past her normal reason. She didn’t budge, waiting for Claudia to give in.

Dido and Livia did not attempt to disguise the fact that they were watching. Several others around them were paying attention now too, shifting curiously and cutting eyes at each other.

‘I cannot,’ said Claudia.

‘Then it can’t be important,’ said Gia.

‘Please, Gia. It isn’t safe for us to talk openly. Not even here. I might be recognized.’

‘I am tired of hiding.’

‘So am I, but there are things that should only be between us.’

Gia’s expression was conflicted, as she struggled against herself, but then she relented, sighing in disappointment at herself.

‘I will not order you,’ continued Claudia, ‘but I *am* begging you. Must I get down on my knees and further humiliate myself?’

‘Fine. We’ll talk outside.’

‘Should we follow?’ said Dido, not wanting to miss anything.

Livia gravely shook her head, holding her back.

Gia and Claudia ducked out into a small courtyard full of colourful plants, forming a rainbow around a small fountain and a pool.

‘You didn’t have to come all the way out here,’ Gia said. ‘You could’ve just waited for me to return.’

'I was afraid that you might not.'

Gia was unsteady on her feet, tripping over a pavement stone. Claudia tried not to find it adorable since they were about to have a very serious conversation, suppressing a smile when Gia looked at her.

Gia only made it halfway down the path before pulling up.

'Is it just me, or is the garden spinning?'

'That would be the wine, I fear.'

'I . . . don't feel so good.'

Claudia guided her to the nearest bench, where Gia hunched forward as if she might be sick. They were still being watched here, which made her cautious to hold and comfort Gia as she wished to. She settled for rubbing her back as Gia sat forward with her head in her hands.

'Is that better?' Claudia asked.

'Why did I drink so much?'

'You wanted to forget.'

'That's just what my mother used to say, too. Ugh, I'm a mess.'

'When we first met, you had just taken a beating to the face, and you were still so beautiful to me . . . This is nothing, by comparison.'

Gia sat up abruptly again and stared at Claudia, her expression somewhere between anger and sadness.

'You kissed him,' she said. 'Why did you kiss him?'

'*He* kissed me.'

'You let him kiss you, then.'

'It was a mistake. An accident, actually. I offered him my cheek to appease him and he went for the lips. You'll be glad to know it was not a good kiss. There is nothing between us. Not a flame, not even a spark. It was like kissing Damocles.'

Gia pulled a face, as if picturing it again.

'That wasn't how it looked to me.'

'You were far away, and it was dark,' said Claudia, 'and I am not convinced your eyesight is that good.'

'Oh, thanks.'

'You are all I thought about, the whole time.'

'You are all I think about, always,' said Gia, still annoyed. 'I still don't understand why you kissed him.'

'He had just finished telling me that I had no choice but to go through with the marriage! It wasn't even slightly romantic. He knows about us. He has been watching me, watching us like we have watched him. He fears Marcellus will overthrow me and start a war with Persia. He told me I have three days to decide. You must believe me. All that kiss did was make me realize that I am all for you, in every way.'

Gia finally met her gaze properly, and Claudia felt her soul drawn into hers.

'And Darius is hiding, just like us,' said Claudia.

'In what way is he like us?'

'Steady yourself for this: I saw him . . . with your brother.'

'Doing what?' Gia asked.

'Doing . . . *it*. What do you think?'

'My brother and the prince?' said Gia, screwing up her face. 'I may be even drunker than I thought.'

'It's true. They seem to have some prior arrangement. It appeared to be . . . purely sexual, in nature.'

'Please, do not put that image in my head.'

'I know I told Cassius to get close to Darius, but this was not quite what I had in mind.' She thought for a moment. 'Darius did say that he was living a lie. Maybe this is what he meant.'

'Did you confront them?' Gia asked.

'No. Perhaps it is something we can use to our advantage, since the prince wants to play games with me.'

Gia looked shaken, before she started laughing.

'You could not make it up,' she said. 'Cassius doesn't want me to be with an empress but he can fool around with a prince? Wait until I get hold of that brother of mine.'

'He is biased, like all men. The prince is a hypocrite, too. He can do nothing to force my hand now, or I could expose him. He has nothing over me, over us. Nothing, except . . . Marcellus. But perhaps we should sober you up first.'

'The shock of my brother's exploits has done just that.'

'Let us go back to the palace, for privacy,' said Claudia. 'Unless you wish to stay and enjoy the party a while longer?'

'I have revelled enough, I think.'

'I fear my arrival has soured the mood.'

They met eyes, silently appraising each other.

'Maybe we could return another day and dance the night away, instead of drinking too much and arguing,' said Claudia.

'I'd like that,' said Gia. 'I was envious, watching you dancing with him. If only we could dance openly, in the palace, like that.'

'Are you okay to stand up now?'

'I think so. Ugh, I am so embarrassed.'

'Don't be. I am the one who watched you in a magic shield . . . again. I should be more embarrassed than you.'

'Okay. We'll both take this one.'

'Deal.'

Claudia stood up, letting Gia lean on her; somehow, this load-bearing stance turned into a drunken embrace.

'I love you,' said Gia, with utmost earnestness, 'more than anything in the world, but I cannot go on like this – always living in doubt, apart from you, behind closed doors.'

'I know. I love you too. I have been a coward, and I have been confused, but no more,' said Claudia. 'I won't let you down again.'

'I won't ask you to choose. I know you can't.'

'We'll make it work. We will find a way. We have to. None of this means anything, unless I have you by my side.'

Claudia realized that music was playing, and that they were in each other's arms anyway – she may as well commit.

Why one day, when it could be today instead?

She began swaying them both, side to side, until Gia realized what she was doing. Laughing, she spun her, as Darius had shown them.

Claudia forgot where she was, as longing took over her. She reached up and cupped Gia's face gently, kissing her softly as she bent down to meet her. Her lips were sweet from wine, and so warm Claudia melted into them.

It was incomparable to her kiss with Darius – the way they blended together, the way their fingers linked without effort, and the flame that burned between them, flickering, tickling her insides.

'Just so you know, I was never going anywhere,' said Gia. 'I lost my head a bit, but I cannot leave you. I wouldn't want to. I would die for you a thousand times, whether you gave me permission or not.'

'I hope it does not come to that.'

Claudia kissed her once more.

When she pulled back, smiling, she heard a gasp and a giggle, looking up to see a crowd of people gawking from the colonnade.

Worse, the hood of her palla had fallen down, revealing her hair and her identity along with it.

She had been recognized. She heard the whispers resounding: *Empress, it's the empress!*

The secret was out now.

'The Empress of Lesbos!' someone shouted, yet this time, it was not an insult but a cheer.

Claudia saw Senator Pappas waving at her across the pool.

'I think we should go,' she said. 'Right now.'

'Solid plan.'

Gia and Claudia made a hasty exit from the villa, issuing a bashful goodbye to Dido and Livia before climbing (with some difficulty on Gia's part) into the waiting chariot. A crowd gathered to watch them depart, talking excitedly about what they'd witnessed. Pappas appeared on the steps just as they drove away, squinting as he tried to make out her face.

They had been seen.

There was no pretending otherwise.

Rumours were rumours and satire was satire, but kissing her gladiator-guard at a party full of people could not be plausibly denied.

Claudia had exposed herself, and denied anyone else the power.

It was strangely liberating.

17. SOME DARK AND MONSTROUS MAGIC

Back at the palace, all was eerily quiet. When the chariot driver saluted her, Claudia noticed that his uniform was dishevelled, as if it had been hastily removed, while a smear of make-up showed on his cheek.

'What is your name, sir?' she asked.

'Amir.'

'Thanks, Amir, you're a legend,' said Gia, shaking his hand. 'An absolute legend, of the ages.'

'I may ask for you again by name,' said Claudia,

'It would be my honour,' he said.

Only a few guards were awake to patrol the grounds. Claudia wondered which of them might be working for the general, or serving Jupiter. She felt the net closing in around them.

She told herself she just had to get through the night. In the morning, the traitors would be called to stand before her and she could remove the threat they posed – whatever it took to do so.

It was almost over.

'Come on, you,' said Claudia, steering Gia inside.

*

As Gia clumsily attempted to make some food in the kitchen, Claudia explained how Darius had shown her who was conspiring against her: the senators and the general who brought Marcellus to Rome. Tacitus. Thelonius. Aquinas.

'It has been them, working for my cousin all along,' Claudia said, as she snacked on olives. 'The Pantheon, the knife you found, the attempt at the Circus Maximus: they were behind it all.'

'How does Darius know all of this, though?' said Gia.

'His goddess, Anahita. She guides him, as Minerva guides me. He has a talisman that gifts him with visions of the past.'

'I hope his gods will not go to war with ours.'

Claudia shuddered. 'Do not speak of it.'

They scavenged a meagre spread of leftovers, taking their feast up to Claudia's room, which was really *their* room. She sent Nadira and her guard away, not caring if they found it suspicious or not.

'I fear Darius is right and Marcellus will return. But if I can prove his treachery, I can make sure my cousin never comes close to touching the crown.'

'Then what?'

'I could have him arrested,' said Claudia, 'or order one of the leagues to capture him overseas and bring him here.'

'His allies might aid him.'

'I could even kill him, if I had to.'

'You cannot kill every man who stands in your way,' said Gia.

'Says who?'

'History won't remember you well for it.'

They lay down on the bed together as Gia pulled her closer, locked in an embrace. When their eyes met, Claudia felt her soul rising and falling in rhythm with her heart, the silence between them surging and flooding, until she could no longer keep the words at bay.

'I'm sorry I pushed you away,' she said. 'I should never have asked you to leave. I regret us sleeping alone.'

'It's in the past now.'

'You're sure?'

'I promise ... There is nothing to fight over, nothing to be sad over. We're here, and we're together ... I love you.'

'I love you too. More than anything in the world.'

They had nothing left to say, but they gazed at each other for as long as possible, as if afraid to fall asleep.

Finally, Gia passed out.

Claudia watched for a while to make sure she was okay, then carefully climbed out and used the shield to learn all she could about the three men of Marcellus.

Two of the men were so morally debased it took only a few hours to find incriminating information on them. The greasy-haired Tacitus paid brothel girls to spank him with wooden paddles as he wailed like an infant, which Claudia was sure he would not wish for his constituents to know, while Thelonius beat his wife and his mistress alike: not unusual for a Roman man but in stark contrast to the public persona he'd donned. It was only General Aquinas Claudia couldn't pin down. He was a family man and deeply reverent to his god Jupiter, with a flawless reputation as a military hero and pillar of the community.

He was a snake, as Gia would say, but he was a boring snake. She had nothing on him. He would not be so easy to disrupt or convert. But she would keep searching, watching him through the shield.

Claudia pondered the best course of action. By firing Hieronymus, she'd created a dangerous and very vocal enemy, one who had turned against her at the soonest convenience. Expelling the general and the senators would make them even more inclined to work against her. Yet she knew she couldn't change their minds. She would never win them over on merit, for they would never recognize it.

The only way to ensure their loyalty was to bribe them.

Rather than accusing them publicly, stripping them of their titles and having them executed, she decided to seize control of them instead, to put their connections and cunning to use for her own gain.

Claudia would call them to her court and tell them, in the simplest of terms, that their secrets would be broadcast to the public unless they agreed to serve her. She would play them at their own game. If they refused, which they indeed might, she could at least ensure their reputations were sullied in the name of protecting her own. She couldn't be entirely confident that the other men would turn against them, based on what she'd learned, but it was the only leverage she had.

To her surprise and concern, Claudia found that she was now unable to spy on her cousin once more, for reasons unknown.

She had seen him in Britannia before, but now, speaking his name returned only darkness, as it had to begin with.

She tried several times, whispering his name to the shield, but Minerva refused to reveal him.

Why would he be hidden from the sight of a goddess?

Unless . . . he was being protected by a god?

Claudia was having a dream in which she and Gia were living together back in Pompeii, running the Via Stabiana taberna together.

Gia was cooking, her face rosy from the heat of the oven. Gia's mother was still there, laughing with Cassius at Lucas and his dog. Claudia served the customers, cleaning the tables, content to live an ordinary life.

Suddenly, Minerva appeared at the door like a customer hungry for food, helmeted and carrying her spear.

'Wake up, Empress,' she said. *'You are needed.'*

Claudia woke with a start, in Gia's warm arms.

She could already hear it – as if the sound had bled through into her dreams – a military procession snaking through the streets: a procession she'd neither approved nor been informed of.

Scrambling to the window, she saw a parade of soldiers waving flags and blaring horns. In the middle of the military mob, Claudia sighted an imperial chariot, framed by golden wings.

Sitting inside was her cousin, waving to the crowd and flashing the sign of victory.

A frantic knocking sounded, accompanied by the soft calling of her name in repetition.

'Empress? Empress?'

Claudia nudged Gia awake.

'Wake up,' she whispered. 'Someone's at the door.'

'What's going on?' said Gia, still groggy from the night before.

'It's Marcellus,' she said. 'He's back.'

Gia grunted unhappily in response.

'Just a minute!' Claudia called.

Though her secret was out and she'd vowed not to hide herself any more, she instinctively drew the curtains, hiding Gia from view.

Better to be safe than sorry.

'I'm coming!'

When Claudia opened the door, it wasn't just her handmaids waiting for her but also Damocles, Rectina and a group of guards, all displaying different shades of alarm on their faces.

'I know. My cousin has returned. I have seen . . . and heard.'

She winced as another horn blared.

'He found the missing legion and brought them home,' said Damocles. 'We did not expect Marcellus to return for weeks.'

'*All* of them? How?'

'We don't know the details yet,' said Rectina, 'but there is something of the divine about it.'

Claudia cursed, anticipating what might come next.

'I'll be right with you, just let me get dressed.'

'Shall I help you, Empress?' said Nadira.

Claudia looked furtively at the curtains. They rustled, indicating that she wasn't alone, but then Princess jumped down, gave a sleepy growl and wound around Nadira's legs.

'No, that's fine,' said Claudia. 'I can do it myself.'

'Yes, Empress. I'll go and fix this sweet baby some breakfast.'

'Please call Marcellus to the throne room, Damocles.'

Claudia shut the door and leaned against it, closing her eyes as her mind raced. When she opened them again, Gia had parted the curtains and was waiting to meet her gaze.

'We have to get up,' said Claudia.

'Must we?'

'I'm afraid so, my lover.'

A loud horn sounded, startling Gia into a sitting position.

'Okay, okay.'

'If I'm still empress by tonight, I'll issue a decree for a longer lie-in,' said Claudia, kissing her.

Gia leaned into it, pulling her closer, but there was no time.

'Alas, I have to find out what Marcellus is up to,' Claudia said, gently pulling back. 'I think he's making another claim to become emperor. The streets are full of soldiers venerating him.'

Gia groaned more dramatically this time.

'I hope I don't have to fight him for our lives, in the state that I am in this morning,' she said.

Once they were presentable to the world, which took considerably longer than usual, they stood at the balcony, watching as soldiers gathered outside in the Forum in great numbers. Their red cloaks, helmet fringes and shields matched the red flags and eagle standards they carried. A drummer played as a priest in red robes commanded the crowd.

'Father Jupiter, as the Sun has born witness, you were not deaf to our pleas,' cried the flamen priest. 'You were not blind to our suffering. You have heard us, and you have fought for us. These men, survivors of the battle, dedicate to you our trophies and the armour of our victories.'

The soldiers cheered uproariously.

'Gods above, we do not pray for peace. Grant rage onto the nations. Bring forth the whole world in arms to war!'

'All hail Jupiter!'

As they made their way downstairs, soldiers filed into the throne room. Many people turned as she approached, whispering furtively. Claudia knew her appearance at Pappa's party would be legendary by noon, and that everyone in Rome would know the truth.

'I gather that you rather enjoyed yourself last night,' said Damocles, appearing at her side. 'Which is good, because I'm not sure you'll have anything to celebrate for a while.'

'Good morning to you too, Damocles.'

'The parade is quite a spectacle, isn't it?' said Damocles.

'It is . . . something.'

'As far as I can gather, the entire legion has been converted after witnessing some sort of miracle in Britannia. An intervention of the gods, to aid Rome's victory.'

Claudia frowned, her mind snagging and spooling.

'I have worse news, I'm afraid,' said Damocles.

He looked into the throne room, nodding towards a group of three men, who stood in league beside her cousin.

Senators Tacitus and Thelonius, and General Aquinas.

'We can't detain them now,' Damocles said. 'Even our own soldiers believe them to be triumphant heroes.'

'Your ability to summon a goddess is the only thing that stood between Marcellus and the empire,' said Rectina.

'You think Jupiter intervened in his favour?'

'If he can demonstrate his ability to do the same and summon Jupiter himself, I fear your reign may end imminently,' said Rectina.

'I have the same fear,' said Claudia. 'Any advice?'

Rectina appeared distraught, shaking her head as if it were an empty box. 'An offering to the goddesses?'

'I have already tried.'

'Perhaps we should flee, while we still can.'

Claudia looked to Damocles.

'Unless you are open to marrying your cousin—'

'Absolutely not.'

‘Then no,’ he said. ‘I am out of ideas.’

‘What of the prince?’

‘I do not think he’ll be a problem for much longer.’

Claudia grew cold with the realization. Marcellus might kill Darius. Her only powerful, if tentative, ally.

‘Good luck, Empress,’ said Damocles.

None of the soldiers saluted her entrance. They seemed to be deferential to Marcellus, looking to him for guidance.

Her cousin stood with one foot on the stairs that led to the seated gold chair, as if he was merely biding his time before taking it from her. He was mid-sentence, holding forth to Cassius and Darius.

‘They’d been spirited away by those painted barbarians.’

‘The natives, you mean,’ said Cassius.

‘Horrible people,’ said cold-eyed Aquinas. ‘Vulgar and filthy, with the minds of rabid beasts.’

Cassius looked at him with undisguised disgust.

‘By the glory of the gods, we will triumph. We must continue to bring civilization to the savages.’

‘We had every soldier in the area looking for the soldiers,’ said Marcellus, trying to return to his monologue. ‘The Legate had given up all hope, until I stepped in to—’

He caught sight of Claudia.

‘Claudia,’ he said.

Not empress, or even princess, but her cold, naked name.

‘Marcellus.’

Meeting eyes with Darius, she gracefully took her seat on the throne, while Gia positioned herself next to her.

‘Have you heard the good news? I have personally delivered the missing legion to safety,’ said Marcellus.

'I have.'

He waited for an acknowledgement that didn't come.

'Aren't you going to thank me?'

Claudia smiled without teeth, suppressing the murderous impulses that tore through her.

'Congratulations, cousin. I did not know doing your duty warranted a prize,' she said.

'Is that all you have to say?'

'I shall have a wreath made especially for you,' she said, in a voice as sweet as syrup and as poisonous as henbane. 'Perhaps you could tell us exactly how you performed this astonishing feat?'

'You don't just have to take my word for it,' said Marcellus. 'The soldiers of the Eighth Legion are all telling the same story. There is no denying what happened.'

'Which is?'

'I prayed to Jupiter for guidance. I made an offering and asked him to find and return the men and prove his might. The next morning, they were back in their camp.'

Gia and Claudia exchanged a sceptical look.

'Just like that?'

'Just like that.'

'Well, where did they go?' asked Damocles.

'They say they were captured by a feral warrior queen.'

Gia's eyes lit up.

Claudia shot her a look that said, 'Focus.'

'They were taken back to her fort and interrogated,' he said.

'Thousands of men were captured by a single woman?' said Cassius. 'They didn't resist? None of them were harmed?'

It seemed he was sceptical too.

'They were vanished away by some dark and monstrous magic. But Jupiter himself appeared to her and appealed for their freedom. She feared the wrath of the gods and let them go.'

'And what of the queen?'

'She was killed, to set an example,' said General Aquinas.

A solemn hush fell upon the room.

The general's eyes were not dark like her brother's, but a cool pale blue. Yet they had the same skin-crawling emptiness.

Claudia recognized it well.

'I'm still not clear on the details of how an entire legion was whisked away and returned like a scroll from a library without a single drop of blood being spilled?' she said, holding his gaze.

'Jupiter blessed us. He aided our passage home,' said Marcellus. 'Our ship moved at four times the speed.'

Claudia looked to Gia, then to Rectina, mutually recalling how Salacia had spirited them to Rome across the sea, faster than any ship could ever sail without divine intervention.

'And what does your god expect in return?' asked Claudia.

'That is between him and me,' he said.

She looked to Darius, thinking of the prophecy he'd foretold: Marcellus as emperor.

'Perhaps we should discuss an appropriate reward,' said Damocles. He gave Claudia a sharp look, which she interpreted to mean that she needed to placate her cousin, but she was sick of coddling men.

'A parade, a public holiday, a new building named after the great Marcellus Suetonius?' Damocles suggested.

'I have a much greater reward in mind,' said Marcellus.

'Which is?'

He looked to the throne, but he didn't say anything.

'I asked you to speak with the Legate, Marcellus,' said Claudia. 'I didn't give you permission to launch a mission.'

'I need your permission to save thousands of lives?'

'You need my permission to take military action. What you and your men did is a capital crime.'

Marcellus's wide smile faltered.

'We could stand here pointing fingers but it would do Rome no good,' he said. 'You have seen the work of the deities for yourself. You have your goddesses, and now I have my gods. The people outside are celebrating. Our soldiers have been saved. Let us just enjoy this moment.'

He had her in a bind. She couldn't arrest and imprison the men whose devotion had supposedly saved an entire legion, including General Aquinas, though he unsettled her flesh.

'We will put it aside, for now,' she conceded.

'We can talk this evening,' said Marcellus. His gaze lingered on the prince. 'There are matters we need to discuss.'

'Then we shall arrange a welcome dinner,' said Damocles. 'It will be our great honour, of course.'

'It shall be done,' said Rectina, less enthusiastically.

'Good, I will see you then.'

It was typical of him to announce an event, then expect everyone else to arrange it.

When Marcellus departed with his soldiers to join the joyous Martian cult outside, Claudia addressed the prince and Cassius:

'You two should remain.'

'Me?' said Cassius.

'Yes, I'm afraid so.' She turned to Damocles and Rectina. 'Leave us, please.'

Damocles huffed in indignation but dutifully left, corralling the other advisors as he did. Claudia waited until the room had emptied before setting her eyes on Prince Darius.

'It's time to discuss our deal,' she said.

'You have come to a decision?' said the prince.

'Yes, but my terms are different now.'

'Oh?'

'I happened, quite by chance, to stumble upon a most intriguing scene late last night . . . What you get up to in your own time is your own business, of course. Isn't that what you said to me, Darius? But, and here I quote: "I am not the only one with eyes in Rome". You're lucky it was only me, who saw you. Roman men will do what they do behind closed doors, we all know that, but you were sent here to secure a wife, were you not? A prince of Persia and a foreign soldier? Your father won't like it.'

'Empress,' said the prince, bowing his head in regret. 'Whatever you witnessed, it was not . . . it did not—'

'It . . . it's not like that,' said Cassius.

He paled, looking to Gia.

'I already know of it,' she said. 'I must say, I am rather surprised, brother, after you expressed such strong opinions about an empress being with a gladiator.'

'It isn't the same,' Darius protested.

'You think a prince and a soldier is different? Or you think it's different because you are men?' said Claudia.

'I am not at risk of throwing away my privilege and power for him,' said Darius. 'He is not my guard, sworn to protect me. He has no loyalty or allegiance with me. It is simply recreational.'

'It *is* the same thing,' said Claudia firmly. 'Both of us are free to choose whom we desire, without being held to the fire for it. You have nothing over me, and I have nothing I wish to hold over you. Certainly not this. This should never be held over a person as if they have committed a crime, simply by loving someone.'

'I didn't say anything about love,' objected Cassius.

'Please, you must understand,' pleaded the prince. 'We must marry. My father will disown me. He sent me away and told me not to return until I am married. If he hears of this, he'll be furious. There are . . .' His face fell further. 'There are already rumours he wished for me to dispel by marrying the empress of Rome.'

The misunderstandings Darius mentioned, back at home. He'd referenced them when they spoke of the graffiti. Claudia hadn't pushed the issue, trying to play her hand too carefully. Perhaps if she had done a bit more probing, they could've come to an easier understanding.

'You wish to hide it for your own reasons and I will respect that, but I will hide no more. My marital status, my preference – it should not reflect on my ability to rule.'

'You would live in the open?' he said. 'Together.'

Claudia looked to Gia.

'I find that I have grown weary of hiding,' she answered. 'Perhaps there is nothing greater to be gained than to live an authentic life, no matter the cost.'

She and Gia exchanged a smile, more secure now, before Claudia turned back to Darius.

'Were they real?' she asked. 'The visions you showed me?'

The prince's solemn expression deepened, became grave.

'All of them. This was the only lie. I promise you that. I swear on my life, on the lives of my animals, everything else was true,' he said.

'How can I trust you now?'

'Because you have seen me, the real me,' he said, holding her gaze firmly. 'You know who I am now, and what I am running from. I saved your life, and I will do it again, Empress. I will fight with you to the end, in alliance, as we are meant to be.'

Claudia paused, nodding softly as she considered it.

'So, here it is,' she said, after a moment. 'Here is *my* proposal, to you, and I think you'll find it quite fair, if you are willing to hear it?'

The prince nodded, his eyes on the ground.

'You will remain here in Rome until Marcellus and his men have been dealt with. We'll work together to ensure he doesn't come to power, thus disrupting whatever dark future your goddess saw. You will return to Persepolis and tell your father we have signed a pax to ensure continued peace, despite our failed engagement. Find another wife to satisfy him, if you wish to live in secrecy. I will not wage a war with you, and you will not wage a war with me . . . but we shall end our engagement today. We can still bring peace to our people, just not in the way that was chosen for us by our families.'

He stared at his ringed hands, helpless as a boy.

'Will you agree to these terms?' she said.

Darius stared off into the distance, his eyes shining with unshed tears. Claudia couldn't work out what he was thinking.

But after a moment, he nodded solemnly.

'I am tired of hiding too,' he said.

She had seen him, and he had seen her.

This time, when he took her hand and kissed it, it was not as a fiancé or a lover but something else.

18. MURDERESS

As Claudia sat down to her cousin's welcome home hero dinner, she found herself thinking about her late brother, Decimus.

She recalled his final dinner party, on the last night of the world back in Pompeii; how they had sat around a table heaped with rotting food as rocks hammered the roof and fire burned rivers down the hillside, her brother screaming about Jupiter's cosmic power.

She remembered when he told her that Gia was dead, and how she had ceased to care that the world was ending thereafter, growing numb as slaves whipped senators and eels ate flesh.

Compared to that, this feast was perfectly pleasant and properly civil, with its soft lyre music, its delicate decorations and delectable menu, all organized with great order and class by Damocles and Rectina.

Yet Claudia felt the same sinister, foreboding undercurrent running beneath the surface as the invited guests took their seats, making her cold, her stomach turning in anticipation.

Claudia, Cassius and Darius joined a table of senators, generals and soldiers, while Gia had been relegated to the servants' table, along with Rectina and the prince's remaining staff. The servants' table was almost entirely women, while, at Claudia's, she was the only one.

Looking around, she noticed Senator Philopappos sitting between Pliny the Elder and another man. He looked anxious too, even ruddier of face than usual, pulling at the collar of his robes.

He met her eye . . . and looked away.

Her cousin was surrounded by his usual triad of patrons. General Aquinas whispered in his ear, as Claudia took advice from Damocles and Pliny.

Marcellus had his people, and she had hers. It was a bit like a gladiator match, with two competitors preparing for battle, but the fight was one of words and politics: persuasion and manipulation. Marcellus would be the favoured competitor, with a clear advantage, but the night was not yet over. She was not yet ready to give in.

At the start of proceedings, Claudia had little choice but to praise the triumph of Jupiter and Marcellus, announcing her intention to make him Commander of the Roman army.

'Thank you, cousin. How very generous of you.'

But he barely reacted to the news, though everyone else in the room dutifully applauded.

Something was off.

Claudia vowed to get through dinner as quickly as possible.

She drank a glass of wine too fast, unable to wait for a servant to pour it. It went right to her head, making her woozy. She tried to fill up on bread and olives, waiting to be served, though her poison taster delayed her, insisting on checking everything.

It was probably wise, in the circumstances.

Servers dished out food, steamed fish and grilled vegetables, and Claudia was so ravenous she briefly forgot that they were in the middle of what might well turn into a coup.

Halfway through the main course of goose, Marcellus stood up unexpectedly and clinked his glass against a vase, making a *ting-ting-ting* sound that drew everyone's attention.

'My esteemed fellows, I assume you've all heard of my heroic rescue of the Eighth Legion by now,' he said.

A round of applause sounded, as Marcellus bowed.

'Yes, thank you. Thank you. General Aquinas and I have brought our troops home to safety. The city is celebrating. Rome is once again victorious in battle.'

Senators Tacitus and Thelonius looked to each other.

Marcellus gestured at the door as some of the lost soldiers filed in – looking worse for wear but very much alive.

'They were captured in Britannia by barbarians,' said Marcellus. 'A wild warrior queen tortured them, but Jupiter came to their aid. Like me, they witnessed a pack of hunting dogs that appeared from the sky, followed by a parade of flying chariots. Archers fired arrows at their captors from the air, setting the barbarian village on fire before the queen was killed and they were whisked back to Rome.'

The guests were rapt, murmuring in awe.

'Jupiter has proclaimed himself my patron. He is backing my campaign to be emperor. Tomorrow, I shall go to the Senate and make my claim as the rightful princeps and ruler of Rome.'

As the room exploded into a riot of support and opposition, Marcellus calmly touched the clasp that held his red cloak together, engraved with a relief of Jupiter himself. He adopted a serene smile, his eyes shining, alight with superhuman confidence.

Claudia stood up immediately. 'You will not,' she said.

Immediately, four soldiers surrounded her, preventing her from leaving her place.

'What are you doing?' she said. 'I am your empress. You do not point your weapons at me.'

But the men remained in position, ignoring her command.

'Unhand her,' demanded Darius.

Still, the men did not release her.

'If I were you, Prince Darius, I would return to Persia and tell your father that the empress already has a husband.'

'I'm sorry?' protested Claudia. 'And who is that, exactly?'

'Me, of course,' said Marcellus, with a bow.

'How many times must I decline your advances before you understand that I am not for the taking.'

'You're not thinking clearly, cousin.'

'I have never been surer.'

'It's the only solution. Step aside gracefully and you will remain at the palace as my consort,' said Marcellus.

'Your consort?'

'I will still need a wife, and the public already knows you. It will enable a smooth transition. As ruler, you won't hold on for much longer. We can all see that you are struggling.'

He gestured around the room, opening his arms, to a chorus of muted agreement.

'A woman simply isn't suited for the position. But you will make a fine enough empress as my consort. The people will forgive your foolish errors, in time. Step aside and Rome will no longer be your problem. Wouldn't that be a relief?'

Some small part of her yearned for it, pleaded for it. She could take Gia and run, escape her responsibilities and the expectations of the goddesses, but what kind of leader would she be? What kind of example would she set to other women?

She looked to Gia.

This was their duty now – for better, or worse. If they gave up, these men would inherit the earth once more.

'Say what you will,' she said firmly. 'Do what you will. I'll not change my mind.'

'Are you sure? You and your friend will be safer, this way.' Marcellus looked at Gia, pointedly. 'I can't promise to protect her, if you are unwilling,' he said.

Claudia swallowed, her mouth sand dry.

She had to be brave. She would not live in shame and cowardice. If she was going to die, she would not die under a bed of lies.

'I refuse,' she said.

'What say you, Damocles?' asked Marcellus. 'You support our union, don't you?'

Damocles made a non-committal noise.

'You're an intelligent man. You know what is best . . . Convince the empress here to go ahead with it,' said Marcellus.

Damocles looked to Claudia, as she remembered what he'd said about playing both sides.

'If you think I can convince her of anything, you have not been paying attention,' he huffed.

He was loyal only to the Senate, and the Senate would fall in line with her cousin.

'You can do better than that,' said Marcellus.

'She will not listen to me.'

'Come on, man. I thought you and I had an understanding. Tell her we must be wed, for her own benefit.'

'I am sorry, but I cannot,' said Damocles, to her surprise.

'Why not?'

'Because she does not desire it. As of right now, she is still *my* empress. If she says no, it means no.'

Claudia gave him a tiny nod of gratitude.

'If you cannot do the right thing and stand by me as your fellow man, then . . . you will no longer be consul.'

'You don't have that power,' said Damocles.

'Don't I?'

General Aquinas nodded at two soldiers nearby, who detained Damocles, holding him in place.

'You are easily replaceable, all of you.'

They served him. Not her, not Marcellus, but him. General Aquinas. He was the real threat, and had been all along.

'You are making a fool of yourself,' Marcellus said. 'Grappling for power is a man's business. It's not attractive for a woman to clamour for it so desperately. You could make a fine wife and mother, if you were being realistic. Enjoy the life to which you are accustomed. This is your last chance to save yourself.'

'Let me make sure I am understood clearly when I say this,' she said, 'but I would rather turn into a tree than marry you, Marcellus. I would rather peel off my own skin, or drink the piss of a lynx.'

Maybe Gia had been rubbing off on her.

'You can ask me a thousand times, and the answer will always be no,' she said.

Marcellus ruefully shook his head.

'I'm not asking, Claudia,' he said.

'I'm sorry?'

'There is no question about it. You must agree. You *have* to agree. I don't think you understand what's at stake here.'

'I said no. Didn't you hear me?'

'I've called everyone here so we can agree to a change of hands, and a peaceful exchange of power. All that remains is for you to step aside gracefully and accept my proposal.'

Consternation rumbled through the audience.

'It is too late for peace,' she said.

'I have the military on my side, along with the majority of the praetorian guard,' he said. 'No one can rule Rome without them.'

'I could live for a thousand years and still I would decline.'

'Last chance.'

'Once again, no.'

'Very well,' he said. 'In that case . . .'

As he signalled for her to be seized, Gia stood up to defend her, yet she was swiftly detained. Guards seized her sword and cuffed her hands at her back as she kicked out.

Cassius looked at her with alarm but didn't move from his spot at the table, his gaze shifting uneasily back and forth.

'Don't forget your place, gladiator,' sneered Aquinas. 'You may have been famous in Pompeii but here you're the lowest class in society, no different to a brothel worker, barely better than a slave.'

'Let her go,' demanded Claudia.

'Your decisions have consequences,' said Aquinas. 'You should know that by now.'

'Claudia, please,' her cousin said. 'They'll kill you, if you refuse.'

'Who is they? I thought you were to be the new emperor.'

He looked to the general, then back to her. His expression grew hard and lined, cold fear in his eyes.

'They will kill her, too,' he said, nodding at Gia. 'They will kill both of you, if you stand in their way.'

'Enough,' said Prince Darius. 'I have heard enough. It is time for you to leave the palace, before I make you leave in a casket.'

'This doesn't concern you, Darius,' said Marcellus.

'I think you'll find that it does concern me, actually.'

He swung his spear around, forming a figure of eight.

'The empress and I have formed an alliance. If you wish to overthrow her, you'll be starting a war with me. You will be waging war with the entire Persian empire.'

'Worry about your own lands, foreigner,' barked the general. 'This is not your country. It never will be.'

'Come at me, man,' Darius said. 'Show me what you've got. I can teach you a few things about valour and honour, I am sure.'

The senators rippled, scandalized by his gall.

The noise of the crowd grew louder as more and more people gathered at the doorway, watching the coup unfolding.

Still, Cassius did nothing, sitting among the other soldiers as if he were one of them.

'It's time for you to go home, Prince Darius,' said General Aquinas. 'We would prefer to keep our blood pure and our women to ourselves. Stay out of our territories and return to your own, or you might find that they are no longer yours to govern.'

'The women do not belong to you,' he said.

The prince's guard seemed to manifest from the shadows, but he was swiftly incapacitated, dragged to the ground. Darius attempted to battle the soldiers who swarmed him, but he too was vastly outnumbered in a swirl of strikes and grunts. His spear was snapped.

Bloodied, the prince was hauled away, shouting obscenities. Some of his staff ran after him in panic. Claudia looked to Cassius for a reaction, but he was staring fixedly down at his plate.

‘I shall take over from here,’ said Aquinas, patting Marcellus on the back like his subordinate.

Claudia felt all the strength in her body melt away.

‘Empress Claudia seeks to turn women into men, to make them soldiers and senators, but look what happens when women are given power?’ said Aquinas. ‘Look what the barbarian queen did to our soldiers. *Our* men. A woman given power is a woman depraved.’

Some of the soldiers crowed in agreement.

‘Women do not belong in the Colosseum,’ he said. ‘They do not belong in the Senate. They do not belong in the palace.’

‘That’s right.’

‘Say it louder.’

‘There is good reason why no woman has ever ruled Rome, and Princess Claudia here is the embodiment of it. We must remove her tonight and liberate the empire from this fashionable new derangement.’

The soldiers were beginning to rouse, catalysed by his words.

‘We have all heard the rumours. She lies with her gladiator as if she were a man. They cavort around the palace like lovers. Even her own handmaids have been forced to witness it. It’s indecent. To show off such perversion while wearing the crown . . . It’s an embarrassment to Rome.’

Some of the soldiers looked to her with disgust. Others chewed their lips to prevent from laughing. Their eyes were craven yet revolted, licking the lips of their grimacing mouths. But one by one, their faces fell still and solemn, their gazes hard, unified against her.

Aquinas had a command over them, directing these men as if they were a part of him - as if, Claudia thought, he himself was a god.

Perhaps Jupiter had possessed him.

‘The gods have shown us who Claudia Caesaria truly is, and given us the power to protect Rome from her wickedness,' he said. 'Beneath the attractive veneer, there is always poison. Whenever women are given a pinch of authority, they turn into witches, harpies ... murderesses.'

As his speech continued, he began to seem less human, his face twisting into a monstrous slit. His eyes were wide and white, his expression only an approximation of a real emotion.

'You have seen this wickedness in the women all around you. You recognize this corruption in our own society.'

The general drew his sword and pointed it at Claudia.

'Claudia Caesaria speaks of peace, but she killed her father by poison,' he said.

'Back off,' said Gia, still held prisoner.

'Claudia Caesaria speaks of law and order, but she killed her brother by the sword.'

'You are playing a dangerous game, Aquinas,' said Claudia.

'Claudia Caesaria speaks of what is right and good, but she is guilty of *infamia*.'

'That's enough,' Claudia shouted.

'She is not fit to rule. It is clear to you all. The two previous emperors both died in suspicious circumstances in a short space of time. The body of Decimus may never be recovered. We have only Princess Claudia's account of how he died. Many of us have questions, and she has no answers. We can no longer ignore it.'

The crowd murmured with interest.

'My god has spoken, and he has accused the empress.'

'True or false, her reputation is sullied,' said one senator.

'She calls herself empress, but she is no better than the savages.'

'This is not the way,' said Pliny the Elder, as he was bustled out of the room. 'Prejudice and division shall get us nowhere.'

'Your soul is not yet lost,' said Rectina, as the guards cuffed her. 'You can still do the right thing, Marcellus.'

Cassius remained silent, though his expression was hard, a muscle twitching in his cheek.

'The Senate will never let you get away with it,' said Damocles.

'It has been good to see you again, Damocles, but it is time for you to retire,' said the general.

He thrust his sword forward without hesitation, so quickly that it took Damocles a moment to realize he'd been stabbed. She watched his eyes popping, his face greying, before Aquinas roughly withdrew his weapon, with such force that Damocles slumped down to the ground.

'No!' Claudia cried. 'What are you doing, you maniac?'

It took her right back to the night her brother died: the smell of death, the sound of panicked breaths, the cold animal fear in her heart, the way every tiny sound was amplified, becoming monstrous in contrast with the weighty silence.

She tried to move towards Damocles but was prevented by the guards. His gaze met hers and he reached out his hand to her, too far for her to touch, his fingers curling up before the light left him.

General Aquinas stood up and walked away impassively, wiping his bloodied hand on one of the table napkins.

Damocles, poor Damocles. His last act as consul had been to stand by her, and he had been sacrificed for it.

'You killed him,' Claudia gasped, tears streaming before she could stop them.

'I didn't think you, of all people, would judge me for that.'

'*Why?* Why did you do it?'

'It is time for a fresh start, and a new consul,' he said. 'One who will be willing to follow the script.'

Half of the people at the table now rushed to Damocles, while the others remained in their seats in terror.

'Does anyone else have any objections?' said Aquinas.

No one spoke.

'Then Senator Thelonius will be the new consul,' said Aquinas.

'I would be honoured to serve,' said Thelonius.

'This man is a murderer,' said Claudia, staring at Aquinas. 'He has killed in plain sight, before your eyes. Have him taken to the dungeon, and his accomplices too. Do it now.'

'Do not do that,' said Marcellus. 'By *my* orders.'

'I am the empress. The ordained and ratified empress,' she objected. 'You shook my hand and conceded. The title is still mine, and you won't take it without a fight. Please, gentlemen, do your job and arrest him.'

'No, men, arrest her instead!'

The guards did neither – looking back and forth, unsure whose orders to follow.

Claudia levelled her gaze at Aquinas.

'Over my dead body will you take Rome,' she said.

'Gladly,' said General Aquinas.

'Claudia!' cried Gia.

Gia managed to break free, but she was prevented from reaching Claudia by Cassius, who dived out in front of her. He held her at sword point, his gaze hard, as if she were the enemy.

'What are you doing?' she asked, in disbelief.

'Shut up, woman,' Cassius replied, in the voice of a stranger. 'Do as you're told. Don't make this difficult on yourself.'

They exchanged a brief look of understanding as Gia struggled against him, though not too hard. Then she turned back to Claudia.

'Say you will marry him,' Gia said. 'Do it. Save yourself.'

But to live meant being prisoner, and to die meant being free.

'I cannot. I will not.'

'It appears that you were wrong,' said General Aquinas, turning to Marcellus. 'You thought she could be brought to heel.'

'I am not a dog,' said Claudia.

'Maybe if you gave her some time to think,' said Marcellus, hopefully, 'she might still come to her senses.'

'It cannot wait. You must stand up as a man, as a ruler, and claim your crown as we have planned. Here – here is a weapon,' said the general, handing a sword to Marcellus. 'Do what you must.'

Her cousin stared at it, as if he had never seen one before.

'You . . . you want me to kill her?' he said.

Claudia's heart plummeted, rolling rapidly downhill like the great boulder of Sisyphus.

'Do it now, before it's too late.'

'You want me to do it . . . right now?' said Marcellus.

'Her prince is banished. Her gladiator is detained. Either she marries you, or she dies.'

Claudia felt weak on her feet, a thick slick of sweat forming on her skin as she shook her head in fear.

'My goddess,' she prayed, hoarsely. 'Please hear me, Minerva.'

'Kill her, I said.'

'I beg you, goddesses. I need you now,' Claudia tried.

'I cannot. You must do it for me,' said Marcellus. 'I cannot bear to do it with my own hand.'

'Are you a spineless coward?' goaded Aquinas. 'Are you?'

'No!'

'Then do it! Do what must be done! This is the test, to see if you are strong enough. It must be you.'

'Please, General. I cannot. I cannot!'

'Will you fail, at the final marker? After everything your god has done for you? You must not let him down.'

'Please . . . sir . . .'

Marcellus continued to hesitate.

'You must not let *us* down, after all we have done . . . after all we have sacrificed. Do it now, boy. Quickly. What are you waiting for?'

Claudia chanted feverishly. Every prayer she could recall passed her lips. She could hear Gia crying out, calling her name, as those who remained in the room whimpered and wept.

'You want to be emperor? Well, this is the price.'

'The people will think me a monster.'

'The former empress will not be remembered well. You will be celebrated for removing her. It will be justice. History will be written so, for we shall write it,' said Aquinas.

He looked to Senator Tacitus.

'Yes, you will be most heroic, in the retelling,' the senator said.

The edges of the room frayed, turning white, as Claudia's vision seemed to tunnel. She swooned, catching herself on the table as guards inched closer, not yet fully detaining her.

Clearly Aquinas didn't see her as a threat, and in this moment, he was correct, for she had never felt so weak or so sick.

'There must be another way,' said Marcellus. 'Can I not just have her expelled, or held in the dungeons?'

'She is the named empress. Her face is on coins and on flags.

Leave her alive and her memory will live on. Her support will persist. You must kill her to rule. You must destroy power to claim power.'

The general's eyes looked even colder than usual.

Claudia was going to throw up. She could feel the bile rising in her throat, so bitter and harsh, burning her insides.

'Please,' she begged.

'Do it, now,' said Aquinas.

Her cousin took the sword in hand, standing up and flexing his arm, but his soul was clearly in torment.

'No, Marcellus,' panted Claudia, searching around for a weapon to arm herself.

She settled on a knife snatched from the table, her fingers slipping over the gold, but it wasn't sharp enough to do harm.

'They'll kill me, if I don't do it,' he said, looking to the general.

Claudia looked to Gia, still battling with Cassius to reach her.

'Then . . . them . . . Fight them, not me.'

Claudia was struggling to form sentences in her fear. Marcellus was talking to her, but his voice sounded far away.

'You're an even bigger fool than I thought . . . if you believe you will last any longer than me,' she managed to utter.

'I have no choice.'

'There is always . . . a choice.'

Marcellus was sweating too, his temple veins popping.

Claudia channelled all her remaining will into making one last plea to reason, though her tongue felt too big, her teeth loose, barely able to speak the words on her mind.

'You will not be an emperor . . . but their slave.'

She was struggling for breath, her chest tight.

'They do not respect you. They do not fear you. You will die the same way you claimed like crown . . . just like me.'

Two soldiers gripped her in place, holding her in position so the new emperor would get a clean strike.

'Go on,' urged the general.

Claudia looked to Gia, mouthing, 'I love you.'

Gia's face was fraught, frantic.

'No! Claudia!'

'Go for the throat,' said the general. 'Make it quick.'

She had run out of time.

Claudia tensed, bracing herself for the stab of the knife as Gia screamed – a raw, dull, hollow sound.

But Marcellus began to sob, falling to his knees.

'I can't,' he said.

'Do it, so help me gods,' said Aquinas.

'She's just a girl,' said Marcellus.

'You're pathetic. It's a good job I planned ahead.'

What did *that* mean?

'Go, get out of my sight. Go and wait in your rooms. I will call for you when it is done. Prepare yourself to face the public.'

Marcellus dropped the sword, still weeping. Those who remained in the room looked to Aquinas, unsure who was emperor now.

Guards ushered her cousin away as General Aquinas walked slowly towards Claudia, appraising her coldly.

'You're going to kill me,' she said – not a question, but a fact.

'I already did,' he said.

Claudia followed his line of sight, fixating on her glass.

The wine she'd drunk so quickly, fast enough that she hadn't noticed the thick, unnatural sediment at the bottom . . .

A dull thud sounded as her poison taster collapsed face down on the table, splattering food and drink.

Poison. She had consumed poison.

Gia was trying to break free again, shouting in horror as she realized what had happened.

'Take the others to the dungeon for now,' said Aquinas. 'We will need slaves to fight in the arenas, so the people will not riot.'

'Yes, sir,' said Cassius.

He was posing as one of them, and neither Marcellus nor the general seemed to recognize him.

Cassius grabbed Gia by the arm. She looked to him, then back to Claudia in helplessness.

Her frightened eyes were like two bolts through Claudia's heart.

Maybe Cassius had a plan, or maybe he was doing what he promised the spirit of their mother: that he would get Gia out and take her far away from this palace of death. Either way, Claudia understood.

Claudia and Gia gazed into each other's eyes one last time as she was pulled away, before Claudia could speak a word.

It was biting, that she would die in the same way she had killed her father, but not unexpected. There was a certain amusing irony to it that comforted her in the final moments, as her organs bled and her skin itched and her body felt to turn inside out.

History moved in circles; its patterns were ever repeating. There would be other emperors, other revolutions, other uprisings and coups. She was just a speck in time, like the prince had told her.

'Gia,' she said, and this was the empress's last word.

19. ESCAPE THE UNDERWORLD

When Claudia regained consciousness, she was still seated at the table in the palace triclinium, as if for dinner, yet she was alone.

There wasn't a guard, not a servant, not a slave to be seen. Not even a torch was illuminated.

'Hello?'

Her voice echoed.

The dark was darker than it ought to be. There was no tone to it. No moon. And yet, Claudia found that she could see everything clearly. The darkness was made of glittering purples, greys and blues, swirling together to paint the palace at night, familiar and yet strange.

Claudia realized that she was bound to the chair by lengths of white fabric, but they were loose – loose enough that she could free herself. She removed them and stood up, looking around cautiously.

The table had been cleared of its feast; the candles extinguished. Everyone had gone. She and the palace had been abandoned. It was unnaturally quiet and still, as if time had stopped.

Perhaps Rome had fallen.

As Claudia walked on, she saw that she was wearing a simple

white chiton, belted at the waist. She wasn't wearing sandals; her bare feet were cold on the dark, stony ground.

'Hello?' she called again.

Hello, hello, hello.

Her voice echoed into infinity, bouncing around her.

It was silent but for her bare footsteps, which was strange for a palace teeming with people at every hour of night.

Her head was heavy. Her soul was cold. She couldn't quite remember what had happened. How had she arrived here? Where was everyone else? The knowledge was just out of reach. Her memories were clouded and muddled.

Everything was effervescent, gloomy, shimmering, tilted.

She wasn't right, wasn't where she was meant to be . . . She couldn't get warm, hugging herself as she explored.

Confused, she wandered the halls in search of a living person but she was still terribly alone in the vastness of the empty palace.

It was like being in the labyrinth back in Pompeii, using a torch to scour every hall and corridor for signs, becoming increasingly frightened and frantic when she couldn't find anyone.

She was not in the palace she knew any more but a shadowy, parallel version of it. The murals were darker, more sinister than she remembered, full of winged creatures and spiky vines. The busts of the emperors all seemed to scream in silent torment as she passed, their mouths wide in horror, as if sculpted at the moment of their deaths.

As Claudia continued along the long hall, filmy spectres popped into being at her side, re-enacting their deaths. Every emperor lived and died before her eyes, including, at the end of the row, her father.

Canicula, he whispered.

Claudia fled, turning back on herself.

In the main hall, pillars were crumbling, the mosaic-laid floor full of missing pieces. In the throne room, the roots and branches of dark trees had broken through the bricks. The palace seemed to be deteriorating before her eyes, dust streaming from the roof. She darted from place to place, but the palace was collapsing around her.

Outside was even more decayed and shapeless. Howling dark clouds blotted out the pale sky. The earth burned reddish beneath the surface as rivers of fire snaked through mounds of bones. They formed familiar sights, taking the shapes of the Pantheon, the Circus Maximus, the Colosseum, the palace . . . all made of mortal remains.

Claudia realized she was no longer in Rome but its underworld inverse. A morbid, macabre mirror of the city.

She was dead.

Claudia waited for the terrible epiphany to hit her. She should be crying, screaming, wracked with grief, but she was none of those things.

Dead? No, it couldn't be so. Minerva would not allow it.

Claudia told herself that she was dreaming, that she would soon wake and leave this place. Still, she didn't dare to leave the palace, so she made her way to the temple, where the statues of the gods surrounded her.

She sought the image of Minerva so she could call to her for help, but Minerva wasn't there. The statues too were not the same. They were made of strange, shiny black stone, with burning red jewels for eyes. They were not the deities she remembered. They were not the Twelve Harmonious Gods, as they were supposed to be.

Instead of Jupiter, there was Pluto or Dis Pater, distinguishable from his brother by his straggly hair and the keys on his belt. Instead of Juno, there was the ever-young, flower-crowned Proserpina, who bore a forced smile. Pluto had stolen her from her mother and made her his bride, forced her to serve as his Dread Queen of the Dead.

Underworld deities.

Their faces morphed into sinister grimaces before her eyes.

She was definitely dead. Claudia tried again to feel something – rage or sorrow maybe, but still nothing came. She, too, was just a shade of herself, a hollow shell.

She ventured out into the garden, watching as dark creatures sailed through the clouds above. Winged, humanoid creatures with sharp talons, they swooped down like owls, snatching up the few lost souls who roamed the city and carried them away.

Afraid that she might join them, she slowly backed off.

'Poor little creature,' came a voice.

Claudia shrieked and spun around to see two women – no, not women: two goddesses.

'Who . . . who are you?' she gasped.

'She's all alone.'

'It's very tragic for her to be so unexpectedly deceased.'

They circled her like wolves, toying with her hair and riffling her clothes without touching her as she shrank away from them.

Minerva, Diana and Venus were golden-eyed with a sheen to their marbled skin, but these goddesses were black-eyed and greyish, matte and faded, as if they had never seen the sun.

One had a sunken face and a tangle of twisted curls made of black snakes. Her robes were tied with a long, blood-red ribbon and her sockets were bruised like eyeshadow. She clasped her hands together in glee.

The other was sickly pale, almost snow white, with the clawed hands of a harpy and the same serpentine hair, a snake curled around her shoulders like a necklace. She had a permanent scowl upon her face, even when she smiled, as if everything in existence vexed her.

Claudia searched her memory for their names, trying to identify them by appearance, but she was certain they had no statues in Rome, that they were not depicted in any palace murals.

'I'm Discordia,' said the wide-eyed one, as if she could hear Claudia's thoughts. 'Eris to the Greeks. This is my sister, Invidia, otherwise known as Nemesis.'

The bored-looking one gave Claudia a cold, searching look, as if trying to decide where to stab her first.

'We won't be offended if you don't know us,' said Discordia. 'There weren't many statues or murals of us to begin with, even before Jupiter tried to remove us from the pantheon.'

'No, I *do* know you,' said Claudia. 'I have studied mythology. You are the goddess of chaos . . . and you are the goddess of retribution.'

They clutched at each other, squealing.

'She knows us, sister.'

'We are *known* . . .'

'Maybe all is not lost after all . . .'

They spoke fast, cutting into each other's sentences.

'We are so glad to be remembered. There are many who strive to forget us,' said Discordia. 'We are—'

'We are the infernal daughters of Nox, the children of night. Our mother once tried to steal the mortal sun,' said Invidia.

'It's a long story.'

They continued to weave around her. They didn't walk but

hovered mid-air, moving slowly and silently in a most ominous way, surrounded by curls of dark smoke.

'Jupiter wishes to hide us away in shame, and so . . .'

'We are stuck here in the dark, for always.'

'If a god or goddess has no followers and no offerings, well . . .' Invidia cut her finger across her neck like a knife. 'We can—'

'We can only exist, as long as we are venerated,' said Discordia. 'We must have followers, or we will cease to be.'

'We risk being forgotten completely. It is a shame you are dead, or you could tell our stories.'

Invidia rolled her eyes.

'Typical. We have *one* mortal supporter, and she is dead.'

'It isn't fair,' said Discordia, reclining dramatically on a rock. 'We haven't done anything wrong.'

'Didn't you start a war among the goddesses?' said Claudia.

'It was a *misunderstanding*.'

'They excluded us from their party on purpose,' said Invidia, menacingly. 'That hurt our feelings.'

'All I did was throw a golden apple for the fairest so they would squabble over it and make fools of themselves,' said Discordia. 'I didn't tell them to wage war over it, yet *I* am blamed for starting the conflict?'

'We're no worse than the sanctimonious Twelve and their greedy children, but they treat us like inferior beings,' sneered Invidia.

Claudia wasn't sure what Invidia had done to enrage Jupiter, and she didn't volunteer it, but she imagined that it was very unpleasant. At the same time, Jupiter was known for being unreasonable. She may only have caused him mild offence to receive so severe a punishment, imprisoned in this nightmarish realm for all eternity.

'I am really, truly dead?' she asked, in a small voice.

She still felt strangely numb, far away from herself, as if her mind couldn't quite grasp it.

'What gave it away?' said Invidia, gesturing around at the apocalyptic décor.

The goddesses cackled, baring their sharp little teeth.

'This was not supposed to happen. It wasn't my time.'

'Too bad,' said Discordia, pityingly.

'Mortal life is brief and futile,' said Invidia, less sympathetically.

'Why . . . why am I in the palace?' Claudia said, looking around.

'This is the place where you died. Now you must begin your pilgrimage, like every mortal soul.'

'Why are you here to greet me?'

'Don't flatter yourself. We were merely bored,' said Invidia. 'We have infinite time to play with.'

'We heard that the new empress had passed violently, and came to see what was happening,' said Discordia, a little too gleefully. 'We don't get much gossip down here.'

'We wanted to see what the fuss was about,' said Invidia. 'You are the one Minerva has started a war with her father for, after all. I thought you would be more impressive. You're not very interesting to look at, but perhaps you are more interesting within than you appear in the skin.'

'What do you know of war?' Claudia asked. 'The war between the goddesses and the gods?'

'Minerva is assembling an army of goddesses, or something,' said Invidia. 'That's the last thing I heard, from Bellona's blessed dead. I wasn't really paying attention.'

Claudia's spirit throbbed with hope.

'We know only that Minerva wants to overthrow her father,' said Discordia. 'But who doesn't?'

'Many have tried and failed. Look at Vulcan.'

'And Neptune. Now they are among the stars.'

'She can count me out,' said Invidia. 'I can think of far better ways to waste away my endless days.'

'You are content, just to put up with it?' said Claudia. 'I thought you were a vengeance goddess.'

'I was, once. But I have no followers, no shrines. My power is waning. The underworld never changes. It is always the same, no matter who rules. Saturn, Jupiter, Pluto, Minerva . . . It makes no difference to us.'

'What if you were no longer banished?'

'It is hopeless. We have tried to change their minds. Minerva will fail, and the pantheon will stay the same.'

'Not this time. This time, she will succeed.'

'You mortals are so optimistic. You wouldn't be that cheerful if you had seen what we have seen. Countless cycles of victory and loss. So many wars and so many kings.'

'That is why I need to go back,' said Claudia. 'How do I return?'

'There is no way back.'

Claudia withered under the glare of their double gaze.

'But my time was cut short,' she said. 'Please, I *must* return.'

'We already told you. You cannot.'

'You don't understand,' insisted Claudia. 'I'm Minerva's charge. I must be there, for when she wages war with Jupiter.'

'No one cares who you were any more,' said Invidia.

'They don't care who you *are*, either,' said Discordia. 'That's one good thing about the underworld.'

Claudia gaped at them feebly, bile rising in her throat again.

The enormity of it hit her at last, all at once, like being knocked down by a wild, runaway horse. Those feelings that had been muted and repressed suddenly came to the forefront in a wave. She stared at her hands – her pale, cold hands – no longer full of life, full of blood.

'I was poisoned,' she remembered. 'By General Aquinas.'

'It's a popular way to die these days,' said Invidia.

Gia's face hit her like a landslide, dragging her under. She would never touch her face, or feel their lips meet again. She would never hear her voice, her laughter, the warmth of her hand in hers . . .

'Gia.'

Claudia gave a strangled little sob, her throat aching.

'No, no, no. I must go back. Please, goddesses, you must help me. I cannot be dead. This can't be happening.'

She clutched at their robes but they were immaterial, made of thin white smoke that slipped through her fingers.

'First of all, you need to calm down,' tutted Invidia. 'You can't do anything now. It's too late. Death is irreversible.'

'That's not true. It cannot be. I have heard of people returning before, in mythology,' said Claudia, speaking quickly and with increasing desperation. 'There are tales of Orpheus, Hercules, Proserpina herself. Surely, there must be a way? I will try anything.'

'You think you're that important?' said Invidia.

'It didn't work out so well, much of the time,' said Discordia.

'Help me and I will pray to you. I will venerate you. I will build your statues in the palace. I will start a cult and name it after you. Anything you want, I will do it,' said Claudia. 'I can do it, because I am the empress. I have that power, so long as I live. Then you will never be forgotten.'

They looked to each other, intrigued.

'What do you think, sister?' said Discordia.

'She is full of it,' said Invidia. 'Just like every other mortal.'

'I swear it,' said Claudia. 'You have my word. I am used to making negotiations and agreeing terms. That is what I do. Just tell me what your demands are, and I will do everything to fulfil them.'

'We'd want our own temples, for one thing,' said Discordia, raising a finger, 'and statues that would be most flattering.'

'I would like an apology from Venus,' huffed Invidia. 'She said some not so pleasant things about me, back in the last millennium.'

'Sure, whatever you want.'

'I don't know. We're not really *helper* deities,' said Invidia. 'We mostly just cause chaos and strife. We get mad and we get revenge.'

'Then help me with that,' Claudia said. 'I want revenge, on the man who poisoned me.'

'There are plenty of terrible men. I could throw a stone over my shoulder and hit one of them. What's so special about this one?'

'If you know who I am, then you will know what I have done,' said Claudia. 'I killed my father and my brother, so they wouldn't reign in terror. I did that for the goddesses. They enabled me to do so.'

'It is just as we heard,' said Invidia, looking to her sister. 'I thought those gorgons were merely exaggerating.'

'I have lived through many labours to claim that throne. I have sacrificed everything. I will not let some . . . some . . . fascist, geriatric, corpse-eyed, Jupiter-kissing warlord take it from me now.'

'She is speaking of General Aquinas,' said Discordia.

'Yes, sister. I gathered that.'

'Yes, *him*! Aquin-asshole! He tried to kill me, tried to frame another man for it, tried to make me marry my cousin. He killed the consul. He poisoned me, attacked my friends and captured my lover.'

'Lover, you say?' said Discordia. 'Remember those, sister?'

'Do not remind me,' she said.

'If you had the chance to be with the one you loved, would you let some mortal idiot take it away?' said Claudia. 'Or would you kill him, claim victory and win back your mate?'

'I would boil his eyeballs,' said Invidia, forming a fist with her taloned hand. 'I would rip off his toenails and make paste of his intestines.'

Claudia blinked.

'Sure. Why not? If you care so strongly about vengeance, you must care about injustice, too. They are two sides of the same coin. An injustice was done to me, and I need your assistance.'

'Come on, Vidi,' urged Discordia. 'Let us have a little fun. It sounds like it will be a most entertaining mess.'

'You must send for Minerva, right away,' begged Claudia.

'Oh. We can't do that,' said Invidia. 'Even if we wanted to.'

'Why not?'

'For one thing, she doesn't like us, and for another, we don't like her. For another still, she does not come here.'

'Does not or *cannot*?'

'I don't know. Either way, she doesn't show her face.'

'What about Bellona's dead? Could they take her a message?'

'They are here on a one-way ticket, like the rest. Not much help when it comes to delivering messages.'

'Maybe Mercury the messenger could help her,' said Discordia.

'No. I cannot trust any of the gods,' said Claudia.

'You might need to change your mind on that. Because if you want to return, you'll have to speak to Pluto.'

'*Pluto?*'

'Plouton. Dis Pater. King of the underworld, ruler of the dead.'

'I know who he is, it was more of an exclamation,' said Claudia. 'He is Jupiter's brother. I can hardly count on him for help.'

'Well, nothing happens here without him approving it,' said Discordia. 'Each day, the underworld guards take the most interesting and important of the dead to the palace for Pluto and Proserpina to assess.'

'Some of them are sent on to the Isles of the Blessed, some are imprisoned in Tartarus, some are punished, forced to toil eternally.'

'I cannot go to him when I am working against Jupiter,' said Claudia. 'No. Pluto isn't an option either.'

'There are only three ways to escape the underworld,' said Invidia. 'The first is to present yourself to him, Dis Pater. Perhaps he would grant you a return. But it is rare. Death makes no mistakes, and if Pluto consults with the Fates and decides your time is through . . . that's it.'

She made the throat-slitting motion again.

'And the second way?' asked Claudia.

'Each day, souls arrive via the River Styx. You might be able to convince the ferryman to take you back.'

'Does he do that often?'

'No, but you could try it. It hasn't worked on any of the billion other times he has been asked, but you could be the first,' said Discordia.

'I didn't even arrive on the river, so I doubt I can go back that way. What's the third option?'

'The intervention of a god, or a goddess, I suppose.'

'Including yourselves?'

'No, silly,' said Discordia, with a wicked giggle. 'If it were that easy, we wouldn't still be standing here discussing it, would we? We don't have that kind of power, sadly. Not any more.'

'Could Minerva intervene to save me?' asked Claudia. 'Or even Diana, or Venus?'

'Maybe, but it can only happen in the moments after death. If you have been gone for a while now, it may be too late . . . and remember, we have no way of contacting them.'

Claudia gave up, sitting down on a nearby boulder.

'Who else can travel between the realms, besides Mercury and Pluto?' she asked.

'Dreamers, but you can't dream your way back,' said Discordia. 'Dreamers aren't really dead, so they are not really here to begin with. There are the psychopomps who reap souls, and Mors, the god of death, but he is hard to track down, and he won't be moved by your story.'

'What about Proserpina?' said Claudia. 'Pluto allows her to go back for the summer and spring. Maybe she can help me return.'

'Her return is only possible because Pluto opens the portal. She would still need him to enable your escape,' said Invidia, as if it was obvious. 'Only he has the keys to the doors that lead to the other realms.'

'I can think of a fourth way,' said Discordia, brightly.

'What is that?' said Invidia.

'We could wait until Pluto falls asleep, distract Proserpina and steal the keys right from his belt.'

No one spoke for a moment.

'That is an utterly insane plan, sister,' said Invidia.

'I know. Isn't it brilliant?'

'Seriously?' said Claudia.

'Imagine the look on Pluto's face if he woke up and the keys were gone,' said Discordia.

'What if he catches us and punishes us?'

'We are already punished, and you are already dead. There is nothing to fear. Sure, he could turn us into birds or constellations or imprison us in Tartarus, but what is death without a little risk?' said Discordia, bobbing up and down in excitement.

'How would we do it?' asked Claudia.

'Pluto sleeps when dawn breaks in the mortal realm,' said Discordia. 'Proserpina will be at the palace, as always. He rarely lets her leave, and she is too scared to go out without him.'

'While he sleeps, she continues to meet with the deceased and judge their worth in his absence,' said Invidia. 'She is more merciful than he. You could join the line and make your case to her in her court. We'll take the keys while you keep her conversing.'

'Then what?' asked Claudia.

'She won't know what to do with you. She'll have to wake Pluto up and ask him, because she won't want to make the decision on her own, but she'll be afraid that he'll be angry at her for disturbing his sleep.'

'If we're lucky, they'll get into one of their notorious quarrels,' said Discordia. 'That should give us enough time to flee.'

'Do you think she could be converted to the cause?'

'Why would she?'

'Because she is a goddess, and goddesses help each other.'

Invidia gave her a sceptical look.

'Try again,' she said.

'Because Pluto stole her from her home, abducted her and forced her to live in the underworld for half the year as his queen?'

'Now you're cooking on fire,' said Discordia.

'Not so fast, sister. Proserpina is both Pluto's wife and his prisoner,' said Invidia. 'She says she chose to stay with him, for love.' Her face twisted in disgust. 'But he gave her no choice at all. She is afraid of him, as we are all are. Proserpina's mother caused a famine that threatened all mortal existence, and still he didn't set her free.'

'She won't be easily persuaded to turn against him, and he won't be easily persuaded to turn against Jupiter.'

'That's why you'd be better sticking to my plan,' said Discordia.

'We should at least *try* to get through to her. Stealing the key can be our backup plan.'

'I don't know,' said Invidia. 'It's a lot of effort.'

'Please, will you take me there?' said Claudia. 'As quickly as possible? Who knows how long I have been dead already.'

'Fine. I am game,' said Discordia.

'It's such a long way,' complained Invidia.

'That's not the real reason, is it?' said Discordia.

'No,' admitted Invidia.

'You just don't want to see her.'

'Why not?' asked Claudia.

Invidia's dark eyes glittered with crystalline tears.

'Because every time I see her, I wish to fill his cup with poison and set her free.'

They silenced. Discordia looked away awkwardly as Invidia quietly fumed. There was obviously a complicated history there.

'You say Proserpina won't easily be converted,' said Claudia, 'but perhaps she has the strongest reason to turn against the gods. She, of all the goddesses, knows that as long as gods rule the pantheon, they will do exactly what they want, with no consideration for anyone else.'

'You won't have long to get through to her,' said Invidia. 'I do not think she will see sense.'

'It's worth trying.'

'If *we* cannot change her mind, why will she listen to you?' said Invidia. 'Even Diana and Minerva have tried. You think a human could persuade a god?'

'It has happened before,' said Discordia. 'Even Jupiter has been fooled by mortals.'

'I can try,' said Claudia. 'I managed to convince the Senate to confirm me as empress, with a little help from a goddess. Imagine what I might do with the help of two.'

20. AN ARMY OF GODDESSES

The streets outside were eerily empty, free of horses and chariots, with only the occasional shade to be seen. Filmy, see-through human forms, they were just fragments of what they used to be. A little boy with a ball. A brothel girl whose robes were stained with blood. An elder statesman who staggered drunkenly across the Forum, eternally intoxicated as he was when he died.

The longer shades were here, the less they remembered themselves. Eventually, they would become mere matter, just ether . . . the stardust that gods were made of. If Claudia could not find her way home to Gia, she would be just like them one day.

That fear pushed her forwards, through the macabre sights of underworld Rome. The city had none of the charm or flavour of its surface counterpart, as everything appeared to be rotting slowly.

Collapsing aqueducts, burned-out temples . . . It was like a vision of the city that could one day be.

As they passed the Colosseum made of skulls, carnal roars arose from within. Peeking in through an arch, she saw two dead gladiators in armour fighting in the arena, as rows of colourless shades cheered and heckled. They couldn't be killed, or even injured, so the fight raged for hours, providing endless entertainment for the Roman undead.

The same was true in the Circus Maximus, where ghoulish riders of broken death-chariots raced around an infinity-shaped track, with a captive audience of ghosts. Each of them reflected their appearance when they lost their lives – from crying babies with mottled skin to men with beast-ravaged faces, cheering on the victors.

Claudia had always hoped that the dead would be reborn and renewed somehow, suspended in a state of eternal youth, and certainly, some of Rome's heroes were indeed forever beautiful and unageing, dancing and dining with the gods of the Isles of the Blessed. But many more were here, among the miserable masses, living a faded second-life that was an inferior copy of reality. She feared that she might see her father or brother among them so she did not pay close attention to their faces.

Thankfully, they made their way out of the city, into the fields and farms that surrounded the outer walls, where there were fewer dead persons to be seen, and far more ghost animals.

Graceful and translucent, moving fluidly, Claudia watched as a hare bounded past, chased by dogs in a never-ending hunt.

Time flowed differently in the underworld. The scenery was always shifting and reshaping, reacting to the presence of those who entered it, formed by the collective consciousness of every dead mortal and deathless god. Hills became mountains. Lakes became seas.

The underworld was a living thing, a kind of beast that fed on the memories of all who dwelled there.

Crossing a single field of weeping, whispering poppies seemed to last for a century, pushing Claudia to the brink of her patience. Conversely, they traversed vast forests of feral centaurs and black-sand deserts in minutes.

Eventually, the land curved into what looked like the crater of a dormant volcano, but as they drew closer, Claudia saw that it was a ginormous dark staircase, spiralling deep down into the pits of the Earth.

It gave her a bad feeling.

'This is the way?' she said.

'There is no other,' said Invidia.

She could no longer avoid looking at its gaping mouth. It was calling to her . . . to her, personally. Claudia couldn't resist it any longer, so she followed the others and began to descend.

She was ready to meet her fate.

She spiralled downwards for so long that it made her dizzy. She could no longer tell how much time had passed – whether it was minutes or aeons or something in-between. When she asked how long it had been, the goddesses told her they did not recognize time.

'Time is a human intervention,' said Invidia.

'Deities live by the clock of the Earth turning,' said Discordia, 'but down here, in the underworld, we cannot even see the days and nights, or the seasons or the weather. Time has no meaning for us.'

'You cannot tell me how long I have been gone?'

'It could be minutes, or days. We do not know.'

If days had passed, Claudia was certainly gone. Her body would be rotting in a cell or burning on the pyre.

She began to think the staircase would never end, that she would never reach the bottom, endlessly spiralling with no destination. The goddesses assured her that it would come to a conclusion, but, by their own admission, they didn't know the difference between a minute and a millennium. By the time they reached Proserpina, it would be far too late.

Claudia thought about turning back and returning to the palace, but she could no longer see the surface, entombed by the dark.

She could only move forwards – or downwards, in this case.

They descended for another century or so, until torches appeared on the cavernous walls. Claudia was gleeful at these primitive signs of life, delighting as carvings and sculptures began to emerge from the rock. They must be close, she thought, but still they plunged onwards. At some point, Claudia stopped thinking, stopped feeling, stopped existing, hypnotized by the motion of her eternal descent.

Just when she had accepted this unfortunate fate, the stairs finally opened out into an enormous chamber.

'I thought it would never end,' she said.

'You mentioned,' said Invidia. 'A few times. This way.'

Claudia rushed forwards with relief, as they navigated a series of caverns decorated with hot-red sculptures made of lava. The twisting structures looked like pillars, while rocky blobs formed crystalline creatures who peeked out of the endless folds of primordial stone, seemingly alive.

Time hurtled ahead of them as they moved through the labyrinthine network of caverns.

Still, it didn't seem quick enough.

'If you want to go home, remember, you can't eat anything or drink anything,' said Discordia, as they passed through a strange, underground cave forest.

Shiny red and gold fruits were suspended from black branches.

'I know,' said Claudia, though she was hungry and thirsty. 'That is the first rule of the underworld. That, and "don't look back".'

The cave path meandered on and on for a lifetime, impossible to quantify. Claudia saw giant creatures swooping through the darkness overhead and volcanic geysers that belched egg-scented gas. She saw great dark beasts rising from the molten underworld seas, and satyrs with pan pipes hosting wild, bacchanal parties.

As they travelled, Claudia sought to know everything there was to know about the underworld, and the goddesses were more than happy to have someone to talk to. She learned that it was just as formless and disordered as the mortal realm, organized into territories where different laws and cultures had emerged. The only thing that united them was the rulership of Pluto and Proserpina.

Eventually, they reached what looked like a port, though they were still underground. Discordia told her that it was the Lake Avernus, entrance to the underworld.

Black seas lapped in through a sparkling void of a cave, with a black, wet jetty at the bottom of an enormous cliff.

Crouching behind a boulder, Claudia watched as recently deceased mortals arrived on the leaf-shaped boat, all of them shrouded in dark pallas. The dead stepped out onto the jetty, many of them still weeping and screaming, before beginning the pilgrimage up a rocky cliff face towards the palace. They were hustled and ushered by strange, skeletal guards in black robes, who carried spears and torches.

'Why did I not arrive with them?' Claudia asked.

'That's a good question,' said Discordia. 'We came here first, looking for you, after hearing the whispers of the shades but . . .'

'You were not here, where we thought you'd be,' said Invidia. 'It was quite suspicious.'

'We heard you'd died in the palace, so we went there in search of you . . . and there you were.'

'Perhaps Mort set you aside.'

'But you have no idea why that might be?'

'Maybe you are not quite fully dead yet,' said Discordia.

'She must be, or she would not look this way. So sickly and faded, as if all the life has been drawn from her,' said Invidia.

Once more, hope pulsated from deep within.

'I will take the chance, no matter how small,' said Claudia. 'I must join the line and meet the goddess. Hopefully no one will recognize me until I reveal myself to her. But how will you two get inside?'

They looked to each other, smirking.

'Don't worry about us,' said Discordia. 'We may not have the power to return you to the mortal realm, but we are still deities.'

She touched Claudia's shoulder, and suddenly she was wearing a black palla, like the other mortals on the boat.

'We have our own ways in.'

'We will distract the guards for you.'

Discordia clicked her fingers as Invidia nodded, and both of them popped out of existence.

Moments later, a rockslide came hurtling over the edge of the cliff, demolishing part of the path. People cried out, diving out of the way, as the skeletal guards who patrolled the jetty ran forward to help.

Claudia took her moment and darted out, keeping her head low as she joined the back of the line. The other mortals were too busy mourning the end of their lives to notice her.

She attempted to look inconspicuous, not drawing attention to herself but making sure to shiver and sniffle like the others, though she continued to feel numb. The path was promptly cleared and the queue of people pushed on slowly uphill, entering the palace in small groups.

Once again, Claudia was reminded of time's rapid passage on Earth. How long had she been journeying through the underworld? How long could she possibly have left to revive herself? But she wouldn't give up until there was nothing left to fight for.

Just as when she'd descended the staircase, Claudia retreated inside herself, going into a trance state until she reached the top of the cliff path and found herself standing before the palace of Pluto and Proserpina.

It was constructed from cooled lava, while the stalagmites and stalactites of the cave system came together to create an architectural masterpiece with many turrets and pillars and spires, all of them a reddish-black colour. It was sinister to behold, and yet someone had planted many flower beds and boxes, which had grown together to create a floral ivy that covered one side of the building.

Proserpina, the kidnapped goddess of spring.

Claudia waited her turn, ushered in by one of those skeletal guards. Along with four others – a soldier, a sailor, a gladiator and a brothel girl – she walked through the red-carpeted interior of the grand palace, decorated with many skulls and bones, like the Colosseum she'd seen. Black pillars lined the aisles, with grotesque statues in alcoves between them, while the ceilings were painted with monstrous scenes of death.

Claudia became aware of a ground-shaking rumbling, which came and went in a repeating rhythm. It grew louder as she passed by an open door, which she peered inside curiously.

It was the sound of a god snoring.

Enormous and half-naked, filling the entire room, Pluto was

deep asleep in his chambers, causing the entire palace to rattle and crumble with his giant snores.

An attendant drew the bed curtain, though Claudia could still see his big head and feet sticking out, too large to be contained.

She carried on, as Pluto's snores continued to shake the ground, until she sighted Proserpina on her throne, guarded by a large three-headed dog. It was, to her great relief, asleep.

Claudia joined a short line leading up to the throne, where the Dread Queen waited to decide their fates. She sat behind a marble table, which had a set of scales on one side and a spindle on the other, where lengths of golden thread were stretched and snipped.

Claudia looked around anxiously as the line grew shorter, looking for signs of the goddesses, but they were nowhere to be seen. She feared they might have tricked her.

They *were* the goddesses of chaos and vengeance, after all.

Once a person's worth was decided, they passed between one of three doors behind the throne. The doors were identical but Proserpina seemed to know which one was which, directing people left, forward, right.

Claudia grew increasingly afraid as Proserpina weighed the soul of the man in front of her.

'Hmm. Let us see now.'

Proserpina was just a young girl, barely older than Claudia, wearing a crown of flowers and a sprig of grain pinned to her flowing robes.

'You will reside in Asphodel,' she sighed, 'with all of the other mortals of mediocrity.'

Oddly, the man ahead did not seem upset by this. Perhaps he had imagined much worse for himself.

'Do not fear,' she said. 'It is nice there. They have flowers.'

He let the guards escort him away without kicking up a fuss.

'Next,' said Proserpina.

Shaking, Claudia stepped forth and met eyes with the goddess. She thought Proserpina might recognize her immediately, such was her ego, but the goddess didn't. Her face remained bored and blank as she tried to weigh Claudia's soul on her scales.

But it seemed there was no soul to be weighed. There was no thread on the spindle either.

Proserpina looked to the empty scales, then back to Claudia, her intimate gaze lingering.

'You are not dead,' she said, in a high, musical voice.

'Am I not?'

'Why are you here?'

'That's a good question,' said Claudia, remembering that she was supposed to distract the goddess for as long as possible. 'It's quite the mystery, actually. I didn't come on the boat, like the others. I woke up in the place where I died, but nothing was the same.'

Claudia saw a flicker of interest in Proserpina's expression.

'Then you must be between life and death,' she said. 'I cannot weigh your worth if your soul still hangs in the balance.'

'Does that mean you can help me return?'

Proserpina frowned, humming, her round, girlish face rumpled with uncertainty.

'I would have to wake up Pluto,' she said, looking to the chambers from which the great rumbling resounded.

'Can't you do it without him?' asked Claudia, eagerly.

'I . . . no. I do not have the keys.'

'But you just said, I am not dead. I don't belong here.'

'If you could just wait until he arises, then—'

'I cannot wait, please. I am needed urgently.'

'Then I will wake him,' said Proserpina, rising to her feet. 'Pluto will decide. He will know what to do.'

In the heat of the moment, Claudia panicked and did the only thing she could think to do.

'Don't,' she said, firmly, flashing warning in her eyes.

'Don't what?'

'Don't wake Pluto,' said Claudia.

Proserpina didn't say anything for a moment. Her face was serene and unreadable as ever, but the flowers that decorated her crown began to bloom as if watered.

'Why not?' she asked, in the slightest of whispers.

'Minerva is rebelling against Jupiter.'

The goddess's eyes flicked left and right, exchanging looks with several of her handmaids. Proserpina had already heard, of course she had. Perhaps Pluto himself had told her.

'What does that have to do with you?' she said.

'I'm Minerva's patron, the empress of Rome,' said Claudia.

Proserpina's face faltered, which was unnerving. There was nothing more terrifying than a frightened goddess, but if there was, it was a frightened goddess who knew her personally.

'I have been poisoned, but it seems they didn't quite finish me off,' said Claudia. 'Incompetent men. I tire of them. Minerva also tires of them . . . Do you tire of them, too?'

Proserpina looked fearfully to the dog, as one of its three heads awoke, blinking slowly. The goddess drew one finger to her lips, signalling for Claudia to silence.

'Come with us,' whispered Claudia. 'Join us.'

But Proserpina shook her head vehemently.

'I cannot,' she said. 'Pluto is my consort. I love him.'

'Love is not love without freedom,' said Claudia.

The second head of the black dog awakened now, looking around the room in confusion.

'He will wake at any moment,' mouthed Proserpina.

'It's not too late.'

'You must go. Hide. Right away.'

'I can't, not without your help,' said Claudia.

'It is not possible.'

'Help us take control of the pantheon, so you can be free . . . so all of us can be free.'

'No! You must go. Go to Asphodel and hide yourself.'

'If he loved you, he would let you return whenever you chose,' Claudia said. 'He would not hold you here, underground, with the dead. He would not keep you from your mother, or from your friends. If he loved you, you would not fear him.'

Proserpina froze, caught on these words, as the third head of the dog woke up and began to growl and bark.

'It's too late,' said Proserpina.

'It's never too late,' said Claudia.

'No, it really is.'

An enormous crash sounded, followed by a thunderous ranting and raving, coming from the god's chambers.

'You! And you! Catch them! Seize them!' bellowed the god.

Discordia and Invidia popped into being next to Claudia, looking dishevelled yet oddly invigorated.

'What's happening?' said Invidia casually.

The serpents in their hair were hissing, striking out in fury. Claudia ducked out of their reach, narrowly avoiding being bitten.

‘Time to go,’ said Discordia, jingling the stolen keys.

Invidia exchanged a brief look with Proserpina.

‘Vidi,’ Proserpina said softly. ‘What are you doing?’

‘I have some anger issues to work through,’ Invidia said. ‘What do you think? We’re here to rescue you.’

Claudia turned to face Pluto as he emerged through the doorway, gigantic and weighty, his footsteps booming.

‘You let that gorgon enter our home so she could steal from me?’ he said, storming over. ‘What have you done?’

‘Darling, please, don’t lose your head,’ said Proserpina, standing in front of Invidia. ‘What can I do to soothe you?’

‘I thought I told you never to speak with either of them again.’

‘If you would just listen—’

‘You expect me to believe your lies?’

‘I am allowed to have visitors,’ she cried, her hands curling into fists. ‘I don’t need your permission to do everything.’

‘You are my wife. You do as I say.’

‘I have had it up to *here* with your rules!’

Pluto reached out and slapped her, the strike echoing as loud as a thunderclap, forcing Proserpina to her hand and knees. Her body twisted as fell, and when she lifted her head, it was them she looked to.

‘Run!’ she ordered Invidia.

But Invidia didn’t run.

A loud shrill cry turned Claudia’s head to the underworld sky, as more and more winged creatures seemed to be gathering.

Invidia helped Proserpina up from the floor. She stretched her arms, revealing widespread black wings, producing a spear from nothing.

‘Go,’ she said, looking back to her sister. ‘I’ll deal with him.’

‘You can’t fight him alone,’ said Discordia.

‘I will not be alone,’ she said. ‘I summoned Bellona.’

‘You could’ve just done that all along?’ said Claudia. ‘Why didn’t you say?’

She shrugged. ‘It made for a better ending.’

Discordia grabbed Claudia’s hand, pulling her away as Invidia and Proserpina faced Pluto together.

She looked back to see Invidia’s snakes attacking the god, as a winged warrior goddess with the same serpent hair as Discordia descended from above, along with three others.

They tore at the god like vultures.

Claudia and Discordia hurtled through an archway as the noise of a fearsome battle echoed beyond them.

‘Do you think they’ll be okay without us?’ asked Claudia.

‘You’d best hope Minerva lives up to her word and overthrows her father, or all of us will be done for.’

‘What happened between them?’ Claudia asked, her voice shaken by their running pace. ‘Invidia and Proserpina?’

‘They were friends, once. They met in the Asphodel meadows. That was as far as Proserpina’s mother allowed her to go into the underworld, because she knew Pluto wanted her daughter for himself.’

Claudia pulled a face.

‘The goddess of spring and a daughter of night. They were quite the pair, always up to trouble. Pluto saw Proserpina there one day and snatched her, driving her into the ground with his black-winged chariot. To prevent them from chasing, he turned her attendants into birds. My sister tried to stop him but she was banished – from the palace, from Asphodel, and from the mortal realm. Jupiter stood by his brother, even after that. I don't know if she and Proserpina ever spoke again.'

'Until now,' said Claudia.

'Until now,' echoed Discordia.

A door flung open, as skeletal guards came charging towards them, the clacking of their dry bones making Claudia's skin crawl.

'This way,' said Discordia, pushing her roughly through another dark archway. 'I think.'

'You *think*?'

Through the dark maze of Pluto's palace, pursued by a horde of guards, they came upon a dark room filled with more locked doors. Discordia attempted to find the right one, and the right key, trying each in turn as Claudia barricaded the door they'd come through, using a large decorative sword off the wall. It was almost as big as her shield.

She peered through the keyhole, watching as the guards smashed up against the door on the other side, their bones breaking and bursting apart, forming a macabre mound.

The sound of a large volcanic explosion shook the room, causing dust to pour through the ceiling. Everything around her was crumbling, rumbling, rotting away to nothing.

It was just like the beginning of her death-dream, back in the collapsing palace. Pillars toppled as the floor gave way beneath her feet.

'What's happening?' she asked, caught by Discordia.

'Sounds like the war is starting. Bellona must've convinced all the gorgons and harpies and furies to serve her.'

The room shuddered again.

Discordia struggled with the endless ring of keys, more keys than

Claudia had ever seen, each one sliding optimistically into the lock before revealing itself to be yet another disappointment.

'Come on, come on. Hurry!' she urged.

'I'm not Janus, the god of doors. I'm going as fast as I can.'

Finally, Discordia found the right combination, the wooden door popping open to reveal a void beyond.

'Go home, and get ready to fight,' said Discordia. 'You are needed there.'

'How are you sure this is the right door?'

'I'm not,' she shrugged. 'But if Proserpina is right, you should be waking up any time now. You'll find your way back . . . Probably.'

'Thank you, Discordia.'

Claudia pulled her into a hug. Discordia didn't return it, standing stiffly in her arms, but her snakes wrapped around them and closed their eyes, joining the strange embrace.

'I will see you again,' said Claudia, passing through the door.

'Sooner than you think,' said Discordia, waving.

In Elysium, the palace of Mars was burning, casting bright red flames up into the twilit sky. Soldiers poured out of the building as the shadows of winged women flocked overhead, scooping the fire up like snowballs to toss at the priests and servants now fleeing in haste. Some rode on the backs of black Pegasi, their equine silhouettes cast large by the growing inferno. Whoops and screams formed a cacophony, as a series of small explosions resounded from within the building, echoing so loudly it could be heard in Asphodel.

In helmet and armour, Minerva crouched on a nearby hill, holding upright her spear as she watched the unfolding carnage. It wouldn't be long before Mars appeared with his armies to fight.

Soon, all of the gods would assemble here, and the war would truly begin.

Fire crumbled another tower.

In this moment, Minerva debated whether allying with Bellona was the right move after all. Her sister would show no mercy and take no prisoners. She had no patience for subtlety. But Minerva had always known it, right from the beginning. She'd shaken her hand anyway. That was the risk she'd chosen to take. Perhaps a part of her knew she needed someone more ruthless than her, to make the first move.

She just hoped it would be worth it, in the end.

'Veni, vidi, vici!' Bellona screamed, as another explosion rocked the palace.

There was no reversing the turn of the wheel. Fortuna had taught her that. What was done, was done. She could only keep moving. If she ended up a constellation, frozen in the sky next to Vulcan and Neptune, so be it.

She had made her choices.

Minerva left Bellona and her women warriors to ransack the house of Mars, while she set out to find her consort Mercury.

As the god of borders and boundaries, commerce and travel, he was a difficult deity to track down. He moved between the worlds above and below, as well as in the mortal realm. But she traced him by following word of mouth, connecting him to the messages he'd been entrusted to deliver. His name was carried by whispers, while birds followed in his wake.

The grapevine worked both ways, however, and by the time she found him, he was already waiting for her.

'Minerva,' he said, though he did not turn to face her.

She approached him from behind, cloaked in his winged hat and holding his caduceus, floating through a lonely red-heathered valley in Asphodel.

'Mercury.'

Their relationship wasn't romantic (Mercury preferred the company of nymphs) but they'd known each other for as long as she had existed, and Minerva found him to be one of the more reasonable gods. She hadn't intended to make any of the gods her ally in this war against her father, but Mercury could still be useful, despite his duplicity.

'I see you've been doing Jupiter's bidding in my absence,' she said.

'I do what I have to, to remain alive.'

'Even if it threatens the foundations of Rome itself?' she said.

'We have had this conversation before, Minerva,' he said.

'Yes, which is how I know your real positions on pantheon politics. This servitude is beneath you. You do not follow him out of honour or admiration. You have no respect for his warfare. You do his duty out of fear.'

'Vulcan and Neptune stood against him, and they are merely stars now.'

'You, a psychopomp, reaper of souls, quaking in your sandals as Jupiter barks orders at you. You should be embarrassed.'

Mercury shook his head, yet said nothing.

'It is time for change. I hoped you would be smart enough to understand the importance of that,' she said.

'Things are the way they are for good reason,' he said.

'The power of the pantheon is just as the power in Rome,' said Minerva. 'It is centred on the patriarchy; the eternal authority of the father. Who is actually fit to rule? Who will protect the mortals? Who will work to build a better world? Not he.'

'The world is not to be made perfect.'

'The words of a coward, if ever I heard them.'

'Jupiter is not the good king, but he is the strong king.'

'Is that why he is killing other gods?' she said, marching closer to him. 'There is no strength in that.'

'But you will kill him, in turn?'

'I will, if I can. If I have to . . . and I think I shall *have to.'*

'You think you would be a better ruler?'

'I know I would.'

Mercury smiled, gazing off into the distance.

'It will not matter. Because you won't succeed,' he said.

'I don't wish to kill you too, Mercury.'

'I hope it won't come to that either.'

'Nor I,' she said. 'But soon enough, I will have little choice. If you stand by my father's side, we'll be enemies.'

He lowered his head, staring at the flower-strewn ground.

'It is but a dream, Minerva. You will pay the price. You will end up just like Neptune or Vulcan, lights in the sky for mortals to tell stories about.'

'Soon, Elysium will be a battleground. It's time for you to decide which side you stand on,' she said. 'Are you with me, or are you with him?'

Still, he did not answer.

'For too long, you have sat on both sides. You speak to heroes and villains alike, as if they are equals, all in the name of peace. But this peace is merely apathy.'

'You have misread me.'

'I think not.'

Minerva raised her spear.

'I have never fought you, Mercury. I have had no reason to. But I think we both know which of us is the better warrior, and how it will end for you.'

She inched closer, as he retreated.

'If you lose, I will let you live . . . but you will serve me.'

As she spoke, the blood-coloured ground rumbled beneath their feet.

'The House of Mars is burning,' she said.

At this, Mercury finally turned to face her, his face seizing with horror. She gazed deep into his soulful, dark eyes, like two portals to the underworld.

'The war of the gods has already begun.'

21. RETURN OF THE EMPEROR

Claudia returned to the world in stages.

Her hearing came first, as muted voices bled through the infinite dark. She heard her name, faded and faraway, but she couldn't talk back. She could hear someone crying – a raw, ragged sobbing. She tried to move her mouth, her tongue, to cry out for help, but her body and her mind were not fully connected yet.

She felt warm hands on her cold skin as someone picked her up and carried her. She was placed on a cold, flat, stony surface. Cold water splashed her face, followed by the warm comfort of some kind of blanket or shroud wrapped around her.

Someone was rubbing her arms, trying to wake her up. She wanted to wake most desperately but she was heavy and sluggish, making slurring noises as she continued in her quest to say something, anything.

'She's coming round,' came an unknown voice.

'Claudia?' came a known one. 'Claudia? Can you hear me?'

She could smell some kind of rousing, spicy incense now, mixing with blood and dirt and sweat – all the carnal smells of people in a state of panic.

She could taste the bitter tang of the substance that was forced down her throat, causing her to cough, splutter and choke, vomiting down herself and staining her clothes.

That was the first thing she saw when her vision returned: a splatter of puke on robes.

Claudia looked up, blinking as her eyes cleared.

'She's awake.'

'Thank the goddesses.'

'The empress lives!'

Her vision was last to return, breaking through in spots of colour that grew outwards, connecting like puddles until she could see her room in the palace, and a crowd of blurry bodies huddled around her.

'She's regaining consciousness,' someone said.

Claudia looked out at a group of soldiers in armour. Thinking them Aquinas's men, she writhed in panic, trying to get away.

'It's us, it's us. Don't be scared.'

One of them pulled off their helmet, as the others copied.

It was Dom. One of the soldiers was Dominic.

She didn't recognize the other soldiers right away, but then she looked to her left and saw Cassius, and, next to him, Celadus the Handsome. She looked to her right and saw . . .

'Gia?' she said.

Claudia blinked again, doing a second-take, because Gia's hair was almost as short as her brother's now.

The other 'soldiers' were Dido and Livia, who had also cut her long dark hair short. Claudia couldn't understand why. Everything was so strange and slow and foggy.

Panicked, confused, she struggled to get up.

'I was poisoned . . . by Aquinas,' she recalled.

'Henbane, in the wine you drank,' said the physician.

Henbane. It was the same poison she'd used to kill her father.

Claudia heaved herself into a sitting position as Gia knelt down before her, pulling her into her arms. Tears streamed from her eyes as she felt the reassuring weight of Gia's embrace.

She was home.

Home was not a place any more – not a building with walls or a country with borders – but a person.

Gia held her so tight her armour dug into Claudia's flesh, but it was a sweet, welcome sort of pain, like love. It reminded her that she was alive, and how close she'd come to not being so.

But when Gia kissed her, Claudia suddenly pulled back.

Gia looked to the gathered crowd, as if their presence was the reason for her hesitation.

'I . . . have been poisoned,' said Claudia, touching her lips with one hand. 'I would not want you to be poisoned too.'

'You're fine,' said the physician. 'It doesn't work like that.'

'Then we are good,' said Claudia, pulling Gia in to her lips.

'It's okay,' Gia said, between kisses. 'You're okay.'

'I thought I'd never see you or hold you again,' said Claudia, reluctant to let go of her.

'Here, drink this.'

The palace physician hovered over her, holding out a cup. She took it into her hands, letting the cold water pour down her throat.

'What's happening?' she asked. 'I assume all is not well.'

'You could say that. General Aquinas has taken over the palace,' said Gia. 'He has control of the army. He's converting the Senate as we speak. Cassius pretended to be one of them, then knocked a general out cold to distract him so we could escape. We had to disguise ourselves as soldiers, to come and rescue you. They got suspicious when we wouldn't remove our helmets. Hence, the hair.'

She ran one hand over her head, self-consciously.

'It looks good,' said Claudia, reaching out to stroke it, though it was hardly the time. 'It is like Diana's.'

'Focus, Empress,' Gia said, clicking her fingers, though she was smiling lopsidedly.

'Yes, yes, sorry.'

'They put you in your room and left you to die. They destroyed Minerva's shield and the evidence of the assassin plot against you. We managed to get you out and bring you here to the valetudinaria, so the physician could treat you.'

Claudia struggled to take it all in, to envision it unfolding in her mind. Her head was still slow and heavy.

'We managed to free some of the prisoners from the cells before they locked the palace down,' said Gia, 'but we don't have much time. We have to get out of here.'

'Damocles?' she asked, hopefully, but the question was met with shaking heads and glum glances.

'Damocles is dead,' said Dom. 'Hieronymus is dead.'

'Rectina,' Claudia croaked. 'Darius, he—'

'Darius fled with his soldiers,' said Celadus. 'Rectina is with Pliny and Athena.'

'Darius fled?'

'His party was seen retreating, back towards the border. The Persian cavalcade is gone.'

'After everything he said about protecting his country?' said Claudia. 'I didn't believe he would be so cowardly.'

'I know.'

Cassius looked unexpectedly forlorn for someone who was just having uncommitted recreational sex.

'And Marcellus?' asked Claudia.

'We haven't been able to find him. He hasn't been seen since dinner last night,' said Gia.

'They haven't announced him as emperor yet?'

'No, they cannot find him either. He might've fled the place, but the general and his cohorts are trying to declare him *in absentia*.'

'Then we must move quickly,' she said.

Claudia looked around, trying to recover herself. It was light outside. Dawn had come, and she was still alive.

In a small alcove, next to the smoking incense, Claudia saw a small carved figurine of Meditrina, the goddess of medicine whose festival she had established.

She'd be sure to leave an offering to her later.

'Aquinas is trying to seize power, for himself and for Jupiter,' she said. 'Marcellus is just his emperor puppet – but all the same, Aquinas needs him. He has no claim to the throne himself. We must find Marcellus and we must stop this.'

'Aquinas has the entire army on his side,' said Gia. 'We don't have the numbers. If we kill him, they will tear us limb from limb.'

'We won't be alone. Others are coming to fight. We will have thousands of warriors to fight for us soon enough,' said Claudia.

'Who are you talking about?' asked Cassius.

'I was in the underworld. I saw Proserpina, and Discordia and Invidia. Bellona came with her furies to overthrow Pluto.'

The others looked to each other with concern.

'Say that again?' said Dom.

'The goddesses are rising up and overthrowing the gods.'

'It might take a while for the effects of the poison to wear off,' said the physician.

'I'm not hallucinating,' Claudia said. 'I'm not intoxicated. The war of the pantheon is just beginning.'

'No, I believe you. After all we have seen, how could I not?' said Gia, nodding in affirmation. 'But it is still an impossible battle. No one would judge you for walking away.'

'*I* will judge me for it,' Claudia said. 'I cannot let the goddesses down – not just Minerva and Diana and Venus, but all of them. If I fail now, everything I tried to do will be lost to the sands of time. They will write me out of history, and women will not stand a chance. It is time. This is it. We rise to the occasion, or we die.'

Claudia fixed them all with what she hoped was a serious, commanding look.

'Are you with me?' she said, looking to them each in turn.

'Always,' said Gia. 'You know that.'

'Yes, Empress,' said Dido, bowing.

Celadus nodded, confidently. 'I do believe I am.'

'I suppose so,' sighed Livia, though she didn't look entirely unhappy about it any more.

'We've come this far, my lady,' said Dominic.

'I . . . don't have much of a choice,' said Cassius.

Gia frowned at him.

'But I guess we're doing this thing,' he added. 'Woo hoo!'

'I am very sadly unable to participate in whatever this is, due to prior commitments,' said the physician. 'But I wish you the very best.'

He hurried away, grabbing all the scrolls he could carry. Celadus moved to guard the door.

'Should I disguise myself as a soldier too?' Claudia asked.

'Do not take this the wrong way,' said Gia, 'but I'm not sure you would be very convincing.'

Claudia pulled the sheet off the hospital cot, wrapping it around herself like a palla, to resemble one of the palace servants.

'Better?'

'Yes, but are you sure?' said Gia. 'You almost died.'

'Not almost,' said Claudia, gravely. 'I *did* die. I have crossed the underworld to return.'

She gave her a look that said *I will tell you everything later*.

'That is why I am so sure that this is what we must do. This is why I have been returned; to fight in Minerva's war for her.'

The gathered group gazed around at each other uncertainly.

'I will rest when it is done, and the war is won. Until then, we fight. As long as I am conscious, I will fight for Rome.' She drew a deep breath. 'Now. Let's go and find my dear cousin.'

Claudia's soldiers marched in formation around her, using their stolen shields to create a wall that concealed her from view. She hoped no one would look too closely as they paraded through the palace in search of her cousin, but she knew they would not remain unnoticed for long.

When stopped and questioned, Cassius was once again ready to take centre stage.

'We've been ordered to join the search for Marcellus.' He gestured slightly in Claudia's direction, as she bowed her covered head. 'This servant says she has seen him in the gardens.'

'Very well,' said the officer, waving them on.

Room by room, they hunted for Marcellus, and though the

imperial buildings were full of soldiers who behaved as if they were right at home, gathering in groups to drink and gamble and discuss future war plans, the new emperor was nowhere to be seen.

'No sign of him,' Gia whispered. 'Maybe he really has fled.'

'It wouldn't be the worst choice he ever made,' said Dom.

'I couldn't blame him,' agreed Cassius.

They paused at a window, looking down on the courtyard.

'If he did, he must've escaped on foot. His chariot and his driver are still parked outside,' said Claudia, pointing it out.

They continued on through the palace, choosing the quietest corridors and halls, concealing themselves between rows of pillars or busts or in the folds of drapes, all the while attempting to appear inconspicuous.

In Claudia's throne room, now bustling with decorated military figures and drunken senators alike, speeches were being written by sweating scribes and flags were being sewn by harried servants and wax seals were being printed on stacks of scrolls for the Archive, and none of it involved Marcellus in any shape or form.

It was clear the principate was a mere military installation, and the emperor just a figurehead. They would drag him out for festivals and official events but he was just a standing man, a seat filler, a foreman of the appropriate birthright. All the same, they needed him. They could not prop a scarecrow in front of a crowd in the Forum and employ a ventriloquist to speak through it. They needed a living man of esteem to sit on the throne and serve their regime. Marcellus was just a convenient pawn.

In the atrium, where they joined a group of naval officers celebrating a victory in the Aegean Sea, Claudia glimpsed General Aquinas talking to a group of commanders – men of higher military rank.

With horror, she saw that he was holding the prince's lotus necklace, the one his goddess had given him. He dangled it between his fingers, inspecting it thoughtfully.

'The rest of his party has fled or been captured,' said one man.

'Good. The prince will be held in Mamertime Prison until we are able to arrange a public trial. For show, of course, and to send a message. He will be our pretext to cross the Parthian Border.'

Claudia snuck a look at Cassius, who appeared equally concerned. Darius hadn't abandoned them – he was being held hostage. She regretted ever doubting him.

'Then it is settled,' said General Aquinas, as they marched by. 'We will formally accuse Prince Darius of killing Princess Claudia. Let King Kamran know he should prepare for a war.'

'Yes, sir. Right away.'

'I will inform the troops tomorrow.'

'I am sure we can persuade the Senate.'

'Leave the Senate to us,' said Senator Tacitus.

Along the colonnade, a group of generals and commanders were discussing the future of Britannia.

'The kidnap of the Eighth Legion proves that the campaign is not aggressive enough,' said one. 'We shall not rest until all of the isles are under Roman control.'

'Aquinas is determined to enslave the barbarians.'

'Send a message to the legates and the tributes, and tell them we will be tripling our numbers. In the new year, we shall conquer the north.'

Each new development was worse than the last, all of the layers of her failure compounding into something truly grotesque.

They marched on towards the stairs, checking the imperial suite her father had once slept in, but it was empty.

'If Marcellus is not there, then where?' she said.

They checked the guest wing, even the servants' quarters, but her cousin couldn't be located. They looked for signs of a plan of escape – perhaps a rope hanging down the side of the building, or a ladder propped up against one of the exterior walls – but they found no evidence of Marcellus. Eventually, they tried the bathhouse and then the palace temple, but both were empty.

'Perhaps we should move forward without him,' said Gia.

'It will be difficult for me to regain power while he is still alive and on the run,' said Claudia.

As they surveyed the gardens, Claudia's attention was drawn to the small temple of Venus, where she'd spied Darius and Cassius in their complex entanglement.

A shadow moved within.

Breaking out of the defensive formation, Claudia crossed the lawn towards the shrine as Gia and the others ran to catch up. As she drew closer, reaching the top of the short steps, she saw her cousin huddled inside the shrine and charged towards him.

'Hiding, are we?' she said.

'I was, but it seems you have found me,' he said, turning to face her quite calmly. 'You look dreadful.'

'I have been to the underworld and back.'

'I knew you wouldn't be killed so easily.'

'It's over, Marcellus. Give up.'

'You know, Jupiter was never my favourite god,' he said. 'I was always a supporter of Mars.'

'Oh?' said Claudia, unsure how this was relevant.

'But after Aquinas and the others came for me, Jupiter began visiting me in dreams. He converted me, to serve him.'

'Save it for your memoirs,' said Gia.

'I should've known what he promised was too good to be true. He tricked me, too. I am a victim, as much as you.'

His face contorted, making him unrecognizable.

'I wish I'd never listened to him. But all the same . . .'

Before Gia could reach her, Marcellus grasped hold of Claudia, pulling them backwards as he held a knife to her throat.

'Don't . . . move,' he said.

Everyone froze, on the precipice of the temple.

He dragged Claudia towards the entrance, but Gia and Cassius held out their swords, blocking him.

'What are you doing, Marcellus?' said Claudia. 'You couldn't kill me before. You won't do so now.'

'I have found my courage now. See? I have nothing to lose. I am a man on the edge.'

Gia inched closer, causing Marcellus to retreat further into the temple, his back pushed up against the wall.

'Back off!' he yelled.

He pressed the knife in deeper, causing Claudia to cry out.

'Let her go, right now,' said Gia.

A rustling noise alerted Claudia to a presence nearby.

They all seized up, awaiting attack – when Princess the lynx skulked out of the shrubbery.

'Oh. It's just a cat,' laughed Marcellus.

Princess leaped gracefully up onto a mounted statue. She eyed her mistress below, struggling in Marcellus's grip.

And then she pounced.

Claudia wrenched away as Marcellus fell backwards. He gave a wet gasp of a scream, trying to pull the lynx off as her sharp fangs dug into his neck, forcing him to drop the knife. It skittered noisily across the floor towards Gia's feet.

The lynx sprang away, leaving Marcellus on his knees, clutching at his wound in shock. Princess trotted up to Claudia and wove through her legs, purring, as she and Gia looked to each other in bewilderment.

The prince was captured but his beast was still protecting her.

'Darius *did* tell me she was trained to kill with a single bite to the throat,' said Claudia, passively, as she watched her cousin dying.

Nadira burst in, breathless. 'I'm so sorry, Empress. She broke free of her leash. I couldn't stop her,' she said.

'It's all right, Nadira,' she said. 'You did well.'

'This is how it ends for me, isn't it?' said Marcellus, ashen.

'I think so,' said Claudia. 'Sorry, dear cousin.'

Marcellus slumped down onto the floor, losing all strength and will as his blood waterfalled down his chest.

'Save me,' he begged of Claudia. 'You could still save me.'

Claudia shook her head. 'Unfortunately, I can do nothing for you. The palace physician has fled,' she said. 'Thanks to your own uprising. Oh, cousin. I still remember you as that little boy I asked to play with me as a child.' She mirrored his words at their first meeting. 'You are much changed, of course.' Claudia paused, for effect. 'You have grown up to be even more of a parasite.'

He laughed ruefully, half sobbing.

'I see. That is how you wish for it to be. You won. You won again, Claudia.'

'It was never a competition,' she said.

'I hope the power is everything you dreamed of.'

'The power is a duty, a calling,' she said, as strong as she'd ever been. 'This, you will never understand.'

'You think you're different to me and the ones who came before. You think that you are kinder, less ruthless, because you are a woman … but you are a dictator, just the same. A killer, just the same. You are no better than us men.'

But Claudia was unmoved. 'I shall not mourn you, Marcellus, for you made your own choices. Any last words?'

'Let me … just think of something …'

Her cousin slumped forward, laid face down in a crimson pool.

Dom carefully bent down beside Marcellus, checking his neck for a pulse, then shook his head.

'He is gone,' he said.

They all looked at the lynx with a mixture of fear and affection.

'Well,' said Dido. 'That was unexpected.'

'Good work, cat,' said Gia, impressed by the beast's combat. 'You would do well in the arena, with moves like that.'

Livia murmured in agreement.

The noise of clanking armour sounded. They huddled into the shrine, hiding from a passing troop.

'What now?' asked Cassius.

'They'll notice his absence before too long,' said Dom. 'We cannot remain hidden while we are still in the palace.'

'Where should we go?' asked Livia.

'Marcellus is dead. We are not hiding,' said Claudia.

She threw the sheet she'd been wearing as a palla over her cousin's body, so she didn't have to look at his face.

'It's over for them,' she said. 'They are in there writing his proclamations for when he is declared. What chance do they have of taking Rome without an emperor?'

'Aquinas still has an entire army at his command,' said Gia. 'We cannot fight every soldier in Rome.'

'We may have to,' said Cassius, darkly.

Claudia followed his gaze to the other end of the garden where Aquinas and his men were gathering, calling for Marcellus.

'They're coming!' Livia hissed.

Gia pulled Claudia behind her, as her soldiers shuffled around in a square, to hide the incriminating body.

'Get ready to fight for your lives,' said Celadus.

'I am always ready for that,' said Livia.

'Halt!'

Aquinas and his men moved towards them, unhurried. They hadn't seen Claudia yet, hidden by a shield of mostly pretend soldiers, but they would soon enough.

Just as they drew close enough to sight her, a distant noise sounded, strange enough that Aquinas pulled up.

It was disguised by the breeze at first, by the clank of armour and the stamp of boots, but the insistent sound cut through, causing the soldiers to pause.

An otherworldly chill ran through Claudia's blood, causing her skin to prickle.

'Hush!' shouted Aquinas. 'What is that?'

They all fell silent, listening.

It was the beating of a drum, getting louder and louder, though no military procession could be seen.

They looked around, seeking the source of the sound.

'Perhaps Darius has returned?' whispered Cassius.

A dull, droning horn cut through the air, then another, and another, creating a crashing cacophony of brass. It was so unfathomably loud that they all gripped their ears in pain.

It was not a joyful, celebratory sound, but a warning.

They looked up as a bright flash of light shot through the storm clouds, followed by a tremendous thud.

Thud, thud, thud.

Each explosion getting closer.

Another flash, and another, turning the whole sky white.

And then a lightning spear descended at speed with a bone-shaking roar, striking the east wing of the palace from above.

22. JUPITER RETURNS

The palace building exploded, spraying bricks and plaster into the air in a dusty cloud. For a moment, Claudia was back in Pompeii, witnessing the force of Vesuvius erupting. At the same time, the ground cracked and trembled, shattering glass and smashing pottery.

The entire universe seemed to shake. Claudia was thrown to her hands and knees. Servants poured like water out of the nearest entrance, all screaming as they fled.

'Fire!' someone yelled.

Flames burst from the outbuildings, spreading as colossal white bolts continued to light up the sky, creating a percussion of explosions.

'Jupiter,' breathed Claudia.

The war had finally come to Earth.

'There's no way out,' said Gia, looking to the crowd on the lawns. 'We must go through them.'

Aquinas's ice-cold eyes caught on Claudia, now visible between fighting, fast-moving bodies. She watched the recognition click in his mind.

'Detain her!' he roared.

More soldiers crossed the gardens at speed, just as another spear struck the west building.

A pillar cracked and slowly toppled between them, like the trunk of a giant tree, creating a barricade that blocked the soldiers from advancing, but also prevented Claudia and her party from escaping.

With a groan, one of the soldiers was crushed beneath it, while Dom and Celadus were cut off from them.

Trapped between the fallen pillar and the wall, they had nowhere to run as another hot, white flare streaked past them, hitting a wall. It burst open, sending pillars toppling and bringing down one of the portico balconies. Screams filled the air, with soldiers and servants alike attempting to scramble for cover.

When Claudia looked up, she saw something flying through the reddening sky above her. She shielded her eyes to make it out.

At first, she thought it was merely a piece of stone, thrown up from one of the impacts, but it was swooping and spiralling, drifting right as it avoided another lightning spear.

It was a chariot. A flying chariot, pulled by white winged horses that soared on the wind. Another joined it, then another, in formation, until the skies above were crowded with chariots.

It was an extraordinary sight, beyond mortal imagination. The dull, thunderous roar of utmost chaos filled the streets for miles around as Romans fled for the hills.

'It is Jupiter's army,' Claudia said, clutching Gia's arm in fear. 'He has come for us.'

His aerial soldiers hurled lightning bolts down at the palace in a shimmering, luminescent rain. They fired indiscriminately, striking servants and soldiers alike with the carelessness of a god for whom all mortals are expendable. Like shining javelins, the bolts pierced each body they hit, cutting through their armour like pins through wool.

Claudia and the others crowded back into the shrine of Venus, where Marcellus still lay bleeding like a sacrifice.

They stood in silence – panting, numb.

As they watched, something fast and fiery appeared from nowhere and struck one of the flying chariots, sending it into a frantic spin. Its rider lost control of the vehicle as it plummeted downwards, striking the ground just beyond the palace with a resounding boom.

They looked up, seeing more chariots moving through the sky overhead. Another red-hot spear sent a second chariot crashing, its Pegasi horses breaking free to save themselves before the vehicle struck the rear palace wall, smashing a hole right through it. Gia and Cassius ran towards it and cleared bricks out of the way, until there was a gap large enough to squeeze through.

'Go, hurry,' gasped Cassius.

One by one, they squeezed through. On the other side, Claudia looked up at the sky to see more chariots, red in colour, pulled by black horses. Their archers were firing at the white chariots. Claudia could see the symbols of Mars and Jupiter on their vessels.

Mars and Jupiter were at war.

Gia, Cassius, Dido and Livia successfully escaped the palace garden, piling out through the hole and into the road, but as Claudia looked back, she saw Celadus and Dom being cuffed by Aquinas's soldiers.

'Dom!' Gia cried.

Celadus the Handsome had been recognized, though he was attempting (unsuccessfully) to charm his way out of trouble, smiling broadly and gesticulating, as if there had been a misunderstanding.

‘We have to go back,’ said Claudia.

The soldiers turned, spying the hole in the wall and pointing at Claudia as they charged towards them.

‘No time,’ said Cassius, pushing them on.

Gia stared back with regret for a moment, before following.

Beyond the palace, the city was in even greater disorder as the skies filled with warring gods and their monsters. Spectral red hunting dogs as big as wolves attacked the Pegasi pulling white chariots, as soldiers of Mars battled soldiers of Jupiter, both vying for control of the pantheon at any cost. Meanwhile, the goddesses were nowhere to be seen.

One of the majestic horses fell to the ground, its mighty wings wrapped around it like a chrysalis. Claudia covered her eyes, but she heard the dull impact as a cry of horror resounded.

They pushed on, advancing towards the Forum, as thousands of terrified Romans filled the streets, all gazing upwards at the strange celestial spectacle that filled the sky.

High above, thousands more chariots appeared between the clouds now darkened and bloated by rain, darting back and forth, light as leaves carried on the wind.

‘Where should we go?’ Gia asked.

‘The Pantheon,’ said Claudia. ‘Maybe we’ll be safe there.’

With a lightning crack and a thunderous rumble, another white-hot spear struck the domed roof of the building, just visible in the distance.

‘Or, not,’ said Gia.

Claudia looked around, frantic, as another flaming red chariot hit the ground nearby, pierced with a shining white spear.

They backed away, retracing their steps.

As they rounded the corner, she saw something streaming, water-falling down from the sky, poured from a giant amphora-shaped craft. It wasn't water, but stone: stone of every kind and colour, from the dull grey of granite and the pearly shine of marble, to a rainbow of gemstones and hunks of pure gold.

They clumped together as they fell, to form enormous arches and pillars, constructing a colossal temple right opposite the palace.

A temple for Jupiter.

A triangular pediment topped four sturdy columns, decorated with many small, gold statues, all of them holding thunderbolt spears in slightly different positions.

Chryselephantine statues made of black ivory and gold arose from the ground, forming an autonomous army to guard the temple. They stamped and thrust their weapons in unison, coming to life.

'Stop!'

Claudia's party had been surrounded by soldiers and praetorian guards. Their formation now blocked escape in every direction, creating endless walls of men holding enormous shields, and at the helm was . . .

'There is nowhere left to run,' said General Aquinas, stepping forward. 'Unless your goddesses are willing to descend from the heavens to rescue you personally, I'd say you were done for.'

Claudia and Gia moved closer together. Claudia reached out a hand and found Gia doing the same.

They looked up hopefully at the sky, but there was no sign of Minerva et al amid the chaos.

When Aquinas clicked his fingers, the entire troop took two steps forward, the square of soldiers shrinking, closing in.

'Women were never meant to rule. I hope that is clear to you now. You cannot fight the military, Claudia.'

He snapped once more, and his soldiers stepped closer.

'It's over,' he said. 'I am the new ruler of Rome.'

'Spare me from your delusion,' she said. 'You are nothing, Aquinas. A mediocre man of little acclaim and even less personality.'

'I am the new emperor,' he chuckled. 'You did my job for me, by killing Marcellus.'

'You are a mere general.'

'And you are a mere whore. The people of Rome would pick a monster to rule them over a woman like you.'

'And you are that monster? Not much of a boast.'

'If I have to be. Real strength is cruel, it is ugly. It is something you can neither fathom nor possess.'

'Certainly, it is ugly,' she said, looking at his cold-eyed, haggard face. 'But you will not hold the empire with brute force alone.'

'Your ignorance would be pitiful if it wasn't so infuriating.'

'You think mighty Jupiter will choose you to represent him?'

'I am the last man standing.'

'Not for long,' said Gia.

'You have offended the gods, and made a mockery of all men.'

The circle of soldiers tightened around them.

Aquinas raised his arm, about to signal his men to charge, but he was cut off mid-word by the rumbling sound of an approaching brigade.

A horn blared.

A hundred voices began chanting . . . in Persian.

Through a cloud of dust, kicked up by a dozen horses, Prince Darius appeared, riding atop a well-decorated steed and holding his ornate shield, surrounded by soldiers and the more fearsome of his menagerie beasts, which immediately began attacking Roman soldiers.

Aquinas directed his soldiers to greet them, as the two parties erupted into the carnality of warfare.

Gia and Cassius guarded Claudia, trying to manoeuvre her out of the mass, but the conflict was getting closer and thicker, more ferocious, pressing in from every side.

The smell of blood and sweat. The clash of steel. The grunting of the wounded and the last breaths of the dying.

Finally, Darius broke through the ranks.

'You are free,' said Claudia, as he approached.

'I knew you wouldn't leave us,' said Cassius.

Darius offered his hand, pulling Cassius up on the back of his steed. He could not stop himself from smiling.

'I swore I would fight until the end,' said Darius. 'My goddess Anahita came to my assistance. It seems she has made a pact with your goddess Minerva. We shall fight together, for Persia and for Rome. If you will agree, that is?'

'Gladly,' said Claudia, shaking his hand. 'I want nothing more.'

As another legion of Mars's soldiers appeared above, the Persian archers began firing arrows up at them in kind, but they were as harmless as pine needles, bouncing off not only the chariots but the drivers themselves. The gods were impervious to human weapons.

A terrific roar sounded, shaking the ground. Claudia looked back to the temple, watching as the largest of the sky chariots descended.

Inside were Jupiter and Juno, king and queen of the gods, golden-crowned and side by side. He in pale blue robes and carrying his distinctive thunderbolt staff, she hooded and holding a sceptre.

An orchestra of cherubs played trumpets and harps, creating an unnatural melody that silenced the city, as Aquinas and his soldiers moved to greet their royals. But before Jupiter could land, another chariot glided down to meet him, drawn by black horses with ruby red eyes.

This one was driven by a man in rust-coloured armour, his helmet fringed with an exuberant red plume.

Mars. The consort of Venus. The ruler of the Roman army. Mars had fathered the twins Romulus and Remus, the patrons of the sacred city, after raping their mother. Like father, like son.

A frenzied battle began, as both parties fired arrows. Jupiter and Mars, both struggling for control, their shouts and cries ringing through the sky above the battlefield of Rome. As above, so below: men warred on the streets and among the clouds alike.

Well, mostly men – for Gia, Dido and Livia had also launched into battle, inspiring the women around them to do the same.

The gods were making themselves visible to mortals, and Rome was the collateral, for many fallen chariots and cannons had wrecked some of the city's most famous buildings.

Lit up by fires, shrouded in black smoke, it reminded Claudia of the underworld Rome she'd recently traversed.

'My children have disobeyed me for the last time,' said Jupiter, loud enough to be heard on the ground. 'I didn't bring you into existence just so you could overthrow me.'

'Like you did to your own father?' said Mars.

'You have no respect for tradition, for authority, for order,' said Juno, her face souring.

'You reign is over,' said Mars. 'Now it's my turn.'

'Never.'

'Give it to me. I deserve it.'

'No! It is mine!'

It was like watching two children fighting over a toy, as Mars rode closer, trying to snatch his father's staff while Juno chided them. Claudia thought of her own father and brother.

'Step aside, old man.'

'You are not even a man, but a boy.'

'Both of you, stop it!' shrieked Juno. 'We must stick together!'

As fighting slowed on the ground, the human crowd watched the scene above with interest. The gods had revealed themselves on Earth in more ways than one – for while they were undeniably powerful, dangerous and fearsome, they were also recognizably flawed, a mere mirror of mortal foibles made supernaturally large.

As Mars and Jupiter continued to battle, their armies resumed fighting. Thousands of soldiers rained down from the clouds, including men made entirely of plates of metal. They landed on their feet, quickly arming themselves and ploughing through the screaming crowd.

Now, Claudia had no choice but to fight, arming herself with the sword of a fallen soldier as the people descended on her, sweeping her up into the manic mob.

She swung the sword wildly, inexpertly, trying to stay low and keep her eyes on Gia. Every man was her enemy now, mortal or immortal. Her sword stuck in someone's thigh, in someone's arm, as she ducked and dived to avoid being struck, eventually taking shelter in a doorway.

Gia had fallen out of sight.

'Gia!' she cried. 'Gia!'

She couldn't see her anywhere.

More falling chariots smashed to earth; fallen Pegasi scarpered and scattered, breaking up the brawling Forum.

When another lightning bolt destroyed his chariot, Mars fell back as his soldiers swarmed around him. They raised an enormous white flag, stained red by a god's blood and signalling peace.

Jupiter was victorious.

Claudia saw Gia across the crowd and ran to her. They climbed up onto the podium of a large bronze statue, keeping them out of the affray, and held on to each other like they were shipwrecked again.

Hovering above the newly constructed building, Jupiter now addressed his citizens, in a voice that could be heard across all of Rome.

'It is I, Jupiter, king of the gods. Lay down your weapons and bow before the almighty.'

Juno descended from her chariot to float at his side, drawing the attention of the women of Rome.

'Where are the rest of the goddesses?' asked Gia.

'They must be dead, or detained,' said Claudia.

'Then this might be it for us.'

Claudia pulled her into one last, end-of-the-world, kiss, her fingers digging into Gia's flesh. She didn't want to let go, if letting go meant accepting defeat – not just the kind of loss that would see her dead and dethroned, but the entire world enslaved by gods.

'I regret nothing,' said Claudia, holding her gaze. 'Even now.'

'I would do it all again, and again, and again,' said Gia. 'If this is how it ends, then so be it. We did our best to save the world from men.'

'The war is over,' Jupiter boomed. 'My army is triumphant. All above and below will serve and obey.'

Atop the podium, Claudia felt herself forced forwards, bending at the middle as she bowed against her will. She watched as everyone did the same, all of them compelled by a supernatural force.

Jupiter was *forcing* them to bow to him.

'There will be no more mortal emperors. Rome will be ruled by me, and me alone. Only the king of the gods is fit to rule.'

A deathly silence fell. Claudia could not hear a single bird. Even the winged horses had stilled. She looked to General Aquinas, just visible in front of the temple. As he turned to mutter with his soldiers, she was certain that he too had been betrayed by Jupiter, just as he deserved.

'All others will fall in line, or Rome itself will fall.'

Her journey through the underworld had been a kind of prophecy, she realized, like the one she'd seen of Vesuvius erupting in Pompeii. It was a vision of Rome, should she fail to save it. A terrible nightmare that was now coming true. If Minerva failed, if Claudia failed, Rome would be ruled directly by the gods and the city would be rebuilt on the bones of many mortal sacrifices.

It was her responsibility as empress to protect the people, but she could do nothing as the king of the gods enslaved them all.

'Pray to me!' Jupiter commanded.

In perfect synchronicity, Claudia and everyone around her dropped to their knees, unable to resist his control. Beside her, Gia tried to fight it, straining against the god's power, but it was insurmountable.

Every Roman who had ever prayed to him or made offerings was now under his direct control.

'Now we shall see who rules the world,' he said.

At his command, every statue in the city groaned and creaked to life, becoming animate as Romans fled.

Claudia turned and looked up, aghast, watching as the giant athlete stepped down from the podium they were standing on. He kicked them aside with his enormous bronze legs as he moved forth, throwing Claudia and Gia to the ground.

Claudia crashed down onto the cobbled stone with a painful jarring of limbs, winded and grazed, watching in cold horror as the statue threw his giant discus into the crowd in the Forum.

People parted in screaming waves, diving out of its path. Those who didn't were struck with the force of a cannon, their bodies flying through the air.

Gia scrambled up, dragging Claudia to her feet.

As they raced past, an enormous statue of a chariot rider burst through the Colosseum, breaking its exterior wall. Drawn by titanic horses, the vehicle cast a terrifying shadow upon the street ahead, tearing up stone as it hurtled forwards and crushing people under its colossal gold wheels. The snapping whip of its charioteer echoed horribly, making the road shake.

Gia pushed them out of the way again as it careened towards them, headed for the palace.

Every god, emperor and warrior cast in marble or bronze now stepped down from their podiums and moved through the crowd, tossing people to the side with their inhuman strength.

Neptune climbed out of a fountain as a giant Venus strolled down the Appian Way, already missing one arm. A marble Augustus in armour rallied the troops, while the hollow-eyed Orator addressed the crowd with a speech. A massive bronze equestrian statue galloped past, trampling mortals underfoot. A bronze Capitoline wolf stalked the streets, pursued by two stone gladiators who crumbled as they fought each other. Even the carved figures of pillars who held up roofs walked away to join the affray, leaving their buildings collapsing behind them.

'Do you see?' roared Jupiter. 'Even the statues are loyal to me. I command the heavens and the earth. I have dominion over the elements. There is no force in the cosmos more powerful than the king of the gods. First, the empire, then all the world will be mine to rule.'

Gia nudged Claudia. 'Look,' she hissed.

Claudia followed her line of sight.

Jupiter was now much larger than any man, looming over the city and casting an enormous shadow, and yet he was no different to a human male in his hubris and ego. He was so busy extolling his virtues and his victory to the crowd of gathered gods and mortals, he didn't notice the large hole that had opened up in the middle of the Forum behind him, where one of his own lightning spears had struck the ground.

Claudia watched as the abyss grew larger, until every head turned towards it. It swallowed up the road and the nearby buildings, pulling everything into the swirling, glittering void.

The crowd shrank away, murmuring fearfully, clamouring not to be swallowed up by the growing hole.

Jupiter paused his speech, looking to the cause of the collapse.

'Who dares to interrupt me, in the middle of victory?' he said.

Mercury emerged from the hole, looking slightly sheepish.

'It is I, my king,' he said, bowing.

'It's about time, Mercury,' said Jupiter. 'I assume that you finally located Minerva?'

'I did,' he said.

'And?' pressed Jupiter. 'What did she say? Does she submit? Does she accept defeat?'

'Not exactly,' said Mercury.

Suddenly, something flew out of the hole in the ground, rising high in the sky: a winged woman holding a bow. An arrow struck one of Jupiter's soldiers in the head, his chariot plummeting to the ground.

'What is this?' Jupiter roared.

In response, a dozen other winged warriors emerged, sweeping through the air as they fired an endless stream of arrows.

Gia grabbed hold of Claudia, pushing her out of the way just as one of them crashed through the rows of people packed into the Forum, now emptying hastily.

Arrows rained down, fired by the creatures emerging from the ground. Claudia recognized the flying warriors she'd seen briefly in the underworld, soaring over the Forum as they targeted the soldiers of Mars and Jupiter. Furies and harpies, attacking in feral flocks.

Among them, Claudia saw Discordia, Invidia and red-haired Bellona, helmeted and raising her bloodied sword in defiance.

She moved straight towards her father.

'You! Didn't I banish you and tear down your temples?' he said.

'I am the plague you cannot cure, father,' said Bellona. 'I am the famine you cannot survive. I am the pestilence you will never be rid of. I am the war you created me for.'

Roaring, she joined the mass that now attacked Jupiter, as her aerial army commandeered a number of his chariots.

His spirits renewed, Mars withdrew the white flag and launched into a second attempt at overthrowing his father, which only added to the confusion of the conflict, but he too was surrounded by harpies and furies.

A black chariot flew up to block him, and, for a moment, Claudia feared that it was Pluto come to defend his brother. But then she saw Proserpina, wearing Pluto's keys on her belt and carrying her husband's black staff, as winged Invidia flew beside her. She waved enthusiastically at Claudia as they passed over, her sullen pout replaced with a toothy smile.

'You know her?' said Gia, in awe.

'That would be my dear friend Vidi,' said Claudia, grandly. 'We met when I traversed the underworld. Long story.'

Proserpina faced off against Jupiter, though he was enormous and she was human in size.

'Where is my brother?' he said. 'Bring him to me.'

'Pluto is dead. I killed him with his own weapon,' said Proserpina, with a ferocity that existed in spite of her cherubic maiden face. 'I made sure he was really gone.'

'You should've seen it,' said Invidia. 'Vengeance is sweet.'

'But chaos is sweeter,' said Discordia, launching herself at a group of Jupiter's soldiers.

'You'll pay for this,' raged Jupiter, struggling to fight off the winged warriors. 'All of you will be punished.'

'You're not *my* father,' said Discordia.

He broke free, charging towards the Dread Princess of the Dead as she drove her chariot in circles around him.

'You owe me your existence,' said Jupiter. 'You owe me your power. You owe me your freedom.'

'What do I owe to you, but nothing?' said Proserpina. 'You did nothing when your brother stole me away and raped me. You did nothing when he made me his bride and kept me prisoner. I owe you nothing, as you have given me nothing. The underworld no longer serves you.'

As if heralding her announcement, another bone-shaking horn blared. Minerva herself floated gracefully out of the abyss, flanked by Diana, Venus, Fortuna and an assembled army of goddesses, including Proserpina's mother, Ceres, who launched herself towards her daughter, embracing her tightly. Each of them wore the most spectacular armour Claudia had ever seen, all of it forged with the symbol of Vesta.

She was, it seemed, the pantheon's new armourer.

Jupiter shrank, floating down to the ground to greet them.

'I knew you would be behind this,' he said.

'As did I,' said Minerva. 'This is the destiny that awaited me from the moment I burst free from your mind. You know as well as I that I was born to kill you.'

'Of all of my children, you are the most deceitful, the most devious, the greatest disappointment,' said Jupiter.

'It is my honour,' said Minerva, bowing slowly.

Discordia popped into being, hanging in the air beside Mars's chariot as she waved at him.

'Look out,' she said, tossing one of her famous golden apples.

BOOM!

The apple of discord exploded, shattering the chariot into a thousand pieces as Mars fled away on one of his flying horses. An army of chubby cupids followed in pursuit of Mars, firing arrows as Venus directed from her own white chariot.

'It is over between us, by the way,' Venus yelled at Mars with a surprising amount of venom.

'You'll be back,' he called. 'You always return.'

'Not this time. I thought you a better man, but I was wrong.'

She fired an arrow at the front of the chariot, causing it to sink down towards the ground.

'What I really needed was to become a better woman.'

'Ao! Claudia!' said Discordia, saluting her, as Gia once again looked to her with curiosity and a shade of jealousy.

'When did you meet all these flying warrior women?' she said.

Gia and Claudia ran for cover, as Minerva closed in on Jupiter.

'This time, there will be no submission,' said Minerva, as war erupted around them, in the air and on the ground. 'There will be no stalemate, no armistice. I will be the new ruler of the pantheon. Proserpina will rule the Underworld. You will step aside, to be detained in Tartarus, or you will be destroyed. You will hang in the sky alongside your brothers.'

'You would kill your own father?' Jupiter said.

'I should've done it millennia ago.'

At this, Bellona gave a shrieking battle cry that roused her army of winged women, as a menagerie of underworld beasts burst out of the ground, including the three-headed Cerberus.

'Don't forget about me, Daddy!' she cackled.

Aquinas's remaining men fled for their lives, though they were met by all manner of undead monsters. In the chaos, the general broke through the crowd and advanced towards Claudia, extending his sword.

'You,' he raged, gnashing his teeth. 'You are responsible! You did this! The graveyard of Rome shall bear your name.'

Claudia backed away, raising her palms innocently.

'I am but a mortal woman,' she said, meeting eyes with Gia over his shoulder, 'and this is not the end . . . but the beginning.'

When the general lunged at her, Gia leaped forwards and slid her sword into his back.

Aquinas made a feeble whimpering noise in shock and shrank

into himself, curling up and collapsing to the ground. Spitting up blood, he could only watch as the monstrous canine approached. Cerberus.

The general's eyes popped as the giant rabid creature tore him to pieces, limb from limb, cracking his skeleton and spitting out his bones.

Claudia found that she could not look away. There was something almost beautiful about such poetic violence.

She startled when Diana sounded a horn, watching as women flocked towards her, their expressions fixed in awe, seizing the weapons and armour of the fallen as they joined the parade behind her.

At last, Minerva met Claudia's gaze. 'Empress,' she said.

Minerva grew enormous to match her father's great size, laying her hand on the ground. 'Come.'

Speechless, Claudia climbed into her palm. When Minerva stood up, Claudia was lifted high above the battle below, held in the hand of a colossal living goddess.

As Claudia rose slowly into the sky, she saw many lower their weapons, transfixed by the sight.

'Call to them,' said Minerva. 'You are the Empress of Women. I will make sure you are heard.'

Claudia gazed up at her for encouragement, like a child.

'This is what you were chosen for,' said the goddess.

Claudia turned to behold the packed Forum below, still in chaos. It was the moment every ruler longed for and feared, the moment when she was needed, to lead the people to victory at war. Her actions would decide how she would be written in history.

'Women of Rome,' she roared, channelling the strength and wisdom of the goddesses, 'as your empress, I command you to pick up arms and defend your city. Channel the bravery that already exists within you, and become the fearsome warriors you are destined to be.'

From high above, she could see members of the Cult of Diana following her word. The group's leader punched a soldier in the face to steal his sword, then used it to skewer his second in command.

'But I am not just the Empress of Women. I also call upon every man, every child, every senator and every slave. In the name of Minerva, queen of the gods, and all of our sisters above and below, we will topple the gods who have endangered our children, who have risked our freedom and our peace, and we will reclaim it, in the name of Roma!'

The Forum erupted again, as every woman who could, rushed to join the fight.

'Viva Roma!'

Claudia had lost sight of Gia in the scramble, calling her name.

She could see Darius and Cassius riding horseback through the crowd, battling the soldiers still willing to fight.

In the pandemonium, Claudia saw many unbelievable things. She saw Diana strike her twin brother, the infamous Apollo, her loaded arrow pointing at his throat as he begged for mercy. She saw Venus kill Mars with his own burning sword as her cupids fluttered around her, weeping. She saw Mercury turn on Jupiter, ordering his messengers in winged hats and sandals to fight for victory.

She saw strange deities she didn't recognize – winged warrior women in colourful armour and golden helmets shaped like different animal heads, who seemed to serve the Persian goddess Anahita.

She wrenched her gaze to Jupiter, hurtling towards her.

Minerva placed Claudia on top of the temple he'd built as she drew out her sword to greet him.

'It ends here, Father.'

Their swords clashed, spewing a volcanic eruption of light, a cataclysm of rebounding sound, spraying up sparks that caught the sun.

Each time their weapons met in combat, it created a clang so loud it shook the ground, catalysing earthquakes. Human spectators dived out of the way, as colossal gods brawled in the Forum, battling until their stone bodies broke to pieces.

Down below, Livia and Dido fought beside Dom and Celadus, who'd broken free of the palace. Claudia scanned the crowd frantically for Gia, but she couldn't see her.

The battle unfurled around her, as giant deities wrestled in the Colosseum, as black and white Pegasi flew free through the clouds, as the waters of Roman baths and pools and rivers began to froth, and mortal men were dragged to their deaths by nereids.

A carnival of satyrs and fauns snaked through the battlefield now, playing rousing songs of war, as nymphs danced behind them, chanting in euphoric fervour.

The most vengeful of the goddesses formed the frontline of Minerva's army, while the goddesses of medicine and peace moved through the crowd, treating wounded mortals.

But Jupiter was gaining control, summoning more and more gods to his side. Even the most minor of deities were glorified as his soldiers in this, the final moment of his victory. Claudia even saw Aristaeus, the Roman god of crafts and beekeeping, joining the affray, though he quickly submitted to the goddesses.

Jupiter fired a lightning bolt that struck Minerva's shoulder, causing golden blood to pour out and down onto the ground. As she struggled to right herself, he cast another, which glanced her neck. When she dropped her shield to stop blood from the wound, Jupiter launched a third at her, taking her down.

'No!'

They struggled together, and Claudia heard a loud, splintering crack as Minerva's shield smashed, exploding into shards of otherworldly metal that dissolved.

Jupiter had her pinned against what remained of the temple he'd built, as she struggled for purchase on her sword. Claudia struggled to hold on, as the foundations shook with the force.

'Minerva!'

Unclear who was winning or what a victory for either side would mean, the citizens of Rome could only take shelter and pray.

And then, Fortuna arose into the sky, wingless and golden.

Older than Jupiter and far more powerful, Fortuna carried no weapon but her experience. He tried to bat her away like a fly, but she glowed brighter and expanded, her light filling the whole sky like a sun.

'Fortune is not in your favour,' she said.

In a sudden explosion of bright, brilliant light, Fortuna pulsated like a supernova, creating a powerful burst of energy that reverberated in waves across the city, downing chariots and dragging soldiers to their knees.

With a groan that split the ground, Minerva sent Jupiter flying, snatching up his dropped staff. The enormous god staggered, collapsing backwards into his temple. Claudia was thrown into the air as the building dramatically collapsed.

She felt strong arms catch her as she was swept up by Invidia and lowered slowly down to the ground below.

Minerva hesitated for only a moment, allowing Jupiter's staff to charge up with lightning.

'A new era begins today.'

She plunged the staff into her father's chest as he roared in celestial pain and fury.

As Jupiter hit the ground, his body broke apart into pure white-hot energy as the world throbbed and tilted. A forceful aftershock moved through the city, toppling several more buildings.

The sun wept red tears.

The sky over Rome turned scarlet, bathing every dome and spire in the imperial red of a god's blood.

Jupiter's chariots fell to earth like cannons, too, spewing up plumes of black smoke. His archers went down firing. The thundering, ground-shaking booms grew louder and the sky spectacle became more frenetic as the remaining chariots burned up. The rest of the chariots descended or disappeared, fading into the daylight sky until they became the glare of the sun.

As the dust settled, Claudia gazed around, and an unsettling fact came to the front of her mind.

Jupiter was dead.

The war was won.

But Gia was no longer standing at her side.

23. IRREVERSIBLE

Though peace had been called by Minerva, bringing an end to the conflict, the city of Rome was littered with the bodies of hundreds of soldiers, most of whom had served Marcellus and General Aquinas. Claudia recalled that Gia had been dressed as one of them, fearing that she may have been mistaken for the enemy in the commotion.

Shouting her name, she ran through the streets in a heart-pounding, gut-dropping daze that blanked her mind. She moved from body to body, both living and dead, turning them round or over in hysteria, checking their faces before moving on to the next.

She came across Livia and Dido, both tending to their injuries as the leafy-haired goddess Meditrina healed the wounded nearby, attracting a large crowd of devotees.

'Have you seen Gia?' Claudia cried, her voice high and shaky with panic. 'I cannot find her.'

Livia sprang to action immediately. 'Not for a while.'

'She was with Diana,' said Dido.

'We'll help you search for her,' said Livia.

They continued moving through the crowd of panicked citizens, who looked to her for guidance, and while she tried to comfort and reassure them, she was consumed by her own fear.

Where was Gia?

She saw Darius and Cassius, standing by the Pantheon. Athena was there too with the dog Viatrix, and Pliny and Rectina, all marvelling over a particularly beautiful Pegasus.

When Claudia saw Diana and Venus, she ran towards them as the entire group turned to greet her joyfully.

'Gia,' she panted, before they could speak. 'Where is she?'

'Gia?' said Cassius, already fraught. 'What's happened?'

'I don't know,' said Claudia. 'She isn't here.'

'Last I saw, she was fighting the good fight alongside my other warriors,' said Diana. 'She cannot be far.'

'We shall help,' said Venus, putting her arm around Claudia. 'Do not worry, we will find her.'

They picked up Dom and Celadus along the way, forming a strange party of mixed mortals and divinities. They continued turning over bodies, allowing Venus to heal all those she could.

Athena was already crying. 'I have a bad feeling,' she said.

'She'll be fine,' said Rectina, comforting her. 'It's okay. We'll find her soon.'

'What if . . .' Claudia began.

'Do *not* say it,' said Cassius, scowling.

'Maybe she was dragged into the abyss,' Claudia said. She laid her hand on the shoulder of a soldier lying face down in the gutter, shaking her head in sorrow. 'Maybe she . . .'

She rolled the soldier over and came face to face with her lover's cold, lifeless brown eyes.

'No,' she choked.

An arrow protruded from Gia's chest.

Blood congealed around the wound. Claudia's mind went cold

and white. She was aware of the others rushing forward and of someone screaming. It took a moment to realize it was her.

'Gia! GIA!'

She shook her violently, slapped at her face, but she didn't blink or breathe, her skin already cold.

It couldn't be . . . wouldn't be.

They were at the end . . . the war was over and they had won. She was victorious. It was just as the goddesses had foretold, back in Pompeii: the warrior who would protect her, lay down their life for her, and love her as she loved them. That was the prophecy. That was their destiny, or so it was supposed to be.

It wasn't real, she decided. None of this was real at all. She was still poisoned, dreaming, back in the underworld.

But Gia's eyes were still open, unblinking, and she saw nothing. The blood on her chest had begun to dry.

With every second, the reality became too hard to deny.

Gia was dead.

'No, no . . . you cannot leave me.'

Cassius pushed past Claudia to try and rouse her, shaking her even more violently than Claudia had.

'Gia . . . Gia . . . Gia,' he cried, like a prayer.

It did no good.

'Who did this? Tell me who did this? I will kill them. I won't rest until they are dead,' Cassius raged.

Darius put a gentle hand on his shoulder.

Dazed, Claudia focused on the fletching of the arrow. It was of a similar style to the arrows that had been fired at them at the Circus Maximus, but instead of bronze it was made of gold – forged by the gods.

'One of Jupiter's men,' said Diana, mournfully. 'The arrow of a divine archer. She died in battle beside me, and I didn't even notice.'

She knelt down, laying her cloak upon Gia as if she was asleep.

Through tears, Claudia looked to Darius, as she recalled what he'd said about choosing between power and love. She could only have one, and she had won the war. She was empress, she was powerful, and she was victorious, but Gia was the price.

'What victory is worth such loss?' she said.

'I am so sorry, Empress,' he said, his eyes wet too.

Gia was the sacrifice, just as a part of her had always feared.

'She cannot have died alone,' she sobbed. 'I cannot stand it. Not without me by her side. I will not allow it. I will not . . . allow it.'

She broke down in tears, crying into her hands, her head filled with flashing images of Gia – from their first meeting in the arena to their last kiss, which seemed to have been just minutes ago.

'Her last moments, her last thoughts . . . I will never know them. How can I have not witnessed it? How can I have missed her?'

Gia would never hold her again, or laugh, or cup her cheek. They would not lie in bed together, their hair entwined. They would not touch or make love. They would make no more memories.

Their story was over.

'If someone had to die for this, it should've been me,' she said.

All that she had ever felt, and all that she had ever loved, was gone in an instant.

She had won the world, and she had lost the world.

It was all meaningless now, for even little Athena was broken by it, her love and courage coming undone.

Cassius looked to her, his face twisted in grief. Claudia braced for his rage but he held out a hand to her instead, pulling her close and holding her as they rocked back and forth.

'It is my fault,' she cried.

'If not for you, she may already be buried under the destruction of Pompeii,' he said. 'You cannot control the path of a single arrow. You cannot control destiny.'

Gia was right there, and now she was gone.

'She is with Mother now,' said Cassius, his voice breaking.

'There must be something we can do,' said Venus, her face streaked by silvery tears.

'Please.' Claudia moved to her, clutching her hands. 'You are goddesses. You created us. You made our world. You can bring her back. Just bring her back. I will do anything . . . anything.'

Everyone was crying now: Dido and Livia, Dom and Celadus. They moved close to her and Cassius, holding them without touching them, making space for her insurmountable grief.

Venus called the leafy-haired medicine goddess, Meditrina, who knelt down beside Gia. She gently touched her, as if she might revive her.

Claudia's heart clamoured so hard she thought it might stop beating as hope swelled inside her unbearably, but Meditrina turned back and shook her head.

'It is too late,' she said. 'She is already gone.'

'No,' Claudia screamed, tearing at her own robes in desperation.

'I'm sorry, Empress,' said the goddess.

'No, you are wrong! You are all wrong!' Claudia whirled around to face them. 'I will go to the underworld and get her back. I have done it before. I will do it again.' She ran towards the hole in the ground. 'I must find Proserpina, and Invidia. They will help me, and . . .'

'It is too late,' said Proserpina, approaching. 'Her soul has been weighed; the thread has been cut.'

'Do not say that. You cannot say that,' sobbed Claudia.

'I'm so sorry.'

Claudia felt as small and as lost as she was when she was a child, clutching at her ugly doll while she listened to her father and brother laughing at her, her mother only recently gone.

Loss consumed her, rotting her stomach. If she'd had poison to hand, she would've swallowed it. Her eyes landed on the sword Gia had been carrying and she wished she was brave enough to spear her own heart.

It was too terrible to be believed.

Claudia shook her head stubbornly, unwilling to accept it.

'If you could bring me back, why not her?' she said.

'You could return because you were not dead,' said Proserpina, gently. 'It is not the same. I cannot reverse the death of a mortal. I cannot reclaim a soul that has been permanently severed from its bonds. I do not have that power.'

Claudia's desperate cries attracted Minerva, now wearing Jupiter's crown and carrying his staff. She had returned to her normal size, allowing Claudia to run into her arms in distress. The goddess embraced her like a mother, stroking her hair as Claudia cried desperately.

'What has happened here?' she asked in anger, as if someone had done something to hurt her.

'Gia is dead!' Claudia sobbed. 'After everything I have done, she is gone. Jupiter has taken her from me. How can it be so?'

Minerva looked past her shoulder, seeing Gia on the ground as Cassius held on tight to her body.

Gently, she moved Claudia aside and went to Gia, kneeling down. She laid a hand on her face.

'How could you?' sobbed Claudia. 'After all she has sacrificed, to deliver your fate? What good is a goddess who would take her from me? It should've been me. Please, take me instead.'

'It does not work that way,' said Minerva. 'We have lost, in this victory too. We have lost Fortuna. She was a primordial goddess, older and more powerful than all of us. She cannot be replaced or reborn. We owe our success to her . . . but . . . perhaps she can still help us?'

'What?' sniffed Claudia. 'How?'

'Everything in existence is made of stars, you see. You, us, the cosmos itself. Death and life are part of the same system. Our energy lives and dies, and lives again.'

'Is this really the time for a lecture, Minerva?' said Venus.

Diana silently shook her head in disapproval.

'It is important, for her to know! That is what we mean, when we say we are immortal. We do not live for ever as we are, but our energy never dies. It only changes form. In death and destruction, lies creation and rebirth. The energy that made Gia Valerii exists no more. She can never be again, not in that form. But the energy that created her is free, to become whatever it wishes to be.'

'I don't understand,' Claudia cried. 'I just want her, only her, exactly as she was. Please.'

'I cannot do that,' said Minerva. 'Well, not exactly. Honestly, I'm not sure yet. But I will do all I can.'

Minerva turned back to Gia.

'What are you going to do, sister?' asked Diana. 'Only the king of the gods can reverse death.'

'Jupiter is dead,' said Minerva, matter-of-factly, 'and I am queen of the pantheon. I have his staff.'

'She does have a point there,' said Venus.

'You think you can bring her back?' said Cassius.

'We do not yet know what I am capable of.'

'Then you must do it, whatever it is,' begged Claudia. 'Whatever sacrifice I must make, I will take it so she can live.'

Minerva nodded, fixed Claudia with a meaningful stare, took a deep breath and raised the shining staff.

24. EPILOGUE

On the festival day known as Romana, Empress Claudia Caesaria made her way through the city just before sunset, accompanied by a small party of colourfully dressed courtiers in matching flower wreaths.

Lively citizens, some already wine-merry, filled the streets and squares, telling tales about the day when the gods descended to Earth.

There were still lasting signs of the battle: statues missing heads and limbs, the sunken wall of the Colosseum and the burnt-out wreck of Jupiter's Temple, but the city was at peace – particularly today, when they celebrated their freedom, protected by a goddess of their very own.

In theatres across the New Republic, actors recreated historical highlights, with flying chariots made of wood and Pegasi horses with stick-on wings. In the colosseums and amphitheatres, gladiators and gladiatrices dressed as the gods and goddesses fought for sport, resulting in matches between mismatched deities. Bacchus fought Hercules, and Pluto fought Proserpina, creating new myths to be woven into the centuries.

In temples, public feasts were held, where servants and senators sat together on long benches enjoying the festivities. Children played games, taking turns to play the bad gods and the good gods, while animals ran free, fed on scraps beneath tables. Prayers were chanted, poetry recited and songs played by bands. No one was enslaved on holidays.

Later, the people would organize themselves into smaller gatherings, including the one hosted by Senator Philopappos, where secret lovers danced wild and free, long into the night.

Claudia passed the shrines of Discordia and Invidia, on opposite sides of the road. Their statues were not enclosed by pillars, like many of the others, but standing atop their shrines, their wings outspread, primed and ready to join in on any revolution that might occur.

There were many circular shrines built to honour every deity who had participated in the Great Battle of Jupiter. On Sun-days and their festival days, they inhabited their statues and entered their shrines, meeting with their followers, receiving their offerings in person and listening to their concerns like senators.

The gods were present, and visible in the world again – for better or for worse.

In the Forum, Claudia paused to look at the statues of the new Triad: Minerva, queen of the gods, along with Diana and Venus. They stood, back to back, with their weapons drawn: Diana with her bow, Minerva with her sword, and Venus with her shield. Their trinity had been installed in the Forum in bronze, now surrounded by flowers, by scrolls, by arrows and candles and votive statues.

'Good day, goddesses,' said Claudia, leaving a basket of their favourite treats at their feet. 'I hope you're celebrating in style.'

Diana was probably on a hunt with her armoured maidens. Venus was probably enjoying a hot spa with her nymphs. Minerva was probably in her palace, measuring the threads of fate and studying the maps of the stars that made up the future, or perhaps trying to keep tabs on her wild-child little sister Bellona.

Parting company with the rest of her palace staff, Claudia and a single guard journeyed to her favourite shrine, to make offerings and pay her respects, which she did as often as she could.

As they walked, they discussed an upcoming gladiatrix match between Livia the Legendary and Salma the Superior, an Egyptian woman with an undefeated record, who Livia was now enamoured with.

The shrine was located out of the way, into the hills, where the goddess who inhabited it could look out over the panorama of Rome. It was the perfect place to watch the sun rise or set, or to see the constellations of the gods at night – when Jupiter, Mars, Pluto and the others could be seen once more, shining bright against the dark sky, forever watchful, yet bound from doing harm.

The uphill trek was part of the pilgrimage, for only the strongest and bravest would be blessed, yet the shrine was well-attended, the winding path littered with flowers and bundles of tokens, along with small figures of women gladiators.

By the time Claudia made it to the top, she was weak-kneed and perspiring, taking a moment to fix her hair in the mirror of the fountain. As she gazed into the petal-strewn waters, she thought of Darius, wondering if he and Cassius were enjoying their grand tour of world wonders. She looked forward to receiving her next message from them, which would no doubt arrive accompanied with a souvenir.

'Would you give us a moment of privacy?' asked Claudia, to her tall, muscular guard.

'Of course, Empress,' said Dido. 'I will be waiting, when you're ready. Take your time . . . and pass on my regards.'

As Dido stood on guard, Claudia ascended the temple steps as she'd done so many times before, stepping into the circular temple known as the Roma Aeterna – part of the larger Temple to Venus and Roma.

A marble statue of a goddess waited within, seated on a throne. She was armoured and wore a mural crown that represented the walls of the city. Short-haired, smiling serenely, and holding the palladium that signified infinity, she was instantly recognizable.

'Hello, love,' said Claudia, bending down to place a bundle of offerings at the statue's feet. 'Happy Romana.'

She gazed at the lifelike sculpture, so detailed that Claudia could make out her eyelashes, the wisps at her hairline, the folds of her robes, even the mole on her collarbone that Claudia had so often kissed.

'I bring festive offerings, my goddess,' she said, bowing. 'I know you love it when I call you that.'

To her, she would always be Gia, or sometimes Viatrix the Victorious, but, to the rest of the populace, she was Roma: the protector goddess of the city, a mortal warrior made immortal. Now she dined on the Isles of the Blessed, with the other deities.

Claudia stood solemnly, admiring her for a moment, listening to the symphony of celebration below.

'Are you there?'

She waited, expectantly, for a sign.

'I was hoping to see you today,' she said. 'It *is* your festival, after all. Unless, of course, you are off doing important divinity things.'

The breeze stirred, picking up leaves and riffling her clothes.

'Maybe you are too busy for me, now you are a goddess, and me, a mere empress,' she said, though she was smiling.

The clouds shifted, letting the dying light of the day bleed upon the hills like golden blood. Claudia turned to watch the sun sink under the horizon, swallowed by the curves of Mother Earth.

She sensed a shift, as the veil between the world of gods and mortals thinned, that made her skin prickle and tingle.

When she looked back, the statue glistened supernaturally. It was becoming incarnate. Stone turned to flesh, as the goddess Roma manifested. Though her eyes had a strange golden hue to them and her skin was lustrous and silken, she was still Gia.

Infinite and immortal . . . but still her.

Claudia fell into her arms, grateful that a goddess was still solid enough to be held.

'I missed you,' she said.

'I saw you on Sun-day,' said Gia.

'That is all it takes for me to miss you,' said Claudia, recalling the first time they made love in Herculaneum.

It was not quite the same as squeezing a fragile mortal but it was a deeper, firmer, more reassuring embrace, the kind that made Claudia feel as if she would never know fear again.

'Sorry I am late,' said Gia, pulling back to stroke her hair fondly. 'I was with Diana.'

Claudia's whole body buzzed and sang at her touch.

'I thought as much.'

'One of the gods came hunting in her woods, letting his dogs attack her deer. He disguised himself as a stag to try and get away from her. It . . . did not end well.'

'I would think not.'

There were certain advantages to dating a goddess, some of which she never discussed in public, but one of them was knowing that a deity was always watching over her. She was always safe, and she was always loved – and a goddess's capacity for love was unparalleled.

'For a moment, I thought you weren't coming,' said Claudia.

'I'll always come for you, until the end of time,' said Gia. 'Happy Romana, my lover. I do find it to be the best of all the festivals.'

Minerva had used her newfound power to resurrect Gia from death. She couldn't make her human again, so she made her something else, something more: the patron goddess of Rome.

The world was no longer the same; it would never be the same again. Part of Claudia mourned the simplicity of it, when she didn't have to deal with problems like demigod babies and drunken deities, but it kept her busy. There were still earthquakes, maritime disasters, and all manner of catastrophes, but with the goddesses watching over them, the people of Rome enjoyed an era of security and peace.

Gia had died a warrior, and she had been reborn as a goddess. Now she travelled between Elysium and Earth, where Claudia ruled as the benevolent empress, hand in hand with the Senate, where women now sat on the benches, bickering with the men.

Claudia and Gia.

Together, they were the rulers of New Rome: the eternal lovers of the Eternal City.

ACKNOWLEDGEMENTS

The hardest part of writing a book isn't the middle or the ending but the acknowledgements, because it's the only bit the author writes in their own voice. Writing the acknowledgements means sitting quietly with your gratitude and expressing it earnestly. So much love is poured into every book, and the acknowledgements is where it's all bared.

To my agent, Hannah Sheppard: I know you hate when I say this, but I really think my life would've been quite tragic if you hadn't walked into it. I needed someone exactly like you to push me forward. If not for you, I'd never have finished anything. I wouldn't have believed in myself enough to go on. Always honest, always protective, always willing to hear the next wild idea, it's an honour and a privilege to be your client.

To my editor, Yasmin Morrissey: it's amazing to see your ambitious, visionary, badass-self in action. I'm so proud of everything you are and everything you do. You chose to be my patron. You chose to back me in this industry, for better or for worse, and there's nothing more beautiful than that. You're my Roman Empire. May she live eternal.

To Genevieve Herr: your ability to interpret and elaborate on my unspoken language is a gift. All of my books are better because you were involved in them. Thanks for always getting it.

To Tierney Holm: your enthusiasm for *Empress, Goddess* boosted me right out of the gate. Thanks for seeing the vision and helping me to refine it. I've enjoyed every part of the process, even the parts where we talked about fish or cosy video games. *Especially* those parts. All best.

To Millie Monaghan: forever a joy to see your name pop up in my inbox. Thank you for being on this journey with me. We'll always have our trip to the printers. I look forward to reading your contemporary fiction one day because I already know it'll be cracking.

To Simi Toor: I look back on that day at the Roman baths and grin. Thanks for making my job such a good time. Thanks for always being so friendly and enthusiastic, even about the little things.

To Tom Roberts, Holly Macdonald, Jesse Green and Patrick Knowles for the incredible visuals in these books. Any author would be thrilled to get covers so beautiful and maps so intricate. Extremely thankful to you all for bringing this story to life.

To Ali Dougal, Lauren Atherton and everyone else at S&S: something about being published by a Big Five name you've grown up with is too big to behold. It's hard to believe that this actually happened to me and that I'm not just in the Matrix, but thanks for making this dream simulation such a realistic experience! Seriously, thank you for taking a chance on a sapphic gladiator story that means so much to me. These books and these memories will live with me for ever.

To all of my friends, simply for existing, but particularly Danielle Curtis: I don't think anyone has ever looked happier for me about anything than you looked on the day I told you I was being published for the first time. You're the person who makes sure I have a giant cookie with colour-coded icing to eat on my publication days. You're the funniest person I know. You're my one call from prison. We've never been too sentimental in our friendship but I love the hell out of you, dude. I simply wouldn't be me without you.

To Jessica Jacobs: blessed to have you and the girls in my life. Thanks for always making time and space for me. Thank you for reading my books, but also for the impromptu mornings that turn into accidental days. My world is better and sunnier with you in it. Love you all.

To Lucy Wainwright: whether it's brainstorming a name for a medieval gay inn or taking me mini-golfing, you're always encouraging me to put myself out there. You make me want to be a braver, bolder person. Thank you for the day ratings, the outings, the vents. There's no one I'd rather have an emotional breakdown with.

To Saz and Emily: two of my earliest, keenest readers. You always make me feel like I'm actually good at this. That's probably why you're both therapists. To many Love Island summers and writing holidays in your barn yet to come.

To Pat and John: thank you for inspiring me consistently throughout the decades and introducing me to a world of creative possibilities. You taught me that a different kind of life was possible.

To all of my author pals and everyone in my writer group chats, but especially Mina Ikemoto Ghosh, Sophie Jo, Philippa Leathley, Ann Sei Lin, Alison Weatherby, B Wheeler, Shanna Alderliesten, Bori Cser, Alison Stockham and April Doyle for reading GG.

A special thank you to Lizzie Huxley-Jones for jet skis, mosaics, penning my favourite sapphic rom-coms and being first class company even at short notice. Thanks for showing up for me, but also for showing me who I am.

To Mom and Dad: look, I promise I'm trying to move out of your house but you made it so nice for me to stay. If you didn't want your adult author daughter living with you in your golden years, you shouldn't have made home such a safe and comfortable place.

If you've read this far, you probably love Gia, Claudia and the gang almost as much as me, so thank you too.

To the queers: this one was for us.

Veni, vidi, vici.